Vicky Zimmerman lives in London. She worked in advertising and as a food tester at a major UK supermarket before leaving to write full-time. She has written four novels under the name Stella Newman, as well as writing for publications including the *Guardian* and the *Observer*. She's a passionate foodie, and when not writing enjoys talking about food, cooking it and eating it.

The
WOMAN
WHO
WANTED
MORE

Vicky
Zimmerman

ZAFFRE

First published in Great Britain in 2019 by
ZAFFRE
80–81 Wimpole St, London W1G 9RE

This is a work of fiction. Names, places, events and
incidents are either the products of the author's
imagination or used fictitiously. Any resemblance to
actual persons, living or dead, or actual
events, is purely coincidental.

A CIP catalogue record for this book is
available from the British Library.

ISBN: 978–1–78576–532–2

also available as an ebook

1 3 5 7 9 10 8 6 4 2

Typeset by Palimpsest Book Production Limited, Falkirk, Stirlingshire
Printed and bound in Great Britain by Clays Ltd, Elcograf S.p.A.

Zaffre is an imprint of Bonnier Books UK
www.bonnierbooks.co.uk

In loving memory of Matt Janes,
an exceptional friend

Prologue

CECILY FINN IS NINETY-SEVEN and a half years old. Her hair is as stiff and bright as a firmly beaten egg white, and her dark eyes hold the look of a permanently unimpressed owl. She claims that all she wants is death, because boredom and institutional fish pie are worse than dying – but Cecily has endured far greater horrors than overcooked haddock.

Over the many weeks Kate Parker has been coming to visit her at Lauderdale House for Exceptional Ladies, Cecily has shared with her a smorgasbord of tales, of love and rebellion, triumphs and travels. Kate used to wonder about embellishments, fabrications, memories warped by time – but not anymore. Cecily's mind and tongue are sharp as lime juice on an ulcer.

Cecily often tries to pass off Shakespeare quotes as her own. She talks in metaphors that take an age to decode. Nothing's ever good enough for her: no biscuit crisp enough, no posset set right. She never holds back, and if there's a choice between bitter and sweet, she'll take bitter every time. Still, Cecily has taught Kate several valuable lessons – not least the perfect menu for what Kate craves most in the world.

Kate turns forty today. Last night she cooked for friends – the meal was delicious, everyone had fun – and tonight she'll be celebrating with Nick, gentle, handsome Nick. He's taking her to an amazing restaurant, and if there's one thing Cecily and Kate *can* agree on, it's that good food matters. In a few weeks' time Kate and Nick will move in together, it *is* happening, and all the doubts Cecily has scattered in Kate's mind will be brushed away like black pepper spilled on a pristine tablecloth. Just because you're old doesn't mean you're always right about *everything*. There are many ways to find happiness in this world, to beat loneliness, to live well.

So why does Kate feel, as she stands outside Cecily's door, that in spite of all the barbs and bristle that come with the package, Cecily is the one person who can help rid her of this gnawing ache that's lodged itself deep in the pit of her stomach? That if she doesn't speak to Cecily *right now* she might lose herself completely?

Kate takes a deep breath and knocks on the door, waiting for that familiar haughty voice to tell her to come in.

Come in.

PART ONE

Hunger is never delicate.

Samuel Johnson

Chapter One

Five months earlier . . .

KATE PARKER IS RAVENOUS. She sits on a deck chair in Nick Sullivan's tiny patch of North London garden, gazing contentedly at his back as he stands by the barbecue. The smell of chargrilled meat is making her stomach audibly rumble but there's no point hurrying him, this man does things in his own sweet time.

Dinner's a prime example – tonight it's taken forty minutes but in real terms it's taken a whole year. Nick embarked on Project Burger last July. Nick's a database engineer (Kate still can't explain fully what that means) and he's applied his intellectual rigour and ceaseless enthusiasm to honing every element of the American classic. Kate's never seen a face light up the way Nick's had the night he mastered The Order of the Seven Layers.

He was a solitary eater before they started dating, relying on takeaways and the odd home-cooked sausage sandwich. Kate had been saddened by the loneliness this seemed to imply, and the missed culinary opportunities. She'd offered to teach him some favourite recipes, he'd accepted, and over the last eighteen months he has emerged from his culinary shell – slowly at first but with increasing confidence. Kate isn't the greatest cook but her mother Rita is such a dire one that Kate learned to fend for her stomach from an early age.

Kate loves cooking with Nick, and has watched him flourish with gentle pride. Normally she chooses the recipe, he the music, and whatever they're cooking they both agree: the more butter used the better. They have compatible styles – he's hard-working and patient, and can chop a dozen onions without making the slightest fuss about eyes watering or hands smelling; she's more chaotic but can juggle multiple tasks, and although he's smarter she's always two steps ahead – nothing's ever burnt on her watch.

It's a beautiful summer's evening, and Kate savours a moment of sheer happiness – the warm breeze scented with jasmine, the sky only now fading from blue. She closes her eyes and thinks about tomorrow. It's been a long time since she's been in a relationship where she's felt relaxed enough to think about tomorrow. Tomorrow Nick will wake up early and pop out to buy the ingredients for breakfast burritos. They'll cook together, go for a walk and in the afternoon, if the weather stays fine, they'll sit back out here, Kate devouring a novel, Nick reading one of his incomprehensible coding books. Their life is not lavish but it's full of priceless treats: lemonade poured into glasses he keeps in the freezer for extra coldness; box sets and BLTs on rainy Wednesday nights; elaborately competitive games of cards, with Minstrels used for gambling chips.

When she opens her eyes, Nick has turned to give her the 'Mustard, now!' look – one brow raised in mock severity. She springs up with a smile and hands him the French's Classic like a scalpel to a surgeon, watching intently as he traces parallel lines of acid yellow onto the meat, the finishing touch.

This burger has taken time but it's worth the wait: six ounces of minced steak, crowned with bacon and a perfect square of melting, tangy Cheddar; delicate concentric bangles of red onion; tomato, lettuce and Magic Sauce – a mixture of Tabasco, mayo and ketchup, to add heat, creaminess and tang. Then the bun: Kate and Nick have spent more time researching this bun than some couples spend choosing a car. Initially, Nick enquired whether the buns they sold at Fletchers, the supermarket chain Kate works for, were any good? She'd laughed a mournful response. Fletchers' buns were cheap but flavourless and papery, and though they claimed to be brioche, on the back of the pack was the ominous phrase 'brioche-style'. After much trial and error they'd found perfection at a bakery near Kate's flat in Kilburn. And the final ingredient – one sour dill pickle, for added crunch.

Kate is not religious, but looking down at her plate makes her want to say grace: thank you, Universe, for this man, who has a lovely flat with a reasonably clean bathroom; who has restored my faith, after several years of late-thirty-something dating starvation, that there are kind, clever, decent men in London. Thank you for a man who puts so much effort into making my dinner; into making me happy.

She picks up her burger – oh, such heft – and holds on for dear life. Once in motion there's no stopping – hesitate or show fear and it'll fall apart in every direction. Nick looks at her tenderly. It's impossible not to love him. Not only does he cook her spaghetti with meatballs if she's having a bad day, but she can eat them with full abandon and he won't judge her greedy or unfeminine; he relishes her appetite almost as much as she does.

Sated after their last bites, Kate reaches to wipe a smudge of mustard from the faint stubble on Nick's jaw. He has such a sweet face, handsome in an unassuming way, a button nose that enhances his boyishness. His brown curly hair is thinning but the short cut suits him well. That old blue Atari T-shirt makes his eyes even greener, and when their eyes meet now he flashes her that smile of his that rarely falters, no matter what's thrown at him. She's so impressed with how he's handled these last three months of unemployment; his optimism is extraordinary.

'Not long now till France!' says Kate, moving to clear away the plates.

'I can't wait – think of all the baguettes,' says Nick, his eyes lighting up. 'Are you positive Kavita doesn't want any money for letting us use her holiday house?'

'She had a fit when I even suggested it.' Kate hasn't told Nick she's bought Kavita a case of good wine as a thank-you. He'd offer to pay half even though he's skint, and the thought of embarrassing him when he's always so generous is intolerable.

'That was a perfect dinner,' says Kate, as they stand contentedly at the sink, washing up. 'Those were particularly fine burger accoutrements.'

'Burger Accoutrements . . . one for our list?' he says. It's one of their running jokes – ridiculous names for their future children.

'Burger Accoutrements Parker-Sullivan? Fine, but *you* can pick him up from the school playground when the other kids beat him up.'

'If we have twins, please can we call the other one Pickleholic?'

'I'm not sure a pickle addiction is a sound aspiration for our firstborn,' says Kate, laughing. She gazes at him standing there in his T-shirt and Levi's, with his forty-four-year-old burger-lover's slight pot belly and feels a sudden throb of love so intense it makes her heart hurt.

He catches her look and returns it with a smile, suddenly self-conscious. He pauses, then reaches for the spatula she's washing. 'You've got a wider one of these at home, right?'

'Yup,' she says, reaching for it as he moves it slightly out of reach.

'We need yours here – for the barbecue.'

'I'll pick you one up from John Lewis in the week.'

'Kate,' he says, putting down the spatula as he turns to face her. 'I think we need all your utensils here.'

'*All* of them?'

He nods decisively.

'Why?'

'And your clothes. And shoes,' he says, tenderly tucking a stray strand of hair behind her ear. 'And your three hundred cookbooks and seven million novels . . .'

'Two hundred at most,' she says, struggling to contain the burst of joy blossoming in her chest.

'Oh, and one other very important thing that John Lewis doesn't sell.'

'Which is what?'

'Which is you, Kate, you,' he says, his smile as big as the world.

Thank you, Universe, thank you. Finally: a man she loves, who loves her too. He's been worth the wait.

The following night Kate stretches out in her bed, her normal Sunday-night blues replaced by excitement. She and Nick are off to France in two weeks. She'll move into Nick's the weekend they return.

She'd been anxious about breaking the news to her flatmate, but then the thought of never again having to clean Melanie's fish fat from the splashback had given Kate a surge of courage. Nick has his flaws, but passive-aggressive, slovenly and light-fingered with other people's special-occasions-only olive oil are not among them.

Melanie had been surprisingly encouraging, and had even suggested Kate start moving her stuff before France. Their conversation had gone far better than Kate had anticipated.

It's always the things you worry about most that turn out fine.

And vice versa.

Chapter Two

KATE FASTENS HER SEAT belt and turns to Nick, who is already engrossed in the Listener, a cryptic crossword so fiendishly difficult it makes Kate's brain ache. Week in, week out, Nick sits absorbed for hours, chip-chipping away – he's obsessed. If he ever reveals a kinky side, she suspects he'll make her dress up as a complex puzzle.

'Four solved already,' he says, holding it out to her proudly. She glances at the grid and shakes her head: how on earth does *that* word fit *that* clue?

She settles back in her seat and closes her eyes, tired from a 3 a.m. alarm but excited. This will be their first proper holiday together and if she's honest with herself, which sometimes she isn't, she'd have liked to have gone somewhere with Nick before now. There are legitimate reasons why it's taken eighteen months to get Nick on this plane. Until he lost his job in April he was a work-aholic, often *choosing* to work weekends (*so* not Kate's style). Then recently he's had no income. And finally, Nick is s-l-o-w-moving. She's analysed this a lot, and her mother Rita's had her two pennies' worth too: 'children of dysfunctional parents always need to feel in control'. Well, who doesn't?

Nick had entered into their relationship so cautiously, it had triggered Kate's commitment-phobe alarm after one month, and so she'd asked him straight out: what do you want? He'd told her he didn't know how to do relationships; he'd only had one short one in his twenties, and another failed interlude in his thirties. A tiny red flag had waved in Kate's head, so she'd offered him an out before anyone (i.e., Kate) got hurt. He'd looked at her for so long she'd blushed, then he'd held her tight and said, 'I want this. I want you.'

From then on they'd gone for it, albeit at a measured pace – one bite, one meal, one day at a time. In the last few months she's felt him move ever closer. Even so, the moment the offer of cohabitation was on the table, Kate had felt a pressing need to take something significant and heavy round to his flat, as a precautionary measure: a couple of boxes of cookbooks and her hardback copy of *The Goldfinch* had done the trick.

Her best friend Bailey had helped her move them last Saturday when Nick was away hiking. Bailey and Kate have been friends since they were four. Kate sometimes wonders if people are shaped by their hair – if she'd been born with Bailey's perfect blonde locks, would she be perpetually calm and gracious too? Certainly Bailey hasn't had it easy – a cheating ex, Tom, who'd abandoned her and their young daughters, claiming his duty was 'to explore his desire' with any woman who was game. Yet on the many wine-infused nights Kate had spent round at Bailey's counselling her through her divorce, it was Kate who'd had to be talked down from wanting to murder Tom. Sometimes friends end up feeling the feelings that are too unpalatable to feel for yourself.

Kate opens her eyes again as Nick turns to her with a radiant smile.

'Fourteen across, it's Contiguous!' he says, holding the paper out to her like a winning lottery ticket.

She smiles and reaches over to ruffle his hair but the plane makes a sudden dramatic lurch and she grabs his hand instead. He gives her fingers a gentle squeeze. She imagines their entwined hands growing into old people's hands together, their skin getting wrinkled, age-marked. Old age would be more tolerable with Nick by her side.

Last month at a friend's wedding Nick had drunk a lot and in the cab home had confessed he wanted them to have three children. He'd patted her tummy tenderly, then rested his head in her lap.

'The only thing you'll hear in there is wedding cake,' she'd said, trying not to dwell on the fact that her ovaries were fast approaching their use-by date.

'I know I'm drunk, Kate Parker, but I utterly love every part of you, I do.'

The feeling is entirely mutual.

By the time Kate and Nick reach San Marcel, a tiny village ten minutes from a slightly larger village, the sun is blazingly hot in a deep blue sky. They stop for provisions, drawn to one store by the sweet, buttery aroma of freshly baking brioche. They linger at a counter sampling ripe cheeses, speckled salamis and glistening inky olives, emerging with bags brim full of jars and bottles, fresh herbs and ripe peaches.

They head to Kavita's place, a simple two-bed farmhouse with a large terrace and, best of all, an icy-cold

13

pool. Nick throws on his trunks and jumps into the water while Kate takes her case to the main bedroom to fish out her H&M bikini. She's never invested in expensive swimwear – why bother? No feat of wardrobe engineering, no high-cut leg could hide the fact that Kate has a normal female body: a big bottom, cellulite and a relationship with gravity entirely in keeping with her age. Thank goodness she'll never again have to be naked for the first time in front of a new man.

She checks the mirror again. Insecurity is so boring at her age. Plus there's not much she can do in the next two minutes about being seven pounds overweight. As Rita always says, 'Focus on the positives – if you can find them.' Kate's hair looks good – caramel brown, shoulder-length and slightly wavy. She takes off her sunglasses. Her eyes, somewhat red from the early start, are still her best feature – greeny-grey and almond-shaped, with an inquisitive look she's inherited from her father. She wipes a nudge of sleep away, grabs her sarong and wraps it tightly around her.

Nick is sitting in the shade, crossword in hand. 'Get in the water, babe. It's amazing.' And it is. Though the initial shock is intense, within moments it's bliss. Kate swims a few lengths, climbs out and arranges herself and her new Anne Tyler novel on the lounger beside him, letting her body sink down into the chair as the heat warms her limbs.

As the day ends they eat out on the terrace, enjoying the last of the sun – a simple tuna salad with green beans and a handful of ripe tomatoes, a fresh, crusty baguette with magnificent French butter and a bottle of chilled rosé. Nick looks at her with a smile of pure joy. She reaches out a finger to straighten his unruly right eyebrow. He pulls her close for a kiss, then another.

How lucky is she? Four more days of reading, sunbathing and jumping into an aquamarine pool – four more days of nothing but sheer happiness.

Chapter Three

They are lying in bed on the second night when Nick tells Kate he feels a strong urge to withdraw. Kate is confused.

They've just had sex, and at first she thinks he's making a rather weak joke, but searching again she cannot find a punchline. The sex that night had been good for her, but she'd felt Nick's attention drifting. She refuses to take this personally; Nick's been unemployed far longer than he'd anticipated – it's natural he's preoccupied.

'Um, what do you mean, withdraw?' she says, trying to sound calm.

'I don't know,' he says sadly and his shoulder blades shift with discomfort. 'It's just my gut . . . says retreat.'

'Retreat . . .?'

He shrugs apologetically, his brow furrowing. 'I've been feeling funny about us . . . for a week or so . . .'

A *week* or so? *Has* he?

'It's here.' He touches his solar plexus. 'When I think about the future it feels . . . weird.'

Hang on, why is he talking like this? He's not trying to lay the groundwork for a break-up, is he? 'Maybe you're anxious about work?' she says, trying to ignore the sick feeling rising in her own body. 'Anyone would be anxious about that.'

'I'm totally relaxed about work.'

Then why were you up half the night last Friday grinding your teeth so loudly you woke me? she thinks.

She pauses. What is going on? 'Oh Nick, this must be linked to you asking me to move in.'

'In what way?'

'Well, you've never even lived with a woman, apart from that moody flatmate you were obsessed with at college . . .'

'*Jo?* You think Jo's moody?'

Jo is dreary verging on morose, but that's not the point. 'It's that thing you do, Nick! Running away. Just like with Tom Brady.'

'Tom Brady?'

'OK, listen,' she says, holding up her finger in an attempt to hold her line of argument. She can pull this back. 'You adore American football, you've repeatedly tried to explain the dumb rules to me—'

'Wow, first Jo and now American football?'

'Look: earlier this year when the Patriots were in the Super Bowl final—'

'The final is the Super Bowl.'

'That's what I just said.'

'No, I meant it's only the final that's called the Super Bowl.'

'Listen to me: when Tom Brady and your guys were losing at half-time—'

'Please . . .' he says, looking pained.

'Exactly! You thought they'd lose, so even though you've been loyal all season, rather than stick by them when it counts, you chicken out and go to bed. It's the Super Bowl final!'

'It's the Super Bowl.'

'Yes, *I know*, Nick, do you get my point?'

'Not really.'

'Discomfort is something you *clearly* can't handle.' Kate is a master of discomfort; frankly, it's where she's most comfortable. 'Nick, even when you love something, you bolt, you're not a finisher – seventh season, *Game of Thrones*? And that book thing? Because the Patriots made the greatest comeback ever and you missed it because you were scared,' she says, more calmly than she feels, but in her stride now. 'This is a classic man-wobble because we're progressing to the next stage in our relationship.'

'Kate,' he says, and in the half-light of the moonlit bedroom she can see there are tears in his eyes. 'I think asking you to move in has made me realise that while I love our time together, I'm equally happy watching TV on my own.'

Oof. It hits Kate in her abdomen as fiercely as if he'd done it with his fist.

'But I've never asked you to choose between me and your TV,' she says, bewildered. 'It's not an either/or, is it?'

'I guess not . . .'

'Nick, is this your way of telling me you don't want us to move in together at all?'

He looks at her with confusion. 'Definitely not – just at the *moment*,' he says with genuine sadness, and while her instinct is to reach out and comfort him, the anger she feels at his feebleness fixes her rigidly in place.

He reaches for her hand and squeezes it apologetically.

She lies in shock for a few minutes, then realises that nothing Nick has said is in any way acceptable to her. She's about to resume their conversation, but turns to see that Nick has already fallen into a deep, and largely untroubled, sleep.

To be fair, Nick does have a great TV. It's a top-of-the-range Sony HD with a huge clear screen, excellent speakers and Triluminos technology, which sounds like a word marketeers have invented to sell women cosmetics. Kate has lain on Nick's sofa countless times, cuddled up with him watching that TV in domestic bliss. Now she lies beside him in bed, her skin blazing from sunburn, her insides churning up. She's hoping he'll leap up, apologise and say he didn't mean a word of it. Kate is prone to hoping for things that statistically could happen but definitely won't.

Realising she's only getting angrier by the minute, she takes herself off to Kavita's daughter's bedroom, places a collection of Peppa Pigs carefully on the bedside table, then crawls into the single bed. She lies in the dark, adrenaline coursing through her. What the actual . . . ? He asked her to move in with him two weeks ago! It had meant so much to her. Kate hasn't done anything wrong since, has she? And why had she gone on and on about him not being a finisher? He's just finished with her.

No, that is *not* what just happened. Nick is having a commitment-wobble, pure and simple. It's 2.30 a.m. She's exhausted, confused, stunned, upset. She'll wait till the morning. Things will look brighter then.

Chapter Four

THINGS DON'T LOOK ANY brighter in the light.

Kate wakes from a fitful sleep, reaches for Nick and instead finds a fluffy toy pig wearing a pink velvet dress.

She tiptoes to the main bedroom. There he is, gently snoring, his elegant feet poking out from the bottom of the sheet. His cheeks are a touch sunburnt, but apart from that he looks as peaceful and content as an eight-year-old who's passed out after lots of birthday cake and an epic session on a bouncy castle.

She crawls back to the single bed, doubled over in pain.

It's Thursday, 6.50 a.m. They fly home on Saturday. She googles her options. An earlier flight will be four hundred euros, plus she's not insured on the hire car, and a cab to the airport will be another hundred euros. Five hundred euros to flee, which might be premature and melodramatic anyway?

Should she insist Nick leave? He can't afford that flight either – not that this should be her concern in the circumstances, but still. Nick is not a bad person. He cannot be dumping her. Not on holiday, not the week they move in together, not when it's her friend Pete's insanely

20

glamorous wedding next month, not when she's turning forty in December. No, no, no – inconceivable that he'd pull this shit right now.

She closes her eyes and tries to calm herself. Nick has never shown any signs of being unreliable. And yet he *did* do that really flaky thing the other day . . . She'd finally persuaded him to read a Kate Atkinson, but he'd abandoned the novel on page 146 because he didn't like one minor character. Ridiculous, to get so far and then ditch it. Kate finds it impossible to abandon books, even bad ones – it feels disloyal; maybe the book will improve, maybe the time invested will ultimately not prove wasted.

Nick's action had bothered her disproportionately at the time. It spoke of a lack of perseverance, an ability to detach too readily. And now, if she looks at his behavioural patterns, his lack of long-term relationships, his refusal to attach to *people*, the whole Tom Brady fiasco – it makes sense, it's all the same thing and it's all his weird parents' fault!

No, no, no, no, no. Abandoning a book is not a crime, even if it is a Kate Atkinson, and it's in no way relevant to her current situation. She's being insane. They are happy, she profoundly believes in their mutual happiness because she has seen and felt it every day. Nick is stable, he is loyal – though perhaps more loyal to his telly than to her . . .

Now the tears are rolling sideways annoyingly into her ears. She mustn't cry, she's overreacting, they're happy, they're solid, this *will* be OK.

Kate's problems are now threefold: firstly she worries that anything she says to Nick to point out his insanity will sound like she's begging. Secondly, an unfortunate part

21

of her psychological make-up means that her instinct is to run towards pain, rather than from it; Nick has hurt her, therefore Nick must mend her. And, finally, she knows she should be 'breezy' in order not to freak him out, but when her tears come they come in giant crashing waves.

The strength of her reaction takes them both by surprise. Of course she's devastated by what he said. She loves Nick. He makes her laugh every day, cooks chorizo burritos as midnight feasts, gets on with all her friends.

Something larger has been triggered, though. She's not good with sudden abandonment. She thinks this is due to the trauma of her father's death, though her mother thinks Kate should have reconciled herself to that loss twenty years ago.

But perhaps the reason this pain is so intense is more to do with her future than her past. It's taken thirty-nine years for Kate to find someone she loves this much – if Nick wants out, will she ever find love again?

It's unbearable being trapped here with him in the middle of nowhere. She hasn't smoked for years, she's not planning to start again, but she desperately needs a cigarette to make it through the next forty-eight hours; just one cigarette. She's heading out to the village that afternoon to buy a pack but at the front door Nick rushes over and insists on walking with her. He holds her hand there and back, and even brings up the plans for Pete's wedding. Is Nick pretending last night never happened?

She must tread softly, mustn't frighten him, but his confusion is making her insane. She gently asks whether he's expecting her to move in at some later stage, or whether last night was his cack-handed attempt at a break-up, but the minute she asks he shuts down again.

'All I know is that for now I want to retreat.'

'To your TV?' she says in despair.

He looks at her forlornly.

If he thinks she's going to try to compete with Triluminos, he can think again.

Anger turns to sadness, turns to pain, then back to shock, as the hours get longer and longer.

How can he just sit there on the next sun lounger doing his crossword, entirely oblivious?

She sits smoking her way through Friday's second pack of Gauloises, feeling anger rise again. Still another twenty-two and a half hours before they can leave for the airport, and she's supposed to just sit here pretending nothing's wrong? The rage mixes with the smoke; she swallows both and chokes. Her cough makes Nick look up with a questioning smile.

'Nicholas,' she says, taking another deep drag. She mustn't show anger – no, no anger, that's *never* allowed. 'I know you're not experienced at relationships, but here's some advice,' she says, poking her cigarette at him. 'You're not meant to pull this *confused* crap *on holiday* . . .' Oh no, a wave of sadness is rising in her throat, making her voice wobble; more tears are imminent.

He puts the crossword down, then reaches over and pats her shoulder that way he does that irritates her. It's how you'd pat a dog if you were really more of a cat person. 'It's fine, Kate, please don't be embarrassed. In fact, it's great to see this sort of emotion. It's not something I've ever seen before.'

She stares at him in dismay. Perhaps she's been going out with a lifelike robot this whole entire time.

The day they're due to fly home, Kate wakes at 2 a.m. She is confused and in pain. Tiptoeing once more to Nick's room in the hope of discovering him perhaps standing at the window, mournful, his torment finally kicking in, her heart sinks as she sees him again fast asleep, his face untroubled.

But looking more closely, she sees he is hugging his pillow tightly, crushing it to his chest as though clinging on for dear life.

Chapter Five

HOW HAS THIS EVEN HAPPENED? Kate stares glumly out of the plane window, her jaw set tight.

She's being punished for allowing herself to feel safe. Recently she's been noticing the amount of unhappy-looking single women her age, always jogging at the weekends, or in jazzily printed yoga gear, and she's felt . . . not smugness, but a sense of relief that she was finally out of dangerous waters and on dry land. Well, more fool her.

The thought of life without Nick's sense of humour, his sweetness, his chicken cacciatore, ices her veins. Her friends are all happily married, or unhappily married but in denial, or divorced and doing half-marathons and online dating. Kate hates running as much as she hates Tinder. Work will provide no respite. Living with Melanie forever, tea bags and wet-porridge clags in the sink, brutal dates with men who cant apostrophise . . .

She has zero appetite for starting over. The thought of going back out there *again* at her age causes a bubble of self-pity to rise up so violently she almost pukes.

She turns to Nick, but he's sitting there next to her, eyes closed, headphones on, mouthing along to every word of Springsteen's *Born To Run*.

*

Back at Stansted the weather is muggy and overcast. Kate feels sweat forming under her arms.

'So . . . what now?' she says with trepidation. 'Shall I come and get my books tomorrow?'

'They're fine where they are.' He smiles gently.

'But . . . what are we doing?'

'I don't know.'

'Nick, if you don't want to live with me now, does that mean you don't want to live with me full stop?'

'That's not what it means.'

'Then what does it mean?'

'It means . . . I'm confused.'

'Are we over?'

'No . . . I don't know . . .'

'Well, when will you know?'

He shrugs. 'I . . . I don't . . .'

She needs to separate herself from this craziness before she goes mad. 'I have to get home.'

'Are you not taking the train with me?' he says in surprise, swinging his bag over his shoulder.

'No, Nick. I'm not. I'll get the coach . . .' She hesitates, rapidly calculating her next move. He obviously needs some space, some time. She'll find waiting intolerable. What's the longest she could bear?

She's scared to say what she's about to but it's her only hope. 'Nick – you've got till the end of September to get yourself unconfused. Either we move forward completely together from then on, or we're done. And in the meantime, I need you to leave me alone. I've got some thinking to do myself.'

His smile falters. 'What – not speak to each other *at all* for almost two *months*?'

'Yes. I mean no. No speaking. I mean: correct – we shall not speak.'

'Can't we just carry on like we were before?'

'I'm pretty sure we can't do that – no.'

He nods slowly. 'OK. If that's what you really want.'

Of course it's not, none of this is!

He reaches in to kiss her on the lips. She stands still, her eyes wide open.

He walks away and she sways, as if buffeted by a strong, cold wind.

On the coach back to London she calls Bailey. Bailey will be sitting in her immaculate white kitchen, dressed in cool, wheat-coloured linen, sipping Evian. Calm, clear-headed Bailey will explain to Kate exactly what just happened and she'll make everything better.

Bailey is actually dressed in running shorts and an old T-shirt, standing in her garden flirting with her hot young gardener. Her phone is on her kitchen counter and eventually goes to voicemail.

Kate calls her friend Cara instead, desperate for re-assurance that things will resolve themselves favourably very soon. Cara gives long odds on that happening. What does Cara know? She dumps a guy if he can't maintain a six-pack; Kate should never seek her advice.

She could call Pete, get a male perspective, but he'll be in pre-wedding mode. She doesn't want to bother him, so she calls her neighbour Emma, who's loved Nick ever since he fixed her laptop. Emma agrees with Cara, and rather than risk running through her entire A-Z of friends only to hear the same negative prognosis, she turns to the girl next to her who has clearly been listening in – who wouldn't? – while pretending to flick through *Grazia*.

'Sorry, but he sounds like a twat,' says the girl.

'I appreciate why you'd think that, but if you met him you'd like him, everybody does. He's just in his own head a lot, self-absorbed. For example, last year he forgot my birthday . . .'

The girl's jaw drops.

'No! But he forgot his *own* birthday too! He's not on the spectrum necessarily but he lives in this bubble of work and computer games. He's not great at emotions, true, but he's not a player. I mean he plays computer games, yes, but you know what I mean . . .'

The girl looks at Kate as if Kate is mad.

'He's an amazing cook, he makes me wonderful food all the time . . .'

The girl shrugs. 'Can't you cook?'

'Yeah I can . . . But . . .'

'Then so what? He doesn't sound like he's worth it.'

But he *is*, thinks Kate. You just don't know him like I know him.

As if life couldn't get any worse, Kate now has to apologise to Melanie, who'll no doubt blow a Schadenfreude fuse. All Kate wants to do is crawl into bed, so it's disturbing to discover, on returning to her flat, that her bags have disappeared from her room, and that her recently crammed bookshelves are now home to a collection of framed photos of complete strangers.

Melanie's obviously told a friend she can stay while Kate's been away, but surely she should have left before

28

now? Kate opens the wardrobe. *What?* There are more than ten pairs of jeans, a dozen dresses . . .

Melanie picks up on the third ring. 'Hiya.'

'Whose stuff is in my room?'

'How was your romantic break, Kate?'

'Melanie, who's been sleeping in my room?'

'Calm down, Goldilocks, that's Steph's.'

'Who?'

'My squash partner. She's taken the room. Actually, the timing couldn't have been better – she had mice at her old place in Tulse Hill.'

Squash? Mice? Tulse Hill? What do these random words mean? 'But that's my room.'

'You're moving in with Nick.'

'That's in limbo, but I've paid rent till mid-August. You'll have to tell Steph to buy some mousetraps.'

'She's signed a tenancy agreement starting the first of August, it's a legally binding document.'

'Fine, I'll buy her the mousetraps, the ethical ones.'

'You were a hundred per cent clear you'd be gone early. Mate, you can keep your bags in the cupboard for another week, if that helps . . .'

Kate hangs up and stares at the bedroom ceiling. She must have done something pretty appalling in a former life to deserve this. There is a high-pitched ringing in her head only interrupted when her phone starts to ring.

Nick? Is it Nick? Please let it be Nick! It is not, and the name on the screen makes her heart sink.

'Aaah, you're back! Was it wonderful?'

Kate struggles to blow out the panic in her chest. 'Could you possibly pick me up from the flat please? No, *not* Nick's flat, mine. No . . . nope . . . I just need your spare room *very temporarily*. No, I'm fine – but I don't want to discuss the details and I definitely do not want any of your therapy bullshit, Mum, *please*, I mean it.'

On reflection, the way this day is turning out, Kate reckons that once upon a time she must have been Genghis Khan.

Chapter Six

COMING BACK TO LIVE at Rita's at her age? This really wasn't part of Kate's plan. Not that Kate's ever had much of a 'plan', but certainly tonight she'd rather been hoping to make Nick chicken fajitas, to celebrate the start of their new life together.

Rita's flat is perfectly nice, a two-bedroom in Heathview, a 1930s block in leafy Highgate, but Rita bought it twenty years ago, just after Kate's father died and Kate can't help but associate it with that awful time. Kate had just started an English degree at Manchester. She'd come home that Christmas. Her father was diagnosed on 3 January. By Easter he was dead. Pancreatic cancer had turned him from her much-loved, jovial dad to a barely recognisable skeleton in a few grim months. Kate had been so traumatised by his suffering, all she could focus on was doing what he'd asked in his last lucid days: 'Look after your mother'.

Kate had planned to return to university but by the time she'd helped Rita sell the house, buy the flat, decorate it, and then advised her on her new glamorous wardrobe and therapeutic courses, more than a year had passed and Kate felt like she'd somehow messed up her own life, pretty much that same glum ache of failure she's feeling right now.

'If you're not going back to university you need a job,' Rita had said at the time. 'Why not consider a holistic career? There are so many people who need compassion and help, and the hourly rates are lucrative.' Over the last two decades, Rita has become increasingly insufferable with each therapeutic qualification. Kate misses her wise, gentle dad every day.

Now, Rita drives into her parking bay at Heathview and pulls up the handbrake with a huff. 'Muteness doesn't suit you.'

Kate swallows and nods. If she opens her mouth she'll cry and she's already bored of crying.

Rita readjusts her rear-view mirror to admire her reflection. She runs a manicured finger over her sleek brown bob and the collection of silver bangles on her wrist tinkle their approval. The noise makes Kate's head hurt.

Kate steps out of the car and slowly, as if sleepwalking, starts to drag her bags from the boot.

'Darling,' says Rita, coming to stand beside her. 'I'd love to help, but . . .' Rita gestures vaguely at her groin.

Kate squints at her mother's get-up – standard Rita: white jeans, a sleeveless hot-pink silk blouse and vertiginous scarlet heels which expose far too much tanned toe-cleavage for a pensioner. 'You could just take off that slutty footwear and help me?'

'It's not the shoes, it's my adductors. Cole and I are doing a lot of lower-body work at the moment.'

Kate drags the bag into the block, Rita scurrying behind her, then sees the sign on the lift door and lets go of the bag handle.

'Oh. Shit,' says Rita, pouting indignantly. 'They're waiting for a part. Not till next Wednesday, apparently, unacceptable of course, but what can you do?'

What Kate does do is press the heel of her palms into her cheekbones and let out a low groan.

'Darling,' says Rita, pulling her close, 'don't take everything quite to heart so.'

But it is my heart, thinks Kate, and it literally hurts.

'There are blessings in our pain,' says Rita with a serene smile.

I will pay for a Travelodge or sleep in your car, so help me God, thinks Kate, struggling to free herself from Rita's embrace.

Rita turns to the lift, then back to Kate's soft body, which seems to have collapsed in on itself like a prematurely removed soufflé.

'Come on,' says Rita, resting one hand on Kate's shoulder as she takes off first one heel, then the other. 'Bring the bags in and I'll help carry them upstairs, it'll work my glutes.'

Kate lies on the faux-fur bedcover in Rita's spare room feeling like she's been in a fight. Her limbs ache and there's a pain low in her torso. In France, the day after The Wobble, as Kate is calling it (sounds a lot less final than The Dumping), Nick had cooked a roast chicken with home-made frites. How dare he make frites when Kate couldn't eat. She'd tried, but after two bites she'd retched. She's never lost her appetite before, but since that moment all she's wanted to consume are fags. At least she'll lose weight, *hidden blessings* indeed.

She stares at Rita's bookshelf. Rita always says she'd swear Kate was adopted if they didn't share a love of books, but Rita's collection is worse than Nick's algebra books: *Mother Your Inner Child*, *Light in Life's Darkest Corners*. Kate looks at her own bags, stacked in the dimly lit corner. No point unpacking, even though, technically, she's now homeless; this isn't the end of the relationship – her gut absolutely screams that. She refuses to take this personally. Nick's a textbook emotion-avoider. Really, it's not his fault, his parents – a hyper-religious mother and a manic-depressive father, both now dead – had been entirely emotionally absent in his childhood. That's why Nick so often retreats into his head, why he's so comfortable spending a hundred solitary hours doing a crossword. Still, none of that stuff is Kate's fault either, and she will not let Nick's past dictate their future. Nick is wonderfully generous, he makes the greatest lasagne; last month they spent an entire Sunday going through old childhood photos, laughing at how geeky their kids would probably turn out. Kate's not going to just walk away without fighting for this relationship.

'Darling,' Rita's voice cuts through her thoughts, 'dinner in five.'

Kate's phone beeps. She scrabbles desperately through her bag and her heart sinks again. Bailey is not Nick.

Enough of this! Time to do something productive. She opens the window and lights another fag.

'Eat something,' says Rita, frowning as she pushes the plate closer to Kate. Rita has assembled Kate's childhood favourites – an M&S Chicken Kiev and two Bird's Eye potato waffles. 'Have a waffle, I made them specially.'

Kate wearily cuts off a bite. It tastes acidic – probably not Rita's fault but more a result of the residual sour nicotine flavour now coating Kate's tongue.

'So what did you do to make him dump you? You said he used the word *withdraw*? What exactly happened?'

'I do *not* want to talk about it.'

Rita pincers an olive with her nails and pops it into her mouth. 'You've left things at his flat?'

Why did Kate do that? So unnecessary – all her favourite cookbooks, her Jamie Olivers, her Nigel Slaters, her beloved Angela Hartnetts – and as a strategy it had clearly proved futile.

'Let's go and get them,' says Rita, pushing against the table as she stands up. 'You need a clean break, to grieve.'

Kate gently touches her mother's arm. 'Mum, it's not over. Nick is confused. At the airport it sounded like he didn't want to break up . . .' She trails off helplessly.

Rita's top lip twitches. 'You need to take back control. Tell him he's either in or he's out.'

'Mum, I did. I'm giving him till the end of next month to sort himself out.'

'So you'll mope around for the next eight weeks till he punches you metaphorically in the face again? Stop being a victim. You need to adopt the mindset of a beautiful, empowered woman with an abundance of men. Sofia Loren wouldn't sit around waiting, Sofia Loren would go round and get her books back. Mind you, Sofia Loren probably wouldn't date a man whose Christmas party trick was doing an impression of a farting robot . . .'

'It was from that TV show we'd been watching! And he was tipsy. He'd just cooked the most amazing meal for us and *that*'s the thing you remember?' Kate's eyes fill with tears again as she remembers how happy she'd been, waking up on Christmas morning, knowing their day was going to be filled with fun, laughter and that feeling of togetherness she's craved her whole life.

'Do you want a yoghurt or something?' says Rita. 'Then we can write a list of all the things you need to fix about yourself before your fortieth.'

'Oh Good Lord, Mum, no, please, not tonight. I'm not hungry. And I'm not forty for several months yet. And in the interim I'll be in my room.'

Chapter Seven

THANK GOODNESS KATE HAS a busy job to keep her mind off the car crash her relationship has just turned into. As she approaches her office on Monday morning her jaw clenches. Her primary thought is: let me get through today without crying. Then: will Nick call today? Her next: is it too early for a fag break? These three thoughts circulate around her head as she passes through the revolving doors of Fletchers and has to stop herself spinning straight back out into the street and home again.

Kate started working at Fletchers supermarket the Christmas after her father died. It was meant to be a temporary job on the shop floor; she'd work for six months, earn money to go travelling, then figure out what to do with her life – preferably something to do with writing or food. Instead, an opportunity had arisen in head office, and because her manager sensed she had potential he'd put her forward. Because Kate felt guilty about leaving Rita, she'd taken it. Nineteen years and three departmental moves later, she's so institutionalised she's rooted in place and can do her job in her sleep. Still, she likes her colleagues and the regular hours mean she can see friends and have a life outside of the office.

As Kate heads to her desk she remembers her first date with Nick and how much she'd been dreading him asking about her job. Mercifully he'd talked all night long, though not in an obnoxious way. He'd started off talking about fractals, then moved on to Fibonacci numbers, Playfair ciphers . . . It was like listening to a fascinating lecture, but by a handsome man with twinkly green eyes who also happened to be buying her lovely red wine. He'd asked her about it on date two, though.

'I'm joint deputy head of copy for in-store marketing for Fletchers Supermarket – Meals and Chilled Solutions!'

'Chilled Solutions? That sounds like a terrible Groove Armada cover band. I'm not sure I know what that combination of words means.'

Kate already knew Nick was the cleverest man she'd ever met but she humoured him nonetheless. 'It means my boss Devron will bound up to me with this,' she says, showing him a photo on her screen. 'And he'll say, "Here's gold-standard. Gimme more of that".'

'A packet of Waitrose dill?' said Nick in confusion.

'Look at the words, Nick, look: *Delicate dill. Feathery fragrant fronds of flavour. Great with gravadlax.*'

'What specifically am I looking at?'

'You can usually get some alliteration on front of pack – rosy rhubarb, perfect pomegranate, oranges are always tricky. But three different consonants and the quadruple F? When you write a line like that it's actually deeply satisfying, it's like using all seven tiles in Scrabble and landing on triple word.'

'Now you're talking. And does the blurb actually make a difference? You either need dill or you don't. Dill or no dill, right?' He grinned.

It's only because she fancied him so much that she'd let the pun slide.

'And that's a full-time job?' he said.

'Two of us do it, me and a rather truculent woman called Annalex.'

'*Two* of you?'

'Yeah, yeah, I know that you, Nick Sullivan, can single-handedly put a man on the moon with the power of maths, but could you convince two warring range managers that they don't need more labelling for Curries or Pies because a third manager needs it for his Coated Protein?'

'I'm too scared to ask . . .'

'Coated Protein? You should be: substandard McNuggets.'

'A whole new world . . .' said Nick, laughing as he broke into song. 'So in fact you're a writer?'

'Yup – just like Shakespeare, but with more BOGOFs. I also write the shelf-edge stripping – that's the stuff that sits under the chicken thighs, and even the occasional wobbler.'

Nick's eyes had lit up as he'd reached for her hand. 'Oh Kate, please – tell me more about these wobblers!'

Well, Nick has now delivered his own wobbler, and a most unwelcome one at that, thinks Kate, miserably shaking off the now tainted memory. She grabs a black coffee then sits at her desk staring into space as the coffee grows cold.

She manages fifteen whole minutes of work before Kavita appears and asks was the holiday amazing? Kate tries to smile but her face crumples and a minute later Kavita drags her to the toast enclave for a debrief. Kate actually doesn't want to talk about Nick, she wants to get on with her job, but Kavita insists, and actually Kavita is happily married and might have a more encouraging perspective.

Kavita listens, her dark brows furrowing at key moments.

'I think I'm still in shock,' says Kate. 'He was giving such mixed signals. To be honest I'm in a bit of a mess about it all.'

'Toast?' says Kavita, offering up her own thickly peanut-buttered slice with a cautious smile.

Kate shakes her head dismally.

'Oh no, this *is* bad. Look, Nick's behaving like a colossal idiot. But . . . Dom and I love him, and we're decent judges of character. Nick deserves a second chance. Just the one, mind you. And you probably do need to ask yourself, if he's doing this before you move in, how reliable will he be if you end up having a kid together, because life doesn't get easier . . .'

Kate can't even begin to think that far down the line – she just needs to get back to where she was one week ago, as soon as possible.

Kate lies on her bed, staring out at the beautiful summer's night. She knows she should see a friend, but right now she's terrible company and, besides, she's so drained from obsessing about Nick, all she has the energy for is lying down and obsessing some more. It's like some weird addiction but with no highs, only lows and lower lows. Every time she looks at a photo of them on her iPhone it feels like an act of self-harm. Perhaps she should delete them. How could she possibly delete a single one?

Kate hears Rita screaming her name and drags herself up. In the living room Rita is sitting on the sofa with Geraldine Marks from flat fourteen and two large gin and tonics.

'You remember Gerry?' says Rita, waving her glass at Kate.

'You poor dear,' says Gerry as Kate stoops to kiss her. 'And while you were on holibobs . . .'

Kate gives Rita a stern look. Rita shrugs. 'Gerry merely asked why you've moved back in at your age.'

'Nothing wrong with living with Mummy,' says Gerry. 'Jeremy's fifty-one next month and he lives with his mummy. We couldn't be happier. Ooh, Rita, did I tell you he's just signed that huge Norwegian crime writer?'

'Tell him to pop over,' says Rita, smiling. 'Jeremy and Kate can talk books. And perhaps other things . . .'

Rita and Gerry exchange hopeful glances.

Yes, Mother, please do set me up with Heathview's answer to Norman Bates as soon as possible, thinks Kate.

'Darling,' says Rita, 'we've got the residents committee here in five. Be a good girl and take notes, you're such a good writer. And you can hand out the nibbles.'

Kate shakes her head. 'Sorry, I've got stuff to do in my room.'

Rita sighs as Kate retreats. 'Kate's gone on hunger strike, terribly oversensitive, my daughter . . .'

With her bedroom door firmly closed, Kate takes out her diary and flicks back to July. 'Feeling funny for a week . . .' OK: the night before France, Nick had made spaghetti carbonara for her; all was well. The night before that, at the cinema, Nick had held her hand continuously, to the point where it had interfered with her relationship with her chocolate raisins. All week long he'd been his usual affectionate self. She tracks back another week, then another, doing full forensics.

She hears the front door open, followed by an amused shriek, increasingly loud giggling, then the pop of a champagne cork – it sounds more like a key party than a residents meeting.

She takes out her iPod to drown out the noise of her mother having substantially more fun than her, but every song reminds her of Nick, of dancing round the living room at 2 a.m. to 'Faith', of singing 'Fairy Tale Of New York' at the top of their lungs last Christmas Eve, of the time he managed to get tickets to that amazing sold-out Phoenix gig at the Empire. Oh, wait. Was *that* it? At the Patti Smith gig in June? When Nick turned up at the Roundhouse bar, and after kissing her hello he'd sat reading his iPad. She'd assumed it was job-related but when she'd asked, he'd told her it was an article in *New Scientist* on dark matter. He'd announced it with such delight that she'd then felt petulant explaining that it made *her* feel invisible if he continued reading an essay during their date. He'd jokingly called her a diva, and she'd jokingly called him a dick, and then they'd laughed because they had both been joking, hadn't they? She can't have hurt his feelings fatally by calling him a dick, surely? He *was* being a bit of a dick . . .

What is her mother up to next door? A series of dull thuds, then more raucous laughter. What is Nick up to? Sitting on his sofa, realising he can't live without Kate? No, it's 8.30 p.m.: he'll be watching *Only Connect* on his beloved TV.

Kate would give anything if he'd turn off his TV and pick up the phone to her right this minute.

'Darling!' Rita screams. 'We need you!'

Kate trudges back into the living room.

'You remember Marco and Rodney? And John Pring from twenty-five, and Lizzette from thirty-three. Lizzette's hurt her ankle, so I've told her you'll walk Cookie.'

'Isn't she pretty?' says Lizzette, taking out her phone and showing Kate her screensaver of a demented-looking Welsh terrier with huge brown eyes and curly gingery-blond fur not dissimilar to Lizzette's hair. 'She's the dearest little thing.'

'Except there has been a report of fouling in the gardens!' says John Pring.

'Cookie would *never* do that. It's Lorna Bleecher's schnauzer, pooping after dark, and she blames poor Cookie – Lorna has a borderline personality disorder, Rita told me so.'

Kate finds herself dragged into a conspiracy theory about whose dog is stealth-crapping in the garden, who in the block is a sociopath (Lorna, and possibly Mikhail, the night porter), and who on the first floor is leaving rubbish in the hallway, exposing them all to risk of mice, rats and bubonic plague. Gerry then makes everyone watch Abbott and Costello's *Who's On First?*, and it is only when John and Lizzette start bickering about the increased service charge that Kate sees a window and excuses herself.

And there it is! The reward for her patience, her suffering and being vaguely polite to her mother's neighbours: a text from Nick.

Her heart lurches as she clutches her phone tenderly.

I really miss you. I told my friends about France, they think I'm an utter idiot.

Huh. What is she supposed to do with this? Was he sharing this information by way of an apology? Because apologies normally contained the word 'sorry'. Kate's thumb twitches as she tries to formulate the perfect response – a text that could undo the past week, make him realise what he's lost, hell, cure cancer too . . .

It doesn't matter what your friends think, it matters what you think. Of course you miss me. We were happy; if you had doubts about your doubts, you should have kept them to yourself!

She doesn't press send. It's not good enough – her response isn't – but that's because neither is Nick's text. It's hardly a man struck low on his knees or bent down on one of them.

She's going to wait, and sit with this horrible painful ache in her chest, and hope that in the next seven weeks, two days and three and a half hours he'll make a more impressive move – because anything less will no longer do.

Chapter Eight

KATE HAS BLU-TACKED a piece of A4 to the wall by her bed and every night she marks a cross with a red pen, another day endured. It feels like she's counting off the days in prison, albeit a rather plush prison decorated with soft lilac throws. Today is only day fifteen, and every one of the last fourteen has felt like she's coming off a drug. Still, she has not relapsed and contacted Nick, which is her main source of pride. This strikes her as a larger problem about her life, but not one she's ready to address yet.

Most nights Kate falls asleep and dreams she's living with Nick in cohabitational bliss. This belief lingers for several moments every morning until she remembers, and the truth causes a wide band of pain to spread across her ribs.

When she used to wake up with Nick, she'd open her eyes and when she saw his sweet face she'd feel safe. When he opened his eyes his smile would widen, and she'd feel a solid surge of joy that she got to sleep next to this gentle soul nearly every night.

Kate lies in bed at the weekends, hugging the duvet. She rests one palm over the other and interlocks her fingers. She tries to pretend she isn't really holding her own hand, wishing it were his.

Come on: out of bed. She draws back the curtains and her heart sinks. Another achingly beautiful summer Sunday. To stay inside and not take full advantage of it would be like wasting her youth, and Kate's already done that. She could go to the farmers' market; nothing's stopping her except that every sight and scent will remind her of his absence. She'd never known she could laugh so hard buying an apple as that time last autumn when they sampled a dozen varieties and Nick made up different silly voices for each; you had to be there, but it really was hilarious. Nick, Nick, Nick, Nick, Nick . . . She is sick of thinking about Nick, of talking about him but not *to* him.

Her phone and her fags have become her dual crutches. She has come to hate herself for being addicted to both. Every time she presses the button on her phone it feels like she's putting her finger on the pulse-point of a corpse in the desperate hope that it will come back to life.

She is stuck, her life on hold, waiting for any further communication from Nick. Of course she *could* accept he's a shit, and that this is the end – but that doesn't fit with the Nick she knows, so why would she do that?

Kate is determined not to waste the entire summer obsessing further – which is a bit like deciding not to let gravity bring you down.

She has written Nick a dozen letters, in her head, in her lunch break. Some are kind, some are furious; fortunately, none are sent.

August drags itself over an interminable bank holiday into September. There are still another thirty days until the deadline she's given him.

Kate is desperate for something else to occupy her head, but it's so full of Nick-white-noise that there's no space left to think. Rita keeps telling her she's in charge of her own thoughts, but that's preposterous. It's like saying Kate's in charge of her own appetite – as if she could stop eating a delicious cake after just one bite. It simply can't be done.

She would give a kidney, she really doesn't need both. Let him call, please just let him call.

Chapter Nine

TODAY IS A PARTICULARLY painful Friday. Devron, her boss, is at their team meeting. He only ever shows up to announce good news (he's heading off on another exotic TV shoot) – or terrible (no more staff discount at Christmas – buy your turkey in July and freeze it, or pay full whack).

Kate is so stuck in her head re-crafting another email she won't send Nick she barely registers the mood in the room, only tuning back in when she hears the familiar euphemism *maximising shareholder value*.

She sits bolt upright and listens with a horrible sinking feeling as Devron explains that cuts are being made across marketing. Either Kate or Annalex will be made redundant this November, along with three other team members – or they can choose voluntary redundancy at any time.

No. Not *again*. Not now.

It's the fourth restructure in the last ten years; she's survived the other three, but every time it causes a miserable few months of low-level fear tracking her like a shadow. And what if she doesn't survive this one?

Devron is currently 'formulating the methodography parameters' of the process and will get back to them next week with an update.

It's irrelevant that Kate has won a dozen copywriting awards, whereas Annalex nicks all her ideas from a creativity manual she stole from her ex-employer, Pharmacore, where she worked for five entire years on a single anti-gingivitis mouthwash campaign.

It's irrelevant that Kate works on forty-six more products than Annalex because Annalex recently played the staunch vegan card to avoid working on the summer barbecue range even though Kate saw her scoff a sausage-and-egg breakfast sandwich the very next day.

It's even irrelevant that Devron makes up words such as methodography and is in no position to be anyone's boss.

Kate's work future will be decided by a man who doesn't yet know what he wants, and doesn't yet know when he'll know. Wasn't one indecisive man in her life already one too many?

As they're traipsing out of the conference room she feels a throb of unhappiness pulsing in her stomach. Dave, the head of production, whispers his commiserations. 'You're too good for Fletchers, Kate. If I were you, I'd take redundancy and run for the hills.'

Kate can't remember what the hills even look like, let alone where they are.

Kate's mood is not noticeably improved when she returns home to find another to-do list from Rita on the kitchen counter:

Water Marco and Rodney's plants – the boys are off in Barcelona. Key with porter.
    Read Healthy Boundaries: How to Create Them; How to Enforce Them – on my shelf.
    Lizzette needs Cookie walked before 9 p.m.

Kate loves animals, so in theory she's been OK with her mother pimping her out as dog walker. Besides, recently she's read online that *Spending time with a furry friend can help lower stress hormones.*

Cookie, like Rita, is affectionate half the time, psychotic the other. Cookie's a jumper and a biter and has already chewed significant holes in several of Kate's most useful cotton skirts. Even though she's only knee high, the other night she was in a particularly playful mood and launched her strong wiry body high in the air, aiming at Kate's elbow and taking a large chunk out of Kate's favourite stripy T-shirt. Also Lizzette is clearly feeding Cookie suspect vitamins and Kate now finds herself crouched in the middle of Highgate High Street, scooping up warm green liquid poo. It's not helping Kate's stress hormones in the slightest.

On her return home, Kate assumes she has the flat to herself and is standing in the kitchen in pants and an old Top Shop vest when she hears the front door open. Kate barely manages to fling on an apron before Rita enters the kitchen closely followed by a respectable-looking fifty-something man dressed in chinos and a pink shirt.

'You're meant to be walking Cookie,' says Rita, sounding annoyed.

'Done that,' says Kate curtly. 'And for the record, Lizzette's ankle is fine, she was in heels earlier. I didn't know you'd have company,' she says in mild distress, then whispers, 'I'm not wearing a skirt, you said you were out for the night!'

'Patrick, this is my teenage daughter Kate. She's not normally an exhibitionist but let me show you through to the living room while she puts more clothes on.'

Kate hurriedly crab-steps from the room, praying this man won't realise he can see half her bottom reflected in the toaster. Her face burns with shame. This is all Nick's fault – she would never be in this humiliating situation if it weren't for him and his imbecilic, selfish wobble. She climbs into bed and composes another furious email to not send:

> Nick – one day you'll realise I'm the one that got away, but it'll be too late. You don't get a second chance for asking someone to move in, then backing out after they've given notice on their flat, thus forcing them to live with their narcissistic, slutty mother. Watch your big fat telly – I'm getting myself a better life.

This is possibly the most bonkers of all her crazy emails – partly because Nick hasn't asked her for a second chance, and also because 'a better life' does not involve throwing a tantrum worthy of a toddler, then retiring to bed at 8.40 p.m. on a Friday night while your mother's in the next room enjoying a raunchy first-date snog.

Kate is too agitated to sleep. She's resisted going near her mother's bookshelves until now, but she's desperate to understand Nick, to figure out what's going on and hence learn how to fix him. Perhaps these books might hold the answers.

Chapter Ten

'DARLING, IT'S 10.15 A.M., you need to water those plants,' says Rita, knocking, then opening Kate's bedroom door to find Kate only now waking up. Strewn over the bed are copies of *Attachment Theory*, *Narcissistic Personality Disorder* and *Why Won't You Apologize?*.

'So you've finally decided I'm not so foolish after all,' says Rita, sitting on the bed and gathering the books back. She picks one out and holds it up to Kate's face.

Kate glances at it, confused. 'Me? Apologise for *what*? Anyway, I read some good stuff about love-avoidants – it's *totally* Nick.'

'Heaven forbid you'd listen to my professional opinion, but Nick is an extreme anorexic.'

Kate squints out of the window and shakes her head. 'Are we talking about the same Nick? Because my Nick sometimes eats a sausage sandwich *before* breakfast.'

'It's not about sausages. Nick's an intimacy anorexic, they can be quite fat. Anorexics starve other people but ultimately themselves of emotional intimacy. They're terrified of closeness, they withdraw when people get too near.'

Kate shrugs. 'Nick obviously has some issues, but *you* know people can be fixed.'

'Sometimes – but not by other people.'

'Apart from people like you . . .'

'They have to fix themselves. On which note, have you thought about *your* issues, given you're enmeshed with an anorexic?'

'En*meshed*?'

'You don't have healthy boundaries, yours are loose. Nick's are too rigid.'

'Oh, here we go. You know what? Thank you for letting me read your books, thanks for letting me stay, but I don't need an attack on my loose boundaries first thing on a Saturday morning.'

'It's not an attack. You have weak boundaries like your father: you're too soft, you're—'

'Sounds like an attack to me,' says Kate, covering her ears.

'You're totally codependent.'

'Not listening . . .'

'And more than anything, you're too hungry for someone like Nick, who doesn't have enough to share.'

'Mum: enough!'

'You're foul-tempered because you're experiencing cognitive dissonance, you're clearly in withdrawal.'

'Withdrawal from *what*?'

'Love. Join a codependency or love addicts support group. I know you won't confide in me but there are other people out there with similar struggles.'

And similar nightmarish mothers. Kate throws back her duvet. 'I've got something important to do today.'

'Don't come back between two p.m. and four p.m., I'm doing lower-body work with Cole. Though you could join us, exercise would do you good.'

'I'm going to be late,' says Kate, grabbing a sundress that looks like it could work for whatever mysterious appointment she isn't going to.

'Water those plants. And let me know when I should ask Jeremy round for dinner, he's a nice man.'

'No matchmaking, Mum, please? Not now, I'm too fragile. In fact, not ever.'

Chapter Eleven

Everybody needs a best friend like Bailey, who will listen to you cry down the phone for weeks on end, and then, when you call on a Saturday morning desperate for an escape, will literally pick you up from a street corner and take you somewhere, anywhere, away from the place in which you're stuck.

'Perfect timing,' says Bailey, leaning towards the passenger seat to give Kate a quick hug. 'I've got two hours before I need to pick up the girls, and I have a plan.' A plan means action; being in motion means Kate won't have to feel her feelings. 'We need to get you out of your head.'

'Drugs?' says Kate. 'Or jogging? If so, can I choose neither?'

'I know how much you love animals. I've found a pet care centre in Hampstead. They need volunteers for kitten socialising; it's the perfect distraction for you, just for a few weeks till things sort themselves out.'

'Kitten socialising?'

'It's the job you were born to do,' says Bailey cheerily.

'Look, I know it's not ideal but they didn't mention there'd be a waiting list,' says Bailey an hour later, biting her lip as she sees disappointment etch itself more deeply on Kate's face.

'But now I've seen those kittens, I've realised I need to be around fluffy, adorable creatures. Maybe there's a less popular pet centre somewhere else. Shall I google?' says Kate, taking out her phone.

'Look, let's just try this Lauderdale place. That woman said they definitely need volunteers, plus it's round the corner, plus – well, I have to pick the kids up in ten minutes,' says Bailey, turning the key in the engine and speeding the car round the corner.

Kate nods rapidly. She feels like Bailey is single-handedly crowd-surfing her around North London, but without the thrills or rock music.

'The main thing is it'll be a distraction. And they'll be all cute and funny, just like in that film your dad took us to see when we were kids.'

'*Gremlins*?'

'*Cocoon*!' says Bailey, pulling up outside Lauderdale House for Exceptional Ladies, and pushing Kate out of the car. Kate is in danger of sinking even lower if she doesn't do something, anything, soon. 'You can teach them how to break-dance,' she says, cheerily waving Kate goodbye.

I'm not qualified to teach anyone anything, thinks Kate sorrowfully as she walks up the stone path, through the neatly manicured garden towards the imposing three-storey red-brick Victorian building feeling like it's her first day at a new school.

It all happens so quickly. She's buzzed into a high-ceilinged oak-panelled entrance hall that smells mildly of TCP and Campbell's cream of mushroom soup. The Director of Care, a middle-aged woman with grey cropped hair and electric-blue-rimmed glasses, strides out of her office, introduces herself with a firm handshake as Jackie Gaffney, and next thing Kate knows she's being formally interviewed.

'What brings you to Lauderdale today?' The kittens rejected me.

'What is your greatest strength?' My ability to tolerate bad behaviour.

'When have you overcome a major challenge?' I managed to get out of bed this morning.

Kate fudges answers to the above, then freezes when asked what she can bring to the role.

'I suppose—' Kate pauses. 'Well, I suppose I understand a bit about loneliness.'

The older woman nods as if it's the first intelligent thing Kate has said. 'And what do you know about us?'

'Nothing . . .'

'Well, I'll be delighted to fill you in! Lauderdale House was set up in the 1950s by Lucinda Winterford, one of the first women to graduate from Oxford. Her mother was a lively eighty-something at that point, and Lucinda felt she'd be better served around equally dynamic ladies rather than rattling around her house with a carer. Lucinda wanted to replicate the companionship of a collegiate experience, with professional high-end care. Residents here maintain as much independence as possible. They have access to a raft of social activities – everything from art classes to cocktail nights.'

'Cocktail nights! How brilliant,' says Kate, smiling for what feels like the first time in weeks.

'Around thirty ladies live here. They're a phenomenally distinguished group, smart, switched on. They've lived full and fascinating lives, and our duty is to make their time comfortable, dignified of course – but more than that – fun. A few of the residents are a little tricky, but their loss of independence can be a challenge. Many of them are highly sociable and take part in our activity programme. Others prefer time in their rooms.'

'And what do volunteers do?'

'All sorts. How's your Scrabble?'

Scrabble, Boggle, cards: all Nick and Kate activities. Kate wants no reminders in this place of why she's here in the first place. 'Not my forte, I'm afraid.'

'Do you play any instruments? We have a volunteer who plays the Celtic harp.'

Kate shakes her head.

'What do you feel strongly about?'

A man who doesn't know if he loves me enough. 'Books,' says Kate. 'I love reading . . .'

Mrs Gaffney looks unimpressed, as if everyone else who walks into Lauderdale is a dab hand at Chinese calligraphy – though the truth is, no one's offered to volunteer all year; she's almost as desperate as Kate.

'You work at Fletchers? Are you a "foodie"?'

'I've always loved cooking, and eating.' Kate rubs her stomach, which has developed a permanent low-level ache. It could be sadness, or the corrosive effects of her new diet of nicotine and black coffee. Not only has her appetite disappeared, but so has her thought for food. The other day she bought a sandwich from a petrol station. A new low.

'But you cook?' says Mrs Gaffney. 'If so, let's put you down for cookery demos on Thursday nights and Sunday afternoons, starting next Thursday at 7 p.m. Nothing too crunchy, spicy, rich or salty. Keep your portions small, be mindful of dentures – and you can use alcohol.'

'I can drink?'

'I meant as an ingredient,' says Mrs Gaffney, looking concerned. 'I suppose you could have a glass, if you're desperate.'

Kate laughs awkwardly. 'Cocktail night sounds great and all, but I'm really not a big drinker. I'm not.'

'You've never volunteered before?'

Kate fears this question is somehow related to the fact that she just sounded like an alcoholic, so she digs deep in an attempt to impress but ends up sounding like a poor man's Gwyneth Paltrow: 'I guess you reach a certain stage in life where you want to give something back – to others.'

Mrs Gaffney's eyes narrow still further. 'Yet you'll only commit for September?'

'I'm not sure I'll be living near the area beyond then . . .'

Mrs Gaffney is a skilled negotiator and realises that now is the time to up the ante. 'Perhaps you don't actually have the skill set we're looking for . . .' Nothing like removing an option from someone to make them want it.

Sure enough, it rapidly dawns on Kate that she could be turned down from a second unpaid role in the space of two hours. 'I think I'm up for it, can I let you know on Monday?'

Kate had rather hoped her mother would be proud. Instead Rita throws her head back and laughs. 'You? Volunteering? At an old people's home? Absurd.'

'Absurd that I should want to help others?'

'Spending your spare time with a bunch of random geriatrics when you should be out living your life? Those are prime dating hours. You're only doing this because you're holding out for Nick. It will be *so* depressing – senility, incontinence, flatulence . . .'

'I can get all that here.'

'Honestly, Kate, wasting time with a group of decrepit people with no future? They'll be more depressed than *you*. Forget this Laudanum place, invest time in meeting a man: join a golf club. You haven't got time to waste, it's rare that a woman gets more attractive with age,' she says, tucking the corner of her bob behind one ear and touching her lobe to check the diamond is still there.

'Mum – if it is definitively over with Nick, I'll be taking a break from men altogether.'

'Don't leave it too long or we'll be competing for the same ones,' says Rita, laughing. 'And you'll still be in the spare room when you turn fifty, you're only minutes from forty now.'

Kate doesn't wait until Monday. She calls Mrs Gaffney straight back to say she'll be reporting for duty on Thursday, at 7 p.m. on the dot.

PART TWO

Friendships should not be hastily formed,
nor the heart given, at once . . .

Mrs Beeton, *The Campaign for Domestic Happiness*

Chapter Twelve

THERE HAS BEEN PROGRESS! Kate has spent the last few days thinking about what to cook for the old ladies rather than obsessing about Nick. She's decided to make raspberry cheesecake brownies, a favourite old recipe from a time before cooking became inextricably 'Kate and Nick's favourite pastime'.

The ingredients are sitting in Rita's fridge, Kate will grab them after work – but on Thursday afternoon as she's sitting signing off Halloween Howlers artwork, her phone rings.

'It's Jackie Gaffney, from Lauderdale. Forgot to mention, ovens are off limits. Bernadette, our head of catering is prepping an Irish stew. You'll have to do something uncooked.'

'Oh, but I've already bought all the—'

'Bernadette rules the kitchen with an iron fist in an iron glove. You don't want to upset her on day one. Or frankly ever. A few other things: don't worry about the food being perfect, it's nice simply for the residents to see a new face. A lot of them suffer from macular degeneration or loss of hearing, so be patient. Don't take it personally if they doze off – some of them do T'ai Chi on a Thursday, they'll be tired. Oh, and come twenty minutes early and I'll show you around.'

Mrs Gaffney is running late and takes Kate on a whirl-wind tour of Lauderdale, every room of which is cosy, softly furnished and slightly too warm. They start in the dining area where Kate will be doing her demo. It houses a dozen tables with a longer table at one end and sparklingly clean French windows looking out on to the beautiful manicured gardens. Down the corridor are the administration offices, carers' stations and nurses' rooms, then there's the entertainment room where half a dozen residents sit watching BBC news on high volume. When Kate enters they sit up in unison, turning like meerkats to examine Kate with wide-eyed curiosity and a few smiles.

Over in the library there's a wide selection of large-print books, board games and jigsaws, and the air smells strongly of rose water. Four of the residents are concen-trating on a round of canasta, another three sit on the sofa, mobility walkers to one side, clearly enjoying a gos-sip as they look up guiltily when greeted, like naughty schoolchildren.

Mrs Gaffney heads down the main corridor to show Kate a couple of bedrooms, which are spacious and com-fortable, furnished with framed photos of children and grandchildren on every surface.

'You can see the gardens another time,' says Mrs Gaffney, checking her watch. 'You're on in two.'

Kate hasn't felt this nervous since her second date with Nick. In front of her sit ten watchful elderly ladies, like a gang of headmistresses. What is the collective noun for headmistresses? Perhaps the same as for porcupines – a prickle?

The youngest resident, Emily Sinclair, is eighty-six – the eldest, Constance Madrigal, a hundred and three. Some have walking sticks, most have hearing aids, all but one wear spectacles on chains or dark glasses. They wear smart blouses, sleeveless jumpers, long-sleeved tea dresses, buttoned up to their chins though it's mild outside, hotter still in here. They have immaculate hair and make-up, most wear earrings, necklaces, gold watches and wedding bands. On the back wall hangs a framed tapestried quote: *First you are young, then you are middle-aged, then you are old, then you are wonderful.* Kate will be chuffed if she gets to eighty-six looking as wonderful as these women do.

Kate's been given a brief introduction by Jackie but she's forgotten most of it – Edith Goldfarb worked at MENSA, Olive Paisner was a sculptor, Maud Rappapot is the widow of a wealthy property developer.

Kate looks down at the ingredients laid out on the long wooden table in front of her: two fresh eggs, the pale greeny-yellow stewed gooseberries, a small mountain of sparkling golden caster sugar and a bowl of luscious double cream. Time to get cracking.

'Hello, I'm Kate. Tonight I'll be making a simple gooseberry fool, ideal for this lovely weather.' She glances outside, wishing she was in a pub garden rather than standing here like a lemon. She decants the gooseberries into a larger bowl, explaining how she's mixed in a smidgen of elderflower cordial, to bring out the floral sharpness.

On the front row sits Bessie Burbridge, who has a delicate bird-like face, piercing blue eyes and thinning white hair combed over her pale pink scalp. Next to her is Maud Rappapot – angrily hunched, neck sunk into her shoulders, with a solid helmet of bleached hair and full *Baby Jane* make-up. Bessie smiles encouragingly as Kate pushes the fruit through a sieve. Maud purses her heavily painted lips as if biding her time.

Kate has been told to chat about her day, the high-light of which was debating with Devron whether they have to have alliteration on every sodding piece of packaging, because Crunchy Carrots was simply too mundane for words (answer: affirmative). She decides to talk more generally about the nineteen years she's worked at Fletchers. She doesn't like public speaking so she's relieved it's a small gathering, and that two of the ladies doze off within minutes, heads tipped for-ward, emitting gentle rhythmic snores. It's not until Kate starts whipping the cream that she hears any voice other than her own.

'Colder bowl!'

Kate looks up. On the back row, sitting alone, is an old lady with a shock of bright white hair, an intense brown-eyed stare and an expression of mild amusement. 'Page twenty-eight!'

Kate smiles awkwardly and carries on beating until the cream has formed beautiful thick ripples. Normally she'd dip a fingertip in to taste it but it could be Dulux today as far as her appetite is concerned. '. . . And every Friday at work we get to try new products, which is a lovely perk of the job.' Kate carefully separates the eggs, putting the yolks to one side.

'Cus-tard!' the voice from the back calls again, as if reprimanding a dog of that name.

'I'm actually doing a fool,' says Kate cheerily.

'No, fool,' says Cecily Finn. 'Use the yolks for custard, don't *waste* them.'

Did that woman just call her a fool? Unsettled, Kate returns to her bowl and starts whisking. 'Ah, now see? These egg whites are perfect.'

'Borscht,' says Cecily, which comes out of her mouth sounding awfully like a profanity.

Kate looks up again and notices that Cecily's hair is moulded into a glossy white peak slightly off to one side, not dissimilar to the stiffly beaten whites in Kate's bowl.

'Dinner for your son's fiancée,' says Cecily, as if reciting a rather obvious lesson. '*Food should be simple but excellent – an example and a warning.*'

Poor woman – Cecily must be one of the ones with dementia. 'Then finally,' says Kate, 'you stir in the fruit purée.'

'*She is not fair to cultural view, as many maidens be,*' says Cecily, with a touch of glee.

'Oh Cecily, do hush,' says Maud Rappapot, turning angrily towards the back. 'Let this girl get on with it, stop interrupting.'

'I'll stop interrupting when you learn the difference between two no trumps and four,' says Cecily, angrily.

'It *was* four! I would have made it if I wasn't dummy.'

'Ne'er a truer word.'

'Ladies, it's fine!' says Kate. 'I hope you're not referring to me, *not fair to view*?'

'Oh, such nonsense,' says Cecily, waving her hand dismissively. 'Read the book.'

It would be unkind to argue with a sick old lady, even if she is rude, thinks Kate, as she dishes out ten portions of dessert. Kate helps the ladies gather round the main table. Their arms feel like pure bone beneath their soft cotton sleeves. She's terrified as she resettles them that one of the ladies will fall and break a limb.

Maud Rappapot grabs a spoonful of dessert tightly, sniffs it, then sticks her tongue out like a tortoise and takes a small mouthful. Her mouth pinches, making the veins of crimson lipstick under her bottom lip intensify.

'What's the verdict?' says Kate, smiling.

'My grandson, lived in Japan for a decade,' says Maud. 'He speaks Japanese, French, Spanish and German fluently, and his Mandarin is passable. He used to bring me back these exquisite delicacies, Mochi, m-o-c-h-i. They were better than this.'

'Number one killer of old people in Japan every New Year!' says Cecily triumphantly.

'How dare you!' says Maud. 'He's a wonderful boy.'

'You stupid woman,' says Cecily, shaking her head. 'He was probably trying to kill you with the mochi. To get his hands on your money.'

'At least my husband earned a lot of it.'

'Well, I earned my own, thank you very much. Besides, what use is it to you now?' says Cecily. 'You'll be the one who takes it with you? *Sans teeth, sans brain . . .*'

Totally bonkers, and scrappy to boot.

'I think this gooseberry thing is wonderful, dear,' says Bessie Burbridge, patting Kate softly on the arm. 'It couldn't be more delicious.'

'Could if she'd used the correct fruit,' says Cecily, pushing her bowl away as if she's poking a dead rat. 'Your gooseberries: too sweet.'

'I'm surprised you can tell that without tasting them,' says Kate, raising an eyebrow.

'It's September, is it not? They'll be too ripe. I'd only use July's in a fool: sharper.'

'Oh, OK, interesting. Thank you, Cecily.'

'*Mrs Finn*!' says Cecily, her heavily lined brow creasing further. '*Anyone who imagines that all fruits ripen at the same time as the strawberries knows nothing about grapes . . .*'

'OK. Yep,' says Kate nodding. 'Grapes ripen later, presumably?'

'Paracelsus. It's a *metaphor*,' says Cecily, shaking her head in disgust.

'Don't mind her, dear,' says Bessie. 'This really is lovely, *thank* you. Won't you even try some, Cecily? You're always missing out.'

But Cecily has already stood up somewhat shakily and is heading to the door like a slow, determined warrior, her walking stick pointed sharply out in front of her like a spear.

Chapter Thirteen

FRIDAY IS PECAN DAY at Fletchers – one of the many acronyms the business uses that bares scant relation to the words represented. 'Proud As Can Be' day involves the food team sampling their latest products. New lines are brought out, greed and post-apocalyptic chaos ensue, and at 5.30 p.m. when people run for their trains, platters of dried-out chicken satay and sticky puddles of lime sorbet sit congealing under the fluorescent lights. Kate is usually keen to try whatever's on the menu but today there's a bad taste in her mouth and an ache in her stomach, anxiety about the impending restructure and heading to Christmas and forty without a job, plus her more immediate personal concerns.

A steady stream of colleagues has passed Kate's desk balancing napkins of multiple beige bites. Kate remains welded to her seat. Pete's wedding is tomorrow, looming like a storm. Rita is convinced Kate should take another guest, namely Rita. Kate shudders as she pictures Rita dragging her to the dance floor for 'Let's Stay Together', the Al Green version, not the Bryan Ferry.

She could text Nick right now and reinvite him, except that she's held out for thirty-six extra-long days already, she only has another twenty-two to go . . . And besides, to invite him to a glamorous celebration would send the message that what he's done is acceptable when clearly it isn't. No – she'll draft him another never-to-be-sent email instead.

Nick,

Please up your game, because every minute you don't fix this makes me hate you – and I don't want to hate you. I refuse to believe you're as crap as your behaviour.

No, far too aggressive. How about . . .

Nick,

I'm sorry you're confused but I'm not. You are a good man but you're having a crisis and you're pushing me away and that hurts. We are a team – I am on your side, I always will be. Come to the wedding tomorrow and let's talk. The food will be amazing – and apparently there's an a-list star doing the music x

Nope, doormat. How is it she can find fourteen ways to describe a potato, yet when it comes to the important things in life she's dumbstruck? It's Nick's fault – he's trapped her in this space where she can't find the words with which to escape, and this realisation makes her angry enough to delete both options.

'Kate – you have to try these new Christmas canapés,' says Kavita, returning to her desk with a napkin laden with putty-coloured pastry. 'The soggy bottoms are out of control. You OK, doll? You look exhausted. You know, you should just call him. You can't get on with your life while it's up in the air like this.'

71

Kate figures Nick's ongoing silence means there's a greater than 50 per cent chance it's over. Of course she *told* him not to call, but he's meant to see through *that*; it's the most basic of ruses. If she forces the issue and calls Nick now, though, she'll remove any remaining delusions she can still indulge in – and while limbo is intolerable, at least in limbo there still lurks hope.

'What are these, hon?' says Kavita, picking up the stack of card strips from Kate's desk. 'Best of *Bir-shit*?'

'October's shelf-edge stripping.' Kate blushes and takes them back from Kavita's hand. 'They're meant to say 'Best of British', but Annalex signed them off wrong again and the printer didn't pick up on it, so this lot are going in the bin.'

Kate tucks them discreetly into her bag; she has plans for these cards tomorrow.

'So is Cinderella going to the ball or what?' says Rita, entering Kate's room without knocking, catching Kate flicking glumly through old photos of her and Nick.

'Sorry, Mum?'

'Am I your plus one?' says Rita, cherry-red fingernails drumming against her hips. 'Call Pete and ask, or I'll call. They'll have paid for Nick's place, I'm sure they'd rather you brought someone than wasted their money.'

'I'm not nagging Pete the night before his wedding,' says Kate, who had been practising relaxing breathing, but at her mother's appearance has regressed straight to huffy teenager.

'Fine – if you'd rather be the only person there alone.' Rita turns her gaze to the pile of bags still in the corner. She looks back sharply at Kate.

Unpacking will make this all too final. Kate will not let Nick's stupidity, his lack of self-awareness, his lack of consideration, his apparent ambivalence, his general and utter uselessness get in the way of their love.

'It'll be sorted one way or another.' Kate glances quickly at the wall chart. 'Soon enough.'

Chapter Fourteen

PETE'S WEDDING DAY HAS arrived. Kate *must* make it a happy day – she must. Pete has been her friend since school. While all their other friends married and some divorced, Pete has been her reassurance that she wouldn't be the last man standing, but now he's abandoning their merry duo and committing to Mia, a girl in her twenties who he's only known for *eight months*. Mia comes from West London media royalty – her father's a film producer, her mother works at *Vogue*; Mia is a beautiful, tousle-haired girl with size four shoes who dresses like a Parisian – she'd be hateful if she wasn't so nice.

Kate could have done without the dream she had last night which has left her out of sorts already. In the dream she and Nick were getting married. Kate was at the altar, Nick beside her, missing his vows because he was too busy reading an article on his iPad about SpaceX rockets. Why does her subconscious have to be quite so unhelpful? Couldn't she at least have dreamt it was Ryan Gosling missing those vows?

Outside the sky is stormy. It's already hot and humid. Later it's due to chuck it down.

Pete's wedding is in Surrey – a train, bus and another bus away. Kate rummages through her pile of bags till she finds her favourite heels: three-inch, purple, suede. They bring good cheer every time she sees them – not least because they were reduced from £400 to £40 in the sales, and are implausibly comfortable. She puts them into a cloth bag, then puts her trainers on for the journey and gathers her essentials in her handbag: tissues, fags, phone . . . This phone will become a time bomb later. She scrolls to Nick's name and changes it to DO NOT CALL WHEN DRUNK.

One final bag check – oh, she'd almost forgotten her shelf-edge stripping cards. There'll be guests at the wedding who only know Kate as 'Kate and Nick'. On the back of the cards she's written various communiqués in black Sharpie:

> We're on a break, I'm fine but sober, so let's not spoil this lovely day talking about it.
> We're on a break and now I'm too drunk to discuss it.
> Nick is a confusing, commitment-phobic man-boy.

These subtitles should head off any conversation at the pass. She is going to enjoy this wedding if it kills her. She grabs her two bags and heads out, her face as grim as if she's funeral-bound.

Kate sits under the fluorescent glare of the Overground train, transfixed by the ugliness of the orange seat covers. She's been on this train an hour already with two stops still to go. She rubs her diaphragm; it's feeling particularly bruised today. She'll start taking better care of herself tomorrow – stop drinking so much coffee, cut the fags – but today she's allowing herself one final booze-soaked round of self-destruction.

It's good she didn't cave in and contact him. That would have been weak and she is not weak, she is strong – or at least it might look that way, though not if Nick could see inside her head. She should be proud of her self-control and she nods her approval, then catches sight of her reflection nodding violently like a mad girl on a train, and her face reddens.

She takes the wedding invitation from her bag. On the front is a patchwork collage of selfies of the happy couple – in photo booths, in the Glastonbury rain, kissing in Day of the Dead Halloween costumes. In every shot they look like there's nowhere they'd rather be. Nick rarely takes photos, though he's always the first to pull a funny face in a group shot. Rita had used the word 'inauthentic', and though Kate tries not to engage with her mother's psychoanalysis of every boyfriend, she'd asked Rita what she meant: 'It's never Nick's true self. He doesn't know who he is.' 'Good grief, Mum, he's just having fun.' Kate is so anti-therapy because Rita's always shoving it down her throat – but actually, perhaps a skilled counsellor might help crack Nick open. Maybe Kate should buy him a session, he's too short-sighted to see the benefits without a push . . .

Shit, bugger, *shit!* She looks up to see the train doors about to shut, she leaps and runs for them, swerving a couple of teens who've just boarded, thank goodness she's in trainers, she only just clears the doors before they close, her heart racing as the train pulls away.

Jeez, that would be pure Darwin Awards – dragged under a train by her own dress because she'd been too busy analysing what a moron her boyfriend was. She forces a deep breath. It's OK, just two more buses in this sweltering heat. On the bus she tries hard to switch her focus to *positive* thoughts: she is losing weight, primarily through swapping fags for food. Has she remembered her lighter? Panic. She reaches, feels it at the bottom of her handbag: relief.

She changes buses and stands at the new bus stop, smoking and counting her blessings: she is fantastically lucky. She is healthy. She has a mum, a decent job – actually, best not to rely on her job for solace at the moment . . . She has a home, good friends. Perhaps even if it doesn't work out with Nick, *they* can still be friends. It's the nothingness, the void, that overwhelms her. Rita is right, she thinks, stubbing the butt under her trainer – why does Kate have to *feel* everything so much?

The second bus winds through the suburbs as Kate gets stuck in the cul-de-sacs in her mind. She almost wishes Nick had said it was over, at least then she could move on. Could she even get past this, though, if they did get back together? It feels like he betrayed her, it was *so* unexpected that punch to the gut – ENOUGH! She will go mad if she doesn't stop this loop. She googles a meditation website, then spends the next five minutes thinking about Nick's toes wiggling.

Next stop Halewood House – a beautiful eighteenth-century Palladian villa set in acres of manicured grounds. She walks towards the entrance pondering where to change into her heels, maybe in the car park, or the – oh no. No! She freezes in horror. A sudden nausea rises up as she remembers wedging the shoe bag beside her on the train, but not grabbing it when she dashed for the doors.

It's not even as if her trainers are cute plimsolls; they're what Nick calls her 'Florida tourist' shoes – zinging yellow Nikes which embarrass her even when she runs.

Right: she'd passed a newsagent on that last leg of the journey. She still has twenty minutes before the wedding starts. It is conceivable that a newsagent in the height of summer will sell flip-flops, or a magazine with a free pair on the cover. She hitches up her dress and jogs back the way she came. Intense smoking has done her lungs no favours. The sun beats down. By the time she reaches the newsagent, she's breathless, her hair damp at the temples.

Small independent newsagents in Surrey do not sell flip-flops, and this one doesn't even sell cold water because the fridge is broken. Kate speed-walks back to the venue, panic rising, four minutes to get there but her phone says it takes six. She arrives glistening with sweat, decides that no shoes are better than trainers, stashes them behind an umbrella stand and is panicking trying to remove her socks when the music starts and she hops to a seat on the back row, still in one sweaty sports sock and here comes the groom!

Kate hears the opening bars of Cat Power's 'Sea of Love' – one of her and Nick's favourite songs – and bursts into tears. She is overwhelmed – happy for Pete, but heartbroken – and the tears flow freely. She gasps and swallows, making a gurgling splutter like a small frog being squelched under a DM boot. The guests in front turn to stare. She hangs her head in shame.

Kate stands alone on the terrace, surveying the sea of couples on the lawn below. Another glass of champagne should take the edge off this overwhelming loneliness.

She grabs her third from a passing waiter, which means necking the glass in hand, which she promptly deposits on his silver tray with a loud clink and a 'woops!'

This wedding's like a Richard bloody Curtis film – in fact, Mia's parents live on the same street as him. Mia's father worked in music before film, and there is a bona fide rock star here whom Kate has loved since forever. Mia's mother is formidable – stick thin, high-fashion, air kisses. Mia's friends are like Mia – waifs who could pass off the shoeless look far more convincingly than Kate. And this venue is so unnecessarily romantic, terraced gardens leading down to a secret maze. Later there will be fireworks and coloured sparklers.

If Nick was here they'd be having a blast, but he's not, so Kate lights up a cigarette and sucks on it like it's oxygen. A woman passing in a gold fascinator turns to frown. Kate shrugs apologetically – cigarettes have become her medicine.

Kate downs the champagne. The humidity and nicotine are making her wobbly. The thought of canapés piling up in her stomach doesn't appeal, though normally she's the one hovering by the kitchen doors waiting to pounce. She will eat dinner and hear out the speeches – and then she'll put her trainers back on and trek home, because no one will notice if she misses the dancing, but they will notice if she voms on the dance floor or immolates herself with a sparkler.

Kate walks back through the reception room and her eye is drawn upwards. Ten wooden hoops hang from the ceiling with pink ribbons criss-crossing them. Each hoop has a table number in the centre, and captured within the ribbons are smaller cards with the guests' names. Kate scans for her own – Lettie and Matt, Vicky and Nathan . . . where is she? Oh, there she is, on table nine – Kate and Nick, suspended in mid-air. Damn Nick for turning this special occasion into an ordeal in which the metaphors are quite so in her face.

More champagne *immediately*. She grabs another glass, takes a swig and a flourish of bubbles burns up her throat. It's too acidic, but Kate's not going to leave this drink, no indeedy, *she*'s not a quitter.

She heads to the bathroom, ah, sooo good to sit down. But her feet, they need a scrub! In the sink, of course, that makes total sense! She has one leg raised when the door opens and a woman in head-to-toe Chanel enters and Kate dashes back into the cubicle. For some reason (ABV 12 per cent) she decides to wash her feet in the toilet instead, but after washing her left foot she real-ises the process is ticklish and cold, and that the toilet flushes a violent blue bleachy water. Love isn't patient, love isn't kind; love is hopping out of a toilet, trying to muster the smile that says, *Having one blue foot is all the rage in Milan*.

By the time Kate heads back to the party the clouds that were threatening have turned into a downpour. Couples shelter arm in arm inside the conservatory. 'Winter is coming!' says one man, and his girlfriend giggles and nuzzles his neck. Kate's winter is less than three months away now, her forties: becoming invisible to men, spinsterdom, cats, then death. She'd mistakenly believed she and Nick had agreed to shelter from that storm together.

Two of Mia's friends, a couple in their twenties, suddenly burst out of the conservatory doors and run, laughing, into the garden. Holding hands they sprint across the lawn, shrieking with joy, their faces raised to the downpour, the girl's long red hair streaming down her back. The entire wedding party gives them a massive cheer, apart from Kate, who thinks, *show-offs*.

This is why Nick dumped her – because she's a mean, ungenerous person – that, and she has one most peculiar bleachy Smurf foot.

By the time they finally sit down for dinner, Kate is officially toxic. To Kate's right is an empty seat with Nick's name tag on it. To her left are an engaged couple, mouths glued to each other, the man wearing Nick's distinctive cedar aftershave. It's too much; the pressure in her head is making her crazy. She fears she'll do or say something more shameful. Already behind her ear is a peony she's snapped off a bouquet – first flowers Nick ever bought her, peonies. Her card strips now line the bottom of her bag, angry confetti. And there'd been that awkward moment earlier when she'd told Pete's pre-teen nieces, who were busily discussing their own future sparkly wedding dresses, that they'd be better off investing in sparkly lab coats and a science degree, because it was only a matter of time before a man proved how utterly disappointing and un-Disney-like he truly was . . . Not ideal, but Kate's right, isn't she?

She needs to pull herself together. She forces herself to stop drinking. She eats as much of the dinner as she can; it's probably delicious but the dauphinoise potatoes feel like lumps in her mouth, the lamb like tangled flesh.

Pete is besotted with his new bride. In his speech he talks about their first holiday together, how beautiful

Mia looked as they were driving around Sicily, her little finger twitching with excitement whenever she caught sight of the sea; how this made him realise he wanted to share every adventure with her, to spend his life making her happy.

Kate fears she'll be sick, not from booze but from sheer envy. It's not a cool sentiment – Pete is a great friend, he deserves happiness; she just wishes he could have got married a month before The Wobble rather than after it.

Just because they're happy doesn't mean Kate won't be happy one day; there's not a finite amount of happiness to go round.

Just because they look blissful now doesn't mean they won't be arguing about who's taking the bins out in a year's time. You don't know someone after *eight months*; people can surprise you horribly at any time.

Kate does not want to be here, wallflower at the wedding, having bitter, uncharitable thoughts.

Oh, and here comes the music – and it's her absolute favourite, it is actually Debbie Harry up on the mic! – a friend of Mia's dad – and she's going to sing, and Kate can't bear not to share this with Nick: it will break her.

All very well Kate commending herself on the train earlier for her superhuman self-control, but that's only because she hasn't been this blind drunk since New Year's Day when she and Nick drank far too many White Russians while watching *The Big Lebowski*.

She goes to dial Nick, then curses: she's deleted his number. Oh but she hasn't – she's merely changed his name to prevent her doing precisely this. The problem is she's now too drunk to remember what he's saved under.

That's OK – she doesn't need his number: she has his email. She has to tell him about Debbie Harry and also ask once and for all if it's definitely over, because it's better to know, even if the truth hurts – at least then this madness ends.

She types: *Can you please phone me? x* presses send, instantly regrets the kiss mark, then the entire email. She sits on the toilet floor and rests her spinning head on the toilet lid. She will wake tomorrow and all that will remain is an imprint of shame. She's lost her favourite shoes, but most of all she's lost her beloved. Actually, those shoes are a pretty close second.

She lets out a small sob. It doesn't matter. This too shall pass. We're all going to die one day, possibly sooner rather than later in the current sociopolitical climate. She rests her head and is instantly asleep, but then her phone rings, caller ID: DO NOT CALL WHEN DRUNK.

Adrenaline kicks in. She sits bolt upright. She's too drunk, she should not answer his call. She answers his call.

'Hey!' says Nick, and Kate's heart aches from missing his voice. 'You must be at Pete's wedding?'

'I lost my shoes,' says Kate. 'I lost my other shoes too. And Debbie Harry is here! And I feel rotten.'

'Debbie Harry? What do you mean you lost your shoes? Are you drunk?'

'I'm asleep in the toilet,' she sobs. 'I wish you were here.'

'Oh babe, so do I. Not necessarily in the toilet, but I wish I was there to take care of you. How are you getting home? Do you have money for a cab?'

'I was going to get the buses and the trains and the planes and the automobiles . . . It's like the middle of nowhere, Nick, it's not even London, I can't afford an Uber.'

'OK: what's the name of the venue?'

Kate blows out hard. 'That is such a difficult question.'

'It's in Kingston, right?'

'It's . . . Hale . . . Hen . . . Halewick . . .? It's white.'

'OK, stay on the line . . . Heatherington House or Halewood?'

'Yes.'

'Which?'

'It has a maze full of Vogue-shaped monsters, an amazing maze, a noisy oyster.'

'Definitely a maze?'

'Uh-huh . . .'

'OK, I'm pretty sure you're at Halewood House. Listen to me carefully, Kate: go and get a pint of water and drink it and then go and stand in reception and drink another, an entire pint. Be careful not to tread on any broken glass. I'm calling you a cab.'

'No! You've got no job, it'll be millions of pounds.'

'I had a final interview at Allsom this week, it's going to be fine.'

'Oh, Nick. You're so sweet. Nick, why did you set fire to what we had? Why did you burn down our entire relationship like it meant nothing?'

'I didn't, I didn't mean to. I really need to talk to you, when you're sober. Look – go and stand in reception. Keep drinking water. Try and find a bread roll to soak up the booze. You're not going to be sick, are you?'

'No, I'm OK,' she says wearily.

'OK, so stay on the line with me till you're back home.'

'I've lost my Florida tourist shoes, they were by the umbrella stand. Who would even steal them?'

'Probably not Debbie Harry . . . Listen: I'm staying on the line till I know you're safely back in bed, OK?'

'You'd do that for me?'

'Of course! I'd come down and rescue you but I think you need to get home quickly.'

'Nick,' she sighs.

'Kate, I've been waiting for you to call for over a month, I didn't think you wanted to speak to me. It's so good to hear your voice. I think about you every day.'

'You do?'

'I didn't realise how big a part of my life you are.'

Kate feels an epic wave of relief wash over her. Kavita was right and Rita was wrong and can piss right off.

Nick does love her. It's all going to be OK.

Chapter Fifteen

THE SOUND OF THE front door slamming wakes Kate: Rita, off to bridge club for their Sunday social. Kate runs her tongue over her teeth in an attempt to find moisture. Her entire body feels like it's been soaked in vinegar and left to air-dry, like a Japanese shrivelled pickle.

This morning she doesn't need to check her phone to see if Nick's texted. Of course he's texted, several times:

Hope your hangover's not as big as the Big Lebow-ski . . .

Please let me know you're OK?

Eat some carbs x

What can she cling to from last night's phone call that might stop her drowning in mortification? He'd called four minutes after receiving her email – that was hugely encouraging. She'd blabbed and blubbed and he hadn't hung up – that was good too. He'd definitely said he missed her. If he hadn't rescued her, she'd probably still be asleep in that toilet, locked in the venue till Monday.

She rubs her forehead. She needs water, food. She'd cooked Bailey dinner every night for that first hideous week after Tom's affairs were discovered. Bailey's always vowed to repay the favour one day: well, today's the day! Kate's halfway through dialling Bailey's number to plead for a bacon sandwich, when she remembers with a sudden dread that she's committed to preparing tea for the Lauderdale ladies this afternoon – and with a heavy heart puts the phone back down. *Such* a dumb idea to volunteer there – she can't let old people down, and that is so annoying.

Why is daylight so bright? She slowly gets out of bed. She washes, makes coffee and a slice of buttered toast with Marmite. It tastes surprisingly brilliant, possibly because she's so desperate for salty carbs, possibly because now that there's a thin scraping of Nick back in her life she might be able to eat normally again.

What's her next move? She feels like she has some power back because Nick sent the last text; she must hold on to that power for as long as possible. More pressingly, however, she needs to buy the ingredients for tea. She wants to go via Karma Bakehouse in Hampstead for their challah bread. It'll be lovely and soft, and avoids a hard crust issue so hopefully that crazy Cecily Finn won't have anything to moan about.

Kate only has two hours to do that, and it's taken her two whole hours to get from bed to dressing gown. She needs to move.

She is dozing on the bus to Hampstead when Nick texts again, fourth text in a row:

Fancy a sausage sandwich to help soak up the booze?

Oh she does, she does! She could get off the bus, take a cab straight to his flat, eat that sandwich with ketchup and mustard, lie down on his sofa and let him stroke her hair till she passes out. That is everything she ever wanted in life right there – but no, she's going to stay on this bus and make the grannies their tea, because she said she would and also because how dare he think he can just waltz back into her life without some sort of penance?

In the reception area at Lauderdale, Kate sits waiting with couples young and old and the occasional baby being brought to meet a great-grandmother. Most visitors carry flowers or cakes, and there's a lively bustle, the visitors chatting with familiarity and a shared camaraderie.

As a consequence of families visiting, Kate's audience is even smaller today, only seven ladies – probably a blessing, given her delicate state. There's Bessie again, beaming at her from the front row, and Maud, wearing lilac eyeshadow that makes her look like Michael Winner in drag.

Kate had rather hoped Cecily might be entertaining her family, but no such luck – there she is again, alone on the back row, wearing a crisp blouse as bright and white as her hair, and navy slacks. She raises her chin towards Kate and frowns, adding a hundredth crease to a face already more creases than skin.

Kate and Nick once ate at a posh pub that served miniature toasties on challah topped with perfect fried quails' eggs. Kate's fine motor skills are definitely not up to cracking a quail's egg right now, but she can handle a Breville. She's picked up the challah and bought good ham and cheese from Sainsbury's. She sets up the equipment on the long table. All she has to do is slice the bread, butter both sides, layer on the ham and cheese, grill for two minutes with a flip halfway, then cut into delicate squares – a five-stage process even Rita could pull off.

'Are we not having mochi?' says Maud before Kate has even unpacked. 'You promised, you wicked girl.'

Kate smiles awkwardly. 'I'm actually doing savoury today. I did look up a mochi recipe, but you need a Japanese red bean paste that's hard to find. It's probably easier to ask your grandson to buy some.'

'He's far too busy! He's very successful – his company now supply wine to all the finest hotels. And now he has the children half the time, I wouldn't dream of asking.'

Kate notices that Cecily has turned to face the wall, away from the direction of Maud's monologue.

'Just a thought,' says Kate, putting the bread on the table.

'My eldest great-granddaughter has won a scholarship to The Mayhew,' Maud continues. 'She plays tennis for the county too. She's fantastic at everything.'

'Except coming to see you,' says Cecily, chuckling.

'That's because her mother makes it so difficult,' snaps Maud. 'I told him that's what happens when one marries beneath oneself.'

'Pardon me! I keep forgetting you're royalty,' says Cecily.

Oh please, not again. 'Er, Bessie, do you have children?'

'Oh yes,' says Bessie, straightening up in her chair. 'My son lives in California with his second wife and they have twins who are at university. My daughter lives in London, she visited yesterday. She and her husband didn't have children. Are you married, dear?'

'No,' says Kate, frustrated to find herself blushing furiously as she reaches for the cheddar. 'I'm . . . not with anyone at the moment.' There. She's said it.

'You're not one of those strident feminists, are you?' says Maud. 'One of those women who's so dismissive of other women who choose motherhood?' Maud looks pointedly at Cecily.

'You utterly dreadful harpie,' says Cecily, shaking her head. 'Dreadful!'

'Gosh, no, I very much want a partner,' says Kate, stumbling in. 'I'd love to be in a relationship again, I was – well, it's a bit . . . it's not something I need to burden you ladies with.'

She feels Cecily's focus on her sharpen as she struggles to find the end of the plastic wrap on the Cheddar. Kate turns redder and redder as she wrestles with this most basic of tasks and ends up stabbing the cheese open instead.

'Oh well, dear, I'm sure you've still got time. Girls nowadays seem to do things so much later.'

'I'm sure it'll all work out the way it's supposed to,' says Kate, swallowing down the wave of sadness that hits.

'*The hope I dreamed of was a dream, was but a dream . . .*' says Cecily from the back row, in a singsong tone as if crooning. '*And now I wake, exceeding comfortless and worn and old.*'

That's pretty much how Kate is feeling – a coincidence she could live without.

'"Mirage" . . . Rossetti . . .' says Cecily.

Random, incoherent babbling; no point in trying to decipher any meaning, Kate's head is throbbing as it is. Instead, Kate turns her attention to buttering the bread. 'So I've chosen challah—'

'Not a patch on Grandpa's,' says Cecily.

'It's like a brioche dough and it's very—' Kate grabs a glass of water; her brain is moving too slowly. 'Versatile. Yup. Here we go, let's stick that in the Breville. Ladies, Mrs Gaffney mentioned some of you cook for yourselves sometimes?'

'Occasionally I'll microwave a soup,' says Bessie. 'Or an egg, if I fancy something light.'

'Mrs Finn?' says Kate with trepidation.

'Why bother? *One morsel's as good as another when your mouth's out o' taste*. Are you acquainted with Eliot?'

'Eliot . . . I don't think I know him,' says Kate, trying to keep the cheese from spilling out of the sides of the bread. 'Does he work in the kitchen?'

'*George* Eliot.'

'George Eliot, nope, haven't met him yet.'

'Good grief, you are a halfwit. Scrap that, a quarter-wit!' says Cecily, and this thought seems to amuse her greatly.

'Marvellous, OK, time to flip these sandwiches,' says Kate, her face colouring. Seriously, she could be on Nick's sofa right now rather than being a punchbag for this mad old cow. She came to Lauderdale to escape a difficult woman – not swap one directly for another.

The toasties have turned out surprisingly well. Bessie Burbridge announces that they are the nicest she's ever tasted. Maud Rappapot eats two and doesn't mention the mochi again. Olive Paisner takes tiny bites like a mouse, her jaws working overtime, and ends up eating four. Cecily sits at the table silently.

'Won't you at least try one, Mrs Finn?' says Kate. 'I know you don't like food going to waste.'

'They're not salty enough.'

'Again, why not taste the food before forming an opinion?'

'My eyesight isn't what it once was, even so: challah contains a lower salt ratio than other breads – not as low as what we used to eat in Tuscany but, nevertheless . . . And cheap supermarket ham and cheese cannot provide an adequate salty crystalline underpinning. I am ninety-seven years old, I have eaten sandwiches on *thousands* of occasions, on every continent on this wretched earth, so I do not need to taste *your* sandwiches to form my opinion because my opinion is based on observation and ninety-seven years of experience.'

'Fine. Then add salt now.'

'Now they're tepid.'

'Mrs Finn . . .'

'A deluxe rarebit would have had sufficient salt. From the bacon. Page 148, I think.'

'Of what?'

'Every continent on earth?' interrupts Maud, her scarlet lipstick curling into a vicious smile. 'You haven't been to Antarctica, you absolute liar, Cecily Finn.'

Cecily takes a deep breath as if her patience has never been quite so tested. 'We visited King George Island in the South Shetlands in the spring of 1973. We were served peculiar food, possibly a penguin sandwich, but we felt it impolite to question our hosts, unlike certain people who don't seem to comprehend the concept of impertinent and vulgar questioning.'

'But Cecily, aren't the Shetlands in Scotland?' says Bessie, her brow furrowing in confusion.

Cecily looks straight through Bessie as if she's invisible.

'Of course the Shetlands are in Scotland,' says Maud. 'Harold and I had a friend who owned a castle there.'

'The *South* Shetlands,' hisses Cecily. 'You are a shamefully unintelligent creature, Maud. Ho-rren-dous,' she says, rolling the word around her mouth like a mint imperial.

'Ladies, ladies!' says Kate, holding her hands up in an attempt to calm the group down. 'Please, let's be gentle with each other. Mrs Finn,' she says, turning to Cecily with a pleading look, 'I'd *really* like to make you something you'll actually eat next time.'

Cecily shrugs. 'It is of such little consequence to me – but if you insist, you could attempt a dark chocolate soufflé.'

Kate nods. 'A chocolate soufflé. With a salty crystalline underpinning?'

Cecily raises an eyebrow.

'Everyone happy with that?' says Kate.

The others nod enthusiastically. Kate glances at her watch – ah, thank goodness.

She starts to pack up as the ladies slowly head from the dining room. Now that Kate's distraction is over, her thoughts switch straight back to how to respond to Nick. She turns to leave but Cecily remains sitting, palms resting on the table, her intense brown-eyed stare focused on Kate.

'Buried down the road, of course,' says Cecily. 'In High-gate Cemetery.'

'Sorry, Mrs Finn, who is?'

'George – dear, clever George.'

'Oh right. Was George your husband?'

'Young lady, do you have *Alzheimer's*?'

'Do *I*?'

'Are you mentally subnormal? I'm talking about George Eliot!'

'Sorry, my mind was drifting. You mentioned him before.'

'*Herrr*!' says Cecily with a roar.

Best just to humour the old bird. 'That's nice. High-gate Cemetery's near me.'

'I'm hoping to be there myself, in a week or two.'

'Oh, on one of their cemetery tours?'

'No. Dead. In the ground. Mortal coil: shuffled off.'

'OK, then,' says Kate, grabbing her handbag and swinging it onto her shoulder. 'See you next week, Mrs Finn.'

'Not if I'm dead,' says Cecily.

'If you are, I'll swing by Highgate and pay my respects.'

'Touché,' says Cecily, and although Kate doesn't turn around she could swear Cecily is smiling.

Kate is desperate to leave, but as she's walking past Mrs Gaffney's office she hears her name called. Kate prays she doesn't still reek of alcohol, particularly after that whole interview misunderstanding.

'How was your second session?' says Mrs Gaffney, her nose wrinkling. 'You look . . . tired?'

'Late night . . .'

'Oh. But you're enjoying the volunteering?'

'*Enjoying*?' says Kate, before she can stop herself. 'No?'

'It's a little more challenging than I was expecting, that's all.'

'If you're thinking of letting us down, I'd ask you to honour your commitment till the end of September,' says Mrs Gaffney sternly.

'I wasn't planning on quitting.' Quitting has never been Kate's style.

'OK, then,' says Mrs Gaffney, giving a small nod to indicate their conversation is over.

'The thing is, Mrs Gaffney, one of the ladies is being a little . . . disruptive.'

'Ah, a nemesis! And so soon. Presumably it's Mrs Rappapot being horribly racist again?'

'Maud? No, it's the lady with dementia, Mrs Finn. I feel bad saying it, I know she can't help it, but she can be quite . . . inappropriate.'

'Mrs Finn? White hair, swirled to the side, big brown eyes, only ever smiles after she's verbally skewered one of the other ladies?'

'That's the one. She's been heckling me. Today she called me a quarter-wit. And, er, mentally subnormal. Last session she called me a fool. I'm not taking it personally, I saw a documentary – I know it's the disease talking. Dementia makes people say things they don't mean.'

'Cecily hasn't got dementia. She always says precisely what she means.'

'Oh. But it sounds like random murmurings.'

'Poetry probably. Or quotes. Cecily's the sharpest resident here, that's her problem. She's extremely bored but she's too proud to ask for help. She'd rather sit in her room doing nothing than acknowledge her dependency, so instead she busies herself being provocative.'

'Are you sure she doesn't get confused?'

'She has a brain the size of a planet, and an extraordinary memory. She's terrified of losing her faculties but she's actually in great nick, apart from her eyes and some mild Parkinson's.'

'Oh. In which case, should I answer back or just ignore her?'

'Entirely up to you. When she senses weakness she attacks, so whatever you do, don't be timid.'

It only occurs to Kate as she's walking home that of *course* she knows who George Eliot is: she studied *Middlemarch* for A-level. It's not fair, Cecily had been talking completely out of context, and Kate was trying to focus on her toasties. What was it Cecily had said?

Kate googles and eventually finds the quote, from *Adam Bede* – 'one morsel's as good as another when your mouth's out o' taste'. Funny. That's what Kate's been feeling recently.

She googles 'George Eliot grave'. Sure enough it *is* in Highgate – lucky guess, everyone's buried there. Kate googles Eliot's tombstone inscription:

Of those immortal dead who live again
In minds made better by their presence.

Kate stops in her tracks: *The dead who live again, in minds made better by their presence.* That line reminds her of her father. He's been dead twenty years now – more years than they had a chance to share. She's learned to exist alongside the huge void his death opened up; what choice did she have? She's found precious comfort in the parts of him that have survived. Today's been a prime example: the best part of her, the part that made her go to Lauderdale rather than stay under the covers, comes from her father's voice telling her to always be kind.

Perhaps Cecily might know a thing or two. Kate would never admit it but she's almost looking forward to what Cecily will come out with next week.

Chapter Sixteen

NICK HAS BEEN TEXTING Kate frequently since Pete's wedding. He'd offered to cook spaghetti Bolognese for her on Monday night, her favourite – and while she'd almost been hooked by the food bait she'd said no, Monday and Tuesday were reserved for soufflé practice. Besides, she's needed more time to get her thoughts in place. She won't go to his flat either – the prospect makes her anxious, the space haunted by too many ghosts of happiness past.

She's counter-proposed neutral turf in the hope that a public place will magically prevent anything traumatic happening again, so they're meeting at Aposta, a lovely café five minutes from Rita's – the coffee's great and the acoustics will provide the necessary background noise to drown out any screaming or wailing.

In the earliest days of their relationship Kate had once looked up something on Nick's iPad, pressed the wrong tab and consequently seen a page on which was written one of the texts he'd sent her. It had been a cute, funny message asking if she'd like to go for Sunday lunch. Kate remembers feeling touched by his sweetness, the fact that he'd been so nervous he'd needed to draft a simple text message before sending it to her. Yet here she is, the night before they're due to meet, pen and paper in hand desperately scribbling her thoughts as if she's revising for her finals, writing lists of pros and cons, different approaches she could take to their 'chat'.

The stakes are high. Kate must gain two things: clarity, and a return of power, or at least a shedding of the powerlessness she's felt since France. Nick once claimed emotions were a waste of time, and of course he's a maths geek from a super-repressed background, but, damn it, Kate will prise him open, if only a crack. She's hungry for insight into his behaviour. Nick made her feel safe; if she totally misjudged him, then how can she trust herself in future?

Perhaps she could make all this easier for him? Hand him a biro and ask him to mark an x in the boxes which apply?

Nick Sullivan, are you:
A) deeply regretful of your wobble;
B) incapable of being unemployed and in a relationship at the same time;
C) a narcissistic sociopath lacking any empathy;
D) all of the above;
E) going to have therapy and become an emotionally open, articulate and all-round fantastic boyfriend;
F) going to continue being an un-self-aware emotional dirty bomb capable of exploding at inopportune moments and leaving me to deal with the painful debris?
G) I don't understand the question.

Their meeting will either end in that dreaded but much-needed state of 'closure' – or it could open up a brighter, more intimate future.

She's anxious and hopeful and angry and excited, and as much as Nick doesn't like feeling emotions, turns out neither does Kate.

When she arrives at Aposta, she's surprised to see Nick sitting at a table wearing a smart navy suit. He looks great – younger than he did a month ago, he's lost weight, his skin is tanned and glowing. His eyes light up when he sees her, and she can't help but beam back.

'You're looking lovely,' he says, standing to greet her with a kiss she slightly steps back from – then into – causing an awkward little dance which ends with them both laughing nervously. He grabs her hand and gives it a little squeeze. The small gesture makes her heart throb with all the weeks of pent-up longing.

'Have you just come from an interview?' says Kate.

'An induction, with my new team. I got my old job back.'

'At *Marshalls*?'

'At Allsom. I rang Ivan a couple of weeks ago, he said to come in for a chat.'

Kate had suggested months ago that he try to get his old-old job back. He'd loved that job, she'd never understood why he'd quit.

'They've got a new database integrative role that's my dream job.'

'Ah, I'm really happy for you. That must be a relief.'

'To be honest, yes,' he says, nodding fervently. 'I didn't realise how hard it is being unemployed. You end up feeling a bit useless.'

'Of course you do. So you must be feeling better? You look well.'

'I've lost a bit of weight.' He shrugs. 'Been running, just 5k round the park every day.'

News of Nick's job and his fitness regime bothers Kate. It would appear that during these long, long weeks she's been carrying around an outdated version of Nick. In her constant thoughts he was on the sofa, despondent – but in fact she was the despondent one, merely going through life's motions. Nick's been taking immaculate care of himself while she's been busy generating lorryloads of whatever the opposite of an endorphin is.

They sit staring at each other lovingly, but with confusion on their faces. Why are they even in this mess, when they both look like they want to reach across the table and kiss and make up?

Eventually, Kate breaks eye contact for a moment, trying to take control of herself. 'Nick – I don't understand what happened in France.'

'I don't understand it myself, Kate. I've missed you every day; you're the person I'm closest to in the world.'

'I know that, Nick, but what you did really hurt me.'

'Kate, I'm clueless about all of this,' he says, waving his hands in the air as if referring to the whole of human existence.

'I know that too, but clueless does not mean harmless. In France it felt like I was run over by a driverless car. I know you're not behind the wheel on this one, Nick, but you are still the bloody car.'

'I was as surprised as you were about what I said,' he replies, looking at her intently.

'What does that even mean?' she says, feeling irritation start to rise.

'I didn't plan to say it, I really didn't.'

'But you didn't take it back either.'

'Kate,' he says, taking her hand, 'whatever happens, I don't want to hurt you again, but I don't know how to do this.'

'Nick, no one does, but love is an act of faith. Look, don't you think that *now* might be a good time to deal with some of your issues? Your parents, with all due respect, have done a total number on you – lots of parents do – but you can get professional help.'

'It's just so difficult to talk about . . .'

'I understand that but you are forty-four years old, not eight. You're totally un-self-aware, you're incapable of talking about your feelings. Sometimes I think you're so repressed you don't even feel your feelings – and it's not good enough, Nick, it just isn't.'

Nick looks utterly forlorn, and a little scared. Kate feels like she actually *is* beating up an eight-year-old. How has *she* suddenly become the bad guy?

Nick shifts in his chair, then perks up again. 'I managed to get tickets for Radiohead at the Roundhouse!'

'What?'

'I queued for five hours – I know you love them.'

'That is a massively unsubtle way of changing the subject,' says Kate with incredulity.

'No, I only just remembered – I wanted to tell you,' he says, taking out his wallet and trying to hand her the tickets. She bats them away.

'Nick – we were talking about us. You can't just shut down in the middle of this conversation.'

'But I don't know what to do about us.'

'Well, do you want us to have a chance together?'

'Of course!'

'Then go and see a therapist. As soon as possible.'

'You're right.' He nods. 'I'll look into it. As soon as I've got my new work routine sorted.'

Kate shakes her head. 'I know you. You'll put it off and avoid it like you avoid everything else that's uncomfortable.'

'I will do it, Kate. I know I've messed up. I want to change, but the last thing I want to do is muck you about again.'

'Then *don't* muck me about again. Talk to a professional. Nick, I won't nag you about this, but unless you sort yourself out I can't have you in my life, we're over. I'm going to go now.'

'No, wait,' he says, reaching for her arm.

'What?'

'Kate – you're my favourite person. I'm sorry. Please, take the tickets at least,' he says, trying again to put them in her hand. 'The gig's next month, we don't have to go together, you can take Bailey or someone. I want you to have them. Please? I queued in the rain . . .'

Reluctantly, Kate takes them and puts them in her bag. She can't bear to leave him here alone, suddenly looking so vulnerable. She wants to wrap her arms around him and tell him it'll all be all right, but she stops herself, and instead walks out of the coffee shop. She feels his gaze following her as she heads down the street.

Before she's even at Rita's door he's texted:

I've found three therapists near work. I will call them first thing tomorrow. I will do whatever it takes to sort myself out.

She enters Rita's flat and collapses on the sofa with a sob of relief. He's going to fix himself. It will all be all right in the end.

Chapter Seventeen

KATE HAS HAD TO ASK Mrs Gaffney for special permission from Bernadette, head of catering, to allow her to do the soufflé demo in the kitchens on Thursday night. Kate's been staying later than normal at the office recently, trying to prove her dedication, and arrives feeling rushed and slightly too sweaty. She is met by Bernadette, a formidable woman of around fifty, with dyed black hair pinned in a tight bun. Bernadette's kitchen is spotless stainless steel, and the warm air holds the not unpleasant aroma of freshly baked pastry and lemon cleaning product.

'You'll be wanting not to indulge Mrs Finn,' says Bernadette as she bustles around, pulling sheets of aluminium foil over leftovers and placing them in the fridge. '*I* certainly don't have time to whip up soufflés on demand. We plan our meals months in advance.'

'It's just a one-off,' says Kate, arranging the dozen chairs from the dining room in a neat semicircle in front of the counter.

'We serve extremely well-balanced, nutritious menus – everything is cooked fresh daily. The ladies always get their veggies, whether they like it or not. They had a fine gammon pie for tea tonight, summer fruit jelly with fresh cream for afters.'

'It's not your food Mrs Finn has a problem with, it's mine.'

'Mrs Finn enjoys complaining more than she enjoys eating. The Parkinson's, it affects the taste buds, you know. Mrs Paisner also suffers but Mrs Paisner has the good grace not to complain every five minutes. I can't begin to tell you how demanding some of those women are. This isn't a five-star hotel,' says Bernadette, though there's warmth in her voice. 'Right, I'm off to Zumba, so you'll clear up after yourself. I'm not coming in to dirty dishes in the morning. And if Mrs Finn gives you a hard time, rise above it – like one of your fancy soufflés,' she says, her face creasing with laughter at her own joke.

Kate didn't think Cecily could be any ruder than she was on Sunday – but it turns out she can. Tonight, having specifically ordered the soufflé, she hasn't even bothered to show up.

The entire time Kate's been melting the chocolate and whisking the eggs, she's been expecting Cecily to make a grand entrance with some new and exciting insult. Every time a nurse or carer has walked past, Kate's hopes have risen, but now as she removes the soufflés from the oven and turns again to her audience, she feels the sting of being stood up.

'These look delightful,' says Bessie. 'You're such a clever girl.'

They do look perfect, puffed up gloriously into light, delicate crowns. Kate has dusted the tops with sprink-lings of icing sugar, and the occasional cracks in the surface reveal rich, dark seams of gooey molten choc-olate. If Kate knew which room was Cecily's, she'd go there now and show off these triumphs.

Kate sits feeling increasingly deflated as the ladies eat. By the time they've finished it's 8.40 p.m. Cecily had mentioned she was hoping to die imminently. Kate pre-sumed from the set of Cecily's jaw that she was in no danger of dying anytime soon and would probably out-live everyone here, including Kate.

Kate will do the washing-up later, but first she should probably check with Mrs Gaffney that everything is OK.

'She did leave you a note,' says Mrs Gaffney, shaking her head in apology. Then, seeing Kate's crestfallen face, she adds, 'Oh no, she's fine, she's in her room.' She hands Kate a heavy cream envelope. 'She'll be awake if you pop by now. Room thirteen, at the end of the corridor.'

Inside the envelope is a short poem written in elegant, looped handwriting:

> *'Tis seldom or never the good and the clever*
> *Hit it off quite as they should*
> *The good are so harsh to the clever,*
> *The clever so rude to the good!*

Kate raises her eyebrows. Clearly she's not the clever one, but she thinks Mrs Finn has the harsh base covered too.

Kate hesitates outside the door to room thirteen, then dashes back to the kitchen to retrieve a soufflé. It's sunk in the middle, but at least she can prove she tried to please Mrs Finn, though she doubts Mrs Finn will feel remotely guilty.

She raps lightly on the door with the dessert spoon, then more loudly, then a third time, and eventually Cecily calls out, 'What fresh hell . . .?' which is probably the warmest welcome Kate's likely to get.

Kate puts on a smile, steps into the warm, bright room and her forced smile becomes an entirely natural one before her jaw drops open. Cecily's living area contains a single bed covered in a peach satin quilted bedspread next to a small wooden side table. Every other object in sight is a book. Every inch of wall space from carpet to ceiling is fully lined with shelves; Kate counts eight shelves high along the main walls. There are shelves entirely surrounding the large bay window that looks out on to the garden. Kate catches a glimpse into the bathroom and laughs in delight. There are shelves covering the area above the sink where a mirror would normally be; there are even books stacked neatly under the sink.

The books are arranged broadly in size order, the spines ranging from murky green and brown leather bindings from the nineteenth century, through to colourful, modern paperbacks. There must be thousands of them, but because there is good natural light, and because the vertically stacked rows are frequently broken up by neat horizontal piles, the room feels magically uncluttered.

Cecily sits in a beige wing-backed chair in the far corner, back straight, as if on a throne. A tray table next to her houses a small portable radio, a hands-free telephone and a pair of glasses. The strong, familiar smell of old paper and ink reminds Kate fondly of her father's tiny study, but here there's a sweeter, powdery note Kate recognises as Chanel No. 5, and, sure enough, one minor concession to anything other than the written word is a black-and-gold tube of talc on the bedside table.

'*I wondered much to see: that all my wealth should be confined in such a little room . . .*' says Cecily, sweeping her hand in the direction of the wall of books behind her. 'Traherne, one of the metaphysicals. He lives in the bathroom.'

'This is the best room I've ever seen,' says Kate, staring up at the top shelves in wonder. 'I could happily spend all day in here.'

'I had a couple of falls in my lovely old home in Finchley after I turned ninety. I only agreed to come here on the basis that I'd be dead shortly after. Two thousand and something days I've been trapped in this tiny box surrounded by books I can no longer read. "Happily" would not be an accurate adverbial summation.'

'I've brought your soufflé,' says Kate, holding out the dessert to Mrs Finn, who turns her head as if the sight is offensive. 'I'm surprised you didn't show up today.'

'I'm tired,' says Mrs Finn. 'Besides, I couldn't bear another session listening to that interminable Bessie Burbridge.'

'*Bessie?* How can anyone not like Bessie?'

'Inane people-pleaser.'

'I thought it was Maud you didn't like?'

'That clown-faced, flatulent show-off? *I've* had tea with Ingrid Bergman, got drunk with King Edward the Seventh and drunk Bellinis with Richard Burton at Harry's Bar in Venice – or his doppelgänger, I was quite merry so I can't be sure which – but you don't hear me dropping all that into every conversation. Anyway, why should I have to like any of those women?'

'It might make your life easier.'

'*Au contraire*, it would make this deluxe knacker's yard even less tolerable. So – what did you think of the poem?'

'Did you write it?'

Cecily grunts. 'Did *I* write it? Hardly. It's Wordsworth.'

'Really?'

'Not *the* Wordsworth, another Wordsworth, his great-niece Elizabeth. Well?'

'Honestly? I don't think it's great – the second line doesn't scan properly and I'm not sure it's particularly true. Am I to assume it contains a veiled message for me?'

'And if I told you it was, in fact, I who wrote it?'

Kate laughs awkwardly. 'I wouldn't put it past you to embarrass me like that, but I suspect you could write a better poem.'

'Hmm,' says Cecily, and she pulls a face to try to hide the fact she's secretly pleased with the compliment. 'Anyway, I need to go to bed now, so you can leave. I wanted to say one thing: don't bother with the half-baked volunteering nonsense, I can smell a rat a mile off.'

'Sorry?'

'It's a waste of time.'

'Well, you've voted with your feet – the other ladies seem to enjoy it.'

'They know nothing about food, but I meant it's a waste of *your* time.'

'Why?'

'Living with your mother? Doing a job half a monkey with half a typewriter could do in half an hour? No wonder you have a constant expression of haunted misery.'

'I do not – do I?'

'As far as I can see, you're doing life all wrong, blundering around like a fart in a pickle barrel,' says Cecily, pointing a finger at Kate.

'You know what? I'm going to go now because I do not like the way you speak to me. You have no idea what I've got on my plate right now.'

'You should be grateful for all of it. You have freedom, opportunities, your eyes work, your mouth works—'

'So does yours . . .'

'You are young, attractive, you can bathe without the indignity of a heavy-handed Filipina midget in the room. Every single book in my library could be in Cyrillic for all I can see. I haven't eaten anything worthwhile since 2005 and even without the Parkinson's, each meal served here has been a war crime. Everyone I've ever loved is long dead, and as for the other residents? Intolerable, each in a distinct way. The only interesting one, Dora Bassett, went and died of pneumonia in May – it was *my* turn next, she was only ninety-two!' she says, furiously. 'I have been starved of decent conversation far longer than is humane, so, frankly, I will speak to whom I want, howsoever I choose, but anyway, please go now, I am extremely tired.' Cecily closes her eyes, takes a deep breath and her bony chest lifts up and down.

Kate stands watching as Cecily breathes heavily in and out. 'Cecily, are you OK . . .?'

'It's *Mrs Finn*. Now go.'

Kate backs out of the room carrying the soufflé, her face burning with indignation. How dare she speak to her like that? It's not Kate's fault the old woman's decrepit. If Cecily doesn't want to show up to another demo, brilliant – everyone's a winner. Even if there was a gram of truth in what she said, it's none of her business. She's not Kate's grandmother, she's just a bitter old woman who takes sadistic pleasure in tormenting people.

Kate is standing by the kitchen sink, washing up the ramekins, still smarting from the conversation, when she hears footsteps behind her.

'You had an interesting chat, then?' says Mrs Gaffney, with barely concealed curiosity.

Kate shakes her head. 'Sorry, but that woman is bloody difficult. How do you put up with her?'

'Normally she doesn't put up with us. Take her interest as a compliment.'

'Fresh meat more like,' says Kate, lifting the last of the washing-up onto the draining board.

'She phoned me just now.'

'Did she?' says Kate, wiping her hands on her jeans. 'Bet she didn't say I was timid.'

'She said she'd like you to visit on Sunday, and something about training a monkey.'

Kate shakes her head and stares out into the dining room and beyond to the garden. 'Mrs Gaffney, I find her really quite vicious.'

'Mrs Finn is a lot of things. We all are. We "contain multitudes". That's Whitman, one of Cecily's favourites. You have to get past Cecily's bite.'

'Do I?'

'I think she'd appreciate the company more than she might show, and I think you might get something out of it too.'

'I don't need the aggravation.'

'The thing is . . . the weekend numbers are so small there really isn't justification for your Sunday slot, and then it doesn't make sense only to do Thursdays, so the cooking thing isn't going to work for us.'

'Are you blackmailing me?' says Kate, laughing.

'It would be a great kindness. Cecily is the only one here with no visitors.'

'Well, that's because she's mean.'

'I'll cut you a deal – come back and see her on Sunday and if you can't handle it—'

'I can *handle* it. I just don't *want* to handle it.'

'Come and see Cecily on Sunday and if you don't enjoy it, I won't mention it again.'

Kate folds the dishcloth and puts it neatly to one side. 'I'm afraid I'm going to have to think about it.'

Chapter Eighteen

Kᴀᴛᴇ's ʀᴇᴀsᴏɴᴀʙʟʏ sᴜʀᴇ sʜᴇ had a life before Nick, yet somehow she's forgotten how to have fun without him. After a Saturday spent as errand girl, queueing for an hour in Aldi for a cheap posh candle for Rita, then typing up the minutes of the last residents' meeting, she agrees to meet Cara in a bar in Soho for drinks.

Kate and Cara joined Fletchers on the same day nineteen years ago, and instantly bonded over their shared view that a food business really should offer better milk than those pesky UHT sachets that *always* spurted on your clothes. Cara quickly abandoned ship and now runs a glamorous food PR firm; all Kate can do is look on in awe.

Cara arrives late looking immaculate – her dark hair scraped back, her smoky eyeshadow contoured to perfection. 'You're not texting that dickhead, are you?' she says, settling down opposite Kate and taking a swig of Kate's wine.

Kate puts her phone back in her bag. 'He's not a dickhead, he's confused.'

'What makes you think he's confused?'

'Because he said he was, in France. And since then—'

114

'Maybe he only said that because he didn't want to hurt you.'

'He was in the middle of cheese-grating my heart and you think he paused to comfort me? Anyway, I met up with him last Wednesday and—'

'Er, why would you meet up with a confused dickhead?'

'And we had a great chat, and he's going to sort himself out.'

'You're mad to still be talking to him.'

'He had a panic, partly because he's scared of intimacy and partly due to work stress. Nick's a terrible multi-tasker. . . .'

'Oh yeah, like the time he forgot your birthday?'

'That was not a big deal.'

'Let's write a list of crap things about Nick – knock him off that pedestal you've stuck him on,' says Cara, grabbing a pen and a cocktail napkin. 'Number one – Forgets birthdays. Two—'

'Cara, this is not how I want to spend my Saturday night.'

'Plays PlayStation at *forty-four*,' says Cara, heavily circling the numbers with disdain.

'He doesn't play shoot-'em-ups, he plays puzzle games – it's like doing a crossword.'

'But the point is he chooses to play them instead of spending time with *you*.'

'Cara, you expect a man to worship at your altar 24/7. I'm far lower maintenance, and I accept Nick likes his own space.'

'Stop making excuses for him and accept he's just not that into you.'

'Oh for goodness' sake, that is the *most* simplistic, unhelpful phrase ever. This . . . *incident* didn't happen after a first date, he'd just asked me to *move in*. It is complex.'

'There are so many men out there. That guy in the red T-shirt's totally been checking you out.'

Kate doesn't bother turning her head. 'Look, Nick made a mistake, he's not perfect. And I can write lists till the cows come home about how he should trim his toenails or buy me more flowers, but pen and paper are not going to stop me loving him.'

'Fine.' Cara shrugs. 'If you're not up for talking to hot guys, I'll have to do it for both of us.'

By 10 p.m., Cara is in the corner of the bar snogging a hunky Danish man. Kate is stuck in another corner fending off a sweaty married letch from Croydon. Cara is more than happy to be left with the Dane, so Kate heads home, cursing the fact that she didn't take Nick up on his offer of steak and chips and a DVD.

Cara's totally wrong about Nick. He's been sending loads of chatty texts since they met up. He had a fantastic first session with a therapist on Friday and he's going to go every week. Kate is hugely hopeful he'll sort himself out, but she'd be foolish to go straight back into the relationship, which is why she turned down his invite tonight. They've agreed to just be 'friends' while he's figuring himself out. Kate will be compassionate and patient, stay close, yet at a safe enough distance until he's sure about their future. She figures if she speaks to him but doesn't see him, she can't get hurt.

The following morning Kate wakes with a hangover of grumpiness, playing Cara back in her mind. There's no point visiting Mrs Finn when Kate's already in a bad mood, it would be masochistic, and besides, she doesn't owe that woman anything. No. She's going to read a good book and maybe go for her own little jog around the park.

She's about to head out in her running gear to buy cigarettes when Rita intercepts, insisting Kate accompany her to the recycling centre in Kentish Town with an old microwave. Their journey starts innocuously enough. They drive to the dump, Kate takes some primal satisfaction in hearing the crash and smash of glass and metal. As soon as Kate gets back into the car, Rita claims she needs Kate's advice, though actually she just wants a gossip. John Pring, the pettiest of Heathview's residents' committee – a man who once denied Mrs Ren, who walks with a stick, a parking permit because her application had a typo – has been complaining vociferously about the rodent problem. Mikhail, the night porter, was called to Mr Pring's on Friday after another sighting and uncovered a vast nest of baby mice in a wardrobe bursting with Mr Pring's stash of yellowing 1970s porn mags!

'That is totally gross,' says Kate.

'And I only know this because Mikhail told Sonia, Gerry's cleaner, but now we all know, how do we broach it with John?'

'Ew, just ignore it, Mum.'

Rita has successfully managed to lull her daughter into a false sense of security and she catches her own reflection in the rear-view mirror and smiles. 'Gerry and I think it's time you had dinner with Jeremy. If I were five years younger, I'd make a play for him myself.'

'Er, even if I fancied Jeremy – which I don't – I don't want you setting me up with anyone.'

'He's got an excellent job, he's now publishing *director*. Of a *very* large publisher.'

'Not a small one? You should've said.'

Rita's hands grip the steering wheel tighter.

'Look, Mum, I do appreciate you trying to help but please don't fix me up. And anyway, I don't need a date, things with Nick are looking up.'

Rita's eyes narrow and Kate turns to look out of the window. She shouldn't have given her mother a crumb, such a basic error.

'You saw Nick on Wednesday, didn't you? I knew you looked guilty when you came home.'

'I was *not* looking guilty, I was looking preoccupied. He's finally got a job, and he's agreed to therapy. Aren't you happy, vindicated at last?'

'What type of therapy?'

'I don't know – the type where you sit in a chair and slag off your mother.'

Rita barks a laugh. 'I've always said his mother sounded emotionally negligent.'

'I agree it was the mother's fault,' says Kate pointedly.

'Ah! You and your Larkin, though you never do blame your father The Saint.'

'Nice.'

'You'll have to take my word for it that I did the best I could. Read Winnicott on good-enough parenting, on my bookshelf.'

'Your bookshelf is full of reams of psychobabble – if any of those books could fix heartache, it would have sold more than *Fifty Shades* and *Harry Potter* put together.'

'Darling, I'll be honest with you.'

'Please don't be.'

'You're at the bargaining stage of your break-up on the Kübler-Ross curve. It comes before acceptance, but you should have moved through that by now. You were like this after your father died.'

'Sometimes it takes as long as it takes to deal with grief,' says Kate, forcing herself not to rise to her mother's bait. 'Anyway, Nick and I are no longer in a break-up situation.'

'You probably are – just in a messy, protracted one. Nick isn't going to change overnight,' says Rita, indicating left as she turns right. 'He's lived dysfunctionally for forty-four years. There are no miracle quick fixes. He'll take years to heal. He may never be a fully integrated adult. Meanwhile, you need to read up on codependency.'

'I know what codependency means – it means allowing difficult people to take advantage of you.'

'You're always saying Nick is the problem child, but Nick seems perfectly capable of taking care of his own needs.'

'That's only because he doesn't realise what his real needs are.'

'Darling, that's pure codependency talking. You need therapy too.'

'I do not . . . I just need Nick to love me.'

'You give your energy to all the wrong people. Right, I'm going to head down to Selfridges to take back those L. K. Bennett wedges. It's a bugger to park round there, so you'll need to sit in the car while I dash in.'

'And that would be a perfect example of me giving my energy to the wrong people,' says Kate triumphantly, her thoughts crystallising as she speaks. 'Besides, I'm having tea with someone.'

'Nick?'

'Someone who needs me more than you do.'

Kate waits for the next set of traffic lights to turn red, then jumps out and makes a bolt for freedom, feeling a small thrill of rebellion as she turns and heads towards Hampstead.

She's been rude to Rita. She needs good karma. She's off to befriend the dragon.

Chapter Nineteen

'YOU MUST BE A GLUTTON for punishment,' says Mrs Gaffney, coming to greet Kate in reception with a warm smile.

'You promise Mrs Finn isn't going to give me a hard time?' says Kate, scrambling up from her seat. Kate could do without spending her entire Sunday arguing.

'Oh I'd never promise the impossible. But why not get her to talk about her life, her beloved husband, her adventures? It's the only thing she still enjoys doing.'

Cecily is sitting straight-backed in her chair, a half-eaten bowl of beige soup from lunch on her tray table. Her expression softens slightly when she sees Kate, and her brown eyes sparkle with mischief.

'I brought you some biscuits, Mrs Finn. Sorry I didn't make them myself, but I figure you won't eat them anyway,' says Kate, handing her the fancy lemon short-breads she's bought en route.

Cecily holds the packaging up with her left hand, squints, then discards it on her side table. Cecily's right arm has a constant low-level tremor and Cecily re-clamps her left hand over the wrist to hide the fact. 'I can't see properly,' she says. 'I almost thought it said lemon short-bread, which would be preposterous.'

'What have you got against lemons?'

'Citrus has no place in a shortbread. Leave those at the carers' station on your way out.'

'What, now?'

'Shortly. First, tea,' says Cecily, picking up the phone and ordering a pot of Earl Grey and a plate of 'unflavoured, unpretentious shortbreads'. Kate turns her gaze to the well-worn Persian rug. She'll save herself the fiver on biscuits next time; in fact, there won't be a next time.

'How's your weekend been?' says Kate.

'Dreary and interminably long. Yours?'

'Not far off,' says Kate, smiling. 'Anyway, back to work tomorrow, a monkey at a typewriter . . .'

'Explain to me why you do that job?' says Cecily, leaning forward with genuine curiosity.

Kate shrugs. 'Why does anyone do any job? For the salary. I know how to do it. I have friends there.'

'But such a singularly pointless job? What did you want to be when you were young?'

Kate tips her head back and strokes her neck. She hasn't thought about that for a long time. 'A journalist, like my father. I used to sit in his study while he was working. I loved the sound of his typewriter. If he ever made a mistake, he always used to let me do the white-outs. My dad loved words, so he was always encouraging me to be creative. I'd write stories and make up little radio shows for him on his tape recorder.' Kate feels a dull ache as she remembers a younger version of herself for whom any future seemed possible. That version disappeared the minute her father was diagnosed.

'Did you go to college?' says Cecily. 'Presumably you don't need qualifications to write about sausages?'

Always a dig. 'I started an English degree, but then Dad died and I went to work.'

'Oh, he died young?' says Cecily, looking suddenly troubled. 'How old was he?'

'Forty-six.'

'Oh,' she says, momentarily chastened. 'Forty-six is hard. And you never went back to your education?'

'I was a bit broken for a while, and then it felt too late, I'd missed so much. And Mum pointed out I could read and write on my own time. Oh, hang on,' says Kate, as she hears a knock at the door. She takes Cecily's soup bowl and swaps it for a tray of tea and biscuits the carer brings in. 'How about you, Mrs Finn?' she says, settling back down. 'What did you want to be when you were young?'

'Me?' Cecily taps her chest with a flourish. Even though she's wearing a shirt, jumper and sleeveless cardigan, her curved fingers make a noticeable hollow thud against her bony chest. 'I wanted to be a movie star, so that I could stand out, and a Catholic, so that I could fit in,' she says, reaching for a biscuit. 'Neither came to pass, although I travelled the world and married a spy – oh, my dear Samuel. We were so very happy.' She sighs. 'I perfected the art of *fiskepudding*, danced the hula in Kauai under the midnight stars . . . and I did make it to Hollywood in the end.'

Kate will take the spy part with a pinch of salt, the Hollywood part too – and she has no idea what a *fiskepudding* is, but a long and happy marriage? Sounds encouraging. 'How far back do you remember?'

'Oh, all of it! But you don't want to hear my boring old adventures, do you?' says Cecily, with a sparkle in her eye indicating that she'd very much like to share her stories.

'I can think of nothing I'd rather be doing.'

'Then you must have a dire imagination. No, dear, run along and play Scrabble with Maud, God knows she could do with winning for once.'

'I came to see you, Mrs Finn. I want to hear about your life.'

'About the time I flew in a bomber in the war? Or the time my car broke down on the way to my own wedding? You don't want to hear about the time I met Groucho Marx, do you, surely you'd rather go home and think about carrots?'

'Absolutely not! Groucho Marx? Seriously? Tell me everything.'

'Really?'

'Really, yes, one hundred per cent. Please?'

Cecily struggles to contain a smirk of victory. 'Well, if you insist.' She settles deeper into her chair and takes a breath. 'My father, Joseph Polonsky, was a renowned maker of treats, famous across all of London and even parts of the Home Counties. His life was tough, but he and my mother brought happiness to everyone around them. I was born in Forest Gate, a terribly dull suburb in East London. I was the last of three, my arrival entirely unplanned, but I obstinately refused to be got rid of by traditional gin-based methods, though Mama tried hard. Papa was Lithuanian – a brilliant man, a free thinker and a socialist – but when he arrived here his English was so poor he ended up working in a sweatshop in Leeds, making buttonholes.'

'Making buttonholes – that's so strange, like making the holes in a Polo.'

'Nothing like it,' says Cecily dismissively. 'It was there he met Eva, my mother.'

'She was from Yorkshire?' says Kate, checking the tea has brewed before pouring it.

'Half a cup at a time for me.'

'Half-full?'

'Half-empty.'

'Same thing,' says Kate, catching Cecily's eye with a smile that is returned with an imperious glare.

'Mama was from Poland. Her father was the village baker – she grew up in a house sweet with the smell of freshly baked challah.'

'Ah, you mentioned your grandfather's bread the other day . . .'

'Mama was a wonderful cook too, and a beauty, with luxuriant hair and piercing blue eyes. My father loved beauty. He always preferred my sister May to me – she was pretty and she never answered back. He used to say, "Cissie, you have a head like Bismarck and a brain like a Bismarck herring".'

'What's a Bismarck herring?'

'A pickled one. Papa once invented a contrivance made from a chicken bone and fixed it to my nose to make it a better shape: failed miserably.' Cecily turns to show her profile, running her nail down the length of her aquiline nose. 'I digress. Mama was summoned to Leeds to make a match with her brother's friend who owned Papa's factory. She took a violent dislike to this suitor but fell deeply in love with Papa. They would meet secretly after his shifts, and she would stare into his dark, intelligent eyes, captivated by his passionate opinions. He always expressed himself so beautifully, and even though her English was very limited, she drank in his words and flourished. After six months he gave her a sapphire ring he'd saved for since the day they met, and he proposed. My uncle was outraged at the engagement. His sister had chosen this nobody, and he literally threw Papa down the stairs, but Mama was in love. The next morning they packed their bags, eloped and fled to London.'

'That's so romantic.'

Cecily frowns, her mouth forming deep creases. 'Their life was hard. Papa was unwell on and off for most of his life. Mama, soon pregnant with May, was forced to scrub floors and take in washing. Papa ended up working in a sweet factory. I remember visiting him and seeing these incredible long ropes of sugar paste being twirled on enormous hooks, emerging as clear sticks of barley sugar, the most fabulous treacly smell in the air. I must have been three at the time.'

'You remember that far back?'

'I remember with great clarity things people insist are impossible – my stately green perambulator, wheeled by my nurse Clara who died four weeks after being jilted.'

'From being *jilted*?'

'From consumption. Bad timing, though. Papa took me to the hospital and there she lay, burning black eyes, her twisted fingers plucking at the sheets.' Catching the disturbed look on Kate's face, Cecily laughs bitterly. 'Papa didn't believe in what he called "Hampstead" methods of indulgent child-rearing. How he'd laugh to know I've ended up in Hampstead, mollycoddled like the most useless of infants: *Have you eaten your mush today, Mrs Finn? Do we need a little trip to the bathroom?'*

'Tell me more about the sweet factory,' says Kate, fearing Cecily will sink into a darker mood.

'Papa didn't stay there long,' says Cecily, nudging herself forward in her chair with her elbows. 'He'd noticed a confectioner's near us for sale. He had twelve pounds in savings, the lease was four hundred pounds, but he was a much-admired man, renowned for his intellect, and everyone loved Mama – she was as gentle and warm as Papa was intimidating. Their friends and neighbours wanted to help, so they gathered together to lend him money and he bought 25 Woodgrange Road, E7, and turned it into Polon's Treats.'

'From sweatshop to sweet shop . . .'

Cecily raises her cup to Kate, who blushes. 'Is that the type of dreck they force you to write at work? That's why Papa always said to be your own boss. He said his idea of happiness was *being able to tell everyone else to go to the Devil*,' she says delightedly. 'So now he was the boss, though of course it was Mama's hard work that built the business. They opened a salon in the back room, and became famous for their ice creams. Mama would rise at 5 a.m. to stand in our little yard, churning the ices by hand in these small salt-packed vessels. In summer, if I was up early enough, she'd let me turn the handle and as a reward she'd let me sample the custard. Toffee was my favourite, though one summer she made strawberry and cream flavour, which was the best ice cream I've ever tasted, and we lived in Italy for years.'

'Your family did?'

'No, that was some years after Samuel and I were married. Mama used to make English madeleines too, different from a Proust one. These were the prettiest little pink-and-white towers, the fluffiest sponge, made with jam and coconut and a cherry on top, marvellous,' she says, bringing a trembling hand to her lips, which quiver at the memory.

'Your mother sounds like a domestic goddess.'

'She did everything – cooked for Papa, nursed him, supervised the shop, charmed the customers – so my early days were presided over by the shop girls. Emmie was my favourite, what a virago.'

Kate is too embarrassed to ask what a virago is, she's forgotten – though when she looks it up later she sees the description neatly fits Cecily.

'Our shop was next door to one of the earliest cinemas, the Grand Theatre – Emmie used to sit me down on the front row while she went off to see her boyfriend.'

'She left you alone? How old were you?'

'Legend has it I would only drink my bottle if it was given to me on the steps of the entrance. I saw every film twice, I fell in love with storytelling when I was young. I spent a lot of time living in my imagination.'

'Hence the books too . . . You brought all these with you when you moved here?' says Kate, heading to inspect the main wall of bookshelves more closely.

'We had twice this collection at home. That's one of the worst things about the whole indignity of getting old – things are taken from you constantly: your possessions, your hips, your eyesight.'

'Then surely you'd rather not be surrounded by reminders of what you've lost?'

'What I've lost? My books remind me of everything I've had – a lifetime of adventures.'

Kate looks at the rows of books in front of her and her heart soars. All these stories, all these endless discoveries to be made. She traces her fingers along the spines in front of her – a vast selection of fiction, art, poetry and travel.

'Look to the right,' says Cecily. 'They're probably to your taste.'

Kate scans the titles and her eyebrows rise. Cecily has almost every cookbook Kate has stored at Nick's, plus several hundred more – everything from Mrs Beeton via Fanny Craddock through to Nigella. It's not only recipe books, but books on the history and science of food, and fiction with food at the heart of it. 'Nora Ephron!' says Kate, excitedly pulling the slim volume of *Heartburn* from the shelf. 'This is my favourite book ever,' she says, beaming with happiness.

'I take it you're a fan of cookbooks?'

'Very much so,' says Kate, longingly. 'I adore them, I've got loads at home. Well, actually, I haven't got any at the moment,' she says, suddenly crestfallen.

'Was there a fire?' says Cecily with concern.

'Yeah, in my relationship,' says Kate, wincing as she shakes her head.

'That sounds painful.'

'Oh, I'm sure I'll get them back at some point,' says Kate, biting her lip.

Cecily pauses for a moment with a pensive look on her face. 'Well, then,' she says decisively, 'if your shelves are empty, you must borrow one of my books.'

'Oh, I couldn't.'

'I insist. Otherwise it's yet another weekend I'll have spent utterly without purpose.'

'Can I really take one?' says Kate, though actually, she'd love to. Oh, she's always wanted to read these Howard McGees . . .

'Hurry up and choose. I want to rest,' says Cecily abruptly.

'Oh, OK . . . how about this Elizabeth David?'

'No, that's a first edition,' says Cecily. 'Pick another one, any other you like.'

Kate scans along the shelf. 'This *Silver Palate* one?'

'Under no circumstances is that to leave this room.'

'I thought you said take any one . . .' mutters Kate.

Cecily frowns, straining forward in her chair to see where Kate's focus is. 'Try the next shelf down.'

For some reason Kate feels like she's playing a game of hot or cold. Her hand is drawn to a colourful hardcover on the shelf below. 'This?' she says, fishing it out. *Thought for Food: A Cookery Book for Entertaining Occasions* by Esther Shavin, its title written in a jaunty 1950s font. The cover illustration shows a dinner party with a vivacious hostess presenting a stern guest with a platter of chops. Another guest has his fingers crossed in an exaggerated comic twirl. Kate's never heard of the book but it looks interesting.

Cecily smiles and her whole body relaxes into the chair. 'Perfect. I couldn't have chosen better for you myself.'

Later that night, Kate wonders if Cecily did indeed stack the deck. Kate had thought it was the colours on the book's spine that attracted her – pink and yellow, like a rhubarb-and-custard sweet – but maybe it was the fact that it was the only book sticking out in an orderly line, almost like it had been dragged across her path.

Either way, Kate can't imagine a more perfect book to alleviate her current anxieties – it's charming, funny and easily digestible. On the bus home she reads the jacket blurb:

A cookery book that will be equally at home on the kitchen shelf or bedside table. A selection of menus chosen for the major occasions of life and love, with analyses of the reasons for each . . . Should appeal to everyone who appreciates good food, good taste and good humour. 15/- net

She flicks to the front – published in 1957 – then to the Foreword:

I've written this book not for those heroic house-wives who, having produced a Cordon Bleu dinner for twenty, emerge from their kitchen triumphant. I address, rather, the more easily dismayed to whom a gastronomic occasion is a challenge and a dilemma. What shall one give to the man one hopes will stay on after dinner? The man one hopes will not?

Kate was planning on tidying her room, but finds herself glued to the book. Cecily's obviously read it several times herself, the edges of the slipcover are well thumbed and there's the occasional time-faded food stain on the yellowing pages.

The book is in six sections including Family Occasions, Social Occasions and Occasions of Emergency.

Each section has a dozen short chapters – 'Luncheon for a Bad-Tempered Client'; 'Supper to Make Peace with Your Sister After a Squabble' . . . Each chapter starts with a relevant quote, then lists the meal's aim, followed by advice on the setting, menu and recipes.

It's the Occasions of Love section that most intrigues: 'Dinner for a Charming Stranger'; 'Dinner for the Man You Hope to Marry'. Under 'Dinner for a New Love, an Old Love and the Old Love's New Love', the aim states:

> Very complicated. Putting it as simply as possible: to flaunt your new love before your old love and at the same time show your old love's new love that, were your new love not so much more attractive than your old, you could bring your old love to heel again with the flick of an eyelash. Setting: Subdued lighting, preferably candles. This will be as flattering to her as to you, but that can't be helped.

The menu sounds delicious: lamb skewers on jewelled rice, followed by Cecilienne Chocolate Pudding.

Kate drifts to Rita's kitchen craving a plateful of lamb, the book carefully balanced in one hand. She's too absorbed to cook but she makes a couple of rounds of toast and peanut butter and returns to her room, entranced.

She falls asleep after midnight with the book on her pillow, her fingers tucked safely between its soft, thick pages, her body curled peacefully under the sheets.

Chapter Twenty

*T*HOUGHT FOR *FOOD'S* cover states that its author Esther Shavin is also a screenwriter, a travel journalist and a children's author. On Monday in her lunch break Kate googles her. There are IMDb references to two films she wrote in the 1960s. Second-hand copies of her books are listed on various websites. There's no indication of whether she's still alive, but if she was middle-aged when writing, she'd be dead by now. Kate buys all nine copies she can find – her friends will love it too – even though some of the food is old-fashioned, the advice and wit are timeless.

Kate leaves her copy in pride of place on her desk when she pops to her meeting with Dave, the head of production, and when she returns, Kavita is engrossed.

'This is great,' says Kavita, turning a page. 'It's like cookbook meets self-help with jokes thrown in.'

'Which bit are you on?' says Kate, delighted her friend is enjoying it.

'I love this' – she flicks back through the book – '*Impromptu Supper After Cocktail Party – Setting: Depends how you left your home when you went out. Either pick up your discarded underwear off the floor with a gay laugh, or ignore any mess in a high-handed* manner and offer your guests Alka-Seltzer while you repair to the kitchen to curse and see what can be done. And this quote, before "*Dinner to Celebrate Thirty Years of Marriage*": *Does the road wind uphill all the way? Yes, to the very end* – that made me laugh. That's clearly someone who's been married forever.'

'Did you notice she makes that same anniversary lamb dish for each of the five anniversary dinners in the book, right up to their fiftieth – but changes it slightly each time? And for that final supper they have small portions, it's so sweet because they're growing old together.'

'The stuff in the kids' birthday party chapter – that was my Saturday afternoon *Aim: to ensure your child is included on the party lists of other desirable parents in your area. All such parties tend to finish in tears and fighting. You must accept this risk and be prepared to dispense rough justice and clean handkerchiefs.* Bloody tiger mothers of Ealing . . . Where did you find this gem?'

'One of the old ladies at the home has a huge library. It was buried in there.'

'Someone should do a modern version . . . "Dinner for When You've Forgotten Your Own Wedding Anniversary and Your Husband Wants You to Cook a Romantic Meal Because He's Bought You the Steam-Iron You Wanted, But All You have Energy or Desire for is Watching *The Good Wife*".'

'Oh, poor Dom – what did you make him?'

'Made him order a curry,' says Kavita as she mimes 'ba-dum' on an invisible cymbal and drum.

'That is a terrible joke,' says Kate, laughing.

Kavita shrugs. 'Meanwhile, has that douchebag Devron updated you on what's happening?'

'Oh please don't,' says Kate, burying her head in her hands. 'I thought work was the one stable thing in my life, but the timing couldn't be worse, with Nick and everything. Devron hasn't said a thing, but I'm just waiting for more bad news.'

'What is the latest with Nick?'

Kate brightens slightly. 'Well, actually it's okay, I think. We're back to speaking every day. It's really nice. He keeps asking to see me but I'm not quite ready yet.'

'Can't you just write off France as a blip?'

'Bit of a painful blip,' says Kate, shaking her head. 'The good thing is he's started therapy.'

'Nick?' Kavita's eyes widen. 'He doesn't seem the type.'

Kate shrugs. 'I told him he should sort himself out and I guess he paid attention. He says he loves it, he says it's the first time he's ever been able to talk to someone about his mum's death. I pointed out that my dad died when I was at college too, and he could speak to *me*, but he says it's not the same. Anyway, at least he's opening up to someone – oh, and he's asked if he can take me somewhere nice for dinner on my fortieth.'

'You said yes?'

Kate shakes her head. 'I'm trying to pretend this particular birthday isn't happening.'

'You have to celebrate.'

'Not if I'm jobless, homeless and single,' she says, shuddering. 'Everything's so up in the air, I'm hoping that if I just close my eyes, it will all work itself out.'

'Yeah,' says Kavita, laughing. 'That's definitely the way life works.'

Chapter Twenty-one

KATE HADN'T PICKED UP on it on her first reading, but now she's read *Thought for Food* twice cover-to-cover, she realises that Cecily has been quoting this book at her, and her random ramblings start to make sense. The heckle during the gooseberry fool session was from 'Dinner for Son's Fiancée'; Cecily was quoting Coleridge, 'She is not fair to outward view' – presumably because there's a gooseberry fool on the menu. And Kate's second session, the quote that had bothered her, 'Now I wake, exceeding comfortless and worn and old', was from a Christina Rossetti poem, and the menu – 'Breakfast With a Hangover' – did feature a toastie, and some sound advice: *The most urgent need will be coffee. Weaker spirits, if able to sit, should be offered bacon.* So true. This book has taken up permanent residence in Kate's handbag; it's her new bible.

For her next visit, Kate's decided to make Cecily a recipe from the book, biscuits from 'Tea for a Crotchety Aunt' – *Aim: if she is an aunt you love, to make her feel cherished.* Kate is nowhere near the love stage, but she'd like to brighten Cecily's day, and the biscuits sound delicious – cherry and almond shortbreads – a Bakewell flavour with a light, crumbly texture. If Cecily won't eat them, Kate will polish them off. After weeks of food tasting like ash on her tongue, this book's started to make her hungry again.

If Cecily wasn't wearing a different silk blouse and a new cameo brooch, Kate would swear she hasn't moved since last Sunday. Mrs Gaffney says Cecily barely leaves her room. She's lost her confidence as well as her appetite, she never sits in the garden and only occasionally comes to an event, presumably so she can walk out halfway through. She certainly hasn't stood to open a window – the radiators in here feel like they're on full blast, though Cecily looks cool and elegant, her hair once again an immaculate white swirl.

'How's your week been, Mrs Finn?'

'I'm still alive, aren't I?' says Cecily, frowning. 'Order the tea and biscuits, would you?'

'No need,' says Kate, taking the Tupperware from her bag and proudly displaying the shortbreads. 'Cherry and almond—'

'From my book?' says Cecily, with a look Kate could almost mistake for impressed.

'Yes! I loved this book,' says Kate, taking it from her bag and handing it back to Cecily. 'I've never read one like it.'

'Keep it.'

'No, it's fine. I've ordered copies online.'

'You can buy copies of this book online?'

'Mrs Finn, you can buy nuclear weapons online.'

'Keep that copy until the others arrive. I insist.'

'OK. Thank you.' Kate tucks the book safely back in her bag. 'I wanted to ask, your mother was obviously a great cook, you grew up in a sweet shop, so when did—'

'Oh, I was never allowed *in* the shop, it was a forbidden paradise, which only made it more alluring. I once sneaked in to eat the toffee creams, ate rather too many. I was terrified Papa would notice, so I replaced the sweets in the wrappers with stones.'

'Sounds like a recipe for disaster.'

'Mrs Milton broke a tooth! I can still feel the impact of Papa's fingers stinging my face,' she says, gently touching her cheek. 'Still, worth it for those toffees,' she chuckles. 'Get the door?'

Kate helps the carer with the tray, serves the tea, then watches nervously as Cecily reaches for a biscuit. Cecily slowly chews, her eyes narrow, then she gives an almost imperceptible nod. Success, at last: Cecily's finally eating something Kate's cooked and she hasn't spat it out.

'Is your mother a good cook?' says Cecily, blotting the crumbs that have gathered on her bottom lip.

'A terrible cook, she doesn't care about food.'

'I wouldn't care much for her, then,' says Cecily, taking two more rapid bites and immediately inching her fingers towards another biscuit. 'Did your father cook?'

'Dad? The most he'd do was arrange a Ploughman's for lunch.'

'So who taught you?'

'I taught myself, not altogether successfully. When I was eight, my parents took me to Chinatown for my birthday. We ate delicious egg fried rice, and the week after I begged Mum to make it for dinner. She told me to make it myself. I already knew how to cook an omelette, so I didn't think it would be that hard. I fried the rice, added the peas and egg, but Mum hadn't told me I needed to boil the rice first.'

Cecily giggles and her whole body shakes. This part of Kate's anecdote doesn't sting, and Kate secretly congratulates herself on making the old woman laugh so hard.

'Mum joked that I'd inherited Dad's looks but not his brains,' continues Kate. 'At that moment I vowed I'd learn to feed myself properly, and I also vowed that even if I couldn't be beautiful like her, I'd never be cruel like her either.' Kate has told this story several times over the years, and every time she does she marvels at how mean her mother was. Rita strenuously denies her role in this story, claiming Kate has false memory syndrome, but Kate knows it happened because it had cut her straight to the core.

Cecily pauses and turns her gaze to the window. 'I never came close to what my father wanted me to be. The one thing we can't forgive our parents for is their disappointment in us.' She turns back to Kate with a helpless smile.

'Do you feel like telling me about your husband the spy?'

'Not today,' says Cecily. Her eyes narrow and she points to Kate for more tea. 'Tell me more about this man of yours.'

'I don't really want to,' says Kate, staring at her hands.

'I suspect you do. And even if you don't, I'm in the mood for a story, especially one that goes horribly wrong.'

'It's complicated,' says Kate, straightening up in indignation. 'I'm trying to keep my mind off it.'

'Nonsense,' says Cecily, gleefully. 'What's this chap called, and is he handsome?'

'He's called Nick, and I'll show you,' says Kate, coming to crouch by Cecily's side. Kate flicks through her photos. 'Hmm, here's the most recent one . . .' It's the one taken on their second day in France, a selfie of them with sunburnt noses, lying on their loungers. Their faces are pure happiness, yet seven hours later . . . Looking at this photo still feels like pressing on an open wound. She flicks back further. 'Ah, here's a good one.' Back in May, Kate had insisted Nick leave the sofa and crossword and take a day trip to Brighton. 'We went down to the coast, but it turned cold the minute we got there. We ended up buying a pizza and eating it on the beach in a hefty gale. I was using the pizza box to protect me from the wind but it had bacon stuck to the lid and I didn't realise the bacon bits were getting caught in my hair, so this was taken just after Nick's eaten the pork from my hair,' says Kate, laughing at how unsophisticated they sound. In the photo Kate turns to Nick with a half-smile, her face tipped up towards his. He has his arm firmly round her shoulder and is beaming – his green eyes filled with laughter.

Cecily squints at the screen impatiently. 'I can't see him clearly.'

Kate zooms in until her entire screen is Nick's smiling face.

Cecily paws at the picture. 'The temples are grey yet the mind looks childish.'

'How on earth can you tell what his mind looks like from an iPhone photo?'

'Because I can. What's the situation?'

'To cut a long story short, he's not good with emotions.'

Cecily shrugs. 'Men often aren't.'

'Exactly, thank you! So we've been together eighteen months, we get on brilliantly, we have loads in common. He'd just asked me to move in with him but then we went to France for a few days and out of nowhere he says he has an urge to withdraw.'

'What does that mean?'

'Well *exactly*. He said he didn't want to live with me *at the moment*. It was incredibly confusing.'

'And then what?' Cecily leans forward as if something revelatory is about to be delivered. 'Did he do something spectacular to make up for it?'

'Oh, Nick's not a romantic at all. He's analytical, scientific, possibly mildly autistic. He's been single most of his life.'

'These are his selling points?'

'He's completely rational, not emotional – but that's fine, I do the feelings for both of us. Look, Mrs Finn, I don't believe in fairy stories, I don't need him to turn up on a white horse. He's agreed to have therapy—'

'Oh no. No, no, no. Give that man short shrift.'

'Therapy, which is a huge deal for a bloke like him, and in the meantime we've agreed to just be friends. We talk every day, but I'm not going to see him till he's sure of what he wants.'

Cecily waves Kate's comment away. 'Ludicrous – friends help, not harm, each other. Anyway, I wouldn't worry about it; you're not the first person in history to have their heart broken. If this chap is too emotionally stunted to love you, let's find a man who can.'

'*What?*'

'There's more than one man on earth who'll eat pizza from your hair.'

'Mrs Finn, do you have any idea how hard it is to meet a man nowadays? Don't ask me to explain Tinder to you because you'll find it appalling but, basically, the Internet has ruined human relationships. Things aren't normal out there. Every forty-something, pot-bellied male in London thinks he's entitled to date a hotter, younger woman. Men reject perfectly lovely women because they're holding out for unrealistic perfection and they're delusional about their "infinite" choices; women try to cling to these substandard men because they're so beaten down by years of terrible dating.'

Cecily points in confusion at Kate.

'No, that is *not* my situation *at all*,' says Kate. 'I'm lucky to have Nick – he's incredibly clever, a great cook, he's kind . . .'

'Kind? To jilt a girl on holiday?'

'I was *not* jilted. Day-to-day he's a gentle soul, there's an absence of malice to him.'

'And an absence of other key qualities too.'

'He expressed a modicum of doubt about our future. That's not unreasonable,' says Kate, feeling her cheeks colour.

'*I* find it unreasonable. The only reason you'd countenance a man doubting you is if you doubt yourself.'

Kate is silent as she tries to think of a reason to convince herself, and then Cecily, that this is not the case.

Cecily stares at her, then softens slightly. 'In my day you were over the hill at twenty. Papa was frantic, in his eyes I was an "old maid", a disgrace. But I found my soulmate in the end. He was worth the wait. Papa had made me become a teacher—'

'You were a teacher?'

'In one of my many lives. Papa forced me into it. He said at least I'd have a pension as no one would marry me because I was so plain.'

Kate shifts uncomfortably in her chair but Cecily is unfazed. 'Every time I went to a tea dance, he'd say, "If anyone better-looking than a toad asks to marry you, say yes".'

'But you did marry in the end,' says Kate defensively.

'And I married a prince, not a toad.'

'Not an actual prince?' says Kate, wondering if Cecily's about to claim royalty.

'Better than a prince – a man who was always by my side.' She pauses to look at Kate more closely. 'Do something for me, Kate. Find another chap to take you out.'

'What?'

'Hoping and waiting make fools of us. This amoeba chap—'

'Amoeba?'

'Was that not his name?'

'It's *Nick*,' says Kate, spilling tea into her saucer as she places it back on the table.

'He's clearly inadequate. He doesn't realise how lucky he is. Find a better man.'

'I can't do that. We're on a break while he works through his issues. He doesn't want to hurt me again and obviously I don't want that either. We're being responsible. I think he loves me – why else would he waste his time?'

'His time is not my concern. Yours is.' Cecily points a warning finger at her. 'Has he made any firm commitment?'

'He wants to take me for dinner for my fortieth in December . . .'

Cecily shakes her head impatiently. 'Good Lord, when the stomach's empty so is the brain. Listen to me – you need to explore other options.'

'Even if I say yes, you can't meet a man in real life in London – people only date via phone apps.'

'More nonsense. Technology may have changed but people haven't. Next weekend do something, anything, you're interested in. Do the things you love and everything else will fall into place. Go to a museum or for a walk in Hyde Park. Next Sunday, I want to hear that you've at least spoken to a new man. That really isn't a huge demand and, frankly, I haven't mentioned it, but I've been having palpitations. I don't think I'll make it past October. You could do this one last thing for me.' Cecily rests her hand on her chest and makes a low, unconvincing moan. 'I can feel it now, beating too fast. Time for you to go.'

'Mrs Finn, you are OK, aren't you?'

'I will be, but only if you come back with progress next week.'

'You're totally faking it.'

'You couldn't live with the guilt if I'm not,' says Cecily as Kate heads for the door. 'Opportunities are everywhere. Take it from one who knows.'

On Kate's way out a man sitting in reception looks up from his phone as she walks by. He's a few years older than Kate, with dark blue eyes, sandy hair and a long, narrow nose. He smiles warmly at her.

Kate has been getting quite a lot of random male attention recently. She reasons it must be down to the fact that she's lost eight pounds since France, and now has a flat and empty stomach. Or because she's walking around looking vulnerable, a damsel in distress, which is a look some men lap up – sad men who need women to be fragile in order to feel strong. It hasn't occurred to her that men are looking at her because she's an attractive girl wearing pretty dresses in the summer and they might just, well, fancy her.

Kate smiles back at the man. If Cecily is right and this world is full of opportunities – if only you are open to them – then he will strike up a conversation with her right now, and then he'll ask her out. That would be destiny. Kate holds his gaze, possibly for too long as he eventually looks embarrassed and turns his attention back to his phone.

Probably Tindering some thirty-year-old in her underwear, thinks Kate, as she heads for the door.

Chapter Twenty-two

KATE IS IN A VALENTINE'S DAY meeting with the team on Monday morning, running through product lines for next year's menus. The meeting is more like a Valentine's Day Massacre. After sampling the scallop 'Aphrodisiac Soup', Dave launches into a vivid comparison of the soup with the contents of his father's waste bag in hospital after his father suffered multi-organ failure following a routine gall bladder removal. The heart-shaped crab cakes provoke such visceral abuse Devron has to call a time out.

Kate's tempted to go and fetch Cecily's book from her handbag and offer up 'Valentine's Dinner for a True Love After Three Decades Together'. *Aim: to remind your love that while age may start to wither you, it cannot diminish your appetite for life.* The menu has some delicious Italian dishes, but Kate fears that if Fletchers attempted to mass-produce angel-hair pasta with meatballs, the result would be lumpen gristly stodge that would kill off any passion in a single mouthful.

Devron spends the next half-hour taking them through a PowerPoint on a new cross-category workstream called KIPPER – Creativity Yields Profit in Retail. Why is he talking about five-year plans when half the people in this room might not be here in a month? Why isn't he updating them on redundancies? He was meant to get back to them three weeks ago! There's nothing Kate hates more than not knowing where she stands.

Her indignation swells, mixing itself with residual irritation she still feels about Nick which she hasn't expressed satisfactorily. How dare Devron carry on like it's business as usual? He's the most inconsiderate man in the whole world ever – what, are they just expected to wait until he can make up his indecisive little mind?

By the end of the meeting she's whipped herself up into a misdirected and self-righteous rage. Before she has a chance to think, she corners Devron and demands to know the cause of the delay.

'It's unreasonable,' says Kate. 'We're all in limbo. It's impossible for us to move on with our lives with this hanging over our heads.'

Devron looks unsettled. He likes Kate because she's attractive, and normally isn't too pushy. 'I haven't come back to you because HR are debating whether to roll out new psychometrics or keep it Simple and Lean.'

'We should do Myers-Briggs,' says Annalex, nodding encouragingly. 'We used Myers-Briggs all the time at Pharmacore.'

'Except it's a totally unhelpful tool to figure out who's best for a creative role,' says Kate, feeling herself colour as she tries to tamp down her anger.

'You would say that, you're an INFP,' says Annalex, turning to Devron with indignation.

He clears his throat with a frown. 'Girls, girls, you both need to calm down. It's barely October, you've got weeks, and there's always the voluntary redundancy route.'

'But I'd like to know where I stand now,' says Kate, who never feels less calm than when a man is telling her to calm down. 'I don't want to be put on ice till November.' She could do without her P45 hitting the doormat along-side her birthday cards.

'If you want a decision made right now you can always make one yourself,' says Annalex, her small blue eyes nar-rowing in calculation. 'Voluntary redundancy?'

Kate's mouth twitches in indignation. 'I'll wait.'

Chapter Twenty-three

Even though she has absolutely no desire to date anyone but Nick, after considering it further, Kate has decided to spend the following weekend as Cecily has instructed – not to meet a man, but to prove to that manipulative old woman that it's impossible to. Plus she's so wound up by the stasis at work, a weekend of distractions would be welcome.

Nick is spending the weekend with his friends Rob and Tasha at some trendy music festival in Sussex. Rob and Tasha are cliquey hipster wannabes, the only friends of Nick she's not fond of. Nick was their perennially single friend for so long, they see Kate as the Yoko. So if Kate were forced to take a lie-detector test, a third reason she's willing to do Cecily's bidding is because she is mildly bothered by the fact that Nick is off having fun with those particular friends, while she's still in protracted limbo waiting for him, and actually not much better off than she was a month ago.

Kate has no major hobbies apart from food and she's still lacking the appetite for serious cooking, so instead she's planned a Saturday that incorporates a little food, a little culture and a girls' night out.

On Saturday morning she heads off to Borough Market, having woken with a craving for a Bread Ahead custard doughnut. She's waiting in the queue when the man in front of her, a craggy sixty-year-old, turns to ask if she could recommend anything. Kate can't believe she's actually being chatted up but is happy to share her extensive doughnut knowledge. They talk for a few minutes about custard, Kate's Mastermind specialist subject, and Kate's just starting to consider how she'll avoid a coffee if he asks, when a beautiful young blonde sweeps up and kisses the man on the lips.

'Ah, baby, the coffee queue was so long, I couldn't bear to wait,' she says in a transatlantic accent, sticking out a beautiful bee-stung bottom lip. She turns to Kate with a curious look. 'I'm Yanika.'

'Hey, sexy,' says her boyfriend, slipping his hand round the girl's waist. 'This lady says the doughnuts here are great.'

'Oh baby, you know I can't,' she says, tapping an inch of her tanned concave belly.

'Oh you must,' says Kate. 'They're genuinely worth the calories, and besides, you've got a fantastic figure.'

The girl smiles shyly.

'The custard's a dream,' says Kate. 'Heavy but not cloying – and the doughnut part's so light – the balance is perfection.' The girl's face lights up as Kate is talking.

'I'll take four,' says the boyfriend to the guy on the stall. 'And another in a separate bag.' He hands Kate the single doughnut as she's about to order her own. 'For your custard wisdom. Thank you.'

'Oh, that's so nice!' says Kate. One-nil, Kate to Cecily, and one free doughnut – the morning's off to a perfect start.

Kate takes her doughnut and heads east to Bermondsey Street. It's a beautiful day and she takes cheer in the pink and orange buildings popping out against the deep blue sky. She strolls over to Maltby Street food market and stumbles across an amazing greengrocer and butcher under the railway arches. She buys a bottle of wine for Rita from a French deli, then sits at a coffee stand to watch the world go by, inhaling the smells of falafels frying and onions being grilled. All around her, hip couples are getting drunk on gin and craft beers, but Kate has a perfect cheese toastie, a coffee and a Stella Newman novel and she's entirely content – thoughts of work and even of Nick don't trouble her.

Now it's 2 p.m. and Kate's aware she's not doing much to obey Cecily's diktat, so she decides to visit the trendy art gallery in Bermondsey. She has no idea what's on but every time she's visited previously she's been more impressed by the glass and concrete building than the art. Today is no exception. It's a 'mould-breaking, provocatively curated meditation on feminism, examining the politics of genitals'. She and Nick would have a field day here.

Kate is standing, hands on hips, scrutinising one of the paintings of a naked woman. What's going on there? It's so abstract – she does a sudden take when she realises that the orange lines she's been squinting at are supposed to represent female genitalia, the black gouache lump next to them a cockroach.

'Wow, right?' says a man standing next to her, arms folded, staring with concentration at the canvas.

She turns to look at him: not unattractive – brown eyes, short dark hair, designer trainers which cost more

151

than she earns in a week, which she will try not to judge him for.

'Yeah,' says Kate, followed up by a 'Wow', because she cannot think of anything polite to say, and this man's 'Wow' is possibly sincere.

'Extraordinary,' says the man, and Kate still can't figure out whether he's taking the piss.

'You didn't paint it, did you?'

'Me? God, no. I'm a networker, not an artist. You know, when you see a canvas like this, so necessary,' he shrugs.

'Right.' Kate nods. 'Well, always nice to see insects in unusual places,' she says, because that sounds facetious enough to get rid of him without sounding unequivocally rude.

'Micky,' he says, extending his hand to Kate. 'What do you do?'

I seem to attract awful men in awkward situations, thinks Kate. 'My job is to think of alternative ways of communicating that carrots are crunchy. It's a hugely specialist line of work. There's only a few of us in the country with the requisite skill set.'

'That's . . . cool?' he says, looking to her for confirmation.

Kate smiles a neat goodbye and moves with haste to the next canvas. It's by the same artist and depicts a woman's bottom with a wasp edging very close to the danger zone.

Seems Micky's not one to be deterred by sarcasm. 'What I find most relevant about this artist,' he continues, 'is how she's not afraid to push boundaries. Good taste is utterly redundant.'

'Apparently so. I guess I'm old-fashioned, but give me a Monet any day.'

'But that's my point, this is provocative,' he says flirtatiously. 'People are so uncomfortable with challenge.'

'They'd be more uncomfortable with a wasp up their backside,' says Kate, and heads for the door before he has time for a comeback. Really, Cecily has *no* idea what it's like out here.

Kate's due to meet Cara and Bailey at a pub in Clerkenwell for a night out, but when she checks her phone Bailey has sent an apologetic text – her ex-husband 'forgot' he's taking his girlfriend to the opera and he can't have the kids after all, and it's too late for Bailey to find a babysitter. Kate is walking to the pub when Cara texts – she's running an hour late, and she's bringing the hot Dane from the other night.

Kate sits alone nursing a gin and tonic, thinking back to the dates she'd had just before she met Nick. There was the TV producer who was super-chatty, and returned from the toilet with a crescent of white powder round his nose. When Kate had pointed it out he'd claimed it was moisturiser – no second date there. Then there was the host of her local pub quiz who'd taken her to a restaurant in Chinatown that served frozen dumplings filled with meat of dubious origin. When he'd realised Kate wasn't going to sleep with him he'd called her uptight, then claimed he'd lost his wallet – no more pub quiz for Kate.

Cara and the Dane eventually arrive looking like they've just rolled out of bed. Cara sends him to the bar, then whispers excitedly to Kate, 'I'm moving in with him.'

'*What*? You've literally known him two *weeks*.'

Cara shrugs and tosses her hair to one side. 'By the time you're our age you know what you want. Why not just get on with it?'

'Er, because you don't know a person after fourteen days?'

'But what a fourteen days!' says Cara, her brown eyes sparkling. 'We've spent every night together. He's got the most amazing penthouse in Chelsea. Last night we sat on his terrace naked drinking champagne . . . and the sex!' she says, raising her eyebrows almost to her hairline.

Kate can't tell if her abdomen aches because Cara's man sounds too good to be true and she doesn't want her friend getting hurt – or because she can't stomach being around such highly sexed-up lovebirds. She has to excuse herself before closing time because she's worried the spark these two have between them might rub up against something more flammable in her.

On the way home she stands, smoking, waiting for her bus at the Old Street roundabout. The lights and neon from the shops and billboards make the night sky a dull yellow-grey. Traffic's at a standstill. There are people everywhere, couples on dates heading home, buzzing partygoers only now starting their nights out. How many people alone in this bus queue still believe in true love, or is it a fantasy that gets beaten out of you as you get older?

At home in bed Kate forces herself to compile a gratitude list: one amazing custard doughnut. And it was free. Her health. The beautiful weather. A great book. That's a pretty good day.

She pictures Cecily, trapped inside her book-lined walls. Cecily couldn't write any of those items on a list; she wouldn't even have gone outside to enjoy the sunshine. She stays stuck in her room, living in memories. Kate is lucky – even if she doesn't always feel lucky. She still has a future full of possibilities. She just needs to figure out what they might be, and how to go after them.

Chapter Twenty-four

R ITA HAS CALLED AN emergency meeting on Sunday morning to discuss reports that two local youths were spotted by Mr Pring in the communal garden on Saturday night, smoking what looked like 'a marijuana cigarette'. Mr Pring operates a zero-tolerance policy on everything but vintage porn, and has insisted the committee discuss how and when to involve the local constabulary.

Kate needs to escape, so she heads to Aposta for a coffee. She almost has second thoughts when she arrives – the café is crowded with loved-up couples hogging the sofas, reminding her of her old Sunday mornings snuggled up in Nick's bed – but she has to bury that thought because she's here now, and Nick at this moment is probably waking up hung-over in a tent with his idiot friends and won't be pining for her because he is so much better at living in the moment than she is.

She orders a coffee and settles in a low leather chair at the back with the Sunday supplements. Wow, she is a complete failure of contemporary womanhood. Apparently, she should be eating freekeh and spending her Saturdays lifting her own bodyweight while wearing metallic leggings. She throws the *Style* section down on the coffee table in dismay, where it is immediately picked up again by a man who has come to sit a few seats away. She looks up and does a double take – she recognises him, from a Channel 4 comedy last year. He was only a minor character, but he'd performed a hilarious dance to Shakira dressed in glittery lederhosen, which Nick had insisted on rewinding and rewatching a dozen times. Nick sometimes does an impression of this dance when he's naked and fresh from the shower – and this, as much as anything, makes Kate break into a broad grin and then a furious blush.

The guy smiles back. He is six foot and bald, with piercing blue eyes. He's wearing a black T-shirt and Levi's, and his confidence and smile make him incredibly sexy. 'I hope you haven't ripped out the horoscope from this magazine,' he says. 'I need to know what Shelley von Strunckel says the stars have in store for me.'

'If you're a Sagittarius, Shelley says it's time for a new chapter in your romantic life – say yes to an intriguing offer from an unexpected direction,' says Kate, blushing deeper.

'How did you know I'm a Sagi?' he says, looking genuinely surprised.

'Oh, snap!'

'I'm Martin,' he says, extending his hand and holding hers a moment longer than is necessary.

Yes, that's his name, Martin something Italian – sweet lord, it's taking all her self-control not to ask for a selfie she can send straight to Nick.

'I'm Kate.'

'Kate, I don't think I've seen you in here, are you local?'

'Ish. You?'

'Down towards Archway. I love this place, great coffee. I come here in the week to work sometimes.'

'What do you do?' She thinks it's obvious from how starstruck she is that she knows, but somehow she feels it would be even more embarrassing to admit she's watched his Shakira lederhosen dance a dozen times.

He shrugs and pulls a nonchalant face. 'Ah, a bit of, you know, bit of acting, bit of comedy, but I'm mostly writing nowadays. I did a show last year, a pilot I co-wrote, and I'm writing something for HBO. I don't know if anything will come of it, but, you know, all the good writing nowadays is on American TV. What do you do, Kate?'

'I'm a writer too, you might know my work. My last big project was the small print on a range of Fletchers' pork pies.'

He laughs with absolute delight. 'That is the funniest thing ever.'

'It's true, I'm afraid.'

'That's why it's funny, sweetheart.'

Kate's tummy does a little flip when he calls her sweetheart.

'You have majorly intense eyes, Kate. Crazy thoughtful, like there's a lot going on behind there.'

'Let me tell you, Martin, pork-pie packaging does not write itself . . .'

'I can see you're a deep thinker. And you've got these stunning little flecks of hazel right near your pupils.'

Kate blushes deeply. It took Nick about a year to notice this.

Martin's phone beeps and he glances at it and nods. 'What are you up to this afternoon?'

'Me? Why?'

'I've got a spare ticket to see a show a mate of mine did at Edinburgh, it's at a pub in Crouch End. Fancy it?'

Kate takes a deep breath. 'I'm busy.'

'What are you doing that could possibly be more fun than comedy with me?'

'I'm off to visit a grumpy ninety-seven-year-old lady up in Hampstead.'

'A random grumpy old lady, or your grandmother?'

'No, she's pretty random. Actually, grumpy's not entirely fair – she's cool. Well, she's interesting. She's one of those people who has no filter.'

'Wow, you're pretty *and* kind – you're like a hot Mother Teresa. Right, I've got to head off – give me your number, we're going out this week.'

Kate pauses. Should she say she has a boyfriend? Because she doesn't have a boyfriend, she has a *situation* . . . 'Er, this might sound a bit weird, but I'm sort of on a break from a relationship at the moment.'

'Perfect timing.'

'Well, it's just—'

'Do you live with this guy?'

'No . . .'

'Are you currently, you know . . .' He smiles and makes a clicking noise with his tongue.

'That's a rather personal question! But no, no we're not. We're just friends for now.'

'Look – we'll just go to a gallery, grab a coffee, it's no big deal, you are allowed to talk to other men, aren't you? He's not the type to stab me, is he?'

Maybe with his crossword pencil, thinks Kate. 'It's just some art, right?'

'Yay, that's a yes, right? Life's too short to say no to fun.'

Kate tries not to smile as she gives him her details. Cecily will be pleased.

And of course, secretly, Kate is too.

Chapter Twenty-five

'I TOLD YOU SO,' says Cecily, waving her hand in a matador flourish. 'This man was right under your nose. You should listen to your fairy godmother.'

Kate smiles with embarrassment. 'It's pure fluke, Mrs Finn. No one's ever chatted me up in a coffee shop before. The thing is, I'm flattered. And he's very attractive, but I'm emotionally involved with Nick. It feels disloyal. And I did try to explain about Nick . . .'

'*Oy gevalt*, if they put your brain in a chicken it would run straight to the butcher,' says Cecily, bringing her fist down with a small thud, causing her tea to spill. 'You're going to go out with this man. You'll have a good time, and you're not to mention Amoeba, and then you'll see him again and cook "Dinner for a Charming Stranger"—'

'Hold on a minute,' says Kate, raising her voice above Cecily's. 'Are you going to direct my life from here on in? Because you said you'd be dead before the end of the month, so we won't get too far, will we?'

'I am prepared to stick around for a few more weeks, because I cannot abide seeing an intelligent woman be so utterly stupid.'

Kate shakes her head at Cecily. '*What?*'

'Your job, your home life, your namby-pamby boyfriend – I could hardly do a worse job of running the show.'

'I talk to one random man in a coffee shop, big deal – that's no justification to sit there ripping my life to shreds.'

'Call that a life?'

Kate sighs. 'It's not that bad.'

'If I had the opportunities you have . . .'

'Then what?'

'I'd be bold. I'd do anything, I'd do everything. Explore! You're how old?'

'Thirty-nine and five sixths,' mumbles Kate.

'Right – by the time *I* was forty, I'd seen thirty-seven countries. By my fiftieth birthday I'd had three distinguished careers and when I retired at sixty-eight we hiked Machu Picchu. Life is as long as it's short.'

'What does that even mean?'

'It means find what nourishes your soul, discover what you're capable of – live life well.'

Kate has spent many a night lying in bed feeling like she hasn't done anything with her life, but since she fell in love with Nick, those feelings have dissipated. She somehow saw a happy relationship as the finish line of a marathon.

'I'll go out with Martin once,' says Kate, folding her arms, as if that were protection against the onslaught that is Cecily.

'Fine – take it one step at a time if you're the timorous type.'

'But what if Nick turns round tomorrow and says he's ready to commit?'

'Never play chess with a pigeon, and certainly don't play it twice,' says Cecily, drawing her head back in horror.

'Is that *another* metaphor, Mrs Finn?'

'That's surely a rhetorical question,' says Cecily, frowning in confusion. 'Well, I suppose either way it's sage.' She shrugs, reaching for another all-butter shortbread. 'Embark on a game of skill with a flying vermin and it cannot end well.'

Kate is in no mood for metaphors and even less so for Cecily's cryptic nonsense. 'More tea?' she says, reaching for the pot. 'Remind me, Mrs Finn, what's on the menu for "Dinner for a Charming Stranger"?'

'*Boeuf aux Champignons*, then *Torrone Molle* for dessert – that's a nougat you make in advance so you can spend more time on the night being seductive. I learned to make it on our honeymoon in Italy, so it was a bit of a fudge in the book, but still . . .'

'How do you remember every menu from that book?'

'I remember almost every significant meal of my life.'

'Your memory is amazing. Er, what do you mean *your* life?'

'"Dinner for a Charming Stranger"? That's the first meal I ever cooked Samuel – the beef part was. I actually made profiteroles for dessert, entirely the wrong choice, far too labour-intensive when all I wanted was to be sitting at the table listening to him talk.'

'Hold on, I thought Samuel was your husband?'

'My husband and my best friend.'

'Right, yes, but hang on,' says Kate, trying to work out the maths. 'You were almost forty when you met him?'

163

Cecily frowns in irritation. 'I never said that. I was twenty when we married. Papa would have sent me to a nunnery if I'd left it much later.'

'The book was published in 1957, wasn't it? I'm pretty sure you lent me a first edition? The one with the pink and yellow cover?'

'There was only a first edition, more's the pity, or we'd have been able to buy a second home in Capri when we lived there in the sixties.'

'*Thought for Food* was published in 1957, but you were already married to Samuel by then?'

'The wedding was more than two decades earlier. Where is your miscomprehension coming from?'

'Well, how can the first meal you cooked for him be from a book that wasn't published till twenty-something years after you cooked it?'

'You're talking about *my* book?' says Cecily, giving Kate a quizzical look.

'Now *that* sounds like a rhetorical question,' says Kate in utter confusion.

'That book is one of *my* books,' says Cecily, as if she's expecting something more from Kate.

'Well, of course.' Kate feels a small twitch of anxiety. This is the first time she's seen Cecily anything less than pin-sharp. '*Thought for Food*, from right there on your shelf?' says Kate more slowly, hoping this might aid Cecily's comprehension.

'Why are you speaking as though *I'm* the idiot in the room?'

'What have I done now?'

'Why do you think I lent you that book?'

164

'You said choose any book. You thought a cookery book would cheer me up.'

'You didn't choose the book, cretin, the book chose you. I chose the book *for* you, I wrote the damn thing!'

'What?'

'*I. Wrote. That. Book.*'

'But . . . No, you – but . . . *what*?' says Kate, trying to read from Cecily's incredulous expression whether Cecily is winding her up or not.

Cecily blows out a puff of air and looks to her left and right as if seeking back-up from an invisible audience. 'One of us has had a stroke during this conversation and I'm reasonably confident it isn't me.'

Kate's mouth opens and her lips move but her brain hasn't quite caught up with her.

'Young lady, why is this so difficult for you to under-stand?'

'Because I assume you'd have mentioned this fact to me earlier! Because your name is not Esther Shavin. Or is it? Were *you* a spy too?'

'For goodness' sake, it's a simple pseudonym. Esther was my best friend at school,' says Cecily, waving the comment away.

'Oh my goodness,' says Kate, shaking her head. 'I did wonder how you knew all the page numbers by heart.'

Cecily is now the one lost for words. 'You actually thought I could remember every word of every book on these shelves down to the page number?' She lets out a shriek of laughter. 'If so, you have my full permission to sell me to the circus. You'll make some money and I'll get to ride an elephant before I die.'

'So you wrote that book, and a children's book, and several films?'

'I told you I went to Hollywood, did you think I was fibbing?'

'How come you went to Hollywood?'

'Oh, they were interested in remaking one of the films I wrote, *The Man Who Liked Funerals*. We went out there in 1968 and I sat in endless meetings with studio executives for weeks. They were promising Peter Sellers would star, but it all fell through, these things often do. Thank goodness Samuel was by my side. Every night I'd come back to our motel room, thoroughly dejected, but he'd always make me laugh and realise how lucky I was,' she says with a deep sigh.

'So hold on – can we go back to *Thought for Food*? I still can't believe you didn't tell me you wrote it.'

'I credited you with some intelligence.'

'Or deliberately misled me . . . How many copies did you sell?'

'I didn't make a fortune, but enough to eat well, and for us to spend the following ten years or so in Italy.'

'It must have been a bestseller.'

'Not at all. But after the book was published I had the strongest hankering to go back to Italy. Samuel and I had been for our honeymoon, it was the place we'd been happiest. We went to Rome, then decided there was no reason not to stay a while, and *a while* turned into nearly a decade. I wrote another book there, and when money started to run out, I ended up writing screenplays. We moved cities a few times, to Genoa, Florence, Palermo . . .'

'How utterly glamorous! And what did Samuel do?'

'We didn't live in high style, but it was simple and wonderful. The sunshine, those fantastic food markets, the glorious architecture. I wrote in the day and cooked at night, it was an absolute tonic. It was only when they produced my first film that we returned to England, and then there was the failed Hollywood experience. Anyway, now you know I'm the book's author, I trust you'll use it wisely.'

'I'm still amazed,' says Kate, grinning. 'And this was your life? These menus are autobiographical?'

'A touch of poetic licence here and there,' says Cecily coyly, rubbing her fingers together as if sprinkling more salt into her soup.

'Which bits are true? "Dinner for Your Son's Fiancée" – do you have a *son*?' Kate had assumed Cecily had no family, but perhaps they're estranged, which wouldn't be too surprising.

'We had no children. That was a meal my mother-in-law Shindel cooked for me.'

'Ah, so you switched the perspective around. What was on the menu again?'

'Gooseberry fool, and a warning to maintain her standards of cooking.'

'Mrs Finn, please tell me how you met Samuel? He sounds wonderful.'

'Yes, yes, another time,' says Cecily, settling herself into an incredibly long yawn. 'I'm tired, and your foolishness exhausts me.'

'Why are you so mean sometimes?'

'Because I can be,' snaps Cecily. 'Now get one of the Filipinas to bring me a headache tablet.' She closes her eyes and breathes out heavily through her nose.

'Shall I see you next Sunday?' says Kate, hovering awkwardly by her chair.

'If you have progress, yes. Otherwise don't waste my time.'

'Right-oh. Well, let me know if you need me to bring you anything.'

Cecily shoos her away with an irritable flick.

Chapter Twenty-six

'HAVE YOU BEEN OPENING my mail?' says Kate, giving Rita her best outraged face.

Rita finishes stirring sweetener into her cappuccino and stares blankly at Kate.

'I've just sent a stroppy email to that poor bookseller in Lancashire telling him the two books I ordered are late, and here's one of them, which must have been sitting on your bedside table for weeks.'

'People always ask questions they already know the answers to,' says Rita, scraping a thin layer of margarine onto her toast. 'You know I opened your mail because you've found the book – you're holding it in your hand – so why ask if I've opened it?'

'Is that supposed to be an apology?'

'You're living under my roof. You can't expect me to put reading glasses on to examine every single piece of mail that arrives in my own letterbox. I was waiting for a book Patrick sent me, you'd had several packages, how was I to know you had more on the way? It was an accident,' says Rita, giving the marmalade lid a sharp twist.

'You're the one always quoting Freud saying "There are no accidents" . . .'

Rita lets out an irritated sigh.

'And at the point when you realised you'd opened my mail,' says Kate, 'a normal mother would have put the books back in the jiffy bag and put the jiffy bag in my room, rather than steal those books and "forget" she's stolen them, and now front it out like it's *my* fault.'

'Aren't you going to be late for work?'

'Well?'

'It looked like an interesting book. I noticed you'd ordered multiple copies. I didn't think you'd miss it, and I was right.'

'Have you *ever* apologised for anything in your life? Plus, I ordered two copies – where's the other one?'

Rita tips her head back and runs a finger along her eyebrow. 'Gerry Marks happened to pop round. She liked the look of it. I said she could borrow it. She's always bringing me books, it's the least I could do.'

'Sorry, you've *given away* one of my books that you stole because you owe Gerry a favour? In what universe is this acceptable?'

'In one where I pushed you out of my body over an excruciating twenty-hour labour. Anyway, she'll give it back once Jeremy's had a look. Why were you ordering so many copies?'

'Because it happens to have been written by the old lady I visit.'

'Oh! Really? You didn't tell me she was a writer.'

'Because you've never asked a single thing about her.'

'Was she successful?'

'Why?'

Rita shrugs. 'I wonder if there might be a little windfall coming your way. Is that why you're so attentive, round there all the time, while neglecting your own flesh and blood?'

'I'm not going to dignify that.'

'Oh come on, where's your sense of humour? It's in the book, anyway.'

'What is?'

'A little limerick about ingratiating yourself with a rich old relative – look it up, "Lunch for a Wealthy Benefactor" or something,' she says, grabbing the book from Kate. 'Where are we . . . ah, page thirty-eight, "Luncheon for a Wealthy Aunt":

'My aunt, she died a month ago,
And left me all her riches.
A feather bed and a wooden leg,
And a pair of calico breeches.

'Aim: to express your pleasure at entertaining such
a rare guest, and to intimate that you are unlikely
to squander any monies she'd like to drop in your
lap. Menu: grilled halibut . . . '

'Give that back,' says Kate, grabbing the book and stroking the cover tenderly. 'What do you mean, Gerry's showing it to Jeremy? Why?'

'He runs the publishing company now, they're always looking for good ideas.'

'Oh right – so not content with stealing my mail, you're now planning to mug an old lady for her idea, marvellous.'

'You know what? I think you should move in with Nick and make his life a misery instead of mine. Maybe then I can enjoy a piece of toast in my own home on a Monday morning without being accused of being a criminal. Oh, and while you are still here, we've finalised a date for the Heathview AGM.'

'Why are you telling me this?'

'You're in charge of catering. Put it in your diary, it's the Thursday after your birthday. I'll be back from Lanzarote the night before.'

'Lanzarote?'

'Breathing retreat.'

'You're missing my *fortieth*?'

'No point buying in sandwiches for the AGM when you can do it better.'

'I'd like my book back from Gerry, please.'

'We'll give you fifty quid for it.'

'For the book?'

'For the catering, silly.'

'Oh, you don't need to pay me.'

'I want you to do a good job.'

'You don't need to pay me because I'm not doing it.'

'Nothing too greasy – some elegant salmon one-bites might be nice.'

'I am not interested.'

'Oh fine, we'll give you a hundred pounds and you can't say no because you're living here rent-free. Now hurry up and go to work before you lose your job as well as your boyfriend.'

Chapter Twenty-seven

Project: Eggcellent Easter at Fletchers

Launch/upgrade of 12 x Easter Eggs.

Pack copy to include 6 x alliterations – Sophisticated Salted Caramel, Marvellous Marmalade; 6 x rhyming adjectives – i.e., Silky Milk Chocolate IS acceptable.

If no solution can be found, the following descriptors must be used: Eggsquisite, Eggcellent, Eggceptional.

K ATE ARRIVES AT WORK extra early on Tuesday, at 7 a.m., hoping to produce a dazzling response to Devron's brief for next year's Easter Eggs. She's had to write the same weary puns year after year, each time worrying that she might be the one to crack, but this year it's essential she pulls something magnificent out of the bag. She cannot be jobless this Christmas, not jobless and single and forty – just no.

After an hour she's finished the copy for the first five eggs but is struggling with the orange and ginger one. If she was allowed a qualifier for 'Orange' – 'Seville', or 'Bitter' – life would be easier, but Devron thinks no one knows what 'Seville' refers to and that 'Bitter' is off-putting, so the descriptor has to start with an 'o'. Overpriced . . .

Odious . . .? She senses a solution just out of reach and closes her eyes to concentrate. She's so close she can almost touch it when Annalex emits a loud grunt, disrupting her chain of thought.

'Have you seen this email about the redundancies?' says Annalex, turning to Kate accusingly.

'What email? Is there news?' says Kate, suddenly on high alert.

'You're telling me you didn't suggest this to Devron?'

'Suggest what?' says Kate, hurriedly clicking on the email in her inbox:

Along with an up-to-date CV, candidates must submit a thousand-word statement on what inspires them in food marketing. NB: candidates can submit for voluntary redundancy up to 30 November.

'Why are you annoyed about that, Annalex?'

A sharp crease forms between Annalex's eyes. 'This whole writing thing is exactly the sort of thing that favours someone like you.'

'You mean someone who's paid to write, so someone like me *and* you?' says Kate in confusion.

'I'm much more of a big-picture person. This is totally unfair.'

Kate rests her head in her hands – O, O, O . . . 'Outstanding' is the only positive O, but having tasted that egg at a PECAN showcase, she can't in good conscience utilise it. It's going to have to be 'Oh-so-delicious' – it goes against her principles but Devron will love it. Besides, it's not as bad as when Annalex wrote Feast-a Pheasant for game season, where the 'a' represented *of*, and it means Kate can start the rhyming doubles; what on earth rhymes with praline?

There must be more to life than this. But catching sight of Annalex manically stabbing at her keyboard like it had insulted her and her immediate family, brings out a sudden competitive instinct in Kate. Yes, her job may not be groundbreaking, but she wants to be in control of whether she keeps it or not. She doesn't want her options taken away from her by Annalex or anyone else.

Chapter Twenty-eight

MARTIN HAS BEEN TEXTING Kate all week. He'd asked to see her on Monday but she was babysitting for Bailey, and every night since she's been working till midnight on her submission for Devron. Finally, they'd made a date for Saturday and Kate can't help but compare how long it took Nick to ask her out to how quickly and persistently Martin has.

It's a stunning early autumn afternoon, the sun still strong in a cloudless sky. They meet outside Tate Modern. Rather than flowers, Martin's brought her the glossy sections of the papers, rolled into an elongated cone. In return, she's brought him an autographed packet of Fletchers' pork pies.

He holds them to his heart: 'I'll cherish these forever.'

'I wouldn't if I were you – they're best before Monday.'

He has a smile that transforms his face from attractive to gorgeous. She still feels guilty she said yes to this date, and even guiltier that she finds him so attractive.

Once inside the gallery Martin heads straight for the American classics, whizzing round, rarely lingering. Kate has come to realise recently how impatient she is, and so she likes this about Martin. In one room he slows to a halt in front of a Warhol of Debbie Harry and nods appreciatively. 'Those cheekbones . . . that eyeshadow. Such insouciance,' he says.

'She was actually at my friend's wedding last month.'

'Seriously? I hope you took a selfie with her?'

'No way, I'd never bother a celebrity in public.'

'You have to, it's Debbie Harry. Right, listen up,' he says, pulling Kate close to whisper in her ear. 'Distract that guard over there, do a little mazurka, I'll get this off the wall and when I give the nod, run like the wind. No? Fine, well, let's get a photo at least.' He gently steers her towards the canvas and puts his arm around her. 'Say cheese!'

He shows her the shot and grins. 'We look great together. You have this tiny freckle – just . . . there.' He narrows his eyes and presses her cheek gently. 'It's the sexiest thing ever.'

Kate blushes, moving swiftly to the next canvas, slightly overwhelmed by the attention.

'Chairman Mao,' says Martin. 'Perfect name for a kitten, particularly one that sits in a chair all day.'

Back in July, Nick and Kate been talking about getting a kitten and had spent several nights discussing names, eventually deciding on Sir-Mix-A-Lot, because it was such a ridiculous name for a cat. The memory of this causes a sudden dull ache in her chest.

'I bet you're a cat person,' says Martin.

'I am indeed.'

'It's a Sagittarius thing, my almost-twin.' He clicks his finger and winks. 'Right – that's enough culture for one day, let's skedaddle.'

He reaches for her hand. She and Nick have evolved a way of hand-holding with such tightly interlocking fingers it's like their hands are one, whereas Martin favours the cupping manoeuvre which reminds Kate of walking in crocodiles on school trips. It doesn't feel right. She must stop comparing these men, but still, his hand in hers, it feels somehow too intimate.

Martin leads her along the South Bank, over Waterloo Bridge, then up through to the narrower streets of Soho. 'I'm meeting my bro at 8.30 p.m. at the Groucho, but do you fancy some food first? Let's eat.'

Ten minutes later they're seated in a corner booth at Kettner's, Martin squeezed so tightly next to her the heat from his legs is warming hers.

'What do you fancy to drink?' he says. 'A cocktail? Wine?'

'Shall we have some wine?'

'I don't drink, but order anything you fancy.'

'Oh. If you're not drinking, I won't either.'

'You must, sweetheart, please, I'm all about the vicarious thrills.' He insists on ordering Kate a carafe, then slips his hand casually to her knee while they browse the menu. 'I'm getting the steak. The sausage and mash is meant to be amazing too.'

'Have you tried it?'

'I don't eat carbs.'

'What, never?'

He shrugs. 'Fattening, innit?'

'I always eat carbs,' says Kate, ordering roast chicken and chips. 'So you never eat pasta? Or pizza? Or crisps?'

'Is it a deal-breaker?' he says, laughing.

'At least tell me you eat butter?'

'No butter, no sugar.'

'Is there anything left worth eating?'

'Protein?'

Kate smiles, but the voice in her head is shrieking: *What a fussy eater.* She chides herself. *I don't eat carbs* is probably better than *I love my TV as much as I love you* . . .

'Tell me about this old lady you visit?' he says, resting his head on his hand and staring deeply into Kate's eyes.

'Mrs Finn? She's ninety-seven. Even though her face is incredibly lined, she's so alert she sometimes looks eighty. Though when she's tired she looks ancient. She has great taste in books. And her memory, my goodness, she can recite more poetry than I've ever read.'

'I can barely remember what I ate for breakfast.'

'Protein,' says Kate, and Martin laughs. 'Mrs Finn can be a little schizoid sometimes – like we'll be in the middle of a perfectly nice chat, then suddenly she'll attack.' Kate looks perplexed. 'I think she's depressed.'

'Ninety-seven though – good innings and all that. I'll be ready to check out by seventy.'

Kate shrugs. 'I guess it depends on your quality of life, whether you have children, grandchildren, a sense of purpose. She's bored – and she can't taste or read properly anymore so she's lost her two favourite things. And she was married for over sixty years. She misses her husband.'

Martin tips his head to one side in sympathy. 'You're obviously making her life cheerier.'

'I doubt it. I seem to annoy her every time I open my mouth.'

'What do you do with her?'

'Do?'

'Do you wheel her around galleries? Take her for walks? Or is she a hip nonagenarian like those ones online, getting down to Biggy?'

'Absolutely not, there are no ironic dance moves with Cecily, she won't budge an inch. We just talk. She tells me about her life, then criticises mine. I think she sees me as her pet project. To be fair, it's quite good to get some perspective when I've spent the entire week bickering with Annalex about whose job it is to write the Yorkshire Pudding packaging – it's clearly going to say Yummy Yorkies, but on principal it does sit in her category,' she says, rolling her eyes at the pettiness.

'So, how long have you worked at Fletchers?'

'Forever. If I survive this latest restructure it'll be twenty years next spring,' says Kate, the low grip of fear returning to her stomach at the thought of leaving the security of the only workplace she's ever known.

'You've worked at the same place your whole career? Do people who don't have a mortgage or school fees still do that?'

'People like me do . . .' says Kate, reaching for her wine.

'What does *people like me* mean?'

'I never got my degree,' says Kate, flushing. 'I'm not ambitious. I don't have any superpowers.'

'I'm sure that's not true,' says Martin, stroking his chin. 'You're scared of risk. And that's probably why you've never married.'

No – *that*'s because she'd made a series of exceedingly poor choices.

'There's no other explanation,' Martin continues, throwing his hands in the air. 'You're attractive, you're funny, you laugh at all my jokes – why else would such an amazing woman still be on the market?'

'*On the market*,' she says, nudging him. 'Makes me sound like cattle. So why aren't *you* married?'

180

'Ah,' he says, cringing and bringing two fists to his mouth in an apologetic gesture. 'Did I not mention? I am . . .'

'Are you joking?'

'I'm not *married* married. I am *literally* married, but we've been separated for months, we're just waiting on the paperwork.'

'Oh. Are you sure about that?'

He wiggles the fingers of his left hand. 'Yep, pretty sure. So, Kate – who's your best friend?'

'Bailey, we've been friends since we were four.'

'And what was your nickname at school?'

'Are these off some Buzzfeed list, *Eight Questions to Ask On a First Date*?'

'Damn.' He reaches into his pocket for a piece of paper and gives it a glance before tearing it in two and throwing it over his shoulder. 'Rumbled.'

'That wasn't . . .?'

'I'm pretty sure that was my dry-cleaning slip. Or the cure for Ebola,' he says, choking on his giggle, which makes Kate warm to him again.

The food arrives, and they eat and flirt. Over the next hour Martin asks her more questions than Nick did in their first three months. He's trying to get to know her but she finds it exhausting, and yearns for the familiarity of Nick who knows her so well they finish each other's sentences.

The meal ends, Martin insists on paying and they slowly head out to the street to say their goodbyes.

'I had such a good time,' says Martin, beaming at her.

'So did I,' says Kate, smiling at the realisation that it's true.

'So . . . shall I give you a ring when I'm done? I can swing by on my way home.'

'*Tonight*? I'm living at my mum's – temporarily. And besides, I'll probably be asleep.'

'Ah yeah, no, fair play. Is your mum in most nights?'

'I feel like I'm fourteen again,' says Kate, covering her face in embarrassment.

Martin pulls a face of frustration. 'I'd offer to make you dinner next week but my flatmate, she's . . . well, a bit funny about me having guests round.'

Kate nods sympathetically. 'My old flatmate was the same.'

'OK, so let's say next Saturday afternoon? How about a picnic on the Heath, if the weather stays good?'

'I could make food . . .' says Kate, thinking of Cecily's instructions. 'Would you eat carbs if I make sandwiches, or will you lick the fillings and leave the bread, like some supermodel on a bikini shoot?'

'I'll happily eat anything you make. You know something?' he says, leaning in closer. 'I think you're rather brilliant.'

He leans in and kisses her tenderly. Her heart is beating overtime, but she is so out of sorts because of Nick she can't understand if her body is for or against this particular kiss.

'Ah,' he sighs. 'You really are damn sexy. Right, gotta go. I'll see you Saturday for sandwich-licking.' He winks, and he's off.

On the bus home Kate leans her head against the window, watching the lights of Tottenham Court Road speed by. On their first date, Nick and Kate met for dinner at 7 p.m. and ended up being the last ones in the restaurant, chucked out by the manager at midnight. Afterwards, they'd stood in the street and Nick had said goodbye, then he'd run off without even a peck on the cheek. She hadn't been able to sleep that night because she was so confused – had that just been a great date, or a total non-starter?

She probably should see Martin again, because until Nick comes back convincingly, she is, literally, single. Martin may be a little full on but he's also funny and charming and interesting – and, most importantly, interested in her.

Chapter Twenty-nine

'I TOLD YOU SO, *again*,' says Cecily, clicking her fingers irritably as Kate pours slightly more than half a cup of tea into her cup. 'Spoon that straight out or you'll never learn.'

Kate sighs and replaces three teaspoons of liquid back into the pot. She's yet to see Cecily spill a drop due to her tremor, but Cecily is adamant.

'The minute you stop fixating on Amoeba . . .'

'I'm going to bring Amoeba in to meet you one of these days – I guarantee you'll like him.'

Cecily's nostrils flare in response.

'And could you please stop calling him Amoeba?'

'Fine, then I shall call him Pigeon, but let's not dwell on him. When are you seeing him again?'

'Martin? I'm not convinced I should. I believe in "Do as you would be done by", so I should tell Nick, but I don't want to.'

'Oh stop being such a coward.'

'It's loyalty, not cowardice. Besides, I don't want to mess Martin about. And he is a bit intense . . .'

'He's keen – as well he should be.'

'Probably because I'm not. That always makes someone keener.' Kate realises with dismay that this describes her and Nick – except she's the one on the back foot.

'And you'll make him "Dinner for a Charming Stranger". You'll cook at your mother's?'

'No, and no. Martin suggested a picnic – I'll make him the one from your book.'

'That's not the intention of that picnic.'

'But it's the principle, right? You make it sound like a spell book,' says Kate, rolling her eyes.

'Which would make me a witch,' says Cecily, chewing the thought over. 'I've been called worse.'

'Anyway – I'll do the second date, and I'll cook, but that's as far as I can take it. Now please, could you tell me how you came to be a writer?'

'Are you really interested?'

'Of course – I always wanted to be a writer,' says Kate, settling back into her chair.

'OK, then. Well, I'll have to start at the beginning, which was one rainy Tuesday in the sweet shop when I was five. I was hiding behind a curtain waiting for the perfect moment to steal more toffees when the Farragher sisters, who ran an exclusive prep school, came in with their beagle, Fred. They liked to discuss politics with Papa, but on this particular day Fred sniffed me out.'

Kate laughs as she imagines a young Cecily hiding behind a curtain as a dog's wet nose pokes through.

'After the initial embarrassment Miss Ann said to Papa, "You have an exceptional child here, I can see Jesus in her eyes". Papa saw no such apparition, quite the contrary, but he didn't want to lose a customer who bought a pound of fudge every week. The sisters were willing to take me at the reduced fee of three pounds a term—'

'A *term*?'

'Papa thought it extravagant but Mama finally persuaded him, she'd heard the children at the local elementary had nits. He agreed but with fearful threats of what would happen if I didn't come top of every class. It was an excellent school, we were taught manners, elegant copperplate writing, poetry and, above all, to love Jesus, which scared me as the only Jewish girl there.'

'I didn't realise you were Jewish.'

'Oh my family weren't religious, I'd never been to a synagogue, Papa loved eating bacon. But I wasn't Roman Catholic, so I was the only one going to limbo, which bothered me immensely. I lived in perpetual shame of my difference, which forced me to live on two levels,' she says, nibbling her biscuit thoughtfully. 'The top layer embraced the everyday challenges – lost hair ribbons, difficult homework – but underneath I lived in my imagination. At bedtime I'd hide under the sheets and picture myself as Jo in *Little Women* or Anne of Green Gables. The world of make-believe often seemed a happier place to be.'

'Books were my escape too,' says Kate. 'I'm an only child – and as I grew up, books felt like my companions – they saved me from loneliness. I suppose in some ways they still do.'

'Who did you like to read when you were young?'

'Oh anything and everything. When I was about twelve my father was really into Raymond Chandler; I read all of Dad's copies the minute he finished them.'

'Chandler's a masterful writer. Samuel bought me that copy of *The Big Sleep* for one of my many, many birthdays,' says Cecily, pointing to a shelf high behind Kate's head.

'I love that book,' says Kate, turning her gaze in the direction of the grey-and-white hardback. 'So did you start writing at primary school?'

'No, then I won a scholarship to West Ham Secondary, where I had new problems. I was desperate to be a femme fatale but all the boys loved Dolly Atkin. I felt alone again, but then something good happened: our English teacher, Mr Moffat. In our first class he read a Cowper poem, *Oh that those lips had language* . . . I already loved reading, but Mr Moffat sparked my love of writing. Eight decades later, I still have boundless gratitude to him for a lifetime enriched by words.'

'Surely having such an inspiring teacher made you want to become one?'

'Goodness no – that was all Papa's decision. In my day being a teacher meant being a badly dressed spinster. I wept and argued but he threatened me with all manner of humiliations, so I ended up spending two miserable years at Saffron Walden Training College. I remember on the day of the practicals, our examiner, Miss Clelland, was observing me teach an art class at the village school. I'd finished setting up the still-life models but just as we were about to begin, the hunt went by, hounds baying, hooves clopping. I'd never seen a hunt before and rushed to the window; those scarlet jackets, the prancing, glossy horses, they fascinated me. I shouted for the girls to come and watch! Once the hunt had passed I told them to ignore the still life and paint what they'd seen, the colour, the movement, and to have fun. Afterwards Miss Clelland dragged me to her study, her face grim. "You broke every rule in the book," she said. "Why do you want to teach?" When I told her I didn't, she looked pained. "It's rare I discover a true teacher, someone who can bring light in, and when I do, she can't wait to leave. It's an unjust world." And she wasn't wrong about *that*.'

'I bet your pupils loved you though.'

'They were fond of me, and I of them, but I was consumed by a desire to escape the dreariness of it all. And my parents, who'd retired to Bournemouth, worried. The fact that I was unmarried spoiled their peace of mind.'

'My mother's the same.'

'She shouldn't be. I learned to truly value my independence.'

'So, hang on, is this when you met Samuel?'

'We'll come to Samuel another time.' Cecily breaks into an epic yawn. 'Go now. All this talking's worn me out. Good luck with the picnic. Don't under-season the pâté.'

Kate wonders if Cecily keeps interrupting her own story as a way of enticing Kate back for another serving.

Chapter Thirty

RITA IS OUT WITH Patrick on Monday night and Kate sits down with a glass of wine, her paperwork for Devron and a large bowl of spaghetti carbonara. She twirls her fork through the pasta, the crispy chunks of bacon clinging to the luscious strands, and takes a large mouthful. Ah, it's totally delicious, salty and creamy, with that perfect bite.

She looks at her CV and frowns. When Annalex first joined the department she'd circulated her CV – three pages of A4 that positioned herself as the lovechild of Sheryl Sandberg and Steve Jobs. In her mission statement Annalex described herself as 'a proactive team player, equally at home innovating and driving step change'. (There isn't a phrase in the English language Kate hates more than step change, though proactive comes a close second.)

Still, while Kate may not have as jazzy a CV, nineteen and three quarter years of selling food – from the shop floor upwards – means she knows her stuff: cut her and she bleeds Fletchers.

Kate turns her attention to her essay. She's written about the award-winning campaign she worked on last year which doubled sales of Fletchers' Italian range.

She's given the piece many more hours than is required, re-crafted it a dozen times. But rereading it now for the umpteenth time, it's just . . . it's polished, it's professional, it's very Fletchers, but it isn't very Kate.

She looks down into her now-empty pasta bowl, thinking back to her recent trip to Borough Market – how inspired she'd felt. She takes her copy of *Thought for Food* from her bag, pondering the weight of it in her hands. She gently flicks through it and smiles – on every page the passion for its subject shines through. Her thoughts turn to Cecily, teaching that art class all those decades ago, breaking the rules, following her gut, being true to what thrilled her.

Kate takes a sip of wine. She opens a new blank document on her computer and feels a weird tingling in her body. It's adrenaline – fear that she could write something dreadful and muck up her chances – mixed with hope that she could actually write something better, something true to herself, something that sings.

She closes her eyes and in her mind walks through Borough Market, starting at the amazing fruit and veg stall with its bounty of squashes and mushrooms; the wonderful smoky, chargrilled smell from the chorizo sandwich seller – a pile of fresh, warm, flour-dusted bread rolls stacked ready to be filled; then on to the custard doughnut man, with rows of golden sugary doughnuts – luscious vanilla and chocolate cream erupting from the top, just waiting to have someone's teeth sink into them.

She starts typing about her love of food, the role it plays in life and in the lives of Fletchers' customers. She writes about sharing, pleasure, generosity and appetite, and the words flow. Before she knows it, it's well past midnight and she's written 1,400 words, which can easily be trimmed in the morning. When she's doing what she loves, it doesn't feel like work – it feels like coming home.

When she rereads her piece first thing on Tuesday she feels a small swell of pride – the writing is better than good, it's great. She presses send.

Devron's not due to make any decisions until the following week, but something tells Kate he's read her piece when he rolls in to work. Perhaps she's reading too much into the tea leaves, but when he comes over to her desk in the afternoon he smiles a reluctant smile of defeat and nods at her.

Kate feels a small sense of victory, something she hasn't felt in quite some time.

Chapter Thirty-one

Picnic for Friends, English Summer Rain Notwithstanding

Aim: I can think of none but pure masochism, entailing, as it does exposure to wasp attack, hazards of the climate and the discomforts of sitting on inhospitable ground. However, the fact remains that everybody else seems to love a picnic.

A S IT TURNS OUT, Cecily's menu is pretty close to what Kate would create if she was devising 'Picnic for a Fussy Carb-phobic Actor': pâté, ham rolls stuffed with creamy mushrooms, peppers filled with scrambled egg.

Kate's shopping for the ingredients after work on Friday when she notices the pâté recipe contains alcohol, so she texts Martin:

Are you strict AA or is cognac in pâté OK?

He replies instantly:

If you can get me drunk on pâté, you have permission to take full advantage of me. Can't wait to see you xxx

Kate figures the food will take four hours' prep – she can do it all tomorrow. They're not due to meet till 3 p.m., and she's treating herself first thing to a haircut and a new dress from Zara. Since The Wobble, she's forgotten there's a point to looking good for anyone except Nick. Time for her to get back in the game.

Kate stands in Rita's kitchen, hands on hips, head throbbing slightly as she runs her finger down her order of prep. She can't remember the last time she prepared a multi-part menu alone. Looking at Cecily's recipes, her mind had gone fuzzy when she'd thought about how to juggle the timings – should she make the pâté first, as it needed to set? Or the ham rolls – they were fiddly and might eat up too much time. She used to be good at this before Nick, preparing delicious feasts for her friends at every opportunity. She'd once cooked an eight-course Spanish extravaganza to celebrate Bailey's divorce papers, in memory of an amazing meal the girls had enjoyed on a weekend in Barcelona for Bailey's thirtieth. But Kate's lost her culinary independence, becoming reliant on being half of a partnership in the kitchen.

Creamy mushroom and mustard filling for the ham rolls – she'll do that first. She peels the lid off the cream and spatters herself with dairy. Why is she even going to all this trouble for a date she's not sure about? She stirs a spoon of wholegrain mustard into the cream and adds a pinch of salt. She should stop making a big deal about this – Cecily wouldn't encourage her to do anything foolish, and even Bailey had agreed it was smart to keep her options open.

On to the pâté: she takes the chicken livers from the plastic tray and shudders, the slippery organs heavy in her fingers. Nick always handles food Kate's too squeamish to deal with. For his birthday last year she'd bought him a butchery course. She'd happily upskilled Nick, yet never considered doing the course herself – far too expensive. Nick wouldn't blink twice at investing in himself. Was that a male/female thing, or just a Nick/Kate thing?

Right – time for the red peppers. Kate had to go to the specialist greengrocer in Camden to find these pimentos, but she's so glad she made the effort. She'd forgotten how wonderful that shop is eleven varieties of pepper, pale green, almost luminous orange, deep scarlet – fat, skinny, short, wonky. Browsing their fruit and veg gives her the same excitement she feels in a bookshop – imagining the infinite possibilities. Whatever the outcome of this picnic, she's glad Cecily bullied her into it.

As she's chopping the onions she feels a dull ache swell in her chest. Nick would really love this food. But then her sadness is hijacked again by anger, at the fact that he was so careless with something that wasn't his to break – he was careless with them.

Kate's mood swings are all over the place, as are these ham rolls. Sod it. She's going to make a delicious picnic. She's going to go out for a fun afternoon with this sexy actor. She's going to remind herself that she's an attractive, capable woman who can roll a piece of ham round a rather squidgy filling into an almost acceptable-looking cylinder.

Two hours later Kate surveys the final spread, packed in a wicker basket on Rita's kitchen counter: she's done well.

In the bathroom mirror she sees the wear and tear of the last few months. She looks slimmer but tired. She practises a smile. Her teeth are mildly stained from all the cigarettes and black coffee. She must do a Rita and focus on the positives. She traces a thin line of navy liner over her eyelids – that always makes her eyes look greener. She curls her naturally long eyelashes with immense diligence rather than her usual two-second squeeze. She puts on lashings of mascara, two small blots of pink blusher. She takes a deep breath and straightens the shoulders of her new dress. She feels a small dart of excitement crackle through her. Life is not scary, life's a great big abundant universe full of possibilities.

To be honest, this wasn't one of the possibilities she'd considered.

Kate checks her watch again: 3.28 p.m. She's sure they said 3 p.m. but perhaps they said 3.30 p.m.? She rereads the last text from Martin, sent yesterday at 11 p.m. – no, definitely 3 p.m. It's most strange.

She tries calling him again but his phone rings out. That's the second call she's made – any more and she'll look like a bunny boiler. She sneaks her hand into the hamper and surreptitiously grabs a stuffed pepper and wolfs it down; she's starving.

Her phone pings, that *must* be him. No – it's Nick:

Fancy a curry tonight? It's way more fun eating with you x.

This is all Nick's bloody fault. If he hadn't had The Wobble, she wouldn't be standing here with an increasingly heavy hamper, waiting for a c-list actor who was slightly too handsy on the first date.

She texts Bailey and Cara:

How long do I wait before I assume I've been stood up?

Cara replies:

7 minutes, max.

Bailey:

40 minutes.

She'll give it a little longer. There's so much food that will go to waste. In the meantime, she googles Martin. She's googled him before, to check which other TV shows he's been in – but she didn't bother deep-googling, and now she gets to page three of the search she kicks herself for the incompleteness of her stalking. Martin Saponara, age 43, date of birth 14 May. *May*. Not December, not a Sagittarius *at all*. It's possible Wikipedia is wrong, but it's unlikely *Heat* magazine is too – here's a pap shot of Martin coming out of the Groucho on his birthday, in *May*, with a gang of slightly more famous friends.

He's lied about his star sign and birthday, no doubt just to get in her pants. What else has he lied about? Kate places the hamper on the pavement and folds her arms in indignation. What sort of reasonably successful forty-three-year-old man can't have a woman round to his flat – unless his flatmate is, in fact, a girlfriend, or even his 'ex' wife? He probably only suggested this pic-nic so he could have a fumble in the grass because they can't go to Kate's place or his!

And now she thinks about it, it was pretty creepy of him to suggest swinging by for a visit after he'd been out with his brother last Saturday night. Was that why he'd stood her up – he'd thought she was a sure thing, and she sure wasn't?

Ah, panic over, finally, *there* he is, waving at her from the bus stop in the distance. She's got all carried away in her imagination about how he's such a love rat, when really all he did was tell one small fib about his birthday, to charm her – is that *so* bad? She waves back, but as the man approaches she realises with a sinking feeling that he's the same height and build as Martin but is waving at the girl standing behind her – the one who hasn't been stood up.

Kate feels her face burn with shame. She sends Martin a text:

Are you en route? I have a hamper of protein with your name on.

The text says 'delivered', so he's not submerged under water, but there's still no response by 4.10 p.m.

She has never been stood up before. She has wasted her time, effort and far too much money on this food and now here she is standing in the street with her basket like Dorothy in the Wizard of Cocking Oz. She handled those disgusting slimy livers for this man and *this* is what she gets in return? She should have learned by now that no man is to be trusted. But, actually, Nick would never, ever have done something this rude and flaky. Really, the devil you know is so much better than the one who chats you up in a coffee shop – that's true or else it wouldn't be a cliché.

She feels angry, depressed, irritable; but buried underneath all that she feels hurt, then embarrassed for even caring. It doesn't matter that someone has let her down. So what? Who does she even think she is that some cool, handsome actor would be interested in her?

She takes out her phone again and types a text for all the wrong reasons:

I'll be there at 7 p.m., need to un-hamper myself.
Don't forget the poppadoms.

What's so wrong with trying to make herself feel better?

She treats herself to a taxi and gives the driver Lauderdale's address. She finds Bernadette in the kitchen overseeing a store-cupboard inventory.

'You're not normally in on a Saturday,' says Bernadette, checking her watch. 'Are you here for Mrs Paisner's ninety-fourth? They're all in the garden having a sing-song. They'll be finishing in five.'

'I didn't know about her party. I'm just bringing some home-made food, it's untouched.'

Bernadette pokes around in the hamper. 'We can put it out with dinner – the ladies will like those ham rolls, and the pâté, if they're not full of cake from tea. I'm not sure about those peppers, though, probably too spicy.'

'They're very mild.'

'I can't risk any upset tummies, housekeeping would never forgive me.'

'Can I go and see Mrs Finn? I'd like to show her the food, she inspired me to make it – well, ordered me to. Is she in the garden?'

Bernadette's smile turns to a frown. 'Mrs Finn is not in the garden, Mrs Finn is never in the garden. Mrs Finn is having a rest. She had a bad night's sleep and decided to take it out on one of my girls.'

'Oh no, is she OK?'

'Mrs Finn didn't hit her, but she was "unimpressed" with her vichyssoise and made some obnoxious comments. Jeanie was a little shaken.'

'Sorry, I meant is Mrs Finn OK?'

'Mrs Finn? She thrives on conflict. She's asleep, that's all.'

'I'll just take her some food for when she wakes up. If she didn't eat her soup she might be hungry.'

Bernadette shakes her head. 'She's fast asleep. Besides, I don't believe in rewarding bad behaviour. She can take her pick at dinner. I'll tell her you stopped by.'

Chapter Thirty-two

KATE'S HEART IS RACING as she stands outside Nick's flat and reaches for the doorbell. She must try to act nonchalant, but she's mildly traumatised just standing here, memories of a hundred hello kisses on this doorstep ricocheting in her chest. She's said no to all of Nick's invitations since the coffee shop, even though she's wanted to say yes. It's only because Martin's stood her up that she's here now. Still, perhaps all those fridge magnets are true, and everything happens for a reason.

Nick opens the door looking nervous and hopeful, then looks at her and breaks into a huge smile. She breezes past him into the living area and he follows behind her like a puppy.

'Lured me here under false pretences – you said curry,' says Kate, though she's delighted at what's on the kitchen counter. Seven bowls of ingredients – all perfectly prepared: sour cream, chopped jalapeños, home-made salsa, grated cheese, sliced avocado, chorizo and scrambled eggs. He must have raced out as soon as she texted back to buy all this, she thinks tenderly.

'I know it's not breakfast, but I thought you might like one anyway.' He smiles sheepishly. 'There's no point making breakfast burritos if you're not around to share them.'

Her heart responds with a solid surge of hope, which she tries to ignore. She turns to flick through the papers on the kitchen counter where he keeps his crossword drafts. 'I see your crossword pile is in order.'

'I got a clue wrong the other day,' he says, pulling a distraught face.

'That's because you dumped the brains of the operation on holiday,' she says, smiling as she runs her finger down his nose.

He shakes his head in shame. 'Kate – honestly, what happened in France, I still feel dreadful.'

'Join the club,' she says, laughing. 'Why don't you warm up those tortillas? I'm famished.'

He bounds over to the hob and she stands for a moment gazing at his back, at the place where the collar of his white T-shirt meets his neck, that tender stretch of skin. She looks at his broad shoulders, his strong arms, his elegant fingers. She misses being held by his body; she desperately misses holding his hand. She wants to go over and scratch his back the way he loves, but instead she turns and wanders to the mantelpiece, where he keeps his upcoming invitations. There's a photo of his friends Rob and Tasha, though that's not immediately clear because they're wearing pirate hats and fake beards. Kate picks up the card – it's an invite to a Hot-Tub Pulled-Pork Pirate Party for Rob's birthday. She imagines a hot tub with shreds of pork floating on the surface. It's very Rob and Tasha, trying so desperately to be hip. Mind you, those guys are ten years younger than Nick; they do things Kate's either done already or never wanted to do in the first place. Either way, it's none of her business. 'You going to this?' she says, trying to strip the judgement from her voice.

'To what?' he says, turning to look. 'Oh. No. I didn't tell you.'

'Tell me what?'

'Those two broke up.'

'*What*? When did *that* happen?'

'Just the other day . . .'

'Why?'

'Rob kind of slept with someone else, about a month ago.'

'*What? Who?*'

Nick shrugs with discomfort. 'He went to The Hawley Arms when Tasha was away on a hen do, picked up some random—'

'God, what a creep. How did Tasha find out?' says Kate, suddenly feeling deeply sorry for her.

'He kind of caught something off this girl.'

'*Seriously*? That is disgusting, that's beyond disrespectful. I always thought Rob was a bit of a dick, but what a total wanker.'

Nick shrugs. 'He's generally a good bloke. He did say it was only a minor STD . . .'

'A *minor* STD? Like *that* makes a difference? Give the guy a medal because it wasn't super-strain gonorrhoea?'

'He was pretty drunk, apparently.'

'Nick, you can't actually be defending him? He's a pig.'

'Babe, I'm not defending him. He feels really bad.'

'I bet Tasha feels worse. Bloody hell, what a major bellend, with *a minor STD* . . .' She shakes her head in disgust. 'I guess you won't be needing this, then?' She takes the invite and dumps it in the recycling bin as Nick lays two plates down on the kitchen counter.

'I find the whole thing crazy,' says Nick. 'I was talking to my therapist about it this week – how other people seem to have such dramatic break-ups.'

Kate looks at him in disbelief. '*Other* people? *We* had a pretty dramatic break-up. Do you actually talk to your therapist about me?'

'You're the reason I see him!'

'I'll take that as a compliment,' she says, laughing.

'Kate – I'm trying to make sense of all of this. I don't even consider what happened between us a break-up. I know I have issues, but my life is much less fun without you. I miss you every day.'

'You know what? I actually don't want to talk about this, because this middle-ground stuff will do my head in. We've agreed to be friends until you're certain what you want.'

'OK, yep, sure,' he says, nodding, then setting about the precision construction of his burrito. 'Shall I build yours?' Nick builds a better burrito than anyone; Kate's attempts always end up in a giant, wet, leaky ball.

Every few moments as they're eating he turns to her and smiles contentedly, as if they're right back to where they should be. Sitting close on their familiar kitchen stools, in this space they've inhabited so care-freely, Kate's muscle memory is in overdrive. She has to restrain herself from reaching over to touch his arm or ruffle his hair.

Final bite taken, she reaches for the kitchen roll and wipes the last of the sour cream off her fingers. 'That was delicious, thank you.'

'Oh, speaking of delicious, I've booked Le Montrachet.'

'What for?'

'For dinner, for your fortieth. I know you've always wanted to go, and you have to book months in advance, so I went down and booked in person.'

Wow, Kate really should let Nick muck her about more often if it means he's going to up his game like this. 'Thank you, Nick, that sounds great, it's just that I haven't really thought about what I want to do that weekend. I'm still thirty-something for a couple more months.'

'It's a special birthday. We can always cancel nearer the time, but this way at least we have an option. Anyway, what shall we do now? Do you fancy watching some *Modern Family*?'

'No,' she says, catching a glimpse of Triluminos in the corner. Definitely no TV. She knows she sounds prickly, but she can't be here without her guard up to some degree.

'Scrabble?'

'Sure,' she says, her voice softening.

He clears the plates then beckons her to follow him through to the spare room where the Scrabble set is.

'You've had a tidy-up,' says Kate, heading over to the bookshelves to check whether her books are still there.

'Yours are on the middle two shelves,' he says, flashing her a tender look. 'I've refiled them alphabetically for you.'

Kate pauses to decode this. They haven't even begun to discuss whether Kate will be moving in, and yet Nick's acting like he has no doubt about their future, the books, the restaurant reservation . . . Kate follows Nick back out to the living room, trying hard to ignore the hope that's now throbbing aggressively in her like a tooth infection.

They sit together on the sofa and Nick takes the tile bag from the cardboard box and shakes it in the air like a single maraca. Kate never used to like Scrabble but Nick adores it and his enthusiasm is contagious. The fact that Nick had geeky hobbies was one of the reasons she'd always felt safe with him; Nick would never do a Rob. But as she picks her tiles from the Scrabble bag, she realises that Nick's squareness has not proved he is a stable bet for a boyfriend; it seems geeky hobbies can coexist with emotional unreliability.

Inside the Scrabble box is a long score sheet of their historic games. Nick flicks the pad over and narrows his eyes. 'Ready to lose again, babe?' he says, breaking into his own version of the Bee Gees.

Thanks to his crossword obsession Nick has an amazing knowledge of obscure words, peculiar plurals, words beginning with Q that are not followed by U. Kate has been watching and learning, and on a good day she can almost beat him, but not quite.

Nick scrutinises his tile selection, rearranging the order repeatedly before flashing her a grin. Kate frowns at her tiles – four Ss, three vowels. By the time she looks up, Nick has already set down his tiles with an expression of delight.

'*Lariat?*' says Kate in despair. 'Is that another made-up Nick word?'

'It's a South American rope,' he says, nimbly totting up his score.

She looks at her own tiles: S, S, S, S, E, E, I – this just isn't her day. She places an I in front of his T.

'*It*? That's your best shot?' He laughs. 'You sure you don't want to make this a cash game?'

'One day I'll be better than you, Nick.'

'You sure will – those guys at Google are working on eternal life as we speak.' He reaches out to rub her cheek. It's only his finger and thumb touching her face but their eyes lock and she forces her head down to her tiles as her heart starts thumping in overdrive.

She studies Nick studying his new tiles, the familiar creases in his forehead as he works out the best way to destroy her. 'Come on, Nick,' she says, ostentatiously looking at her watch. 'I'm not getting any younger.'

'Yes!' he says. 'D-I-P-S-H, dipshit.'

'Bollocks,' mutters Kate, who's forgotten to pick up a new tile after using her I. Marvellous, another vowel – though hang on just one minute . . . U, E, E, S, S, S, S. Her fist clenches in victory as she lays her letters around his L. 'Useless! Or not, as the case may be.'

'Good work,' he says, high-fiving her. 'Low score, but still, a clean start, right?'

'A clean start,' she mutters, as she picks more letters.

Nick shifts ever so slightly on the sofa, moving an inch closer so that their knees are gently touching. Is she imagining it or is he deliberately pressing his knee against hers? She looks at him and he smiles back. She feels a dull throb of longing.

She turns her attention back to her tiles. '*Useless* . . . *dipshit* . . . If you lend me an O, I could make *asshole* . . . It's Ouija Scrabble – all words lead to Nick in France,' she says, laughing at her own bitchiness, but she can't contain herself.

'Ouch. I guess I deserve that,' says Nick, squinting at his tiles, then nodding as he lays more letters down.

'*Tache*?' says Kate. 'You're not allowed slang.'

'Tache is also an archaic word for a buckle or clasp, but feel free to challenge if you're happy to lose points,' he says, rubbing her knee and giving it a little squeeze.

'Don't worry,' she says, brushing him off. 'I'm over it already. I've moved on.' She lays down H-E-A-R in front of it.

'Hear-tache?' he says in confusion.

'Heartache, dummy! I thought *you* were the bright one,' she says with a jubilant whoop.

'Amazing!' He laughs and instinctively reaches for her, and instinctively she leans in to him, and they kiss, then pause as they simultaneously remember they're pretending they're just friends – and then they kiss again and it is a phenomenal kiss, the sort of kiss you lose yourself in, so much so that it takes Kate minutes before she is willing to pull herself away.

'Kate,' says Nick, running his fingers through her hair. 'We're so right together. This is so right.'

'We always were, Nick . . .'

'I'm so sorry about what happened.' He shakes his head and there is a look of confusion on his face she recognises from the coffee shop. 'I hate that I've hurt you.'

She nods and swallows the surge of sadness and happiness that have collided in her throat. He takes her face in his hands and kisses her again. She can't be stand-offish or feign indifference because right here on this sofa, playing Scrabble and kissing Nick Sullivan, is exactly where she wants to be. It seems clear, from the fact he won't take his mouth from hers, that he misses her, wants her, loves her. That's what it means when a body does this.

She slowly pulls away once more, then stands up, staggering slightly from the head rush. 'Nick, I'm going to go home,' she says, gathering her coat and bag as she heads for the door.

It would be the easiest thing in the world to follow this man through to his bedroom, to lie down on that bed she's lain on a hundred times, to put their bodies back together again to mend her broken heart. But she's been patient beyond what she ever thought herself capable of. If she has to wait just a little longer to feel convinced that France was just an unfortunate wobble, it'll be worth it. This man is her future. She is sure of it.

PART THREE

Patience is bitter but its fruit is sweet.

Sir John Chardin, *Travels in Persia 1673–1677*

Chapter Thirty-three

'IT'S CALLED GHOSTING, Mrs Finn, and you can add it to your list of things you don't ever need to know about, alongside Snapchatting your bottom, Instagramming your avocado toast and every single one of the Kardashians.'

'Are you sure he didn't try to contact you another way?' says Cecily, scraping the last mouthful of chocolate soufflé from the ramekin Kate has brought her, and giving a small contented sigh.

'I sent a final text this morning, checking if he's OK – you never know, people do get hit by buses. I could see he started to reply from the dots on the screen, and then he blocked me!'

'I don't understand what that means.'

'It means he let me cook him an elaborate picnic, then not only did he not show, but he has now evaporated.'

'Oh,' says Cecily, her face falling in disappointment.

'This is what I keep telling you: London is full of horrifically ill-mannered, incomprehensible men, which is why when you meet a half-decent one with solid personal hygiene you hold on for dear life.'

'Why do they call it ghosting?'

'Because people disappear into thin air.'

'Ghosts don't disappear, they stick around to haunt you. They should think of a better word. By the way, the peppers were good – though you do always under-season.'

'Once, Mrs Finn, it was one toastie . . .'

'I must admit I'm impressed you didn't take that feast straight round to Amoeba's.'

Kate blushes. 'Well, if I had done, we could have traced that back to you.'

'To me?'

'If you hadn't insisted I go on a date with some idiot in the first place, then I wouldn't have been stood up – then felt rejected and irritable, which only makes me more vulnerable to Nick.'

'Why on earth would you let one man's bad manners influence your opinion of yourself?'

'I know you said go on that date as a way to boost my confidence, but it had the reverse effect. Anyway, it's made me realise how reliable Nick is. Was that your plan all along?'

'Good grief, since when do two wrongs make a right? Besides, if you could muster the enthusiasm to make me a reasonable chocolate soufflé, you can't be that upset.'

There's clearly no point updating Cecily on how the rest of yesterday panned out. Kate turns to gaze out of the window. 'Mrs Finn, it's almost like summer out there. Could I persuade you to drink this tea in the garden? You'd only need a light cardy.'

Cecily shakes her head. 'Rappapot's out there with the grandson. The other day she tried to cheat me in the film quiz. Burbridge's hearing aid wasn't set correctly and Rappapot took advantage, shouting the wrong answers to her, thinking I'd overhear and try to copy *them* – incontinent imbecile – as if I couldn't name all five Marx brothers. I met two of them myself in Los Angeles!'

'The garden's big enough for you and her.'

'And has she mentioned she grew up in Keen-yah? Can't pronounce it Kenya like a normal person, and that she had a mansion full of "obedient" servants and a cook and a driver and a this and a that. No wonder her daughter emigrated to New Zealand, she'd have moved to the moon.'

'We could sit in a quiet corner?'

'She loves this prison, captive audience, no one can escape her.'

'Just for ten minutes? You never leave this room, some fresh air would do you good.'

'No,' she says, pointing sternly at the teapot.

'Anyway, Mrs Finn, it would never have worked out with Martin,' says Kate, pouring more tea. 'I can't date a man who doesn't like food.'

'The next one won't be so particular.'

'Nick loves food. He makes these phenomenal burritos . . .'

'Did you find the peppers easily?' says Cecily sharply.

'The peppers?'

'The pimento for the picnic?'

'Actually, I went to this amazing greengrocer down on Parkway to get them.'

'Parkway?' says Cecily, her eyes widening in delight. 'In Camden Town?'

'Do you mind if I open the window? It really is too warm in here,' says Kate, feeling the sweat under her arms.

'Keep it shut. Do you ever go dancing?'

'Me? Sometimes, why?'

'I used to love dancing. We'd go to tea dances down on Parkway, they were the highlight of my week. If you were lucky enough to find a partner who'd take you to Lyons Corner House afterwards for an egg mayonnaise sandwich, you were queen for a day,' says Cecily, clasping her hands to her bosom.

'Did you go dancing often?'

'Whenever possible. I was so lonely back then, my nights and weekends were a frantic hunt for pleasure.'

'Weekends are the worst,' says Kate.

'I would not relive those years again for anything. I felt so desperate, marriage seemed the only refuge from my tedious job and my own sense of failure,' says Cecily, shaking her head in pity for her younger self.

Kate shifts uncomfortably in her chair; it's all sounding a little too familiar. 'So did you give up teaching after you married Samuel?'

Cecily nods. 'Not because Samuel was some silly chauvinist – he wanted me to do whatever made me happy – but because his job took us to the continent.'

'Will you please tell me how you met? Was it romantic, like your parents' story?'

'Samuel and I? It wasn't my doing, it was another of Papa's grand plans. Papa had gone to visit a friend and Samuel Finn happened to be there. He'd recently arrived from Poland, from a decent family. He was single and intelligent, with good teeth. Papa immediately invited him to tea, threatening to throw me out if I failed to impress. He said, "This is your last chance" – and I thought, well, if that's the case, then I'd better take it.'

'Oh. That doesn't sound romantic at all.'

'Oh, as soon as I saw Samuel I hoped he'd marry me,' says Cecily, her eyes lighting up. 'He was six foot three, with wavy black hair, huge brown eyes and a serious expression that would break into the most magnificent smile at the smallest delight. Papa did most of the talking that day, I think Samuel was more taken with him than me – still, he invited me out for the following week. Papa said I mustn't let him buy me more than a Bath bun lest he think me extravagant and unsuitable for a wife.'

Kate laughs; she never holds back on a date in a restaurant – maybe that's where she's been going wrong.

'Samuel took me for dinner to a little Greek place in Soho where the proprietor greeted him with affection. Everywhere we went people were drawn to Samuel, he had a laugh that warmed a room like sunshine. I remember being so nervous – Papa had told me to keep my mouth shut – but I could never have done that with Samuel, we laughed from the moment we sat down,' she says, patting her cheeks tenderly at the memory. 'I felt instantly comfortable. He told wonderful stories about growing up the youngest of five siblings. His father Leon was also one of five, so there were dozens of cousins. Samuel and his youngest sister Sophie had written a song with all of the family's names in, which they added to frequently: Leon, Shindel, Lilli, Oskar, Izzy – every meal in the Finn household had at least fifteen hungry diners.'

'His mother must have been a good cook.'

'Shindel? Meh, average,' says Cecily, pulling a face. 'As a young man working at his father's sawmill, Samuel had dreamt of seeing the world. He also felt deeply concerned that Europe was becoming increasingly anti-Semitic, and so he left Poland for England. While he loved London he desperately missed his family back in Warsaw. Even though he had a far more exotic background than mine, he seemed genuinely interested in me, and when he discovered I loved to dance, he asked me dancing the very next day. I remember he looked so uncomfortable on that dance floor, shuffling those long, skinny legs of his. I thought he didn't like me, or didn't know how to dance. In fact, he'd had to borrow a pair of fashionable shoes from his neighbour and they were two sizes too small. He was embarrassed to admit it, but I thought it marvellous he'd gone to that effort. With a little prompting we were engaged within six weeks and the wedding was fixed for six weeks later.'

'Er, can I have the recipe for *that*?' says Kate. 'So really, it was love at first sight!'

'There's no such thing. In fact, that's one thing books have misled us on. People confuse physical infatuation with love, but lust never lasts. Yes, Samuel had a pleasing face, but that was immaterial. Samuel was an exceptionally kind man, and what ultimately counts is having a true friend, someone to hold your hand when you need it most.'

Kate has a flashback to Nick reaching for her hand the day after he'd told her he didn't want her moving in. How strange and confusing it had felt – how, in fact, it is the opposite of what Cecily is talking about. Kate promptly dismisses the thought. 'Tell me about your wedding.'

'It started disastrously. I arrived an hour late, in a beat-up old Ford truck. Papa, economical to the last, had asked his friend with a car to put a white ribbon on it and drive us to the West End. The car broke down on the

Mile End Road and the only vehicle I could find to give us a lift was the truck. By the time I arrived, the Patou dress I'd borrowed from my best friend was crumpled, and the tea roses I clutched had wilted terribly. When I saw Samuel standing there, he looked so nervous – the poor man must have worried I wasn't going to show. But then he saw me and his eyes filled with joy. I felt a rush of elation like I'd never experienced before. The reception was magnificent. Samuel's family were there, his parents and siblings had come from Warsaw – Leon, Shindel, Lilli, Oskar, Izzy, and Sophie. Sophie was a great beauty, terribly glamorous and now a jazz singer who had moved to Nice with her ten-year-old daughter Gisele. Sophie wore the most magnificent emeralds that set off her beautiful green eyes. Gisele looked so much like her mother, and she'd made herself a copy of Sophie's dress – even back then she was an excellent little seamstress. Papa thought Sophie's jewels were fake, but those stones saved Gisele's life during the Occupation.'

Kate shakes her head in wonder.

'We had the most delicious salmon with dill, wonderful sauté potatoes, and Mama had made us our wedding cake, a fabulous six-tier toffee sponge,' says Cecily, her hand rising to demonstrate its height. 'Then there was the music, ah, so much music. Sophie had the most beautiful husky voice, and she sang our first dance, "The Very Thought of You". It was magical, I felt like I was in a movie, dancing in Samuel's arms. And he'd bought some dancing shoes that actually fitted this time,' she laughs. 'We left for our honeymoon in Italy, Mr and Mrs Samuel Finn, setting off for a lifetime of adventures together. We had such a blissful time. We went back thirty years later and stayed for a decade. I knew as we headed off that first time that Samuel would always be on my side, and he *was* by my side for everything that mattered in my relentlessly long life.' Kate notices Cecily is clasping her own hand tightly, the knuckles white, the veins and liver spots having taken over the surface. Kate wonders when was the last time anyone held Cecily's hand.

'So: forget this foolish ghost,' says Cecily, decisively. 'Use that book to pursue something better.'

'I'm holding fire on the man front. You said yourself that you were too hung up on finding a husband.'

'Who said anything about a husband? My book has many chapters – work, friendship, travel. Find one and sink your teeth into it.'

Chapter Thirty-four

Dinner for Husband's Managing Director (Solid Type)

Aim: to make it clear that while basically you are just the 'little woman' standing dutifully in the kitchen preparing a delectable meal, you are able (and, God knows, willing) to exchange the sink for the mink immediately, if the boss would deign to promote your hard-working husband.

KATE TRIES TO IMAGINE inviting Devron round for a slap-up meal at Rita's in a last-minute attempt to salvage her job, then shakes her head. She might need to find inspiration on a different page . . .

'Kate, Annalex – can I have an urgent catch-up?' Ah, it's the man himself, who has suddenly appeared and is now hovering awkwardly by their desks.

Kate subtly shifts a pile of paperwork over Cecily's book. 'Is this about redundancy or is it a Christmas catch-up?' says Kate, reaching for her files as she looks up at Devron with a smile. Devron refuses to catch her eye and this sudden evasion makes Kate's stomach drop.

What on earth had she been thinking, writing that whole heart-on-her-sleeve piece about food being essential to happiness? It was Mrs Finn and her art class, filling Kate's head with ideas of bravery, of integrity. No wonder Devron won't look at her. And of course Annalex's submission will be crammed with data rather than actual words, and nothing gives Devron the horn more than a Mintel report he can quote to sound knowledgeable.

She traipses behind Devron and Annalex, head bent low as if bound for the gallows. By the time they're seated either side of Devron in the boardroom, he still won't meet Kate's gaze. She's starting to wonder if they'll march her out of the office immediately like they always do with redundancies, and if so is there anything she should have taken off her computer? Or have the last two decades of work been entirely disposable?

'Ladies,' says Devron, sniffing loudly then wiping his nose with his hand. 'I've had a read of your submissions, and in the interests of best practice I thought now would be a great time for you to read each other's pieces – give each other some three sixty feedback.'

'Why would you suggest that?' says Annalex, as if she's just found out Christmas has been cancelled.

'Does that mean you haven't made a decision yet?' says Kate, equally disturbed.

Devron looks taken aback that the women are for once aligned, against him. 'If I can finish? You've each approached the challenge quite differently, and I think it's always positive to have transparent dialogue. You'll have your decision soon enough.'

This must be the final hurdle, thinks Kate. *He's testing whether we'll be supportive or back-stabbing. That, or he literally expects us to make this decision for him.*

Annalex grabs the two documents, passes her own essay to Kate, then frowns as she reads Kate's title aloud: '*From astronaut bars to custard doughnuts – how our passion for food can help us inspire and nourish our customers. Is this your submission?*'

'Yes,' says Kate, glancing at Annalex's title: *Building POWER BRANDS through KISM (KEY INSIGHT STRATEGIC MESSAGING) and VIBFOM (VISUALISED BENEFIT FOCUS MESSAGING).*

A heavy silence fills the room. Kate reads Annalex's essay: *A BRAND BIBLE is a functional, process-led tool to springboard CREATIVITY which flourishes best within CONTROLLED PARAMETERS.*

No wonder Annalex is off once a month with a migraine. Kate glances at Annalex, who has pushed Kate's form away and is busy chewing the inside of her cheek.

'You want to go first?' says Devron, flashing Kate a look of apology.

'Someone has to,' she says, pondering whether to be honest or diplomatic. 'I think it's . . . quite . . . Procter and Gamble-ish? Lots of acronyms?'

Devron and Annalex both look pleased.

'OK, Annalex, your turn.'

Annalex shrugs. 'Hers is just . . . it's emotional. I'm used to a much more rigorous FMCG approach to marketing: brand the product, show a demo of how it works, repeat the branding.'

'A demo of how a banana *works*?' says Kate. 'Surely you just stick it in your mouth and chew?'

Annalex lets out a long sigh. 'My approach is functional and benefit focused: that's how you sell product.'

'But that's my point,' says Kate. 'Chocolate cake isn't the same as anti-bacterial mouthwash. People don't buy it for its functional benefits. They eat it because they like cake, or they're celebrating a birthday, or they feel sad because the person they love doesn't love them back. They don't think of cake as product – they think of it as something which makes them happy.'

'Really? How can you prove that?' says Annalex.

'Because I've been eating chocolate cake for a long time.'

'Yeah, we can see,' says Annalex.

'I beg your pardon?' says Kate.

'What? It was a joke! Look, I worked on the UK's number one mouthwash. We were market leader for the entire five years I was on it, I do know what I'm talking about.'

'Yep, well, *I* know that mouthwash is something you spit out, so it's actually the opposite of food, is it not?'

'Girls, girls, let's not lose sight of our goal here,' says Devron, looking alarmed. 'You sure neither of you is interested in voluntary redundancy?'

'No way,' says Annalex, folding her arms.

Kate folds her arms even more tightly.

There will be no voluntary about this. If Annalex wants a fight, then she's got one. Kate will not be told by one single other person in her life that she is not good enough.

Chapter Thirty-five

Supper for a Friend Who is Slimming

Aim: to take the opportunity of giving your friend
a serious talking-to on the evils of diets, pointing
out that all the famous enchantresses of history
inclined to embonpoint.

KATE IS DUE TO MAKE supper at Bailey's that night,
and Bailey's on a diet, but Bailey doesn't need to be
on a diet, and besides, sole Veronique and grilled tomatoes are simply too virtuous. Instead, Kate has chosen
to make 'Dinner Cooked at a Friend's House after an
Arduous Day' – lamb stew, tiramisu and a lot of red
wine – a far more appetising line-up.

She arrives at Bailey's as Bailey is putting her daughters to bed. Kate reads Franny *The Gruffalo* for the
eleventh time, then hovers at Tabby's bedroom door
as Bailey spends a moment with her younger daughter,
stroking her blonde curls and telling her something that
makes her giggle so much they all end up laughing.

It's been two years since Bailey's ex abandoned them for
the woman who sat next to him at work, buying the mis-
tress a tonne of flammable overpriced underwear on their
joint credit card in the process. Kate still cannot fathom

how such a distinctly average man could fail to cherish the grace, beauty and all-round excellence of her friend.

They head down to the kitchen and Bailey pours two large gin and tonics and shakes her head with exhaustion. 'Cheers – to single motherhood!'

Kate sighs and clinks glasses. 'I brought you a present.'

'You brought dinner; you didn't need to bring a gift.'

'It's just a copy of that book I told you about, the one this menu is from.'

Kate hands Bailey a copy, then starts to unpack the Tupperware. 'Page eighty-eight – *Let thy foot be seldom in thy neighbour's house, lest he be weary of thee* – from Proverbs. She writes a relevant quote at the start of every menu.'

'My friend, thou art welcome in this house anytime – you're better than Deliveroo,' says Bailey, as she admires the cover of the book then turns to the page in question. '*Setting – another woman's kitchen. There is nothing more demoralising than cooking in a friend's kitchen. You cannot avoid thinking: a) how much better organised you are, and, dearly as you love your friend, there's no denying she is slapdash; or b) how much better organised she is – and how soon can you rush home to tidy your kitchen.*' Bailey laughs. 'I'm sorry, it's a complete tip.'

Kate surveys the spotless white counter, the shiny copper pans hanging over the hob, the wine glasses lined up, sparkling.

'Trust me, it's messy,' says Bailey, following Kate's gaze. 'Particularly compared to your mum's.'

'That's only because Mum never cooks. I made the picnic last Saturday and she hasn't stopped moaning about it since.'

Bailey empties a packet of crisps into a bowl then takes a seat at the table. 'What *are* you doing about living arrangements?'

Kate decants the stew into a saucepan and puts it on the hob. 'I told you I went round to Nick's after that dickhead stood me up?'

'You still haven't heard from him?'

'Nothing, but if he thinks I'm going to avoid that coffee shop, he's wrong – their almond croissants are the best in North London. Anyway, Nick was being very amorous when I went over. He says he still doesn't understand what happened in France. I think it really was a commitment panic.'

'Kate, relationships are always unknowns – look at me and Tom, twenty years together, two kids, a mortgage, all that and he still did the most clichéd, midlife crisis thing in the world, humping the most up-for-it woman in his office.'

'I never think of Nick as a midlifer,' says Kate. 'Can you be labelled middle-aged if you still play with Lego?'

'I think it's acceptable if you have kids, but anyway, let's not dwell on Nick's youthful hobbies. Look, Kate, anything can happen at any time, so you might as well be with the person who makes you happy. Nick made a mistake but he's not a bad guy, he isn't a cheater like Tom, he's just inept. You guys are such a great couple, every time I see you together you're laughing. Just get on with it and move in. But in the meantime, you're more than welcome to take my spare room and be live-in babysitter? I could really do with someone I trust.'

'Careful what you wish for,' says Kate, putting the water on for the potatoes.

'I love the smell of old books,' says Bailey, bringing the hardback to her nose and breathing in the scent. 'Ah, look,' she says, running her finger down the contents page. 'This is fabulous, I need *this* menu, "Dinner for Important Client (Female and Tough)" – *Aim: to break down your guest's habitual sales resistance by the administration of good wine and food and to induce in her such well-being and possibly slight alcoholic daze that she will sign your contract without a murmur. Table decoration – a glass of cigarettes, chocolate peppermints.* Those were the days . . .'

'How is work going?'

'Manic but good. I've started working with a new ceramicist in Leeds, she makes the most beautiful vases. I only put them on the site at the weekend, but there's already a waiting list.'

'Ooh, I'll have a look, maybe I'll treat myself to one if – well – wherever I end up living.'

'How's your work going?'

'Oh, usual bollocks. I told you we're in the middle of another restructure? Devron's pitting me against Annalex like it's the Judgement of Solomon, without the wisdom part.'

'Take the redundancy, you'd get loads of cash.'

'It wouldn't be loads, but anyway, I'm not a quitter.'

'Seriously, freelance is the way forward. Listen, I meant to ask – what are the plans for your birthday? Did you get my email?'

'Sorry,' says Kate, taking a large gulp of her drink. 'I wasn't ignoring you. Well, I was ignoring my birthday more than you.'

'It's not long now.'

Kate shudders. 'Nick's booked a restaurant on the Saturday night, but I think I'd rather do something with all my friends together.'

'Where's he booked?'

'Le Montrachet.'

'He managed to get a table? Kate, go! It's supposed to be amazing. I was going to say I have a trade show in Paris that weekend – I can take the first Eurostar out on the Saturday but I'm definitely not around on Saturday night. I feel terrible asking, but could the Friday work instead? It'll be your birthday at midnight.'

'Oh, I'll figure something out,' says Kate, giving the lamb a stir. 'She puts pearl barley in this recipe, and loads of fresh thyme, it smells delicious . . . Oh, how is your sexy gardener, by the way?'

'Adam? Still very sexy,' says Bailey, topping up their glasses. 'He asked if I wanted tickets for a gardening show he's exhibiting at.'

'I hope you said yes? Then this time next year you can parade him in front of your jowly, cheating ex-husband at parents' evening.'

'He's twenty-eight and drives a Triumph, and I'm forty with two kids and a clapped-out Volvo. He's probably only asking to be polite.'

'Stop that right now. You're an exceptional human being, Bailey – kind, beautiful, any man would be lucky to be with you.'

'I suppose some men do like an older woman. Wayne Rooney . . .'

Kate laughs. 'I hope you said yes to his invitation? You did say yes, didn't you?'

'Actually,' says Bailey, biting her lower lip, 'I did.'

Kate cheers in victory. 'Invite him to my party, whatever I end up doing. In fact, I've decided – I'll cook for us all on the Friday night. Nothing fancy, I just want to be surrounded by the people I love. And it'll be a perfect excuse to invite him. Tell him you need a plus one.'

'We're getting a little ahead of ourselves, aren't we?'

'Promise, if things go well in the meantime?'

'One step at a time!'

Kate's eaten far too much tiramisu and now lies in the spare room at Bailey's house unable to sleep. With a sigh she turns on the bedside light and grabs pen and paper from her bag. She's going to figure out once and for all if it's even worth hanging around hoping Nick will come good in the end:

<u>*Nick*</u>

Pros:
Love
Investment of time to date
Forty – impending (loss of collagen, general diminution in attractiveness, grey hairs, etc.)
Bailey and Kavita approve
His good qualities (see Appendix 1)

Cons:
He might wobble again at any time – puts me on perma-shaky ground
Therapy can't change a dog into a cat
Various annoying friends' annoying opinions (particularly Mrs Finn)
His bad qualities (See Appendix 2)

Kate has written many lists before:

Alex: gorgeous/drinks too much
Toby: creative, romantic/too young
Maloney: successful/shallow and unkind.

She dreams of being in a relationship where she does not, at some point, have to put pen to paper in order to make facts seem less unpalatable.

Mind you, she'd write down the pros and cons of buying a particular sofa, and a boyfriend is far more complex than a sofa – even a boyfriend nicknamed Amoeba. Especially a boyfriend nicknamed Amoeba.

Cecily keeps telling Kate to be bold. Would the brave thing be to quit, because of one (admittedly hurtful) incident and some rapidly fading pain? No, far braver surely to absorb a knock, get up again and not be beaten – to work through it with Nick – that *was* the braver choice. Cecily can't have been married to Samuel for sixty-odd years without having had to work through their problems, but she never mentions that side of things, does she?

There's no need to debate the matter further. Her mind's made up. She's going to the Radiohead gig with Nick on Thursday and if all continues to go well, she'll agree to supper on Saturday. One step at a time.

Chapter Thirty-six

'I BROUGHT YOU FLOWERS, Mrs Finn. And I made the English madeleines from your book.'

'Flowers *and* cake?' says Cecily frowning. 'You must be feeling guilty about something.'

She really is a witch, thinks Kate, heading off to find a vase. Kate didn't stay at Nick's last night – she's learning what a boundary is, and is ring-fencing herself firmly in the flirty friend zone for a while longer. But that doesn't mean she didn't spend as much of the weekend as possible with him. She'd left him at midnight, tipsy Cinderella, hopping into a cab after a movie and dinner at their favourite Italian, three shared pastas and a bottle of red. She'd met up with him again this morning at Columbia Road flower market, then gone back to his flat to make the madeleines together. It's the happiest she's been since Thursday when they'd been to see Radiohead, then gone to Edgware Road for a late-night kebab followed by a couple of Bourbons in a basement bar. She's desperately trying not to attach hope to all this happiness, but it's so hard not to.

By the time she's found a tall enough vase and returned to Cecily's room, Cecily has vanished. Kate pokes her head back down the corridor – she definitely hasn't gone for a wander. She knocks on the toilet door and a moment later Cecily issues a series of farts as loud as gunfire and demands Kate call for a Filipina.

'Are you OK, Mrs Finn, you haven't fallen over?'

'Stop patronising me and go and fetch one of the girls.'

Kate heads to the carers' station, and waits while the carer heads off to Cecilys' room. Reading the notice-board she marvels at all the activities on offer that Cecily refuses to take advantage of: film screenings, a talk on Matisse, a Yoga and Stretch class.

Kate returns to find Cecily sitting straight-backed, looking more aloof than ever.

'I brought tea roses,' says Kate, placing the vase of pale yellow perfumed blooms on Cecily's bedside table, before laying the cakes in front of her. They look delicious, delicate cone-shaped sponge towers covered in a light scattering of desiccated coconut with shiny glacé cherries on top. Cecily eyes them with suspicion.

'Try one?' says Kate, smiling as she thinks back to a few hours ago, when she'd dolloped a spoonful of the raspberry jam onto the tip of Nick's nose, then dusted coconut on him so he looked like Rudolph with a touch of psoriasis.

'Did you use the correct darioles?' says Cecily, inspecting one of the little cake towers with a deep frown.

'I followed your recipe to the letter. Oh, I saw on the noticeboard there are some events coming up you might like. How about a screening of *Casablanca*?'

'Not with Burbridge shouting all the way through it – if you've gone deaf, don't make life unbearable for those of us who haven't.'

'A talk on Matisse? I could come with you next Saturday?'

Cecily shakes her head violently.

'Suit yourself,' says Kate, throwing her hands up in resignation. 'By the way, the other day you didn't get round to telling me how you came to be a writer.'

'It's a very long story,' says Cecily, still glaring at the madeleines as if they're about to bite.

'I've got time,' says Kate, carefully pouring her half a cup of tea.

'It'll take more than one telling.'

'I'm not going anywhere,' says Kate, placing the cup and saucer on Cecily's side table.

'Well, only if you insist. Samuel's work back then was as export manager for a kitchenware company. He spoke five languages, so it was an ideal role for him, and it suited me very well. He'd often bring me back a new saucepan or egg whisk to try out. The company needed him to sample their products across Europe, so much to everyone's disapproval, after our honeymoon, we set off on a longer adventure, armed with ten suitcases filled with pots and pans. We started in Copenhagen, then went to Denmark, Finland, Germany . . .' she says, counting the countries off on her fingers. 'Holland, Norway – oh the *fiskepudding* in Oslo . . .'

'What is *fiskepudding*?'

'Light as air, utterly delicious. Everywhere in Oslo you'd see white-haired old ladies all looking wonderful, they seemed to survive on a diet of the stuff. I once asked Bernadette to make some, bloody woman served up mackerel paté, as if a mackerel and a pike have the least thing in common. Norway, Sweden, Belgium, Czecho-slovakia . . . I can't remember the order, but the pattern remained the same: innumerable suitcases, waiting at stations, arriving at a cheap pension with a bedroom too small or dark, the towels thin and prickly. In the daytime, Samuel would visit customers, and I'd find the nearest gallery or museum. Once Samuel returned, we'd head out together to explore. We climbed the Fisherman's bastion in Budapest, watched the bridges light up like circles of pearls over the Danube. We danced in the Bois de la Cambre under the beautiful old trees, drank the waters in Franzensbad . . .'

'That sounds wonderful.'

'Oh, it was. But already there was an uneasiness across Europe. I remember visiting Samuel's family in Warsaw. We travelled by cargo boat and I remember a breathtakingly beautiful sunset over the Baltic, the sky navy, purple and crimson with streaks of molten gold. We sat in the captain's cabin drinking schnapps. Samuel rarely drank but he was so excited we'd be spending time with his family that he had a few too many and had to sleep it off. But as soon as we disembarked I started to regret the trip. The cold in Warsaw was savage, the breath froze in our nostrils. Samuel and I had to dodge in and out of shops in order to even breathe. Everywhere there was a sense of depression and gloom. The horses were starving, their ribs poked through their skins, there was snow and slush everywhere. And while Samuel's parents' home was immaculate, the tenement they lived in, with its dirty stairs and dreary hallways, was miserable. We went for Friday-night dinner and when Leon and Shindel opened the door to greet us, I was shocked at how drawn they looked. The shadow of fear fell everywhere.'

'When was this?'

'December of '36. Rumours were seeping out from Germany like tendrils of fog, making our hearts chill. Most of Samuel's siblings and their families had come to the apartment – we were sixteen in total. They embraced us so warmly, Oskar and his wife and twin sons. Oskar was tall like Samuel but strong like a bull, when he hugged you it felt like nothing could ever harm you. Izzy was there, the most handsome of the brothers – he looked like James Stewart, with the most dazzling smile. He'd been a womaniser in his day but was now kept in check by his wife Hannah, a beauty with flaming red hair and a fantastic quick wit. They had brought their four children, all girls, and Izzy looked at them with total adoration. Lilli was there, Samuel's other sister, such a delicate girl, with a smattering of freckles and the same huge brown eyes Samuel had. Lilli had brought along Max, a chap she worked with at the garment factory who was sweet on her, and whenever he left the room, Leon and Oskar would tease her about a wedding. Everyone did their utmost to welcome us. Outside the snow fell in relentless flakes, driving against the window panes, but inside we were wrapped up and warm, and the room was filled with chatter and laughter, everyone talking over each other in their excitement to see us. The glow from the Shabbat candles filled the dark corners of the room with soft light. We said a prayer of thanks for the food and the wine and then we ate, my goodness did we eat. We had wonderful fresh challahs from the bakery Hannah's family owned, and Shindel had prepared all of Samuel's favourite dishes: borscht, gefilte fish, stuffed cabbage, potato and mushroom knishes.'

'What's a knish?'

'Oh, it's a marvellous pastry parcel filled with delicious stuffing, very moreish. The dishes kept on coming. Just when you thought there couldn't possibly be any more, someone would disappear into the kitchen and return with a platter of delights and a proud grin. After dinner Leon insisted on sharing an entire bottle of slivovitz plum brandy. I can taste it now,' she says, shivering. 'That first fiery shock, then warmth spreading up your body like a tree in flames.'

'Ah! That meal's in your book, isn't it? It has about eleven courses?'

'That's right – "Winter Feast for Visiting Relatives".'

'And there's that amazing chocolate babka for dessert. It must have been an incredible feast.'

'Well, the food was plentiful and his family was hugely hospitable, but as the hours went by the evening turned ominous. Samuel was convinced his family's future looked bleak if they stayed in Poland. He sat at that table for hours after the meal was finished, trying to persuade them to leave, but they refused. He begged his father but Leon thought Samuel was overly fearful, which was ridiculous because Samuel was always such an optimist. Lilli seemed to take Samuel seriously, but the following spring she got engaged to Max and he didn't want to leave. Things might have been different for her if she hadn't fallen in love. Ultimately Warsaw was everyone's home. By the end of that evening Samuel was in tears of frustration. I felt worried for him, and scared for all of them.'

'Oh God. It sounded really festive in the book . . .'

'Well, that's editing for you. We had two days in Warsaw and I must admit, I've never been happier than when we crossed the border and were safely out of that ill-fated land. That trip was the only low point of those years. Aside from that, there was always fun and laughter. Samuel was like his father – too generous, always lending money, but in spite of chronic hard-up-ness, our lives were never dingy. Even in the cheapest digs we made great friends, talked art, music, politics,' she says, her eyes sparkling with the memory. 'So when you say you're content spending your life writing about carrots, I find it incomprehensible.'

'Fair enough,' says Kate, taking a large bite of cake, then pushing the plate of madeleines towards Cecily. She's far too content this afternoon to get into a fight. If Cecily thrives on conflict, Kate simply won't give it to her.

'Have you *no* gumption?' says Cecily, forcefully pushing the plate back. 'You're willing to waste your entire adult life unfulfilled because you're scared of the unknown?'

Kate tuts. 'Everybody's scared of the unknown. Besides, I might not even have a job next week, so can we talk about something else?'

Cecily examines Kate, then twitches her head slightly to the left, then back to centre, like a bird about to pierce a worm. 'You haven't mentioned him once today,' she says, pursing her lips. 'Why is that? Clearly you haven't cut him off or you wouldn't be looking quite so rosy-cheeked.'

'I know you're not a fan – but if you do want to know, we've started seeing each other again, as friends.'

'*Friends*?' says Cecily, snorting.

'I am his "person" – he sends me pictures of his breakfast, I send him pictures of my lunch.'

'Why?'

Kate shrugs. 'It's just those little things that make up your day, that make you feel connected to someone.'

Cecily grunts. 'Another's cloak does not keep you warm . . .'

'What's that supposed to mean?'

'This man is a waste of your time. Time is precious. These are not complicated concepts, surely?'

'Why are you so convinced Nick's not good for me?'

'Because he's careless with your feelings. Your relationship crossed the Rubicon on that holiday, and I'm damned if I know how a reasonably smart girl can be so stupid.'

Kate can't remember what the Rubicon is, but having just been called stupid for the umpteenth time she's disinclined to ask.

'You like icing so much you're willing to eat sub-standard cake,' says Cecily in disgust.

'Is that another metaphor?' says Kate, resting her plate wearily on the side table.

Cecily replies with a hard stare.

'So you're saying, percentage wise, Nick's bad outweighs his good?'

'Of course that's what I'm saying,' says Cecily, who is now so angry Kate can see a vein pulsing through the thin skin at her temples.

'Why do you even care?'

'Because unlike that man, *I* am your friend.'

'Friends like these . . .' mutters Kate.

Probably not a good time to mention she's heading straight back to Nick's after this for slow-cooked chilli and a triple bill of *30 Rock*. Nor to ask Cecily about the finer points of the menu she's planning to cook him next weekend when Rita's away with Patrick.

The truth is, Kate can take or leave the cake part of any cake – isn't the icing the whole point?

Chapter Thirty-seven

Dinner for the Man You Hope to Marry

Being your slave, what should I do but tend,
Upon the hours and times of your desire
   Shakespeare, Sonnet 57

Aim: to impress him with your skill in ministering to his comfort, and the promise of an endless vista of delightful meals.

Setting:
Clearly this is the occasion for red roses and candlelight. You cannot do any more without being obvious. Music should be a last resort.

Menu:
Fried scampi
Chicken in cider
Pavé potatoes
American double-layer strawberry shortcake

Method:
Prepare in advance, except for the scampi. No harm can come from the sight of you emerging flushed from the kitchen bearing a love offering of deep-fried golden morsels. Sometimes deep-fried golden morsels are the best way to achieve one's ends.

Nick is going to love this meal. Kate runs a finger down her final list of ingredients; she'll buy the chicken and fish from that fancy food hall in Mayfair after work on Friday. Of course she could buy a Fletchers' chicken for a fifth of the price, but it would taste like traumatised roadkill so she's going to splurge and buy quality – besides, it's an investment in her relationship.

The scampi require Dublin Bay prawns, which are langoustines, more like mini-lobsters. The fishmonger is sure to stock those, and he'll deal with the heads, tails and other gross bits.

Music should be a last resort? Presumably because it fills the silence and means they wouldn't have to talk – but she wants Nick to talk. They've been getting along so brilliantly lately, she just needs a little more reassurance that he's committed to their future.

She commends herself once more on her behaviour since they've been back in contact. She's done a decent job of skating on one leg – demonstrated she's empathetic and patient, but not prepared to put up with any further nonsense. It's been a tricky balancing act, this one-legged skating malarkey, particularly on such thin ice – but Nick has done and said all the right things, booked gig tickets for next spring, told her he wants a proper long holiday together to make up for the terrible time in France. She's finally allowing herself to believe in him again.

Nick is working an overnight shift on Friday – a data transition so complex that no matter how many times he explains it, a drawbridge goes up in Kate's brain. The timing couldn't be better. Rita's leaving for her weekend with Patrick at 4 p.m., so when Kate comes home from work on Friday she can start cooking. That way, on

Saturday she can pop in to Lauderdale and persuade Cecily to go to the Matisse talk; then she has a mani-pedicure and waxing booked – the best deal she could find is out in Harlesden. It makes for a rushed after-noon, but most of the cooking will be done by then; it'll just be finishing touches. She's added home-made bread to the menu – no doubt Cecily would say she's gilding the lily, but Nick adores fresh bread – and the smell of it baking as he walks through the door should set the perfect tone.

This menu is going to work like a charm.

Chapter Thirty-eight

'H E'S FINALLY MADE UP his mind,' says Annalex, arching an eyebrow at Kate. 'So are you coming to find out, or what?'

Kate feels her throat go dry as she follows the dull thump of Annalex's Ugg boots down the corridor to the boardroom. 'I need more time to decide if you're good enough' – it was bad enough Nick basically saying that, but she'd accepted it from Nick because she loves him and besides, he didn't really mean it. But for Devron to say it, when she's proved herself for nearly twenty years? When she's been a loyal and consistently high-performing employee, when she's rated 'Good slash Great' on all her flipping KPIs? She must not get carried away again in a tornado of indignation.

She settles herself opposite Devron, a sudden tight-ness gripping her stomach.

Hang on a minute. Premium chocolate biscuits? Laid right there on the table? Premium chocolate biscuits are normally only dispensed for board meetings or visiting dignitaries.

Devron rubs his hand over his jaw and blows out heavily as his eyes scan his notepad in front of him. 'Right, so, I've spoken with HR and senior stakeholders, and you'll be pleased to hear I've got a decision and it's good news.'

'Good for whom?' says Kate.

'Both of you,' says Devron, giving her a wink. 'It occurred to me after last week's meeting that you have very different core strengths. Kate, you're obviously happy doing creative stuff; Annalex, you're a data-driven thinker.' He glances at the bullet-pointed checklist in front of him. 'It's good to keep home-grown talent like Kate – as well as to attract the best in the marketplace. So Kate, you're going to become Head of Copy, and Annalex will take strategic lead and become Brand Ambassador of In-store Comms.'

'Can I put Ambassador on my business card?' says Annalex.

'So after all that, we're both keeping our jobs?' says Kate. 'But how will that work in terms of the overall restructure?'

'Still ironing that out,' says Devron. 'You'll have your new contracts in December.'

'OK . . . Will we be getting a pay rise?' says Kate, suddenly perking up. 'We haven't had one in three years.'

'You're lucky still to have a job,' says Devron. 'Er, but you will get exciting creative opportunities which are far more valuable for your development.'

That old chestnut, thinks Kate, then laughs to herself as she remembers last Christmas's debacle, when it was discovered that Fletchers' finest Italian chestnuts were actually Chinese, though at least that copy wrote itself.

'So Kate, I'm going to ask you to get involved in the new KIPPER subgroup cluster this week—'

'So, hang on, we'll be starting the new roles now, without a new contract?'

'You're still on the old contract till December, but I thought you might like to immerse yourself in KIPPER sooner rather than later. If that's all right with you?'

'A kipper immersion. What could be finer?' says Kate, aware she should be demonstrating enthusiasm and gratitude a little more authentically than she is currently.

At least Kavita is delighted, and insists on taking Kate for a drink after work.

Kate knows she should feel pleased or at least relieved – but she feels almost disappointed, and for the opposite reason to why she'd imagined.

It's not because Annalex is keeping her job, it's because Kate is.

Chapter Thirty-nine

KATE CHECKS HER WATCH subtly. She's sitting in her first KIPPER subgroup cluster late on Friday afternoon, and so far her colleagues have spent forty minutes bickering about whether the acronym for Creativity Yields Profitable Results should be changed from KIPPER to CAPER. They haven't even started on point one of the agenda, and Kate's starting to worry she won't make it to the food hall before it closes.

The minute the meeting's over she calls and persuades the shop to let her order and pay over the phone, so she can just swing by and collect everything, and thank goodness she does because by the time she's shut down her computer and run most of the way there, it's two minutes before closing. Gratefully she takes the heavy bag from the fish counter and dashes to the meat counter for the chicken thighs, which cost the same as Kate's entire favourite curry takeaway order: not a paltry sum.

Back at the flat, she pops the bags in the fridge, then flops down on the sofa. What a joy, to have a moment of stillness at the end of a long week. She should start cooking, but instead slips off her shoes and stretches the full length of the sofa. Apart from the noise outside of Lorna Bleecher manically hooting her Mazda horn at whichever poor sod is daring to walk near her, all is quiet. Kate wiggles her toes. She can't remember the last time she felt this happy alone. How nice to have a peaceful, quiet home – no surly Melanie, no boundary-invading Rita – almost as nice as the prospect of sharing a home with Nick.

Right – time to start the prep. The cakes first – and she's making an extra one for Cecily. Kate turns on her iPod to her favourite eighties playlist – first up, INXS – and on with the cake! It's a straightforward recipe – two sponge layers baked and left to cool, then sandwiched with strawberries and whipped cream, extra strawberries on top. Diligently she creams the sugar and softened butter, then stirs in the eggs. She inhales the aroma from the vanilla essence bottle before adding a generous swig and giving a sigh of contentment. There's no better feeling than when she's cooking for someone she loves. Gently she folds in the flour, then lovingly pours the batter into four separate cake tins. The baking takes less than an hour, and as the flat fills with the sweet, comforting smell of vanilla sponge, Kate turns to focus on the main course.

Again, the chicken is a simple recipe but the slow braising will ensure the meat falls off the bone. She fries the chicken in the sizzling golden butter with finely chopped shallots, adds the cider, a fragrant bouquet garni and skinned, deseeded Italian tomatoes, then sticks it in the oven on low.

The potatoes are a true labour of love – but that's the whole point. Cecily's recipe involves peeling and squaring off the potatoes, slicing them with a mandolin, soaking them in cream, layering them in a twenty-layer formation in a loaf tin with seasoning and tiny cubes of butter, slow-baking them, leaving them under a heavy weight overnight, then the next day cutting them into neat rectangles and frying them in butter and thyme – resulting in a soft, creamy, multi-layered inside and a crisp, crunchy exterior. They sound delicious, but they are *hard* work, thinks Kate, arranging the fourteenth layer of slices in the tin, then washing her cream-covered fingers for the fourteenth time.

The potatoes need two hours in the oven, during which time she can relax and have a bath. As her final chore she takes the fish bag from the fridge to decant the contents. It's heavier than she'd envisaged, they must have packed it with ice – but when she takes the inner bag from the outer, she sees with despair that London's most expensive food hall has failed to take the prawns from their shells. She'd assumed they'd do that automatically – for the price she paid for twelve prawns they should not only de-shell them, but also come round and cook the damn things, then do the washing-up and fix Rita's wireless-router problems.

These aren't tiger prawns, they're giant crustaceans, each the length of a school ruler. She takes the cold, wet bodies from the bag and lines them up on the counter. Twenty-four shiny dead black eyes stare up at her accusingly – they will haunt her in her dreams. *Fruits de mer?* Fruits de nightmare more like, she thinks, then chastises herself for a pun even Annalex wouldn't make.

She wishes Nick was here to help – he loves fishmongery – but he's enjoying a red-hot night fiddling with Oracle and SQL server, which he's assured her are not strippers. She checks in Cecily's book for the method: *shell and trim the prawns; dip in batter* . . . Huh – she makes it sound easy.

Right: she puts on Rage Against the Machine to psych herself up. Oh but crustaceans are weird – tasty, sure, but as she lifts one up she shudders. They're like armoured slugs, those long whiskery antennae, those angular spiky joints; how anyone can cook a live lobster is beyond her.

She googles 'langoustine anatomy' and acquaints herself with *Nephrops norvegicus*. The head bit is the head, obviously, then there's the carapace – underneath are some walking legs and some swimming legs – ooh handy, two different sets of legs – and inside is the intestinal sac. Has there ever been a less appealing phrase in the history of cooking than intestinal sac? That would not make it onto hers and Nick's shortlist of kids' names.

She googles 'peel and devein a langoustine'. Unfortunately, it is not a straightforward process, or at least not for a squeamish person. She finds a video and starts following along, holding the first prawn down by its thorax, then squirming as she holds the tip of a knife against the centre of its back, bringing it down hard, splitting the prawn sharply in two with a nauseating crunch, snap and crack of breaking exoskeleton.

Kate's pretty sure she's never bisected a once-living creature's head before. She squints at the pale grey insides – an undignified end. She wonders if Cecily created this task to test the strength of her readers' devotion. But no, of course . . . this is what Cecily cooked for Samuel, and she secured an engagement out of it a few weeks later: onwards!

Bloody hell – now Kate has to remove the veins. She takes a pair of tweezers, almost retching as she digs into the slippery flesh and pulls the prawn's glistening veins out. She should have gone to Iceland – two for a fiver on frozen scampi and Nick wouldn't have noticed the difference.

She looks down at her finished prawn halves with a touch of satisfaction before realising that each half is still firmly in its shell, which would make for pretty crunchy scampi. She presses play on the video and curses the presenter as he explains that these prawns are now ready for the barbecue, and he'll move on to demonstrate an entirely different process for deep frying.

She stares at the kitchen wall. She loves Nick, she does, but really, *this* much? She sighs. It's not even about Nick anymore: it's Kate versus prawn. She restarts the video and after much wrestling, wriggling, cursing and further vein detaching, she finally surveys the dozen scampi tails before her, then piles the spoils of her war into the fridge. She washes her hands in scaldingly hot water for as long as she can stand, then sniffs her fingers gingerly. They smell intensely of prawns. She scrubs, then scrubs again. Lucky she made the cakes first or those strawberries would have a distinctly fishy taint. On the plus side, in the time it's taken her to eviscerate the prawns, the chicken has cooked, as have the potatoes, and she can now go to bed.

As her weary head hits the pillow she commends herself on learning a new skill. Also, next time, she'll ensure she asks more clearly for what she wants in the first place – that's a valuable life lesson. And finally, if Nick can't proclaim his eternal love for her after the effort she's put in, she's going to eat his share of the scampi and find a man who can.

Chapter Forty

K ATE SITS IN RECEPTION at Lauderdale, fanning herself with a copy of *The Lady*. Outside it's a crisp October day, almost scarf weather; inside it's tropical, and today there's a faint suboptimal smell of bleach and boiled white fish.

She looks down proudly at the layered strawberry shortcake balanced on her lap. It's beautiful, a kaleidoscope of heart-shaped strawberry slices resting atop the luscious thick whipped cream.

Mrs Gaffney is finishing in her office with a visitor, and as she emerges Kate sees it's the same man she's noticed in reception a couple of times before – the one with blue eyes and sandy hair. He smiles in recognition and she automatically smiles back. Something about his long, straight nose looks rather familiar.

He heads over to a heavily made-up sulky young woman in platform heels who's been taking endless selfies three chairs down from Kate. The girl stands and pouts, and he puts his arms on her shoulders and talks to her in a low voice. Kate has a flashback to the old man at the doughnut stand. It always makes her a little queasy when a man is old enough to be his girlfriend's dad. Kate smooths out her frown; it's entirely none of her business.

Cecily is looking immaculate today in a navy-and-camel-checked cardigan, listening to the radio. She's looking thoroughly miserable, but seeing Kate her expression brightens before her brow furrows. 'You're a day early.'

'I happened to be passing. I brought you a treat, and I thought I could persuade you to come to the Matisse talk. It's on in twenty minutes. We could have a quick cup of tea first?'

Cecily looks confused. 'I told you I didn't want to go. Why would I have changed my mind?'

'I know,' says Kate gently, taking a seat. 'It's just that you were telling me about the galleries you went to in Europe. You have all these art books on your shelves. I just thought if you were bored—'

'I've been bored for a decade. I wouldn't be less bored in that lecture, I'd simply be sitting on a different chair.'

'Mrs Finn, what *would* make you happy?'

'Death, quick and painless, without further loss of dignity,' says Cecily, who is eyeing up the Tupperware resting on Kate's lap. 'What's that?'

'I made you one of the cakes from the book – it's more cake than it is icing. The American strawberry shortcake,' she says, taking the cake out to show Cecily.

'I see,' says Cecily, raising her eyebrows in disgust. 'And was this from last night's "Dinner for an Undeserving Cretin"?'

'Er, no.'

'Tonight, then. I should never have given you my book. I want it back tomorrow.'

Kate feels a little stab in her chest, but nods. 'Was this a recipe you picked up on your trip to California?'

251

'You won't get a story from me today,' says Cecily, folding her arms tightly.

'Did you sleep badly?'

'No more so than every night. My arm's giving me pain,' she says, rubbing her right elbow. 'The last time I fell it broke in three places. That idiot child-doctor did a botched job – it's never been the same since. Also my stomach's a little acid, God knows what that banshee put in my porridge, unspeakable texture.'

'A piece of cake always makes things better, don't you think?'

Cecily grudgingly takes a forkful before wrinkling her nose. 'You've used butter, not lard?'

'I thought you couldn't taste properly?'

'I can tell from the texture.'

'You can never go wrong with butter, surely?'

Cecily shrugs her disagreement. 'And for your information, I didn't cook Samuel the chicken that night.'

'Sorry?'

'I made him lamb, his favourite. But if you're really looking to impress, you should have made *Gigot de la Clinique* in the Toklas.'

'The Toklas?'

'Alice B. Toklas, she took the recipe from Pierlot, who took it from Guegan,' says Cecily, pointing wearily to one of the shelves. 'Though it takes a good eight days.'

'Days or hours?'

'Leg of mutton marinated in a good Burgundy for eight *days*, turned twice a day and injected with syringe-fuls of cognac; I wish they'd inject me twice a day with cognac,' she says grumpily. 'Over those eight days at least you might have seen sense. Take this cake to the kitchen,

252

they can eat it after the Matisse. I'm out of sorts. My stomach is upset, I have a sharp pain. What else did you put in that cake?'

'It's exactly as per your recipe, apart from the lard. Should I fetch the nurse?'

'No, I hate a fuss. I want to be alone.'

'All right, Greta Garbo, I'll see you tomorrow, then.'

'Go away, vulgar girl.'

Fine. If Cecily's going to be like that, Kate's delighted to have an extra hour of her day back.

Kate is in Harlesden, part way through her manicure, hoping the manicurist won't discover any lingering prawn flesh under her nails, when her phone rings. For a moment she panics that it's Nick cancelling, but when she fishes the phone from her bag with her free hand she sees it's Lauderdale and her throat goes dry.

'Kate? It's Bernadette here, from Lauderdale. It's about Mrs Finn.'

'What's wrong?' says Kate, gesturing apologetically to the manicurist that she needs a minute.

'She's had a funny turn.'

'Oh,' says Kate, her heart sinking. 'What kind of a funny turn?'

'She had acute stomach pains and felt faint.'

'Oh. Can you put me through to her?'

'She's resting, but she asked me to call.'

'How can I help?'

'She needs some soup.'

'She wants me to make her some soup?'

'Not make it. I don't know why she can't have the tomato soup on the menu here, it's delicious, but no – it's a very specific Jewish soup, apparently, from a place – have you got a pen? From a place called Steiner's in Stamford Hill.'

'Stamford *Hill*?'

'It's the chicken soup with the dumpling things in.'

'How unwell is she?' says Kate, looking at her watch. Cecily had been complaining of a bad stomach earlier, but it hadn't seemed serious. Not Stamford Hill serious.

'She's called for the nurse twice.'

'OK...' says Kate, trying to remain objective. Stamford Hill will involve multiple buses and horrendous traffic; there are always roadworks around Holloway and she absolutely has to have a bikini wax, she hasn't had one since France. 'Bernadette – could she wait until tomorrow, do you think? I'm seeing her then anyway.'

'I'm only passing on the message. Normally she lacks the humility to ask for help, so perhaps she needs it. She did stress it was urgent, but I can't make your decisions for you.'

Kate stares down at her three scarlet nails and seven unpainted ones. She visualises the state of her bikini line – approaching that of a Greek waiter with a chromosomal abnormality.

It's already 3.15 p.m., she still needs to buy flowers, make bread, tidy the flat and lay the table before Nick arrives at 8 p.m. She pictures the lovely, relaxing, indulgent dinner they're going to enjoy – which will be even more enjoyable if she has good nails and a chance to do things at a reasonable pace.

Then she pictures Cecily, hunched over in her chair, in pain.

She hangs up and asks the manicurist if she can have the rest of the bottle of nail polish to go.

Cecily is lying in bed wearing a pink quilted house jacket, a glass of ginger beer on her side table. Her cheeks are flushed but she looks well rested. She smiles brightly when she sees the tray of soup Kate is carrying.

'No need to bring it this afternoon, dear,' says Cecily, her expression entirely innocent.

Kate's smile falters. 'Sorry?'

'There was no hurry. I'm seeing you tomorrow, aren't I?'

'Right, OK, well, that wasn't the message I received,' says Kate, frowning.

'Was it not?'

'I was *told* it was urgent.'

'Oh well, that's Bernadette for you, half daft, never listens. I told you about the time I asked her to make *fiskepudding* and she made it with mackerel? Why not go the whole hog and make it with horse?'

'Yes, I know about the *fiskepudding* and the wrong fish – and I also know you said you needed this chicken soup immediately because you were very poorly.'

'A misunderstanding,' says Cecily, reaching for Kate to haul her up in bed.

Kate rests the tray on the floor, then holds out her hands. Cecily grabs them tightly, her fingers pinching Kate's as she shifts herself up in bed, then calmly smooths her bedcovers while Kate sets up the tray over her lap, placing a spoon in her outstretched hand.

'Looks like soup,' says Cecily, nodding appreciatively at the bowl of broth. 'Only one carrot, though,' she wades her spoon steadily back and forth through the noodles as if sifting for gold. 'Could have brought it tomorrow . . .'

Kate bites her tongue in irritation, too hard, and tastes blood. 'You know what, Mrs Finn? I think I'm going to double-check with Bernadette what you said.'

'I wouldn't bother, if I were you, she gets quite irritable.'

'I will bother, because it was quite a lot of bother for me to sit in traffic on a bus full of feral teenage girls for an hour and a half, and then arrive at the deli you sent me to only to discover that it's shut on a Saturday.'

'Oh,' says Cecily laughing. 'It's Shabbat, of course it's shut.'

'Of course it's shut, so then I panicked and had to get a taxi because the Victoria line's down, to the next-best Jewish deli that's actually open, which is all the way back in St John's Wood, then on the way back here in a *second* cab, hot soup spilled all over my lap because the idiot in the shop didn't put the lid on the carton properly and there are far too many speed bumps in London, and so the whole enterprise has taken the best part of three hours.' And thirty-eight pounds she could have done without spending, but she restrains herself from mentioning this.

'This is from Harry Morgan's?' says Cecily, pulling a face to say that if she'd known *that* she wouldn't be enjoying it half as much.

'That's right, Mrs Finn – miles away.'

'That depends entirely on your starting point. In that case you *definitely* should have waited till tomorrow – then at least you could have bought it from the right place.'

Kate takes an extra-long deep breath and lets it out to the count of ten. 'I thought you had terrible pains in your stomach? I thought you were faint?'

'I did. I was. Turns out it was trapped wind, terribly painful at my age. The Parkinson's exacerbates it, and those calcium tablets don't help the bowels much either. You really can't strain too hard in your nineties or you're at risk of your tail popping out. I'm sure Rappapot strains herself deliberately down there once a week just so she can have people make an extra fuss over her bottom, attention-seeking hypochondriac.'

'Oh good grief,' says Kate, rubbing her hands over her face.

'What on earth are those fingernails?'

'I was in the middle of a manicure. For tonight.'

'Oh. Doing anything special?'

'You know exactly what I'm doing!'

'Do I? Oh, right, yes, I do, don't I? Oh well, no good deed goes unpunished,' says Cecily, chuckling. 'I presume you've done most of the prep anyway, what difference?'

'The difference, or rather the point, is that you made a whole big deal the other day about being my friend, yet you think it's funny to mess up what's a big night for me. I've been through the wringer with Nick over the last three months, and this dinner matters a lot. And I was going to make home-made bread, and at this rate I won't have time.'

'Oh, don't take it all so seriously, dear. So what if I did indulge myself? I'm bored. Bored, exhausted, full of ennui, which, as you may know, is a French word meaning—'

'Yes, I know what ennui means.'

'And *Weltschmerz*?'

'Welsh who?'

'A-ha! It's a German word, meaning world-weariness, pain.'

'Well, maybe if you ever left this room you might feel less weltschmerzy. You could easily have come to the Matisse earlier, then you wouldn't have had to try to ruin what's left of my love life.'

'If every step you took felt like daggers, you wouldn't leave your room either.'

'Yeah, well, if you walked with a proper frame like Mrs Gaffney says you should, your joints might not feel like daggers.'

'One of those heavy lumbersome frames? Ridiculous, I'm far too young for one of those. Now look, dear, I'm a very old lady—'

'You just said you were too young for a frame.'

'Humour me. I'm touched you came. The soup is fine. Not as good as mine, mind you. I used to make chicken soup all the time for Samuel, it was his favourite. I was still making it well into my eighties,' she says, getting misty-eyed.

'Uh-huh,' says Kate, glancing at her watch: 6.02 p.m. The home-made bread needs two hours for the dough to rest and forty minutes to bake.

'I always used to give him the last *kneidlach*, and he'd cut it in half and give me back the slightly bigger half – technically not a half, but still. Such a shame you forgot the *kneidlach* – I did make it clear to Bernadette. Perhaps she didn't pass that on either.'

'*Kneidlach*?' says Kate distractedly.

'The matzah balls, they're the best bit,' she says, slurping her spoon noisily. 'If I'm being really honest, it's not hot enough. Be a dear, would you? Go to the kitchen and reheat this till it's piping hot,' she says, pushing the bowl with both hands deliberately slowly towards Kate. 'On the hob, not in a microwave, that radiation will kill me.'

If the radiation doesn't, I will, thinks Kate.

'When you come back, I can tell you all about the chicken soup we ate in Hawaii, quite delicious, made with pineapple, of all things! Did I tell you we went to Kauai for a whole month for my seventieth? Hanalei Bay, the most glorious place, we danced under the stars every night. The colours of the sea, what an island! Better than this miserable island, we should never have come back . . .'

'I'm afraid Hawaii will have to wait till tomorrow,' says Kate, checking her watch again – she won't have time to buy flowers either, and if she doesn't leave right now she'll be hosting her seductive dinner in soup-soaked leggings.

'You can't rush off, you've only just got here – it's incredibly discourteous.'

'I need to go now.'

'If you don't have the decency to stay today, don't bother coming tomorrow.'

'Don't be like that. I'll take this to the kitchen, and I'll see you tomorrow, OK? I'll make sure to tell Bernadette you want it piping hot.'

'Fresh bread wouldn't work anyway,' says Cecily, shoulders drooping in defeat. 'It's too heavy – you already have the potatoes with the chicken.'

'I'm going to go now.'

'You might as well surrender all your remaining dignity and beg the damn pigeon to love you.'

'Enjoy your hot soup,' says Kate, walking out of the room without turning back.

Kate takes the bowl to Bernadette, who promptly confirms Cecily's order: 'urgent and immediate soup, don't spare the horses.'

'Would you mind taking it in?' says Kate. 'I've had my fill of her for one day.'

Chapter Forty-one

THE BREAD HAS FALLEN by the wayside, as have the roses. Kate's had to lay the table and tidy up in a frog-like sideways squat-waddle due to the emergency Nair smeared on her bikini line.

Was she too mean to Cecily before? Or not mean enough? Rita's right, Kate does need to enforce better boundaries, certainly with that woman.

It's now nearly 8 p.m. The flat looks beautiful. Kate can't see it herself but Kate looks beautiful too, her hair loosely swept to one side, her cheeks flushed from the heat of the kitchen and residual irritation from earlier.

Nick texts to say he's ten minutes away and she feels the same surge of excitement she feels whenever she's about to see him. It's not butterflies – it's the anticipation of happiness which feels just as good as happiness – it's the thought of being reunited with her favourite person.

The doorbell rings. Nick's standing in his smart navy trousers and a crisp white shirt, shyly holding a bunch of pink peonies. He always has this sweet self-consciousness about him whenever he correctly pulls off anything vaguely romantic. Cara says Kate needs to train Nick, as clearly no woman ever has. This appals Kate, as it makes him sound like a dog – although Cara does treat men like basic animals and she does get results.

Nick's eyes sparkle at the sight of her, and the couple greet each other with a kiss and a look of mutual adoration. Kate feels like she's on a TV show – an almost-domestic goddess with three perfect scarlet fingernails and seven slightly smudgier ones, no longer smelling of prawns, opening the door for her handsome boyfriend on a perfect Saturday night. On the dining table candles are lit; the lights are dimmed. She's doing this dinner entirely by the book.

'Something smells amazing,' says Nick as Kate pours him a glass of white wine and he takes a seat on the edge of Rita's sofa. 'I'm scared of your mum's flat, everything's so pristine.'

'Expect an electric shock off that coffee table if you don't place your glass directly in the centre of that coaster,' says Kate, laughing as Nick flashes a grin and puts his glass straight on the table momentarily before gingerly placing it back on the coaster with a look of fear.

'So how was night shift?' she says, noticing the slight dark circles under his eyes. 'Was it full on?'

'Yeah, but fun,' says Nick, enthusiastically. 'We're doing the big switchover next month so I'm working through trials with the team. The infrastructure is so old, I can't believe they haven't had more system crashes.'

With any other boyfriend she might feel suspicious that these regular Friday all-nighters *at the office* were a cover-up for something more sinister, but she's seen for herself the way Nick's eyes light up when he talks data – it's the same way other men's do when they see a pair of black lacy knickers.

'Will you be working nights a lot between now and then?'

'Once or twice a week – but they pay overtime, and besides, I love it.'

'I think I might be jealous of your job.'

'Because I spend so much time there?'

'No, I meant I'm jealous of you. I wish I loved my job the way you love yours,' says Kate, pouring more wine and recalling her sense of anticlimax when she'd found out she was keeping her job.

'Fletchers pays the bills, though, doesn't it?' says Nick.

'That's about all it does. Anyway, are you hungry?'

'Hell, yeah. What's for dinner? That smell is making my stomach rumble.'

'It's a menu from the cookery book I was telling you about, the one Mrs Finn wrote. Scampi, then chicken – come, see,' says Kate, getting up and heading to the kitchen.

'Home-made scampi? Sounds incredible,' he says, eagerly following her through.

'I wish you'd been here to help undress these,' she says, flashing him a traumatised look as she shows him the prawns. 'Such hard work.'

'I love doing all that. We make a perfect team in the kitchen, don't we?'

'We do.'

'Cooking's way more fun when you're around. I really do miss you. A lot.'

'You don't need to miss me,' says Kate. 'I'm right here.'

He leans closer, then kisses her. He holds her face in his hands and their lips lock tight, a seal of intention. They stay standing in the kiss for a good five minutes before reluctantly she breaks away.

'Give us a hand with the deep-fat frying, then,' she says. 'I've got a fear of chip-pan fire after all those TV ads in the eighties, and Mum definitely won't forgive me if I burn the flat down. I can just hear her now. "Freud says there are no accidents".'

Nick laughs. 'You and your mum bicker all the time. You've done well to live together for so long.'

'I didn't have much choice!' says Kate, cursing the fact that she can't maintain the sweetness and light version of herself for more than five minutes. 'Right, you heat the oil, I'll manoeuvre these poor buggers into their oily grave. I can still see their beady eyes staring into my soul.'

Thought for Food was right, thinks Kate, as she lies on the sofa, Nick's head resting in her lap; you really *can* get what you want with a plateful of deep-fried golden morsels. And that chicken was so tender, and the sauce the type you only ever find in a good French restaurant, so intensely flavourful. The potatoes were nothing short of a miracle. The cake was the perfect ending – light, sweet and satisfying.

Nick has been attentive beyond measure, holding her hair back while she fried the prawns, stroking her knee while they were eating. His appetite was a pleasure to behold – he ate seconds of everything. He'd jokingly tried to feed her strawberries in a *Nine and a Half Weeks* style, before they'd collapsed into giggles. Now they're relaxing on the sofa with two glasses of Bourbon, just like they used to, except they're at Rita's, which makes it feel different and new and ever so slightly naughty.

Kate gently scratches the back of Nick's head. He purrs like a cat with pleasure and she leans down to kiss him. Her heart aches for all the unnecessary nonsense of the last few months, but sometimes you have to go through a storm to reach the shore. Who on earth said relationships should be easy? Finding an efficient, easy-to-clean garlic crusher isn't easy, why on earth would love be?

Nick undoes a couple of buttons in the middle of his shirt and taps his full stomach. 'That was the perfect dinner, those potatoes!'

'And you liked the cake? I changed her recipe slightly and she thought I shouldn't have.'

'Whose recipe?'

'Mrs Finn's.'

'The cake was fantastic. I probably shouldn't have had that second slice,' he says, grabbing her hand and laying it on his belly as if to feel a baby kick.

'I went to see her this morning.'

'Who?'

'Mrs Finn.'

'I thought you normally see her on Sundays?'

'I took her a cake. She said she had stomach ache.'

'After your cake? You haven't poisoned me because of France, have you? Was this your plan all along? Get me round here, you looking beautiful, then you Lucrezia Borgia me?'

'She barely touched her slice – but then I get a call this afternoon telling me I have to go there with emergency first-aid soup. I race to this particular deli in *Stamford Hill*, then to St John's Wood – and when, eventually, I get to her, she's fine, even perkier than usual, enlivened! I actually think she deliberately wanted to disrupt my day.'

Nick shakes his head in confusion. 'Why didn't you just say no to her in the first place?'

'I thought she was ill. Plus, if you met her, you'd understand – she's not the type you say no to. And also she's got no one else anymore – I feel bad for her.'

Nick shrugs. 'But she's not your responsibility.'

'I guess it's never the wrong thing to be kind, though.' Not that Kate was particularly kind today, but she doesn't mention that part, nor the reason why Cecily might want to sabotage Kate's plans. 'You never knew your grandparents, did you?'

'Dad was estranged from his parents, and Mum's folks died when she was still young. I think that's what turned her to religion.'

'Weird, isn't it? How tragedy makes people either have more faith, or none whatsoever.'

'I was talking about this to my shrink the other day.'

'About religion?'

'About Mum – he said having a parent as religious as she was is like having a parent who's an alcoholic. They're both addicted to something outside the family.' His brow creases as he tries to explain the theory. 'So she was addicted to Jesus, not vodka, but he says it amounts to the same sort of thing.'

'Interesting. You're still getting a lot out of therapy, then?'

'Honestly,' he says, beaming, 'it's the best thing I've ever done.' He gazes at her and takes a deep, contented sigh, then grabs her hand. 'Kate – thank you for being so patient and standing by me through all this.' He squeezes her hand and she can see there are tears in his eyes. 'We have such a good thing, don't we?'

'There was nothing ever wrong with us, Nick. I could see on holiday you were freaking out about being so close to someone. At least I think that was it, wasn't it?'

He nods eagerly. 'I couldn't put it into words because I didn't have the language, but I've never been as close to anyone as I am to you, and it scared me.'

'Nick, I have to be honest. *I'm* scared you'll have another wobble.'

'That won't happen, Kate, it won't. Give me another chance. I promise there'll be no more wobbles. I can't imagine anyone I'd rather share my life with.'

Kate's heart throbs with happiness. 'Apart from Laura Marling. Or Kristen Stewart,' she says, running her finger along his unruly right eyebrow.

'Or a life-size high-end Swedish robot sex doll, but yes, you're my fourth-best option in the whole world. No one's ever loved me the way you love me, you are wonderful.'

And she smiles, and thinks: maybe I am.

It is 3.40 a.m. and they lie in Kate's bed on the edge of sleep.

'I've forgotten how perfectly we fit together,' says Nick, stroking Kate's hair, then pulling her closer.

She nods, eyes closed, breathing in the familiar smell of him. She's missed this more than anything – not the sex so much as this bit afterwards, the gentle drifting into oblivion, holding hands, their fingers tightly entwined.

'So . . . how do you feel about trading this admittedly lovely bed in your mum's walk-in wardrobe for the left half of mine? Are you still up for that?'

'You know what, Nick? I think I am,' she says, laughing as she looks up at his radiant smile and meets it with her own.

He squeezes her hand tightly and her heart feels like it's expanding with love. 'When shall we do it?'

'Whenever, soon, I don't mind,' says Kate, struck by a sudden exhaustion from all the hoping and waiting and finally now the relief of getting back what she's been aching for. 'Mum's in Lanzarote for a few weeks at the start of December, so I'll have this place to myself . . .'

'And there's the big birthday . . .'

'The big birthday – yep, that is still happening.' Thank goodness at least now she'll be arriving at that daunting destination with Nick safely by her side.

'And then my project finishes the following week, so shall we say the weekend after that?'

'Sure, sounds good.' Kate nods in contentment, and within moments she has fallen into a deep and blissful sleep.

Chapter Forty-two

Kᴀᴛᴇ ᴡᴀᴋᴇs ᴡɪᴛʜ Nick's arm wrapped around her waist, the tops of his feet resting under the soles of hers. She breathes a deep sigh and her whole body relaxes onto the mattress. Every morning since France she's woken with an uncomfortable tightness in her chest. She'd taken it for sadness, but now she understands it was fear – fear of facing the day, or rather of having to face herself. That feeling isn't there anymore – it's been replaced by one of peace and contentment now she's safely back beside Nick, where she belongs.

Nick is fast asleep, so she gently reaches over to her bedside table and picks up *Thought for Food*. Last night's dinner could not have been better. It was so simple, yet came together in a way far greater than the sum of its parts. Actually, those potatoes weren't simple, but they were worth the effort. It would never have occurred to her to pair them with chicken. She wonders how old Samuel enjoyed his meal. She wonders how Cecily felt the next morning, her father interrogating her – that immense, terrible pressure to shed the burden of singledom.

She flicks to 'Brunch for Newlyweds':

Of all the days that's in the week
I dearly love but one day,
And that's the day that comes betwixt
The Saturday and Monday.

Henry Carey

Aim: to combine the delights of a lazy Sunday morning with the pleasure of an early luncheon, thus leaving a long afternoon for any pursuits the lovebirds care to follow.

The menu itself is not to Kate's taste – kidneys flambé – in fact, she can't imagine anything worse. Besides, whatever they do for breakfast, she has to see Cecily later on, which is the second-to-last thing she'd like to do after flambéing a kidney.

She rests the book back on the side table, resettles the duvet over their feet and happily dozes off again.

She's woken a few hours later by a light scratching noise. It's Nick propped up in bed doing the Listener with his favourite crossword pencil.

'Why are you looking so pleased with yourself?' she says, running her nails lightly over his tummy.

He shivers with delight, then rests the crossword on his side table. 'Just happy to have my girl back by my side.'

'What do you fancy today?'

'Other than you?'

'Cheeseball.'

'I thought we could take a walk, it's beautiful out.'

'How do you know?' says Kate, looking at the still-drawn curtains.

'I've been up already. I've done all the washing-up, and coffee's brewing.'

'Ah, Nick,' she says, leaning in to kiss him.

'It was the least I could do after that amazing supper,' he says, stroking her hair. 'We could walk through Regent's Park to the farmers' market in Marylebone, grab a posh bacon sandwich, then buy food for later? How do you feel about roast beef for supper with all the trimmings, and we could watch *The Lego Movie* again?'

'Yes, except for that last bit.'

'*Lego Batman*?'

'See previous answer for details . . .'

'OK, then, one of your grown-up films – *Chinatown*?'

'Even though it has actual humans in it, not little yellow plastic toys?'

'Sure.'

'Excellent. Oh, but I have to see Mrs Finn at 4 p.m.'

'You saw her yesterday.'

'I know, but Sunday's our day – and also we sort of had a row. Do you want to come with me for a cup of tea? She's very interesting, and she's going to tell me all about some trip to Hawaii she and Samuel went on for her seventieth. I'd really love you to meet her.'

Nick shakes his head hesitantly. 'I do have work to do, if I'm not with you . . .'

'Just for an hour?'

'Another time.'

'Oh, OK. I'll see her, then head over to yours.'

'That sounds like a plan,' he says, taking a deep breath and letting out a loud sigh of contentment. 'There is one thing I'd like to do before any of that,' he says, grinning, as he gently rolls on top of her and nudges her thighs apart. 'One very important thing . . .'

She'd have happily stayed in bed with Nick all day, but Rita is due back with Patrick at 5 p.m., then there's Cecily, of course, and besides, it is the most beautiful of days.

It's been an exceptionally dry and mild October. The leaves have only now fallen, and each one seems perfectly intact as though preserved in an album, every last vein traceable on the surface.

As Kate and Nick walk through Regent's Park, their feet nudge through the carpet of leaves, making a pleasing shoosh, shoosh sound – like a steel brush on a drum. Hands held tightly, they take turns pointing out sights each more breathtaking than the last. The highest branches are an explosion of fireworks – crimson, orange and lime, a blaze of fiery glory. Leaves of glowing amber, an egg-yolk yellow tree! The beauty stops Kate's breath. High above, a jumbo jet scores a crisp white line across the blue, blue sky reminding her of an airline poster from the eighties when flying still seemed exotic. Nick is mildly obsessing about the proportionality of yellow to russet leaves, convinced there's some mathematical principle behind it.

He grabs her arm tighter with a smile that seems to say: I'm sorry, I love you. You're mine and I'm yours always.

'Are you thinking about bacon?' says Kate, laughing.

'Nope, just happy . . . it's because I'm with you. I know that now.'

As long as the sky stays this exact shade of blue, the world is a marvel and anything is possible.

Kate can barely drag herself from Nick's side as 4 p.m. approaches. She considers calling Lauderdale to say she's not feeling too well herself. But then she pictures the glorious shafts of winter sunlight making the entire park look saturated in colour, the crisp, clear air filling her lungs. Then she thinks of Cecily in that stuffy book-lined cell.

Lauderdale is busy today, and as Kate walks through the dining room she sees they're holding a tea party. Bessie Burbridge, dressed immaculately in a red skirt suit, sits in front of a large birthday cake with 'Ninety-Two' written on it in chocolate icing. She's surrounded by a couple in their sixties, a dozen other residents and a handful of smiling staff. Kate stops to say hello, then is cajoled into having a slice of cake, and by the time she's had a lovely chat with Bessie's daughter, who was an English professor at the same university Kate briefly attended, it's 4.20 p.m. She excuses herself and heads to Cecily's door, but when she knocks she's met with silence. She knocks more loudly, and when there's no response she cautiously pokes her head round the door and her heart lurches.

Cecily sits slumped in her chair, her head fallen unnaturally forward, her legs rigid at an awkward Kerplunk angle. Kate notices how desperately frail Cecily's legs are, as fragile and knobbly as Twiglets in sheepskin slippers. She rushes over and gently touches Cecily's shoulder, then again more firmly.

Cecily jolts up, muttering something incomprehensible in Swedish, then jolts up again, before slowly opening her eyes and turning to Kate in confusion.

'Mrs Finn, everything's fine, it's only me, it's Kate.'

Cecily inhales with a snort, then another. 'Didn't your parents ever teach you to knock?'

'Can I get you some water?'

Cecily opens her mouth and a dry, glottal noise comes out. 'Tea.'

Heart still racing, Kate heads to the kitchen. She grabs a couple of plain shortbreads. She should have bought a gift for Cecily at the farmers' market, but she'd been having such an indulgent day the thought hadn't occurred to her.

Kate takes the tea back to Cecily and settles on her usual chair.

'I don't like being woken,' says Cecily. 'You should have knocked.'

'I did.'

'I'm in a bad mood with you.'

For a change, thinks Kate as she pours the tea and smiles patiently.

'I suppose the dinner was a success?' says Cecily, grabbing the cup in both hands, her lips quivering with rage.

'The menu was great, thank you. Those potatoes in particular—'

'Where's my book?'

Kate's hand flies to her mouth. 'I didn't bring it. Sorry, I didn't realise you were serious.'

'I haven't forgiven you for yesterday.'

Kate lets out a sigh. 'Which bit?'

'You know full well.'

'No, actually, I don't. Do you mean the bit where I went considerably out of my way to buy you your soup? Or the bit where I brought you home-made cake and you turned your nose up at it?'

'I didn't realise it was *such* an ordeal, coming to see me, such a terrible inconvenience.'

'Didn't you?' says Kate, and instantly regrets saying it.

'Why have you bothered coming today?'

'I was looking forward to hearing about you dancing with Samuel on the beach in Hawaii.'

'With Samuel? What?' says Cecily in outrage. 'I'm not telling you anything more about my life. You don't actually care about me. Really, why on earth *are* you here?'

'No idea,' says Kate, whose vow to stay calm isn't working. 'Blind, stupid loyalty.'

'Misplaced loyalty, that's the first intelligent thing you've ever said,' says Cecily. 'You don't need to worry about coming to see me anymore because I do not want visitors, I never did. I want to be left in peace.'

'Mrs Finn, if you're trying to push me away by being mean—'

Cecily screeches with annoyance. 'Go away, dreadful girl.'

'Mrs Finn, I thought we'd moved past all this nonsense.'

'I'm not moving anywhere. Go. I don't want you here, ever again.'

Kate's face is burning with fury as she walks out of the room. She's gone from feeling terror that Mrs Finn was dead to wanting her – well, not dead of course, but definitely out of her life.

She heads out into the street. The sky is darkening and without the sun it's distinctly chilly. Why is she even surprised? Cecily is queen of holding a grudge: she hates Maud because of a single hand of bridge played years ago, she hates poor Bessie for being too nice!

Kate was having the perfect Sunday and now the old bat has made her feel guilty, humiliated, worried and angry – feelings that are in danger of ruining her day. She won't have it.

She heads to the tube station bound for Nick's. She must speak to him about Christmas, whether he wants to do something just the two of them, or whether he can handle Rita and her acolytes.

Cecily was once a young woman in love and planning her future. Now she has nothing to plan for. She has nowhere to go; her life is tiny. Kate has tried to coax her out, but she's failed.

Kate doesn't want to think these thoughts – far too depressing. Instead, she remembers the walk this afternoon and it starts to bring back cheer.

Then she recalls another walk she took with Nick, nearly two years ago now. It had been their second date and when she'd met him in the street, her heart had sunk – he'd seemed too keen, he was rather sweaty – and suddenly she'd thought he was an awkward geek, not nearly as handsome as her ex-boyfriend Toby, who had loved the same books as Kate and was far more her type. But then she and Nick had walked over to the secret garden in Hampstead and Nick had talked about his love of Eddie Izzard – he could recite entire routines – and he'd been so enthusiastic and funny (even if they were Eddie Izzard's jokes) that when he'd made her stop walking so that he could kiss her – that first kiss so nervous and sweet – she'd realised she'd been foolish and shallow to think that sweatiness, or the books you do or don't read, actually mattered.

He'd kissed her, to 'claim her', as he'd later confessed, and even though the kiss wasn't the greatest, his sweetness had won her over. Sweetness, and the strong sense Kate had of wanting to be on his side. Something about his innocent enthusiasm had brought out an extreme tenderness in her. He'd kissed her, she'd kissed him and she'd never looked back, until, of course, that horrible, stupid incident in France.

It has been a colossal challenge these last few months, having to be two different people – the surface Kate who's pretended she's OK with The Wobble, who's pretended she's empathetic and relaxed enough to inhabit the suffocating fog of insecurity, all the while struggling under the immense burden of hope she's lugged on her back the whole time; and the real Kate, desperate to know whether she is loved or not – and if not, then needing to rush to a faraway cave to scream about it.

It's pretty exhausting having to be a whole person, let alone two, and so for the relief of being able to just be one version of herself again – as much as for the knowledge that Nick does really love her – she is truly grateful.

And Cecily . . . well, Kate has tried, very hard, but Cecily's just one of those people who doesn't want anyone to care about her, and there's nothing Kate can do to fix that.

Chapter Forty-three

Project: Fletchers' Special Selection
Our growers have worked with our farming partners to select premium heirloom vegetables to delight customers, at great-value price points.

KATE IS SITTING AT her desk on Tuesday afternoon, staring at her inbox in dismay as she scrolls through her new brief:

First category roll-out will be root vegetables, specifically carrots. The following varieties offer margins of 40 per cent or greater: Early Horn, Golden Ball, Little Finger, Purple 68. However, Head of Produce is concerned these names sound pornographic. Therefore the first premium variety for BOGOF will be Tendersweet. Requirements: headline alliteration, plus copy for front of pack. Serving suggestions as per standard: wash before serving.

So much for Devron's 'exciting creative opportunities'. She can just picture the scorn on Cecily's face.

Kate's been in back-to-back meetings since 8 a.m. The decision to change KIPPER to CAPER remains unresolved, and after a three-hour nail-biting debate during which Kate pondered whether her colleagues would notice if she slipped from the room and replaced herself with a giant Alexa or some mist, it has been decided that the decision needs to be escalated to stakeholder level, and has been fed up the chain and thus taken off everyone's to-do lists for now. She was then dragged into Mistakes: We've Made a Few – a 'wash-up' meeting which was an attempt to apportion blame for the failure of the Summer of Sausages promotion. Watching grown men argue wholeheartedly about the failure of their sausages lost its comedic value for Kate years ago.

She'll treat herself to a cappuccino and a Twirl, that'll reinvigorate her while she counts down the hours till she sees Nick tonight. Tuesdays are notoriously the worst day of the week – you expect Mondays to be bad, Wednesdays you're already at hump day, but Tuesdays? Famously nothing to recommend them.

She heads off to the canteen, returns to her desk and resumes her stand-off with her computer screen. The caffeine and the chocolate are gone in minutes, along with their temporary high.

Tasty, tantalising Tendersweets . . . tedious, tiresome Tendersweets . . .

Heirloom carrots are still just carrots. Carrots are crunchy. Carrots are good for you. Sometimes carrots are even yellow or purple (not the Tendersweets, mind you) – but they're still just carrots. The night she'd written her submission for her job she'd felt inspired in a way she's never felt in her actual job, not once. If she has to spend another year, no, scrap that, another week

279

having to pretend to care about carrots, she might lose her mind.

It's really only now, now that Nick is securely back in place and space has been freed up in her head again, that she can focus. These last few months at work, she's been swept along on a tide of ego and principle. She's been competing against Annalex, for what? Every time Cecily made a snide comment about her job, Kate knew in her gut that she was right, and now Kate is calm, confident and strong again, she can see it so clearly: she's made a mistake. She had an opportunity to open the world up for herself – to take a chance on a different type of career – and instead she clung to this job because she was scared, because she had no real concept of her possibilities.

She starts to feel a light panic in her chest but closes her eyes and forces herself to inhale deeply. She thinks of Cecily, all the places she visited, the adventures she and Samuel had – Cecily made the absolute most of her life. Kate can't bear the thought of looking back when she's ninety-seven on a career devoted to carrots and Annalex and oh, so many petty tediums.

Kate clicks onto the original email about redundancy and rereads the terms and deadlines. Even last week Devron confirmed they could still take the cash option up until December. She hasn't had a new contract yet; that will surely work in her favour. She picks up the phone and calls Kavita, who briefs her on exactly what she needs to say to HR, which sinister buzz words to sprinkle in, what tone to take if they start being obstructive.

Then she calls HR, and after a thirty-minute pro-tracted 'hypothetical' conversation, she hangs up with a surge of excitement and heads off to find Devron.

'You've got to be kidding,' says Devron, his smile rapidly fading as he begins to understand she is not.

Kate can afford to be gracious because she's just won herself five months of freedom. 'Devron, I really appreciate everything Fletchers has done for me, but I've worked here longer than I haven't. It's time to move on.'

'Can't you just stay until Christmas? Give Annalex some support in her new role?'

'That won't work for me, I'm afraid.'

'You must have something else lined up,' he says, sourly.

Kate shakes her head. 'Not yet . . .'

'Huh. November's never a good time to be job-hunting.'

'Then I guess I'll have a few lie-ins,' says Kate, smiling at the thought.

'Quitting without a job to go to? Pretty bold move. I didn't think you had it in you.'

It's not a compliment but Kate decides to take it as one. 'Thanks. You know what? Neither did I.'

As she walks out of the revolving door into the cold, clear evening, she takes her phone from her pocket. The first person she'd like to tell is Cecily; for once, Kate thinks she'd be proud, but Cecily refuses to take her call, so instead she phones Nick, who insists on cooking her a celebratory steak-and-chips dinner.

All those times in the past when Kate had commended herself for staying put when she wasn't enjoying herself – that terrible nineties gig at Wembley Arena, that appalling four-hour Japanese art-house film at the BFI, innumerable bad dates with men who only talked about themselves. All those books she'd disliked from the first paragraph but persevered with because the *Guardian* had called them 'exquisite' – when they should have said 'pretentious'. People, places, things she'd stuck with that hadn't improved – that had ultimately proved a waste of her time.

She laughs as she realises that she is now the quitter. It's taken her a long time, but she's finally come to understand that sometimes walking away is the right thing to do. It shows strength and courage, it is not an admission of failure. Or rather, an admission of failure is not really failure; it's the first step towards the future.

PART FOUR

Choosing well is one of the most difficult things in a difficult world . . . whether applied to food, drink, companionships or occupations.

Agnes Jekyll, *A Little Dinner Before the Play*

Chapter Forty-four

KATE HASN'T FELT this good in months. Her fortieth is fast approaching, but she and Nick are firmly back on track – not long now till she moves in. Her new part-time job is surprisingly enjoyable. And tonight she's about to meet Bailey, who's joining her for one of Cara's free-food-and-drink events, and even though the food sounds suspect, surely the booze can't be?

'You look amazing,' says Bailey, greeting Kate at the entrance to the food hall with a huge hug. 'I haven't seen you for a month and now you look ten years younger. Are you sure you haven't been to Brazil for a face lift?'

'What, blow all my redundancy on a birthday present to myself? Fat chance. No, I've been washing up coffee cups and bingeing on Netflix with Nick. It's hardly been the most glamorous of times.'

'Well, it suits you, you're glowing.'

'That's probably irritation, Cara's an hour late to her own event,' says Kate, scanning the room for a glimpse of her friend. 'And surely *A Night Celebrating Dairy and Gluten-Free Food* is an oxymoron?'

'I haven't seen Cara since that taco festival you took me to in Battersea Park.'

'Has it been that long? That was before I even met Nick, that's nearly three years ago. Well, she's still as blunt as ever,' says Kate, laughing.

'Why did she choose Deptford for this party? It's nowhere near anywhere,' says Bailey, who rarely complains about anything.

'Deptford's the new Peckham, or is it the new Dalston? One of the two – it must be true, it says so on her press release,' says Kate, taking the crumpled page from her pocket.

'We're too old for the old Deptford let alone the new,' says Bailey, casting her gaze around the aeroplane-hangar-sized space. It's packed with dozens of food stands adorned with fluorescent graffitied awnings, and mobbed with twenty-somethings drinking cocktails out of Mason jars, nodding along to a heavy bass soundtrack.

'*London's finest dairy and gluten-free pop-ups under one roof*,' reads Kate. '*Bao, bun, poke, pho—*'

'Sounds like Teletubbies.'

'*Bringing global street-food highlights from Sri Lanka to San Francisco—*' She tuts noisily. 'Cara should have asked me to write this copy. San Francisco's a city, Sri Lanka's a country, you shouldn't mix the two.'

'What's the capital of Sri Lanka, then, smarty-pants?'

'Ooh, Colombo, isn't it? Like Peter Falk – hold on, I'll check,' says Kate, getting her phone out. 'Oh no, I'm definitely pronouncing this wrong but it's Sri Jaya-warden-epura Kotte.'

'Columbo's spelled with a "u", anyway,' says Bailey. 'The detective, that is, not the city.'

'If you can find one man in this place without pretentious facial hair, I'll give you a fiver,' says Kate, surveying the group of men in front of them queueing for brisket, all of whom sport frizzy, mid-length beards or spiky waxed moustaches. 'Adam doesn't have a stupid beard, does he?'

'He has delightful stubble on his very square jaw. Did I tell you he's taking me to Kew Gardens next weekend? There's apparently an amazing gallery there, and he's really into art.'

'I cannot wait to meet this man. Meanwhile, I bet Cara's in the back office with the Great Dane. Speak of the devil, your ears must be burning, where have you been? You're an hour late.'

'Guys, crazy night,' says Cara, sweeping over, kissing Kate hello and giving Bailey a hug. 'I had to do a meet-and-greet with the bloggers, entitled bunch of twerps – "Where's my goody bag?", "Don't you know I'm London's premier kale influencer and burger curator?" . . .'

'What's a burger curator?' says Bailey.

'She is,' says Cara, pointing discreetly towards a stick-thin blonde surrounded by a group of over-coiffed men engrossed in their iPhones.

'Wow, she might be curating burgers but she sure ain't eating them,' says Kate, counting the girl's ribs on display.

'You don't get a million followers on Instagram by being honest,' says Cara, checking her phone. 'Shit. I've got twenty minutes before I have to greet the grime artist's entourage.'

'It gets worse,' says Kate.

'Grime?' says Bailey.

'And punishment . . . Cara, isn't there a bar area for OAPs like us that has actual seating?'

'Oh, come to the VIP cocktail area! It's being hosted by Friko.'

Friko? mouths Bailey.

No idea, mouths Kate.

'Can he make me a Piña Colada?' says Bailey.

'Will there definitely be seats?' says Kate.

They head up a rickety staircase to a small bar area done up like a speakeasy. They settle at a table and Cara orders three Negronis which arrive 'deconstructed': the gin served in a giant syringe, the vermouth and Campari as two giant ice cubes and the orange peel in the form of a paper square like an acid tab.

'You look fantastic,' says Cara, appraising Kate. 'Have you changed your hair?'

'Nope, I'm just not miserable anymore,' says Kate, smiling.

'You're back with him, then,' says Cara, taking one of the ice cubes from the dish and sniffing it suspiciously.

'Yes, I am. I cooked him a lovely dinner a month ago and it's been brilliant ever since. You know, I think the break's made us closer. Nick's really opening up,' says Kate, noticing the look Cara flashes Bailey. 'Cara, it would be nice if you could be happy for me.'

'I'm happy that you're happy.'

'Why do you say it like that?'

Cara gives Kate a stare as if surely it's obvious.

Kate takes a deep breath. 'How's the Dane?'

'Dumped him, two weeks ago.'

'I thought you were moving in with him?'

'You find out a lot about a person when you move in with them.'

'Yes, which is why it's generally best to get to know them first – what was the problem, wet towels left on the bed? Cupboards full of Pot Noodles?'

Cara looks at Kate as if she's deranged. 'He's a Harvard-educated Danish banker, not a student.'

'So what was the problem?'

'He's in the gym at 5 a.m. and at his desk by 6 a.m. for when trading starts. He likes to be in bed on weeknights by 9 p.m., *asleep*. 9 p.m.? I haven't even put on my make-up by 9 p.m.'

'Couldn't you have found a compromise?' says Bailey.

'Try wearing less eyeshadow?' says Kate, laughing. 'That's surely a small sacrifice to make for true love. You dumped the last bloke because he didn't work hard *enough*, and that music producer before that because he never went to the gym.'

'Pete? He had zero upper-body definition.'

'Outrage, I hope they've locked him up and thrown away the key,' says Kate, turning to Bailey with a raised brow.

'Kate: I know what I want and *I'm* not the type who's willing to compromise.'

Kate looks at Bailey again but Bailey maintains a diplomatic neutral gaze into the distance.

'You're saying Nick is a compromise?' says Kate.

'I think we can all agree he's punching above his weight,' says Cara, picking up the syringe and squirting alcohol briskly onto her tongue.

'Cara, I'm forty in three weeks. Am I supposed to hold out for mythical perfection forever?'

'Forty, hon – not ninety.'

'Look, Nick's not perfect, but neither am I.'

Cara shakes her head as if the air is too full of craziness to breathe, rather than simply full of smoked Cosmopolitan fumes. 'My dad left Mum for his secretary after thirty years of marriage and four kids. When he came crawling back, Mum wouldn't open the door to him.'

'What on earth has that got to do with me?'

'You deserve better, so stop underselling yourself.'

'I'm sorry about your mum, Cara, but Nick didn't even cheat on me.'

'Exactly, that's worse! He dumped you for *no one*.'

Bailey, having chewed her vermouth ice cube, looks down at her syringe nervously.

'At least if Nick had left you for the office slapper like Bailey's husband did, then it wouldn't be because he didn't want *you*.'

'Wow, thanks,' says Kate, her shoulders dropping. 'And really sensitive – I don't think Bailey felt too marvellous when Tom left her for that particular skank-bag, did you?'

Bailey, who is in the middle of injecting more alcohol into her mouth, shakes her head violently.

'And anyway, for the hundredth time, Nick did *not* dump me, it was a time out.'

'Semantics, it was so a dumping.'

'Cara, you do sound pretty harsh sometimes,' says Bailey.

'Harsh? Me? I've got the biggest heart of anyone.'

'No, you've got the biggest mouth,' says Kate. 'It's not the same organ at all.'

'Don't you remember how devastated I was when Michael Jackson died? And George Michael. I cried for nearly a whole week.'

'Yup, dead pop stars named Michael – then you're pure compassion,' mutters Kate. 'When Michael Bublé dies, perhaps you'll compose a requiem.'

'Cara, Kate and Nick are happy,' says Bailey.

'I do want you to be happy,' says Cara, rubbing Kate's shoulder.

'And I'll be delirious if you keep your opinions to yourself,' says Kate, shrugging her off. 'You're going to have to be polite to him at my fortieth.'

'I'm always charming to everyone, that's my job. What's the plan again?'

'I'm cooking for you lot on the Friday. Bailey's bringing Adam, Pete will be there with his child bride, and Kavita with her husband, Dom. Cara, you can bring whatever hapless beefcake you happen to chance upon in the meantime.'

'Well, I'll bring pink champagne, seeing as it's your ninetieth and all. Right – I'm going for a fag, come.'

'I've stopped smoking.'

'What? You'd only just started again.'

'I don't feel like it now I'm back to my normal self again.'

'Look, Kate, sorry if you think I'm being harsh, but you know I'm always honest. There's someone better for you out there, someone who cherishes you from the start, someone less messed up. Or – just you. Have you ever considered *you* are better for you? Just think about that. Nick's not a project. You don't get brownie points for fixing him.'

'I'm not doing it for brownie points. I love Nick.'

'Oooh, can we please *get* some brownies or something that tastes nice?' says Bailey, wrinkling her nose. 'I think they've put Windolene in this syringe.'

'I think they're doing lentil brownies down in the sweets section,' says Cara.

'Ooh, yippee,' says Kate, clapping her hands. 'How to make a brownie completely undesirable.'

'You could have had a stall here if you'd wanted,' says Cara. 'We had a drop-out last week, I should have told you.'

'Me? What would I have made?'

'Those lush brownies with the cream cheese you made for my birthday? Or that amazing spicy cornbread?'

'Yep, vital ingredients being gluten, dairy and butter.'

'You should get involved in pop-ups now you've got time on your hands.'

'I haven't got *much* time, it's pretty full on at the coffee shop.'

'I'm so impressed you actually decided to leave Fletchers,' says Cara. 'I hope they gave you a good send-off.'

'Are you joking?' says Kate, laughing. 'A stale Bobby the Butterfly cake, two bottles of warm Prosecco and a surly Devron refusing to make eye contact. He was so ungracious. It's weird – the minute you get some distance you start seeing how taken for granted you were. He was trying to make me feel grateful for having that job, telling me *I* was the lucky one – when they were the ones getting *so* much more out of the situation than I was!'

'Hmmm, no parallels between your work life and your personal life there, then,' says Cara, chuckling.

'*What?*' says Kate, shaking her head in annoyance. 'Cara, go and have your fag – in fact, have two. Seriously.' She turns to Bailey. 'Do I have a sign on my head saying "Rude bitches, please attack"?'

'You can be mean to me for a minute if you like, Cara – give Kate a short break?'

'Kate doesn't cope well with short breaks, do you, honey?' says Cara, winking.

'Remind me, why are we friends again?'

'I know you secretly love it or you wouldn't put up with it.'

Chapter Forty-five

AFTER SEVERAL DAYS of unemployment, hitting the snooze button and enjoying the lie-ins, Kate had realised that having no job but no sense of purpose, particularly as the weather turned colder, wasn't actually much fun. After five days of absolute freedom, she'd found herself feeling a little bored, despondent and at risk of getting hooked on Jeremy Kyle, so she'd left the flat and strolled down to Aposta for a coffee and an almond croissant.

She'd settled into a comfy leather armchair and had started to think about her next move. Everyone around her has been making such a big deal about her birthday. Forty feels like such a significant landmark, but surely it's arbitrary in the scheme of things. Rita keeps offering her Botox, Kavita's been sending her links to jobs, suggesting she's better off applying while her CV still says she's thirty-something. Kate doesn't want to panic herself back into corporate life simply because of a date on her birth certificate. Is the clock still ticking if she chooses to put on headphones?

It was quiet in the café that day and William, the handsome silver-haired owner, had come over to chat.

Kate had mentioned her love of his pastries, and then her recent redundancy. He'd asked if she was interested in covering some shifts in the run-up to Christmas, as one of his team had broken her wrist and currently wasn't too handy with the coffee machine.

Kate hadn't worked on a shop floor since her earliest days at Fletchers – and a mean, small voice in her head had said, 'Forty-year-old waitress?' But then another voice had said, 'Forty and no job at all?' and that had seemed more persuasive. Besides, it would be sociable, she could do with the cash – and it would kill time between now and the New Year, when she'll be living with Nick and can start planning her future properly.

It's only been three weeks, and of course it's just temporary, but so far so good. The free coffee is amazing, the team are friendly – no one seems to want to stab anyone else in the back with a teaspoon. At Fletchers, if someone came up to Kate's desk, it was invariably with a problem. When customers approach Kate at Aposta, they're usually quite cheery, and by the time she's served them a buttery, flaky Danish or a cheese toastie and a strong flat white, they're in an even better mood. When she leaves at the end of the day, she gets to take home any leftover bread and pastries, rather than a bagful of fear about the seven things that might go wrong with the in-store turkey dangler roll-out.

Even when she's scraping off burnt milk from the frothing nozzle, or grappling with a particularly heavy bin liner, there isn't a moment when she regrets quitting Fletchers – she only regrets staying so long. Her body feels different, lighter. The everyday anxiety she used to feel as she approached the revolving doors at Fletchers has turned into a low-level tingle of excitement each morning as she pulls open the glass door to Aposta, ties her hair back and gets ready to meet the new day.

Chapter Forty-six

'THAT WAS AMAZING,' says Kate, looking down at her empty plate where all that remains of Nick's epic bacon-cheeseburger is a small puddle of ketchup.

'The beef is better on the barbecue,' he says apologetically, staring out at the November downpour. 'But at least the griddle pan gives chargrill lines; I reckon it was eighty-five per cent as good.'

'Not eighty-six per cent?' says Kate, ruffling his hair as he smiles in contentment.

'We should investigate making our own brioche buns in the new year – what do you think?'

'I think I love this burger the way it is.'

'But it's not perfect, the bun isn't—'

'I think you should speak to your shrink about your perfectionism,' says Kate, laughing.

'I haven't made burgers since the summer,' he says, clearing the plates away. 'That feels like so long ago.'

'Yeah, well, we've had a rather turbulent second half to the year.'

'But we're good now, aren't we?' says Nick, smiling as they snuggle down on the sofa together.

'We are,' says Kate, pouring more wine and stroking his hand that's resting on her shoulder.

'I had a beer with Rob the other day,' says Nick, reaching for the TV remote control.

'Oh? How's he doing?' says Kate, though she couldn't care less.

'Struggling a bit. He's been sleeping on a mate's sofa since he moved out of Tasha's, and he's hurt his back.'

'Ah well, he probably should have thought about that before he shagged the pub Petri dish. Anyway, let's not talk about him. What shall we do this weekend?'

'Friday I've got night shift, but other than that I'm easy.'

'I'll probably do the Saturday shift at the café, but Saturday night we could make that Nigella meatball recipe? Columbia Road on Sunday morning, then come back and clear some space in your wardrobe for my things?'

'You don't want to try and see the old lady again?'

'I've called her half a dozen times in the last month – she won't take my calls. Quite frankly, why I'm stalking her when she owes *me* an apology – by the way, do you think that print I bought at Spitalfields would look good in your hallway?'

'Which bit of wall?'

'I'll show you.'

While they're out in the hallway Kate's phone rings, but by the time she gets to it the caller's leaving a message.

'Oh. Shit,' says Kate when she sees the caller ID. She listens to the message – it's a long one – frowns, then her eyebrows raise and she smiles and nods.

'Everything OK?' says Nick.

'I think so. Apparently, Mrs Finn's been in hospital.'

'Oh. What for?'

'Being ninety-seven, by the sounds of it. She had a chest infection. They were worried it might turn into pneumonia so they took her to the Whittington for a few nights. I bet she hated that.'

'Is she still there?'

'This was two weeks ago,' says Kate, biting her lip. 'She's back, apparently, she's fine, and it's her birthday on Sunday. Normally they give each resident a tea party. She's obviously having none of that, but she told Mrs Gaffney to tell me.'

'Presumably that means she wants to see you.'

'The ice is thawing . . . OK, forget Sunday's plans, I might need you to help me make her a present.'

'Hmm. Do you think she'd like a bespoke computer programme?'

'I was thinking something a little more edible.'

'A burger?'

'A *fiskepudding*.'

'*Fiskepudding*? Cute name for a baby. What is a *fiskepudding*?'

'I still don't know. Some sort of Scandinavian fish mousse? Anyway, it's one of her favourites. We can cook it, and I'll make a little white flag to stick on top.'

'You're on.'

Chapter Forty-seven

'Is THE BIRTHDAY GIRL in?' says Kate, poking her head round the door to find Cecily hunched in her chair. Cecily looks frailer than a month ago, her cheekbones more prominent, the skin at her temples so thin Kate can trace every vein.

'You are who . . .?' says Cecily regally.

'I'm here, and tea's on its way – that's all that matters. How are you, Mrs Finn? I've missed you.'

'Still not dead,' says Cecily with lips that are pinched but struggling not to smile.

'Sorry to hear you were in hospital.'

'Nothing wrong with me, just a small cough,' says Cecily, squinting at the Tupperware in Kate's hand. 'What's in there?'

'A birthday treat.'

'A little premature, isn't it? My birthday's in May.'

Kate pauses, then laughs. 'Silly me. Oh well, I'll save the card, I was going to say your birthday's two weeks before mine but it would appear Mrs Gaffney has got her dates wrong,' she says, presenting the Tupperware's contents to Cecily, then taking a packet of crackers from her bag and spreading a few generously.

Cecily looks at the *fiskepudding*, then up at Kate, then back at the *fiskepudding*.

'Made with pike and plenty of salt, Mrs Finn – not a mackerel in sight.'

'Oh,' says Cecily, swallowing hard. 'That's . . . yes, well, I suspect that'll be preferable to whatever filth that woman has planned.'

'And I brought you a toffee cream cake – I know you're partial to a toffee or two. I've started working at a coffee shop that sells the most delicious cakes.'

'You've done what?'

'Yup, it's been a busy month.'

'Instead of the carrots or as well as the carrots?'

'No – no more carrots: I have to admit, you were right about the day job.'

'I was right about the other things too.'

'Mrs Finn,' says Kate, ignoring the comment, 'I do have one small favour to ask.'

'From *me*?'

'Could you carry on with the story of how you became a writer? Last time we met you were telling me about your European adventures with Samuel.'

'Had I been in the hospital?'

'For your cough?'

'No, in the 1930s.'

'You didn't mention a hospital, no.'

'Let's have that,' says Cecily, pointing at the cake. Kate serves her as she settles back in her chair, fingertips gently tapping together. 'Right – well, Samuel and I had been to Franzensbad as the waters were considered conducive to fertility. We'd been married nearly three years but nothing was happening. Eventually, we saw a doctor who discovered a fibroid the size of a mango,' she says, touching her belly gently. 'I needed surgery immediately if I was to conceive.'

'Did you want children?' says Kate with surprise.

'I was ambivalent – but it's what one did in those days; and Samuel adored children, he was far more patient than I ever was,' she says, reaching for her plate. 'We returned to England for the surgery but it went very wrong. I remember reading the chart at the bottom of the bed after the operation, it said *Chances of Pregnancy – nil*. I felt sick at heart. My surgeon came in and said, "Dear girl, you'd best find other things to do with your life."'

'Oof, bedside manner . . .'

Cecily shrugs as she digs her fork in. 'No choice is also a choice.'

'What do you mean?'

'Life has given you a path, even if it's not your preferred one.'

'Even so. I'm sorry that happened.'

Cecily chews the cake thoughtfully. 'In retrospect, I'm not. My fellow inmates here are an emotional and financial burden, their children are now pensioners themselves, praying their mothers will hurry up and die before their entire inheritance gets eaten up.'

'That's pretty brutal.'

'Generating offspring in no way guarantees happiness – often the reverse.'

'*Generating offspring?*' says Kate, trying not to laugh. 'You can't write off the whole of humanity just because you claim old age doesn't suit you – which it does, by the way, you're in incredible shape.'

'I once gave a speech at the UN and now putting on my cardigan is a triumph,' says Cecily with disgust.

'A speech at the UN?'

Cecily shrugs. 'I became terribly bored in my sixties after I stopped the screenwriting. Samuel had always inspired me to do things for other people, and I realised I hadn't done much of that, apart from teaching. So I joined the board of an educational charity, one thing led to another and I was invited to the UN to talk about education.'

'Hollywood *and* the UN? You're like Superwoman.'

'I didn't feel much like a superwoman back in that hospital bed. There was nothing I could do about my body's failure to reproduce, but I was heartbroken for poor Samuel – I was taking away his chances of father-hood. But he took my hand and his eyes filled with ten-derness. He said, "It's going to be wonderful, you and me and a lifetime of adventures, the two of us." I didn't want him mistaking my tears of gratitude for sadness, so I tried to shoo him off to buy cigarettes but he cas-ually patted his pockets and pretended he'd forgotten his wallet. Samuel never forgot his wallet, not once in all the years we were married. He never forgot a birthday, or an anniversary – he never once let me down. Anyway, he stayed with me in that stuffy ward, my hand in his, until well past visiting hours. The matron turned a blind eye, she'd fallen in love with him as everyone did. Later, I brought up the subject of adoption, but then life had other plans . . .' She pauses, staring down at her plate with a look of such sudden sorrow Kate worries she's asked far too personal a question.

'So you moved back to London then?' says Kate, hurriedly.

'Yes,' says Cecily, shaking her head as if rousing herself from a disturbing dream. 'We rented a flat, a sunny, happy home. They were golden times. We had great friends, we entertained modestly – those were the days when a Fuller's walnut cake at three shillings and sixpence was the height of luxury. But our lives gradually darkened with the increasingly terrible stories from Germany. A year after we returned from Sweden, the Munich crisis blew up.'

'I should remember this from GCSEs . . . That was 1938?'

'September 1938 – and yes, you should. Samuel was back in Stockholm for work. People in England panicked, they thought London would be flattened. Samuel managed to telephone to say he could get me on the last boat out to Esbjerg and I should pack and come at once.'

'What about your family?'

'My parents were in Bournemouth. Leo and May were around.'

'Were your siblings married?'

'Leo remained a bachelor his whole life. They have other ways of saying that nowadays. He died of a stroke ten years ago. May married twice and ended up in New York with husband number two, a significant improvement on the first. She died young, a week before her eightieth. Unfortunate timing, as we'd just booked to fly out to celebrate and instead we had to fly out for her funeral. Samuel helped keep my spirits up but it was peculiar, being the last one of us all left alive. I felt rather abandoned . . .' she says, her eyes clouding over. 'You interrupted me, where was I?'

'About to get on a boat to Esbjerg, wherever that is.'

'Jutland.'

Kate winces. 'Where's Jutland again?'

'Didn't they teach you *anything* at school?' Cecily grunts her disdain. 'I left our lovely London flat with a sad heart and boarded the ship – but halfway across the sea Chamberlain's announcement of "Peace in our Time" came through – oh how we cheered. I bitterly regretted leaving England. As soon as I got to Sweden, I thought that Samuel would say we could go home again, but instead he was furious. I'd never seen him angry. He could barely speak – not like Samuel at all. He thought Chamberlain was a fool, and felt sure war was imminent, so we ended up staying put. The news only got worse. The Nazis swallowed Czechoslovakia, then Austria. Stockholm became a first-class waiting room for the luckier refugees who'd bribed transit visas. Sitting in the cafés we'd see these poor people promenading in a macabre parody of the life we'd all previously enjoyed. Elegantly dressed, they gave no impression of being exiles until one saw the fear in their eyes. They'd fled their homes, investing in furs and jewels – but they didn't have the cash in their pockets for a decent meal.'

'It's so grim, and when you look at the news today . . .'

'That's precisely why I don't,' says Cecily briskly. 'Then in September 1939, on the final day of our summer holidays at a pension in Saltsjöbaden – oh look it up on a map, Kate – Hitler invaded Poland. We were sitting listening to the radio in the parlour along with some Jewish refugees, Swedes and a small party of Germans. Chamberlain said, "We are now at war with Germany". There was a terrible long silence, I could hear my heart thumping in my chest – then, slowly, the Germans rose and stalked from the room.'

'I can picture it now,' says Kate, shuddering.

'Fear crept into my bones. The rumours from Poland were alarming, of all sorts of discrimination, Jews being excluded from jobs and universities, increasing violence against the community. We had no news of Samuel's family and as hard as he tried, he couldn't find any. I'd catch him staring out of the window with such a haunted look, but whenever we talked he tried to reassure *me*. Conditions seemed better in England, so in March we decided to return home. Samuel bought me an air ticket. He'd follow a week later after tying up loose ends. After some debate we decided to change my ticket as I wanted to fly with him. He thought I was being sentimental but I'd had a weird panic that we'd somehow be separated from each other. I went to the Turkish baths, as we had no hot water at home, but as I was sitting relaxing in a cloud of steam, a message came through from Samuel: the airline had no other tickets, I must travel that night. I rushed back to the flat, packed a small bag of clothes and books and hurried to the airport, my hair still damp at the nape of my neck.'

Kate's hand goes to her heart.

'I thought Samuel would be back a week later, but my panic proved prescient – I didn't see him again for three years.'

'Wait, what? Three *years*? Why?'

Cecily leans back in her chair. 'I am fatigued beyond all reasoning today.' She starts a yawn which turns into one of her lengthy cat yawns that lasts a minute.

'Please, Mrs Finn, don't leave me on a cliffhanger.'

'*Surely* you know who won the war?'

'Not the war, you and Samuel! Here, have more cake,' says Kate, hurriedly cutting her another slice.

'Oh, OK, then,' says Cecily, flashing her an indulgent look. 'I arrived home to a blacked-out, depressed England.

Life with Samuel had never been extravagant – money didn't matter, we were simply delighted we'd found each other. Still, I didn't realise how spartan life in Bournemouth with my parents would be. Papa refused to have a phone at home or even curtains. He said respectable people went to bed when it was dark. The week after I arrived, he told me there was bad news. "Hitler has invaded Norway and Denmark, Sweden will be next – you'll never see Samuel again." My stomach dropped. Samuel was due the next day but I heard nothing. I could barely breathe. It was a perfect spring that year, hot and sunny. Every day I'd walk with Mama to the beach and I'd sit passing the warm sand through my fingers, trying not to let my imagination run amok. Finally, a cable arrived: Samuel was OK, and he'd been offered a special role at the British Embassy.'

'Ah, as a spy?'

Cecily nods and raises an eyebrow.

'So what type of spy was he? A jumping-between-tall-buildings kind or an office-based one?'

'*Samuel*? He'd have broken his spectacles if he'd jumped off the kerb,' says Cecily, chuckling. 'Also, far too tall. Whenever he entered a room, you noticed him. No, Samuel was in intelligence. With his language skills and good nature he was the ideal candidate. Everyone thought him a "*lieber Kerl*" – a good fellow, which meant he cultivated connections very naturally. He'd make acquaintances with all sorts of people passing through Stockholm – sailors, engineers, financiers, who'd inform him of what was happening in Germany. He'd report back to the Allies on what new buildings were being planned, what shortages of raw materials existed, information then used to plan attacks.'

'My goodness, so a proper spy.'

'Yes. I already told you that – why would you doubt me?' says Cecily irritably. 'He risked his life every day. Anyway, back in England the war had flared up. After Dunkirk, Bournemouth was flooded with soldiers. The Battle of Britain raged above us, the sound of planes filled the air. Looking up one saw swarms of silver-winged insects flickering in the sun. A silver streak would suddenly burst into a flaming flower and hurtle out of sight, leaving only a trail of evil black smoke,' she says, her hand drawing an arc in the sky.

'Weren't you terrified?'

'Of course, but the thought of Samuel kept me going. He wrote beautiful letters I carried with me until I knew the pages by heart – but words on paper can only do so much. His absence felt like a weight I carried all the time. Papa was convinced Samuel would die, and I lived in constant anxiety until I decided to find a job – far less time to mope when you're busy.' Cecily pauses to give Kate a hard stare.

Kate raises her hands to gesture that she's well past moping. Cecily responds by thrusting her chin forward, a small, sharp gesture that nonetheless indicates a universe of *you know what I mean*s . . .

'When you have a sense of purpose,' says Cecily pointedly, 'other parts of your life regain their true proportion.'

'Uh-huh, yup, got it, thanks. So you found work?'

'At the Metropole Hotel – running the kitchen staff, from the 6.30 a.m. breakfast shift till 10 p.m. I felt in control in those kitchens. Plus it was so exhausting it stopped me fretting about Samuel – and occasionally Arthur, the lovely white-haired manager, would let me take home some bacon, which kept Papa happy as it had already been rationed and it was his favourite, his rebellion against organised religion.'

'Hold on – there's a bacon-and-egg sandwich recipe in the book which is cooked in the dark. Is that . . .?'

'"Dinner the Night the Lights Go Out",' says Cecily nodding. '*The Show Must Go On* . . . Even now I could make that sandwich with my eyes shut,' she says, smiling as her hands gracefully move in a layering motion. 'Arthur and I made that sandwich one night after an air raid. We'd ushered the staff and guests into the basement shelter. We'd been down there keeping spirits up for hours as the bombs fell. The noise was appalling, we thought we'd all go deaf if we survived. You'd think a person would lose their appetite from fear, but the thought of imminent death seemed to make us hungrier, made us revel in the taste more.'

'Oh! I didn't put two and two together. I assumed that recipe was written after a power cut in the fifties, not a blackout in the war. You're so blasé about all this, you make it sound light-hearted – like that dinner with Samuel's family in Warsaw.'

'Would you have preferred the truth? The Luftwaffe bombed the Metropole two years after I'd left, poor Arthur was killed instantly. Writing the menus more than a decade later, I felt it wisest to cherry-pick. My book was intended as entertainment, not a history lesson or horror story.'

'It's not cherry-picking, though, it's like you turn these quite dark things into something else.'

'I'd tasted the sorrow in real life. I preferred to make what was on the page a little sweeter. You're allowed to do that when you're a writer – that's the whole point of *being* a writer.'

'You mean so that you can make things up.'

'So that you can imagine a better version,' she says pointedly. 'Besides, I *was* fortunate: I was safe, with a roof over my head. I'm ashamed to admit that I actually felt resentful, coming home every night to that shabby house with no working bathroom. My life had transformed from a bohemian whirl in Europe, where every day with Samuel was joy and discovery, to Mama's and Papa's mundane routine – the highlight of which was a cup of tea at the ABC. I felt restless and frustrated, like a child again. You understand that, I'm sure, living with your mother in your forties.'

'I've got a few more days yet,' Kate laughs. 'Anyway, at least Mum has a working bathroom.'

'That set-up is not ideal for your independence.'

'Obviously not – but it's hardly like I chose it.'

'Really? Who did choose it?'

'Well, I suppose I did, after what Nick did, but it didn't feel like I had much choice.'

'Curious. You don't see it as your life but as a series of things done to you.'

'You sound like Mum,' says Kate, groaning. 'I beg you, please, tell me more about the war.'

Cecily purses her lips. 'Very well. I returned home from work one evening to find a new letter from Samuel. He was as miserable as I was that we'd been apart so long, but he couldn't come home, his work was too important to the war effort. But if I was prepared to take the risk, the embassy could fly me to Stockholm on a bomber plane. My heart leapt. I had to seize this chance to be with him. I said a tearful goodbye to my parents, took the train to Aberdeen and was taken to wait in a cold, darkened airport. Every night I got my hopes up, every night they were dashed when the flight was cancelled due to enemy aircraft. Those were the longest eleven days of my life, until finally the time came when it was safe to fly. That bomber flew so high I wore an oxygen mask strapped to my face the entire way – and after hours that felt like days, we landed.'

Kate shakes her head in wonder. 'And you were finally reunited with Samuel?' she says hopefully.

'I was. But really, I must rest now, I'm exhausted. Promise me something, Kate?'

'Sure.'

'You'll look for other digs soon?'

'Digs other than yours?' says Kate laughing, but Cecily frowns.

'You won't stay at your mother's much longer.'

'It's all in hand, I'll be moving in the next three or four weeks.'

Cecily nods, pleased, but then her hand floats to her brow. 'Not cohabiting with the pigeon?'

Kate opens her mouth to answer but it gets frozen in an embarrassed smile.

Cecily grasps at her chest as if in actual pain.

'What?' says Kate, trying to control her frustration. 'Can we agree to not discuss him, please? There are *so* many other interesting things to talk about.'

'We can agree on *that*. I suppose people only learn from their own mistakes,' says Cecily wearily. 'I never listened to anyone wiser, but it's infuriating to watch you waste valuable time.'

'But you waste *your* time. I know you don't like anyone here, but you could engage a little more.'

'At my age I've earned the right to do exactly as I choose – and I choose this. Besides, you really wouldn't understand until you're at least ninety-two how tired one feels at a molecular level. The only possible purpose for me now is to pass on something of my life to another human, yet you're a stubborn little mule, you never listen.'

'That's not true. Those mean things you said about my job finally filtered through. And I take advice from your book. I flick through it all the time.'

'You do?'

'Absolutely! It's a real shame it's out of print – you could republish it tomorrow and it would sell.'

'You do talk nonsense.'

'You could! Everyone who's seen it loves it.'

'It's almost as old as I am.'

'It's still relevant, though – well, apart from maybe that grapefruit recipe . . .'

'People have stopped eating grapefruit?'

'They don't tend to serve it to impress their boss at dinner parties. Mrs Finn, you're always telling me human nature doesn't change, "Dinner for your Ex", "Dinner for a Noisy Neighbour" – everyone has an ex, and a noisy neighbour – in London, often two.'

Cecily shrugs. 'That book has sat for decades withering on the shelf, just like me. I'm glad someone's enjoying it at least. Right – time for my nap. Are you off home?'

'To the pigeon coop.'

Cecily sighs but for once restrains herself from further comment.

Chapter Forty-eight

'I SEE YOU'VE DRESSED for the occasion,' says Kate, giving Nick a kiss as she breezes into his flat.

'I put the snooker on after you left,' says Nick, looking down sheepishly at his boxer shorts and T-shirt combo.

'I've had the most interesting afternoon,' she says, coming to sit beside him on the sofa as he throws a blanket over them, puts his arm around her and turns back to the screen.

'With the old lady?'

'Mrs Finn, yes. It was well worth us making that *fiskepudding*, she loved it.'

'Ah, good,' he says proudly.

'And her face lit up like a young girl's when she saw the toffee cake.'

'Uh-huh.'

'Meanwhile, it *wasn't* her birthday, I presume she lied to Mrs Gaffney to lure me back into her web.'

'Sure.'

'She was telling me all about the war.'

'Mmm,' he says, patting Kate's knee and turning up the volume on the TV.

'Her husband was a spy, he actually was! I thought she might have been making that up.'

'Mmm.'

'And he turned into a dolphin after Hitler invaded Argos, and he spoke exclusively in Nickleback lyrics.'

'Uh-huh.' Nick nods and squeezes her hand.

'Nick – seriously,' she says, giving him a gentle thump. 'You're transfixed by Ronnie O'Sullivan's balls.'

'Sorry, babe, this break is amazing, O'Sullivan's on fire.'

I could be too, thinks Kate, frowning as she heads to the fridge. 'Do you want a glass of wine?'

'Huh?'

'Would you like a drink?'

'No, cheers, I'm fine.'

If I were Cara, I'd go and stand in front of that TV and either pull out the plug or do a striptease, thinks Kate, pouring herself a large glass, then telling herself to stop being such a needy diva. She settles back next to Nick on the sofa and takes out *Thought for Food*, tracing her fingers fondly over the cover.

Which of these recipes did Cecily write during the war? 'Early Supper for Parents after a Matinee' – *Aim: to make them feel how much you admire them for not having lost their enjoyment of small pleasures* – that must be after tea at the ABC . . . 'Dinner the Night the Pipes Burst' – quite possibly that was after something far worse . . . Nowadays you'd have a millennial equivalent: 'Dinner For When Your Wifi's Been Down for Like Five Whole Minutes', she thinks, chuckling.

She watches the snooker for a while; it's actually quite exciting. If only Cecily would join the other ladies to watch some TV, or get involved in something more social.

'I can't quite get my head around how bored she must be,' says Kate, frowning. 'And lonely. She just sits there

314

in her memories . . . Though I suppose, if you're going to live in your memories, at least she has plenty of good ones. She was married to Samuel for sixty-something years. And she's had such an interesting life. Nick, please stop making me feel like the most boring person on the planet, I want to talk to you for two minutes.'

'Sure,' he says, pausing the screen.

'That's not even live TV.'

'I'm on a twenty-minute delay, but it's as good as live. What were you saying?'

'It must be miserable being that old and having no family or friends.'

'I guess.'

'Think about it, seriously, the loneliness, the boredom . . .'

'I don't want to think about it.'

'Why?'

'Because I don't like thinking unhappy thoughts.'

'I'm not suggesting we have some sort of emo crying fest, I'm just saying try to imagine what it's like, basically being ninety-seven and waiting to die.'

'It's depressing. I'd rather watch the snooker.'

'Yeah – clearly. By the way, have you told work you can't do night shift on my birthday?'

'On the Saturday?'

'No, Friday week – the dinner at Mum's flat. It is in your diary, isn't it?'

'Of course. That's the week before we launch the new system. I'll be working a couple of night shifts that week.'

'Yeah, I know. I'll be practising the menu anyway, I'm trying the birthday feast from Mrs Finn's book. So on the Saturday we're booked for Le Montrachet?'

'Yep, and I thought on the Friday night after dinner it might be cool to stay in a hotel. That way you wake up on your fortieth somewhere special.'

Kate looks at him curiously – it's so not a Nick idea.

'You know, a posh hotel, breakfast in bed . . .'

'You're the king of breakfast in bed, Nick. You don't need to fork out for it.'

'It's your birthday. Rob and Tasha went to the Ritz last year for Valentine's Day, he said it was a lot of fun. I think it's a good idea – not the Ritz, though. It cost about five hundred pounds with breakfast, apparently.'

'*Five hundred quid*? That is a *lot* of bacon and eggs.'

'There's a boutique hotel Rob mentioned in Covent Garden. It's not that expensive, and it'll make your birthday feel really special.'

Extravagance is something Rita's good at but Kate isn't, partly because Kate's salary has always been below par, and partly because it feels self-indulgent. Maybe turning forty would be a good time to start allowing herself to be spoiled, and if Nick's going to all this effort, why stand in his way?

'Sounds great,' she says, giving him a kiss. 'I can't wait.'

Chapter Forty-nine

'ANOTHER SCINTILLATING WEEK, Mrs Finn?'

Cecily lets out a low snort of disdain. '*This place would be unbearable if it weren't for the loneliness . . .*'

Kate laughs in spite of the solemn look on Cecily's face. 'Did you just make that up?'

Cecily chews the inside of her cheek, contemplating whether to pass it off as her own. 'No – it's a Japanese poet, can't remember his name. They must have slipped me a Mickey in hospital to wipe my memory.'

'No chance, your memory's better than mine. On which note, can you please carry on where you left off?'

'You'll definitely have to remind me where that was.'

'You'd just flown back to Sweden in a bomber plane, to be reunited with Samuel.'

'Ah, that's right – December 1943.'

'That must have been wonderful, after all those years apart.'

'Of course,' says Cecily, perking up in her chair. 'I was terribly excited to see him, so nervous I felt queasy. After I landed I took a taxi straight to his apartment – a beautiful place with thick carpet and elegant furniture, absolute paradise compared to Bournemouth. I had a rest and a wash, but it was still only noon and Samuel wasn't due home till 5 p.m. so I decided I'd cook him a special meal.'

'Let me guess . . . "Dinner for a Friend Who Returns Unexpectedly from the Airport"?'

'Oh no, that was an entirely unwanted guest who hijacked me in my dressing gown some years later. No, for Samuel I made "First Dinner after Returning from Honeymoon". *I wonder by my troth, what thou and I did, till we loved* . . . the same meal I'd cooked the night we came back from Italy.'

'The amazing slow-cooked Bolognese?'

'Minestrone, then spaghetti Bolognese, followed by a delicious almond tart with thick cream. I wasn't sure if I'd be able to buy all the ingredients, but I set out to explore. Stockholm was magical – brightly lit for Christmas, the shops bursting with goods, the air scented with gingerbread. The war felt far away. To my delight I found everything I needed and more and rushed back to the apartment. By 4.30 p.m. the soup and dessert were made and the Bolognese was in the oven. I had put on my best navy wool dress, Samuel's favourite, and I was glued to the window, hoping to catch sight of him. I waited and waited but he didn't appear. At 6.30 p.m., I called the embassy but they said he'd left at 4 p.m. By 8 p.m., I was so anxious I poured myself a large glass of glögg but then I must have passed out on the sofa because at 10 p.m. I was woken by the door opening and Samuel in surprise rushing over to embrace me. I was utterly discombobulated, and Samuel – well, he looked so different: older, worn down, his black hair now almost entirely grey. But when I looked into his eyes I could see the Samuel I'd left behind. He was full of apologies, he hadn't known I'd managed to catch the flight and a key contact had asked to meet with important information about a munitions factory. Samuel had met him at a restaurant and I suspect had eaten too many meatballs, his cheeks were flushed. But when he found out I'd cooked for him, he claimed he was starving and insisted on setting up a little table on the balcony overlooking the city. Even though the pasta sauce was so overdone it was crispy, he ate every mouthful.'

'Ah, that's so sweet,' says Kate, clasping her hands to her chest.

'I must admit we'd been apart so long I feared our re-acquaintance might be awkward but we were at once closer than ever. I couldn't believe I'd managed to live without hearing Samuel's infectious laugh for so long. At one point during that first week I had the most horrible dream, maybe it was too hot in the apartment that night. It was pitch-black in the dream, and there was a thick, choking fog between Samuel and me. I couldn't see his face, I was confused, but I knew he was being dragged away from me by some terrible force. His hand was in mine but the tighter I gripped, the more his slipped away. I kept calling for him to hold on but he couldn't hear me. I shouted until my throat was raw, but he kept slipping and then the tips of his fingers left mine and he was gone. I started crying in the dream, and the crying woke Samuel who shook me awake. He kept telling me it was all OK, but the next day I couldn't stop thinking about it, I couldn't even get out of bed, it wasn't like me at all. I felt a crippling fear of losing him,' she says, shaking her head. 'That dream felt so real.'

319

'It must have been all the anxiety of the war, and your separation,' says Kate. 'No wonder you felt scared.'

'When he came home from work I made him promise he would never let us be apart again, no matter what, and he promised. He said, "Whatever happens, I'll always be by your side." The following night he brought home a beautiful globe and a leather-bound notebook and we spent the next month spinning the globe, planning all the places we'd visit together. Every time we wrote down another country in our book, I felt a little better, like somehow our future was safer because we'd written it in ink. We had a list of nearly thirty places by the time we were done.'

'And it sounds like you made it to most of them.'

'Well, plans changed . . . after my book was published we went back to Italy, for quite some time, then back to England for the screenplays. It wasn't really till the writing dried up when I was in my sixties that we had the time or inclination to revisit the list.'

'Do you still have the notebook? I'd love to see it.'

Cecily breathes out a sigh of frustration. 'I threw the damn thing away in a fit of rage a few years after the war, but I knew its contents by heart. I'd spent so many hours in that Stockholm apartment, dreaming of our future when the war would be over.'

'Didn't you work in Sweden?'

'I did, I needed to keep busy as Samuel's hours were so long. I started teaching again. I learned to speak Swedish and German, and made friends with a rather bohemian crowd – artists and film-makers who threw wonderful parties which always ended in some sort of romantic scandal,' she says, chuckling.

'It doesn't sound like life was too hard?'

'Well, Sweden was neutral. The worst thing was not knowing what was happening to Samuel's family. Samuel tried every connection he'd made but we couldn't find out anything. He became consumed by anxiety. This time the rumours were horrifying, Jews being starved to death in the Warsaw ghetto, shot in the street, or transported to German labour camps. Samuel threw himself ever harder into work – fighting for his family as much as for the bigger cause. The following year, because he was so busy, we decided I'd spend three months out of the city, looking after our friends' two daughters. The Swedish countryside was intoxicatingly beautiful after that long winter, a luxuriance of blossom – violet, purple, mauve and white everywhere. I promised Samuel I'd take him as soon as the war ended, though that didn't happen till his eightieth birthday,' she says, looking suddenly crestfallen. 'I should have done that sooner, I fear I rather let him down.'

'Nonsense,' says Kate. 'It sounds like you were too busy having all sorts of adventures.'

'Well, yes, I suppose . . .'

'Italy, Hawaii, Machu Picchu?'

'Yes, Peru, of course,' says Cecily, frowning. 'And my work kept me terribly busy too . . . Well, anyway, looking back now, that summer feels like a dream. I cooked for the little girls, taught them English, and at bedtime I made up all manner of stories.'

'What type of stories?'

'Oh, what any child wants,' says Cecily, dismissively. 'Real life with the horrid bits made larger, then magicked away at the end. The girls loved them so much I

321

wrote them down and showed Samuel when I returned to Stockholm. He said they were excellent, though I presumed he was only saying that because he was always so kind. But unbeknown to me he showed a few to a contact who had a friend in publishing. The editor liked them and asked to see more. I spent every spare minute of the next two months furiously writing, driving Samuel mad reading him stories in bed at night. Eventually, I went to meet the editor, who wanted me to write even more, and a month later I delivered the stories, then sat trying not to stare at our letterbox. Six weeks later a letter landed on the doormat. I couldn't bear to look, Samuel had to open it for me. He read it, then looked up at me with tears in his eyes.'

'A rejection letter?' says Kate, her heart sinking.

'Tears of pride. The book would be called *Om Igen – Tell Me Again* – to be published in Sweden and England. I could hardly wait to send a copy to Mr Moffat, my old English teacher. '

'Ah, how wonderful, Mrs Finn. So, *finally*. *That*'s how you came to be a writer.'

'No, that didn't work out at all,' says Cecily, her eyes darkening. 'The month after my contract arrived we had the news we'd been dreading for so long, confirmation of our worst fears. Samuel's family . . .' She shakes her head.

'What?'

Cecily's eyes shut tight as she takes a deep breath and exhales heavily. 'His parents, his brothers and sister, his nieces and nephews, those sweet, innocent children who'd shared dinner with us in Warsaw – all of them killed in Auschwitz, herded into gas chambers like cattle. Leon, Shindel, Lilli, Oskar, Izzy . . . And we didn't know. Almost his entire family decimated, not a body to bury, no grave he could ever visit.'

'I can't even begin to imagine,' says Kate, shaking her head.

'My belief in the fundamental goodness of human nature was destroyed. Until that moment, Samuel had always been an optimist but that changed us. Certainly, I had no more appetite for make-believe stories. And yet,' she says, raising one hand, then letting it fall, 'life had to go on. The tide of war was turning. We waited in hope for the second front, and at last VE Day came. Stockholm went mad. Samuel and I held hands tightly as we walked down Birger Jarlsgatan under a snowstorm of ticker tape, but our hearts were heavy with the suffering of so many. Too much had been endured to make this feverish excitement exhilarating. Then we received a dreadful telegram from Gisele.'

'Her mother's Sophie, the jazz singer?'

'Yes, Samuel's last remaining sibling. We thought they'd have been safer living in France. Sophie had sold her emeralds on the black market for a fraction of their value. The money had helped them procure false identity papers, and a sympathetic non-Jewish friend had given them refuge. But a neighbour had found out and denounced them all to the Germans. The neighbour was arrested, and Sophie . . . Sophie was shot. Gisele somehow managed to escape but the Gestapo were still searching for her – she couldn't even attend her own mother's funeral. It was such a terrible time, I'd never seen poor Samuel weep like that. His heart was broken. All I could do was hold his hand but it was beyond wretched seeing a person you love suffering so much, even now it makes me sick to think about,' she says, rubbing her abdomen. 'Then I had a cable from England saying Papa had died.'

'Oh God.'

'In his sleep, a peaceful death at least.'

'But all that loss, all at once.'

Cecily nods gravely.

'How old was he when he died?'

'How old was who?' says Cecily, warily.

'Your father?'

'Oh, Papa? Sixty-seven. Mama lived to seventy. I'm amazed I've outlived my parents by decades – do you think I'll *ever* die?' says Cecily, despairingly.

'I suspect it's the likely outcome,' says Kate, awkwardly. 'You're not religious, are you, Mrs Finn?'

'I don't believe in heaven, if that's your question.'

'Don't you ever wonder what happens next?'

'I expect it all just goes dark.'

'Don't you think there's a chance you'll see your loved ones again?'

'Not for a minute, though I'd dearly love to see Samuel's face again, it's been so long,' she says fondly. 'There's so much I never told him. I've missed him every day he's been gone.'

'Of course.'

'He was the most wonderful husband, I couldn't have imagined a finer one. We never did reach that point where we tired of each other. I wonder if we ever would have . . .' she says, giving a gentle shrug. 'I'm not afraid of dying, Kate. I've been ready for years. And I learned not to be afraid of living. Fear is a terrible thing, it paralyses you far more than being stuck in an old body.' Cecily looks at her thoughtfully. 'Emerson said it best: "What if you do fail and get rolled in the dirt . . . Up again, you shall never be so afraid in a tumble".'

It's another piece of Cecily's advice that comes to seem essential only a short while later.

Chapter Fifty

SPICY TOMATO AND BACON rigatoni? Or fragrant lamb curry? Or maybe a chicken cashew stir fry? Decisions, decisions.

Kate is heading out of Aposta on Tuesday evening pondering what to cook with Nick for dinner when her phone rings.

'I was just about to call. How was your day?' she says, pulling her coat tighter as she heads towards the deli.

'Yep, all good,' says Nick. 'Ivan's confirmed we're doing the switchover next Friday, so I'll definitely be doing that shift.'

'The Friday of my birthday weekend?' says Kate, anxiously.

'*Next* Friday, not *this* Friday,' he says, laughing. 'I wouldn't forget your birthday after the trouble that caused last year.'

'I let you off lightly,' says Kate, laughing.

'Rohan totally messed up the import last weekend, Anjit had to rewrite all his queries.'

Kate has no idea what this means but she makes a suitably sympathetic noise. 'Are you still at work?'

'I finished early because of last night's shift.'

'Oh. Are you typing?'

'Playing *Civilisation V*.'

'Declared any wars yet?'

'I'm trying diplomacy first,' he says, tapping away in the background.

She hovers outside the fancy deli, pondering whether to pick up wine. She should save her drinking for the weekend's festivities – but a bottle of wine with Nick is never the wrong thing. 'Hey, shall I bring some of my CDs round later? Does it make sense to bring a bag's worth at a time?'

'*Tonight*?'

'We're doing supper and cinema, aren't we? Red or white, by the way? I'm in the deli.'

'That's tonight?'

'Yup.'

'Honestly?'

'What?'

'I'm knackered.'

'Oh. Do you want to give the cinema a miss?'

'I could do with an early night.'

'Shall we just get a takeaway curry?'

'I was thinking I'd get myself a Deliveroo. I fancy some ribs.'

'Oh,' says Kate, smarting slightly. Ribs for one, not two. 'OK, then . . . well, I can hear you're playing your computer game so I'll leave you to it, shall I?'

'Cool, have fun, babe, see you Friday,' he says, but she can tell his concentration has already drifted back to the virtual world.

She hangs up with a frown. If it hadn't been for France, she'd be more relaxed about him cancelling their evening so abruptly at an hour's notice. She can't expect him to be keen constantly just because she now has some residual paranoid insecurity. She needs to quieten the annoying little voice in her head saying *this isn't good enough* – because she's over-sensitised, looking for problems. There's nothing whatsoever wrong here, but if she knee-jerks constantly, she'll kick this relationship until it breaks.

She heads to the freezer section for a tub of Ben & Jerry's. That should help her swallow the uncomfortable feeling which that phone call's just left her with.

Chapter Fifty-one

Dinner with Friends to Celebrate a Rather Significant Birthday

It is good for him that intends to feast, to set down the full number of . . . dishes . . . sixteen is a good proportion; first, a shield of brawn, with mustard; secondly, a boiled capon; thirdly a boiled piece of beef; fourthly, a chine of beef roasted; fifthly, a neat's tongue . . . sixthly, a pig roasted; seventhly, chewets baked; eighthly, a goose roasted; ninthly, a swan . . . tenthly, a turkey . . . the eleventh, a haunch of venison . . . the twelfth, a pasty of venison. The thirteenth, a kid with a pudding in the belly; the fourteenth, an olive pie; the fifteenth, a couple of capons; the sixteenth, a custard or doucet.
    Gervase Markham, *The Well-Kept Kitchen*

Alternatively, lasagne works well for a crowd.

E VEN THOUGH IT WAS only five months ago, looking back now, Kate can't quite believe how dramatically she'd lost her appetite after France. Her love of food has been reignited with a vengeance, and she can't imagine a finer way to spend the last day of her thirties than a morning shift at Aposta, then coming home to create a feast for her favourite people.

She's keeping it simple and luxurious, in line with Cecily's menu – mozzarella and tomato salad, duck lasagne and chocolate mousse for dessert – but she's made a few tweaks. The salad has evolved into home-made ricotta and roast tomato with home-made bread. The tomatoes have been slow-roasting for hours, with thyme, olive oil and garlic, until they're sweet, jammy and fragrant. After Nick had cancelled on Tuesday, she'd ended up spending the evening practising making ricotta. She'd been through half a dozen muslins and piles of rubbery beige curds before finally mastering the technique – and tonight a bowl of smooth, creamy cheese sits on the counter as proof.

The lasagne feels like it's taken an entire decade to make, though in reality it's only been six hours, three for the soffritto, another two spent braising the duck legs in red wine, another hour once the meat had fallen off the bone making a rich, thick sauce to be layered between pasta and smothered in Parmesan and mozzarella.

Kate's upgraded the chocolate mousse with cocoa nibs and fresh raspberries. She's licked the spoon a few too many times, but what in this world is more delicious than chocolate melted into double cream? She smiles as she whisks the egg whites, reminded of the bright white crest of Cecily's hair. She's going to drag Nick to meet Cecily soon – then Cecily will understand what all this fuss has been about.

She takes Rita's bone china dinner service from the cupboard and lays the table for ten. When Kate was younger, she'd thought that by forty she'd have a husband, a house, a car, kids and her own posh china set. She has none of these, yet she's no longer dreading tomorrow – she has everything that makes her happy: friendship, food, music, laughter and Nick.

Comparison is the fastest route to feeling inadequate but actually her friends' lives haven't turned out to plan either. Kate had assumed Cara would have ploughed through a minimum of three husbands by now. And she'd never have imagined Bailey's ex would be dumb enough to leave her for the office slapper. Man plans, God laughs . . .

Even if Kate married Nick next year, they'd be hard-pressed to make it to 'Dinner to Celebrate Your Fiftieth Wedding Anniversary' like Cecily and Samuel had. In *Thought for Food*, Cecily had made Samuel his favourite meal, with slight tweaks, for every significant anniversary. Will she and Nick still be eating cheeseburgers when they're in their nineties? Possibly little ones, sliders – easier on the dentures . . .

She chides herself. She's always thinking months or even years into the future, Cecily's always thinking of the past – whereas anyone who meditates will tell you that neither the future nor the past even exist.

Kate's going to pour herself a glass of wine and sit and enjoy *this* moment. In an hour she'll be with her closest friends, and shortly after midnight she and Nick will be at the fancy hotel, and she can't think of anything in the world that would make her happier.

'Three cheers for the birthday girl! More shots all round,' says Bailey, holding up the half-empty bottle of Jägermeister, then touring the table to pour more drinks.

Kate's pre-birthday-into-birthday dinner has been a roaring success. Cara's brought Eric, a new sugar daddy she met in Claridge's Bar a week ago. He's brought a magnum of Dom Pérignon: he's been a big hit. Bailey's brought Adam, who's brought Kate various lovingly potted herbs, including her favourite, lemon verbena. Kavita and Dom brought the Jägermeister, which everyone claimed they couldn't possibly drink at their advanced age but which everyone has. Nick turned up late from work, having left Kate's card on his desk, but he's in the final throes of this project, working twelve-hour days – she's really not bothered about a card.

Pete and Mia have refused to be separated, but everyone else has mingled and discovered common passions. Kavita and Eric are both Larry David fans; Cara has been benignly flirting with Adam, but he only has eyes for Bailey; Nick and Dom, a fellow geek, have been joyously discussing their current favourite book, *Hands-on Machine Learning with Scikit Learn and Tensorflow*.

'I can't believe Dom's reading that too,' says Kate. 'I literally don't understand a word.'

'It's way above my pay grade,' says Kavita, winking at Nick, who's gesticulating wildly in his enthusiasm.

'Convolutional neural nets!' Nick pipes up excitedly. 'Recurrent neural nets, generative adversarial nets – they're the new frontier of artificial intelligence!'

'I'll take your word for it,' says Kate, kissing the top of his head as she moves round the table to chat to her guests; it's pure joy to see her friends having such a good time.

'Order, order,' says Bailey, banging her glass loudly half a dozen times before anyone quietens down. 'Attention please! Tonight we are celebrating a very special occasion.'

'Oh no – no speeches, no,' says Kate, shaking her head violently.

'At midnight tonight, my oldest, dearest friend is turning twenty-one again and I thought it would be nice if we could go round the table and remind her of why we love her so much.'

'No! That's unspeakably embarrassing, no way,' says Kate, returning to her seat and burying her face in Nick's shoulder.

'Nonsense, we love you, Kate. We think sometimes you don't realise how much we love you and why. So, I'll go first because I'm the drunkest: Kate, thank you for being my friend for thirty-six years – yes, I know the sums don't quite add up given how youthful and radiant we look,' says Bailey, raising her glass. 'Kate – you're the most funny, generous, self-deprecating person I know, but above all, you're an exceptional, loyal friend who'll do anything for the people she loves.'

There are loud claps round the table, and Pete lets out a long, whooping whistle.

'I need a bucket,' says Kate, as Nick rubs her back.

'I'll stop now before I really embarrass you,' says Bailey. 'Pete?'

Pete tops up his glass and grins. 'Kate – I can never thank you enough for covering up for me over that pack of Silk Cut Mum found in my room when we were fourteen. Bailey said it already – you're a loyal, generous friend, and I'm sorry I met Mia – I'm not at all sorry I met Mia,' he says, leaning over to kiss his wife.

'Get a room,' shrieks Cara.

Pete laughs. 'But Kate, I'm sorry we couldn't do that whole "If We're Still Single at Forty Let's Get Married" thing.'

'I'd forgotten all about that,' says Kate, shaking her head. 'Forty seemed so old when we were young.'

'Nick – you're a lucky man,' says Pete, raising his glass.

'Isn't he just?' says Cara too loudly, as she thrusts her glass accusingly in Nick's direction.

'And bloody amazing food,' says Pete, finishing his toast. '*Amazing* lasagne!'

There's more applause as Kate shakes her head in embarrassment. 'Next! Let's get this over and done with . . .'

'OK, now we have a message from an exotic foreign location,' says Bailey, wiggling her fingers in the air. 'From your mum – it's like *This is Your Life*. She wanted to do this live on FaceTime . . . but I figured she might not want to see the state of her flat at this point in the evening, so I asked her to email me.'

Kate's blush deepens as Bailey clears her throat: 'Sorry I can't be there to celebrate. You're a wonderful daughter, Katey-Kate, even when you're horrible. There's a bottle of emergency champagne under my bed if you run out, but don't drink it unless you absolutely have to . . .'

'How very Mum,' says Kate, laughing.

'Nick?' says Bailey, smiling kindly, 'Do you want to say something?'

Nick shifts awkwardly in his seat and looks Kate in the eye. 'Erm, Kate, thank you for putting up with me for so long. I know I haven't been the easiest boyfriend, but thank you for loving me the way you do.'

'Ah, well, you have your charms,' she says, laughing and kissing him, then catching the look on Cara's face – Cara's eyes narrowing, her lips pursed. Kate frowns her a warning.

'Say something about Kate, not about yourself,' says Cara, laughing good-naturedly at him and shrugging back at Kate.

'That was about Kate,' says Nick, looking to Kate for confirmation. 'Wasn't it?'

'No, sweetheart, it wasn't,' says Cara, shaking her head. 'It was about how much she loves *you*! Try again, try harder.'

'Oh for goodness' sake,' says Kate. 'This feels like some horrible group bonding exercise.'

'Nick,' says Cara, putting her glass down and clicking her fingers at him as Kate buries her head in her hands. 'Say what's great about *Kate* that isn't in reference to your*self*.'

Nick nods obediently.

'Something . . .' says Cara, 'That does not mention *you* at all. For example, you like her feet, or the sound of her laugh.'

'OK,' says Nick, nodding again, he's got this. 'Her feet are nice. And I do like the sound of her laugh.'

Cara laughs again. 'But obviously not the exact words I've just fed you.'

'Please can we stop this,' says Kate.

'No, it's fine,' says Nick, rubbing her arm. 'Erm . . .' He freezes, his mouth open, and Kate feels her face flush further. It's horrible to put him on the spot like this. 'I think . . . Kate has a surprisingly excellent record collection.' He nods, pleased with himself, failing to see the disapproval on Cara's face. 'Did you know she owns Electronic's "Get the Message" on white label vinyl?' he says to Dom. 'Amazing record, that guitar with those synths, just wonderful,' he says, beaming.

Kate had once asked Nick what the girl he dated in his twenties was like. He'd looked at Kate blankly. 'Was she quiet, loud? Clever, like you?' He'd pondered the question for a while, then replied, 'She worked at a vet's.' Expecting a little more data, Kate had nodded encouragingly, but when met with a wall of silence, she'd probed: 'What was she actually *like – as a person*?' He'd looked at Kate as though she'd just asked what his favourite vinegar-based cleaning solution was.

She glances over at Pete and Mia, faces centimetres apart, and thinks back to Pete's wedding speech, how he'd noticed Mia's little finger twitching with excitement on their car ride in Sicily. The smallest of Mia's fingers. In his peripheral vision. Nick wouldn't have noticed if Kate's entire body was in spasms, unless she was talking about SpaceX rocket launches at the time. It's an unfortunate fact about Nick: if you're not standing directly in his eye-line, you cease to exist.

'I think it's time for a surprise,' says Kavita as she disappears into the kitchen with Dom. They emerge a minute later with a chocolate-iced cake, one pink candle blazing, and the room breaks into a chorus of 'Happy Birthday'.

'Look at this!' says Kate, beaming as Kavita places the cake in front of her. *To Kate: The Icing On Our Cake.* Thank you, that is so thoughtful.'

'Someone's phone's ringing?' calls out Bailey.

'You've got the hearing of a bat,' says Cara.

'Blow out the candle,' says Pete.

'Shit, it's my phone,' says Nick, looking embarrassed. 'Back in a sec.'

'Blow it out, come on, one big breath.'

'Peanut butter buttercream filling?' says Kate, cutting into the sponge with an appreciative sigh. 'Gosh, it must my birthday . . .'

Kate cuts ten generous slices and starts putting them on plates. Nick comes back into the room and whispers to her, 'Not for me, I'm afraid, I have to go back in.'

'A smaller slice,' says Bailey. 'That one's the size of my head.'

'Just a minute,' says Kate distractedly, turning to Nick in confusion. 'What do you mean? Back in where?'

'That was work, they've called me three times in the last hour.'

'And?'

'Ivan can't figure out the coding.'

Kate leads Nick gently to the corner, away from her guests. 'Ivan's your boss, how can he not know how to do the job?'

'I guess the same way Devron wouldn't have known how to do yours,' says Nick, looking stressed. 'Look, I don't want to leave. I'm having a great time.'

'Then don't leave. Tell Ivan tough shit. Tell him it's your girlfriend's fortieth. Tell him we're in the middle of cake. Tell him we've got a room booked that's costing the best part of a week's salary. Tell him it's a sodding database, not open-heart surgery. Tell him no.'

'I'll literally be two hours, max. Maybe three.'

'Why can't one of the others do it? Where's Anjit?'

'He's training for the marathon, he has to be up early. Oh shit, Ivan's calling again.'

Kate gently pushes him out to the hallway and listens as he answers Ivan's call.

'No, it's fine, Ivan – yeah, completely understand, not a problem at all . . . no, nothing special . . . just finishing a bite to eat.'

Kate shakes her head violently as he pulls an apologetic face to demonstrate there's nothing he can do about his own choice of words.

'*Nothing special*?' says Kate, shaking her head. 'Come on . . .'

'Babe, they'll pay me overtime. I'll use the money for us to do something nice, we'll go to the Cotswolds or something.'

'It's not about the money, and I hate the sodding Cotswolds.'

'I can't say no.'

'Yes. You can.'

'I've only been back there a few months.'

'You've done two night shifts already this week. There are other people who could fix the problem – why does Anjit's marathon training have priority over your life – over our life? – The marathon's not till April.'

'I can't make a fuss, Kate. Look, the sooner I go, the sooner I'll be done. Honestly, it sounds like a quickish fix. I'll meet you at the hotel.'

'I'll stay here with my friends till you're finished.'

'Sure, but there's no point not taking advantage of the room. I promise, if it gets any later than 2.30 a.m. I'll walk out. I promise.'

'Promise?'

'Promise,' he says, kissing the frown on her face goodbye.

'Are you sure you don't want me to ask my babysitter to stay an extra hour?' says Bailey as they stand by the front door, saying their goodbyes.

'You've got to be up horribly early for your Eurostar,' says Kate, hugging her. 'It's midnight already.'

'Then an extra hour won't make any difference – my hangover's going to destroy me either way,' says Bailey, pulling her back for another hug. 'I don't want the first hour of your forties to be spent alone doing the washing-up. It doesn't bode well.'

'Things can only get better, right?' says Kate. 'Home, Bailey. You're an amazing friend.'

Kavita and Dom have left already for their own babysitter; Pete and Mia will not keep their hands off each other – and Kate really doesn't feel like playing gooseberry; and she definitely doesn't fancy spending extra time with Cara, whose microscope on Kate's relationship will only ever magnify the flaws.

So yes, she's alone at the start of her fortieth birthday, doing the washing-up: so what? She's *forty*, she's definitely supposed to be an adult, and self-pity is never attractive.

She doesn't need to feel so disappointed. Forgetting a birthday card is genuinely not a big deal. She *does* have good taste in music – it was a compliment. Nick's job *is* important. Nobody's perfect. Our flaws are what make us human. Rita was never one to give her much attention, Kate's used to living without it. She has a cab coming soon to take her to a fancy hotel in town, where they'll no doubt have brilliant mini-toiletries, a fantastically plush bed with lots of pillows and a top-quality mattress, and Nick will be there in two hours, give or take. She'll wake up to a champagne breakfast with the man she loves, and

339

she'll be ashamed at how she's felt in the least bit grumpy about any of this.

But as she covers the remainder of her birthday cake and puts it to one side, she can't help but recall Cecily's comment about substandard cake and living for the icing.

Cecily's wrong, though.

It's not about whether the cake is good enough to justify the icing.

Sometimes with Nick it feels like Kate's living on crumbs.

Chapter Fifty-two

THE SOUND OF PERSISTENT knocking wakes Kate from a deep sleep. She rolls onto her back on the plush king-sized bed. This mattress really is incredible, it feels like a giant marshmallow.

She opens her eyes slowly, they're sore, and sees that the plasma screen at the end of the bed is currently frozen in the middle of an episode of *30 Rock* and Jack and Liz are high-fiving in Jack's office. Kate must have pressed pause as she was nodding off.

She looks at the space beside her where Nick should be: it's him at the door, knocking. She checks her watch. He promised he'd be here by 2.30 a.m. It's *8.30 a.m.* He promised.

She closes her eyes again and breathes deeply. This was his stupid idea; it was meant to be her birthday treat, and at this rate they'll only have two hours together before checkout.

No – she needs to rise above it. He's here now, that's all that matters. Blearily she swings her legs over the edge of the bed and shuffles to the door.

'What time do you call this?' she says as cheerily as she can, as she opens the door. 'Oh,' she says, her heart sinking. 'Sorry . . . I was expecting someone else.'

The waiter looks down at his elaborate trolley of champagne breakfast for two, then back up at Kate in her nightie.

'Yeah, I guess that's for me . . . just leave it anywhere, thanks,' says Kate, hurrying him out of the room.

She checks her phone: three texts and a voice message from Nick. He did try, he did – just not hard enough.

Bailey answers on the second ring. '*Bonjour, ma petite* birthday girl, are you having a lovely breakfast in bed?'

'Yup. Just me, myself and I,' says Kate wearily.

'*What?* What happened? It wasn't about that awkwardness with Cara, was it? I feel bad I put Nick on the spot like that.'

'No, nothing to do with that. And I do have an excellent record collection, I'll have you know,' says Kate, shaking her head with shame. 'I woke up five minutes ago to a bunch of texts from Nick. He lost track of time at work, didn't finish till five,' she says, sighing. 'Then he texted a few times and when he didn't hear back – because I was fast a-bloody-sleep! – he went home and he's gone to bed, but I'm supposed to call when I wake up.'

'Why didn't he just come and join you?'

'I don't know – because he's a moron? Or he was knackered? Or he thought I'd be annoyed because he promised he'd be here and he broke his promise?'

'Oh, honey, that's . . . disappointing.'

'No, it's fine. I mean it's a total waste of this room, which I didn't want him spending money on in the first place, but . . . well, I guess it is a bit shit, isn't it? Though they do have this cute little branded pencil set to take home . . .' she says, picking up the pencil box from the bedside table and sliding it open and shut.

Bailey's prolonged silence feels significant; Bailey always gives Nick the benefit of the doubt.

'Bailey – I don't feel good about this,' says Kate, flopping back onto the bed and rubbing the dull ache that's lodged in her stomach. She gazes up at the beautiful fleur de-lys cornices on the ceiling. 'I don't understand. He said he'd be here. You've gone quiet again.'

'Let me buy you a ticket to Paris! Get the next Eurostar out, there's one every hour. You could do a gallery while I'm at the trade show, then I'll meet you after and we'll go for steak and chips and gallons of red wine.'

'Blow out dinner with Nick and hop on a train?' It's the best idea Kate's ever heard.

'Tomorrow we could go to Le Marais for a falafel? Think about it . . . if you fancy . . . if you did want to change your plans.'

Kate hangs up and googles Eurostar. There's a train she could make at 11.01 a.m., oh, ouch, £150. And every train coming back tomorrow night costs £199.

What is she even thinking? She's totally overreacting *again*. Last time she was trying to flee France to get away from Nick, now she's fleeing *to* France to escape him.

She's grumpy because she has a hangover, and she's being a baby, and those overpriced scrambled eggs on that trolley over there are getting cold.

She texts Bailey back:

If the train didn't cost the same as a week's holiday in Spain, I'd say yes – thank you for the insanely generous offer – I'll be happy if you bring me back a croissant x

Kate doesn't care about a forgotten birthday card. But she does care about this.

Chapter Fifty-three

If you'd asked Kate three months ago who she'd most like to spend her fortieth birthday with, *that bossy old harridan at Lauderdale* would not have made the short-list, nor the longer one. Yet Kate has so intense a longing to visit Cecily that she heads straight over without dropping her bag home first.

Kate is fine, Kate is absolutely fine. She just needs this chaos in her head to quieten down for a few hours until she can talk herself back round to being calm.

'Every time you're here on a Saturday, it makes me think I'm losing my marbles,' says Cecily, her brows rising in delight at the sight of Kate.

'I wanted to share this champagne with a good friend. You do drink champagne, don't you?'

Cecily wiggles her hand from side to side. 'If you can tolerate a belch or two, I can tolerate a glass. Champagne for breakfast?' says Cecily.

'Did Mrs Gaffney tell you about my drinking problem?' says Kate, laughing.

'I wasn't sure if the big day was today or tomorrow, I would have given you your card.'

'Don't worry, I'm not really a fan of birthdays.'

'Neither am I. You're not with friends today?'

'I saw them last night.'

'Ah yes? How was the dinner?'

'Phenomenal, I'd have brought you leftovers but there weren't any.'

'That lasagne takes time to make but it's so comforting – to cook and to eat. I learned the recipe in Bologna, the year before I started writing the book. Wonderful city, Bologna, have you been?'

'I've only been to Florence.'

'Oh, Italy is the most marvellous country, everywhere is colour, beauty, excitement. I told you I lived there for the best part of a decade?' says Cecily dreamily. 'Anyway, that wasn't until the 1960s, but back in 1953 or 1954, it must have been, I'd seen *Roman Holiday*, and a friend suggested I do a tour – Milan, Bologna, Venice. I was in a rather blue mood, but I took myself off. It was the best thing for me, it made me excited about food again. Those little stuffed pasta parcels filled with rich beef ragu, topped with a creamy tomato sauce.' She kisses the air. '*Delizioso!* Exactly what I needed. So your friends appreciated your efforts?'

'It was a good night.'

'You didn't have fun?'

'They enjoyed it.' Kate smiles but Cecily's expression tells her Cecily's fully aware the smile is being held up by scaffolding.

'And tonight you'll have supper with . . .?'

'Yup, that's the plan.'

'The plan?' says Cecily, who is about to say something more biting but stops herself.

345

'Mrs Finn, could you carry on with your story? I'd really like to listen to you. I need to be in a different world from my own, just for a short while.'

Cecily looks at her with such intense sympathy it makes Kate want to cry. 'The war was over,' says Kate, clearing her throat. 'Your father had passed away.'

'Ah, yes,' sighs Cecily. 'That very much marked the end of that chapter of my life. Which bit would you like next, the Italian years? My disasters in Hollywood? Learning the hula in Hawaii?'

'Just carry on where you left off? Or tell me how you first got published?'

Cecily pauses and takes a sip of champagne, then pats her collarbone gently. 'They're one and the same chapter, though it's a rather bittersweet one, not my favourite, actually. I don't think you're in the best frame of mind.'

'No, go ahead,' says Kate, taking another sip and settling herself into her chair.

'If you're sure, then. The war had ended and it was finally time for Samuel and me to return to England. We boarded the ship, together at last. It felt like we were truly coming home to each other. Sweden had changed me; I'd become more confident, accumulated attractive clothes and a new swept-up hairstyle which was more becoming. I'd broadened my horizons and improved my tastes – superficial things, but good for my morale. My brother's face when he met us at the port brought me swiftly down to earth. He'd lived through those last awful years of bombing and rationing. He made a comment about my clothes – I wanted to explain that my beautiful velvet coat was given to me in exchange for English lessons – but there was no point. I felt guilty I'd had so comfortable a war when they'd suffered so much.'

'That was hardly your fault.'

Cecily shrugs. 'When I walked back into that house in Bournemouth my heart sank. Mama looked so diminished. And in sentimental thoughts of "home" the house had seemed larger, warmer – now, after all the modern comforts of Stockholm, it dismayed me. Papa had left me £1,500 in his will and we decided to move to London. We put a deposit on a house in Finchley and Mama moved in with us. She lived the last two years of her life well cared for. I will never forget Samuel's kindness to her. Every morning he'd make her tea and chat for hours, in spite of her incessant grumbling about the smallest things.'

Kate stifles a giggle as she imagines Cecily's mother as an exact replica of Cecily.

'Samuel would take her for a drive every Saturday. He treated Mama like his own mother, even though he was still grieving Shindel. Mama's health gradually began to fail, and sensing she needed more care than we could give, she insisted on a nursing home and died there six weeks later with minimal fuss, the way it ought to be done. It was the great gift of my life to be at her bedside, holding her hand when she died, to know she hadn't been alone. In death she was as beautiful as in life, her fine bones stood out from the wrinkled ivory of her skin. Her lustrous hair was spread out against the pillow as I combed it for the last time.

'You were a very good daughter.'

'No more so than average. I mourned Mama, of course, but I was relieved her final years hadn't been too lonely – there's nothing worse than loneliness,' she says, her brow furrowing at the thought. 'Still, any time I felt down, Samuel was there for me, I knew I'd be OK. After a few months, life started to return to normal. My sister May moved to America that spring, she'd met another fella. Leo bought a flat down in Brighton, he'd met one too. Samuel and I were living in our house in Finchley. We'd made it into a lovely cosy home, planted a garden. Samuel carried his sadness more lightly by then – finally he was feeling more optimistic. He'd found a job he enjoyed working as a translator for a shipping company, and was earning a good wage. I was considering applying for a job in food, I'd enjoyed my work at the hotel. We started talking again about adopting. Having lost his own family he was keen to give a child who needed it a happy home. And we started looking forward to some of the adventures we'd planned. We'd begin with a two-week trip to America, visit my sister in New York, then rent a car and head down to Florida where Gisele now lived.'

'Samuel's niece?'

'That's right. She'd fallen in love with an American GI, Louis, and they'd gone back to live in the States. Gisele had started her own dressmaking business and she'd recently given birth to a daughter whom she'd named after Sophie. Samuel was so excited, he couldn't wait to meet the new arrival. He'd already bought the baby a beautiful pink blanket from Liberty. I'd been to the travel agent that morning to discuss tickets. Samuel wanted us to celebrate and travel in style. I was worried about the expense, but he wanted to treat me. He always wanted the best for me, he was the kindest man. I spent a good hour in the travel agent talking through our options and wrote all the details down to discuss with Samuel later that night. As I was leaving the travel agent, it started to rain – a sudden April shower, though the weather was mild that day – in fact, quite muggy. I'd forgotten my umbrella so on a whim I popped to the cinema to see *Key Largo* – I suppose talk of Florida had put the idea into my head. After the film I decided I'd make Samuel his favourite supper, so I headed to the butcher's for lamb chops. When I came home, as I was taking the keys from my bag, I heard our phone ringing in the hallway. It didn't normally ring in the day. I set my shopping on the doorstep, I remember fumbling for the keys as I rushed to answer, thinking it must be the travel agent. But it wasn't. It was Samuel's secretary. She'd been trying to call for hours. Something bad had happened.'

'Why? What?' says Kate, caught off guard.

'Something quite dreadful . . .' says Cecily, shaking her head. 'Samuel had collapsed, at his desk. I was to come to the hospital immediately,' she says, looking down at her fingers, which have started to shake. 'I rushed into the street in a panic. My neighbour saw me and offered to drive. I kept telling myself it would be fine, it had to be, but when I arrived at the ward I could tell from the nurse's face that something was terribly wrong.' She slowly strokes one hand over the other, her gaze downcast.

'Why, what was it?' says Kate, with a sudden sinking feeling.

Cecily shakes her head, more slowly this time. 'An aneurysm,' she says, swallowing hard. 'He went out like a light.'

'What?' says Kate, holding her breath. 'But he was OK, though, wasn't he? He wasn't – he didn't . . . he was OK?'

'No,' says Cecily, finally meeting Kate's gaze. 'He wasn't.'

'But . . . what?' says Kate, shaking her head in disbelief.

'Samuel died, in the ambulance, on his way to the hospital.'

'But . . . but . . . no!' says Kate, feeling suddenly sick to her stomach.

Cecily shakes her head as her eyes fill with tears. 'By the time they let me see him he didn't even look like Samuel. Mama's body had still looked like Mama, but Samuel? Here was a stranger lying in the bed, eyes shut, skin such an awful colour, cold to the touch. How could this be the Samuel who'd kissed me goodbye that morning, a man of such endless warmth and life?' she says, her head dropping.

'Oh, Mrs Finn . . .'

'I remember feeling dizzy,' says Cecily, biting her lip. 'And the next thing I knew, the nurse was handing me sugary tea and giving me a look I never want to see on anyone's face again. That look made me realise this was real. After some time, it must have been hours, my neighbour drove me home. The bag of shopping was still on the hall floor. I must have been in shock, but all I could think of was letting the travel agency know as soon as possible that we wouldn't be needing their help after all, and I was sorry to have wasted their time—' She takes a deep breath and looks back at Kate, who is struggling to hold back her own tears.

'To live through the worst of the war,' says Cecily, 'to grieve everyone he loved . . . he had been so brave in the face of such senseless horror . . . he was finally starting to live again. How is this world just? It still makes no sense,' she says, suddenly choked with a sadness that makes her whole body shake.

Kate has instinctively rushed over to kneel by Cecily and takes Cecily's clenched fingers in her hand.

'All the years we spent apart in the war – you think you have all the time in the world, but you don't. You know, I think I'd better have a whisky, dear,' she says, fingers trembling as she squeezes Kate's hand tightly. 'Underneath the bedside table.'

Kate pours the whisky, then gestures to Cecily that she'd like a shot too and pours it into her empty champagne glass. She comes to sit back down on the floor by Cecily's side.

'But I had no idea, Mrs Finn – I thought you grew old together? In your book, all those meals together, and anniversary dinners, the menus were always Samuel's favourites?'

Cecily shakes her head. 'A work of fiction, I'm afraid,' she says, forlornly. 'Poor Samuel didn't get to have his future, so I wrote one for him. I imagined the meals we'd have enjoyed. If I could write us sitting down at a table, sharing our supper, I could keep a part of him alive.'

'But Mrs Finn, you said you went to Hollywood *with* him, that he was with you in Italy . . .'

'But he was,' says Cecily, with such conviction it makes Kate ache. 'He was there in my heart.'

'But Sweden – you said for his eightieth birthday you took him back there? To look at the beautiful flowers . . . you *said* that.'

'I said my truth. I went back to the place I'd promised to take him, where he'd have wanted to be. He was with me every step of the way.'

'Mrs Finn, this is just . . . I don't know what to say. I'm so sorry, I'd never have asked you to talk about him if I'd known.'

'Oh Kate, I've lived more than sixty years without him. At times our marriage seems like a dream. Still, you don't stop loving someone simply because they're no longer in the room with you.'

'But you never remarried? You were still young.'

'Hardly young. And I was barren. And Samuel's death so soon after my parents' – it all took its toll. There followed several very bleak years. I must admit, if I'd had any faith in God or a heaven, I'd have tried to get myself there. It wasn't until I was around your age that I started coming back to life again.'

'Oh no,' says Kate, rubbing her heart. 'I'm sorry I made you talk about this.'

'You asked how I became a writer. I never set out to be one. Samuel and I had so many plans, but life had different ones. One thing his death taught me is to embrace life on life's terms, or suffer accordingly.'

'So what did you do?'

'I grieved. At times I thought the sadness would pull me under. But this world keeps spinning whether you like it or not. I forced myself to think about what Samuel would have wanted – he would never have wanted me to stay broken. So I started to write myself out

352

of the pain. I tried to revisit the children's book, but it reminded me too much of Sweden. I didn't pick it up again for a decade. The only thing that comforted me in my sorrow was cooking – the act of creation was healing. And writing those memories, those meals, made them tangible. *Thought for Food* had such short chapters, little bites of life – each time I thought, *This is silly, I should give up*, I knew I only had another page or two to go. It wasn't like writing Proust. That book saved me. I had created something that would endure. After it was published, I could look at it there on my shelf and know that Samuel and I had existed – and I was still here. Everything I thought my life would be, it wasn't, but what I got in its place was wonderful. But the only way I could move forward into that life was to let go of what I'd hoped my future would be. Be brave, Kate. I know it's hard letting go when you're scared.'

'Don't talk like that, Mrs Finn, you sound like you're about to die.'

'Of course I'm about to die, Kate, I'm ninety-seven.'

'No, but, like, today – which would put an even bigger downer on my birthday, if I'm honest.'

'Today's not the day,' says Cecily, her chin falling to her chest as she shakes her head, then emits a small burp. 'Take the rest of this champagne home,' she says, giving Kate's hand another squeeze. 'Have a good day. Don't let *anyone* ruin it.'

Kate grips Cecily's hand once more, then gently kisses her goodbye. She takes the rest of the champagne to Bernadette in the kitchen, who gives her an awkward birthday hug and insists on sharing a glass.

Kate heads back out into the street. It's one of those relentlessly grey winter days; it will rain solidly all afternoon. Paris is beautiful even when it rains.

Nick has texted again, asking if she's OK. She replies:

Fine, see you at dinner.

She would normally worry that this sounds passive-aggressive or cold, but she's so upset by Cecily's story, she is for once unbothered about trying to make Nick feel OK. Instead, she wraps her scarf more tightly around her neck and heads home. She's going to spend the afternoon in bed, reading and eating leftover birthday cake. Hopefully, by the time dinner comes around, she'll have more of an appetite for it.

Chapter Fifty-four

KATE STILL FEELS BRUISED when the cab arrives to take her to dinner. That haunted look in Cecily's eyes earlier . . . the memory of it makes Kate want to weep. She rolls down the taxi window, breathes in the cold night air, forces herself into better spirits. She can feel sad for Cecily tomorrow, but tonight is her night.

Kate's journey into town is disrupted by a voice in her head haranguing her. It's not the normal voice, the one that tells her she's getting old, that her thighs are too big and that she doesn't earn enough compared to her peers – it's worse. This voice is saying Cecily was right all along, Kate is wasting her life on a man who doesn't love her enough.

Kate finds herself arguing with the voice, trying to explain that of course Nick loves her, because he says he does – and you say what you mean, except for those times you don't because it might make you look really bad. But the voice is insistent, telling her it's time to let go.

It's bad enough having her own critical voice in her head, which is really just a handed-down version of Rita's – but three's a crowd. And the reason this third voice is telling her Cecily is right is because this voice *is* Cecily's, a woman whose world may now be confined to one small room, but who has lived an expansive life full of great joys and profound sorrows, and who speaks truth.

The restaurant is fabulous. It only has forty covers and it isn't remotely stuffy even though it's Michelin starred and French. The service is perfect – friendly and attentive without being over the top. The decor is modern and stylish, the velvet chairs so plush they're almost on a par with last night's mattress. Yet Kate keeps shifting on her seat, unable to get comfortable.

Everything on the menu sounds fantastic. Kate's ordered the salmon starter, then lamb chops with gnocchi. Nick's opted for scallops, followed by squab with truffle sauce, which made Kate give a wry smile because actually squab's just a fancy name for pigeon.

Nick's been incredibly generous with the wine, ordering a lovely crisp French white. Kate finds herself reaching for her glass frequently. It's not because the wine is delicious, although it is. It's because she's desperately trying to swallow down this horrible feeling that's back again, the one she's worked very hard to be free of.

Their starters arrive and Kate and Nick each taste a mouthful, then pause, dumbstruck – it's the sort of food that's so good you can't speak until you've devoured every last morsel. It's only after their plates are cleared and Nick starts telling her in detail about the problems of last night's databases, that the thought occurs to Kate that he hasn't yet asked how *her* day has been, her actual fortieth birthday.

Perhaps he hasn't asked because he's still feeling sheepish about earlier. Or perhaps it's because he's so self-absorbed he rarely does ask how her day's been, and suddenly she's not at all sure why she's been OK with this throughout their entire relationship.

She gazes at the waiter wheeling an impressively laden cheese trolley over to a couple in the corner, then turns back to Nick. She sits for a moment, smiling gently at him, hoping it might occur to him to ask: *How was your day?*

She's so uncomfortable with the silence, she decides she's going to have to break it herself. 'Mum rang me from Lanzarote . . .'

'Oh yeah?' says Nick, pouring her more wine. 'What's she doing out there again?'

'Some ridiculous breathing retreat,' says Kate, with a raised brow. 'I don't think she'd have managed to get to sixty-three if she didn't know how to breathe, but still . . . She's back on Wednesday, so I've got two more weekends maximum in that flat and then I'll be free.' She smiles. 'On which note, if your project's finishing next week, would you rather I move my stuff in next weekend or the one after?'

Nick's smile freezes as he looks down at his place setting. 'Sure. So . . . actually, how does Easter weekend sound for you? Is that OK?'

'What?' says Kate, her laugh dying in her throat. 'We agreed mid-December.'

'The thing is . . . Rob asked if he could take the spare room, just till he sorts himself out,' says Nick, scratching an invisible stain on the tablecloth. 'Since Tasha threw him out he's been kipping on a mate's sofa.'

'Yeah, you already told me that,' says Kate, gripping the stem of her wine glass tighter as she feels her face grow hotter.

'Rob's having a hard time.'

She's about to make another knee-jerk comment about Rob's inability to keep his genitals under control, but that comment is obscuring a far more important one. 'So hang on, are you saying Rob would have the spare room and you'd rather it wasn't the three of us?' Kate is definitely not up for living in an episode of *Men Behaving Badly*.

Nick's about to say something but pauses.

'Because I do not want to live there with Rob,' says Kate.

'Yeah, no, that's fair enough.'

'Oh. So you assumed I'd hang around till Rob finds somewhere that suits him?'

'Well, not exactly, but you didn't seem to care about specific dates when we spoke about it at your mum's?'

'*What*? I was reasonably relaxed about when in *December*, but we agreed December, and we've been talking through details ever since.' She reaches again for her wine and takes a long, slow sip. Stay calm this time.

The low, sinking feeling that's swelling in her stomach feels horribly like the one she had in France, but this time she knows: it's not an overreaction, it's her body giving her a huge signal that something is wrong. This time she won't ignore it.

'I didn't think you'd be bothered about a few more months,' he says, reaching for her hand.

'I'm not sure that's the problem,' says Kate, pulling her hand back to her lap as she tries to calm the anger pulsing through her.

'Give me your hand?'

Kate does not want to hold his hand. 'Why didn't you mention this to me before? It affects me enough to warrant a conversation, doesn't it? I know it's your home, but it's going to be *our* home.'

Nick opens his mouth and looks confused. 'I guess I didn't think it through properly, it didn't occur to me . . .'

'But if you were serious about us, after everything that's happened, then it should occur to you. Can you tell Rob he can't stay? He has other friends, it's not like you're his best friend.'

Nick looks pained. 'I can't say no to him now.'

'Yes you can, you just won't. You won't let the database team down, you wouldn't dream of letting that douche Rob down, but you don't mind letting me down.'

At this he looks flummoxed. 'But I know you don't really like Rob, which is why I thought you'd rather move in after he's gone.'

Her old familiar cautionary voice is telling her to shut up and not ruin the night, to pick this battle another time, when they're not in such a fancy restaurant, or at least to wait until she's eaten her lamb chops. But Cecily's voice is screaming for her to speak her truth and to speak it now, because the stories Kate's having to tell herself to stay with Nick are becoming too hard to swallow.

'Nick – how sure are you about us? Because if you were sure, I think you'd have made more effort to turn up at the hotel earlier. And I don't think you'd be putting Rob before me.'

He opens, closes, then opens his mouth again. She's beginning to notice how much like a fish he looks when he does this.

'I . . .' He winces, as if the pain he's about to inflict will hurt him more than her. 'I'm at least seventy per cent . . .'

Kate laughs; she can't help herself. 'Wow – I don't even merit at least *three quarters*?'

'I – well – it's just . . .'

'Do you have a spreadsheet you could show me, Nick? Because your data might be faulty. Surely algorithms can't always be right or computers would never go wrong?'

'That's not technically the fault of the software necessarily, it could also be the hardware . . .'

'Oh shut up, Nick.'

'Kate – this is still hard for me . . .'

'You know what? It's harder for me. I'm not the mathematician you are, but here are my sums: I am one hundred per cent sure that *this*' – she says, stabbing the table as she lowers her voice – 'this, here, *you*, are not good enough. You just aren't,' she says, folding her napkin and placing it on the table.

'I'm not saying it's over!' he says, panicked. 'I'm not, it's just . . . I'm not sure yet.'

'But I am. I'm done. You've ruined my last two birthdays. I will not let you ruin a third. I deserve better.'

He stares at her, wide-eyed, nodding sadly. Even now he can't offer a single word of comfort, dispute or apology – it screams volumes.

'Nick, the thing about our relationship . . .' She looks up to see the waiter hovering, holding two plates of the most delicious-looking food. Kate's shoulders drop wearily. What's the point of even saying what she was about to? If you have to explain how love works to the person you're in love with, they're probably not worthy of it.

'You know what, Nick? It's fine,' she says, pushing herself up quietly from the table. 'Your pigeon's arrived.

I'll get my lamb to go. *Bon appetit*,' which in this instance is French for *hasta la vista*, and also for *fuck you*.

Letting go hurts like hell, but it's the right thing to do.

And so is taking dinner home with her. In spite of everything – or perhaps because of it – it's the best meal she's ever tasted.

Chapter Fifty-five

Dinner for One the Night After a Heartbreak

Nay, I have done, you get no more of me
                                        Michael Drayton

Aim: to nourish and console yourself with life-affirming, buttery food made with minimum effort, thus allowing maximum time to retire early to bed with a good book (or a sleeping pill and a whisky, depending on the extent and flavour of the break-up).

Menu:
Linguine with butter and Parmesan
Leftover chocolate ice cream* – made to Eva Polon's secret recipe (see Summer Party to Celebrate the Departure of Your Snooty Neighbours and Their Yappy Little Pekingese)

*If there is no leftover ice cream in your freezer, this is an occasion wherein it is perfectly acceptable to eat whatever cake is within arm's reach.

'HERE, HAVE ANOTHER TISSUE,' says Cecily, yanking a Kleenex from the box and handing it to Kate with trembling fingers.

Kate shakes her head rapidly in the hope velocity will confuse her tear ducts. She will not cry, she will not cry again over this idiotic man. 'I know I'll be all right. It's OK that he doesn't love me. It's not the end of the world.'

'True – but I know you cared for him deeply.'

'And I know you really didn't,' says Kate, blowing her nose, just waiting for Cecily to add *I told you so*.

'I simply didn't like the way he treated you.'

'I guess you can have your book back,' says Kate, taking Cecily's original copy of *Thought for Food* from her bag. 'It didn't manage to make him love me.'

'There's only so much any book can do,' says Cecily, taking it and looking with curiosity at the cover. 'Still, I think it'll work well for you,' says Cecily, a small smile playing on her lips. 'Let's see what happens next, your story's not over yet.'

'Oh Mrs Finn, I'm so not interested in dating another useless anyone ever again. What's the point of ever loving someone if you're always going to lose them?'

'Love is the point. Give yourself time. It's only been a week.'

'Yeah, time's the great healer, I know, I know,' says Kate, sighing.

'It rather depends on what you do with it,' says Cecily, thoughtfully. 'Oh by the way, I have a present for you. It's nothing much, I'm not even sure you'll be able to use it. Fetch!' she says, pointing to an envelope on her bedside table.

Inside is a card with a short message in Cecily's elegant looped handwriting.

To Kate,

On the occasion of your fortieth birthday.

I'm still not clear what your interests are, though I think you have good taste in food, poor taste in men. You've mentioned you like my attempt at a cookery book, so I thought you might like to own it.

'Take and use my work, Amend what flaws may lurk' – with apologies to Browning.

Warm regards,

Mrs Cecily Finn

'Ah, thank you, Mrs Finn – that's very sweet,' says Kate, picking up the book again. 'Do you mean I should keep *this* copy?'

'You told me you had several copies at home.'

'I do, yes . . .'

'Why do you look confused again?'

'No, nothing, I – sorry – I'm not clear which copy you're giving me.'

'Oh Kate, really?'

'What?' says Kate, laughing with embarrassment.

'I'm giving you the book itself, the copyright.'

Kate's breath catches in her throat as her tears start to well up again.

'Oh please don't get emotional about that too,' says Cecily, 'I'll run out of tissues.'

It is the kindest thing anyone's ever done for Kate, and a rush of gratitude overtakes her. She sits for a moment, dazed by it. 'But Mrs Finn, it's your work, it was your life.'

'That's why it warrants a good home. Otherwise it'll come with me to the grave.'

'Are you absolutely sure?'

'Do you question everybody on their decisions or just me? I always say what I mean – and vice versa.'

'Yeah, I guess I had noticed,' says Kate, sniffing back her tears and laughing. 'You're not just giving this to me because you feel sorry for me, are you?'

'Good Lord, Kate, I've felt frustrated by you, occasionally angry and once or twice bemused, but I've never felt sorry for you, particularly not now. Now I feel hopeful. That's a feeling I haven't felt in some time.'

Kate puffs out a deep breath and nods. 'Mrs Finn, did you ever play rounders?'

Cecily shakes her head. 'Never one for sport.'

'I used to dread rounders. Some days I was lucky – I'd swing the bat, I had a pretty strong swing, and I'd hit the ball and it would go flying, and even though I was an average runner I'd get a rounder or at least get to one of the further bases. But whenever this one girl Laura John bowled, the ball would whizz straight past me. I'd swing and miss every time. I'd feel my face burning red, everyone would stare, and all I'd want was to ask for one more chance – I'd do better next time, I would – because I knew I could do this. But rounders isn't like baseball, you don't get another chance. So instead I'd stand for a moment too long, disappointed with myself, and then I'd start to run, but because I'd hesitated I'd get caught out, I wouldn't make it to the base in time.'

'Kate – why are you telling me this?'

'Oh, it's a metaphor, Mrs Finn. Well, an analogy. It feels like my entire life is just my fourteen-year-old self, standing on the pitch, failing hard in front of everyone, being too slow to realise it, feeling desperate for another chance.'

'Oh Kate,' says Cecily, shaking her head. 'Life is full of disappointments, big ones, small ones, even the best lives are. It's what you do with them that counts.'

'I suppose you're right. Oh, *shit*. Oops, sorry, Mrs Finn,' she says, blushing and covering her mouth.

'What now?'

'Nick's still got all my cookery books. And I did this rather dramatic flounce out of the restaurant last week, like a South American soap star – I really don't want any contact with him. I guess that's why people say a clean break is best – I should have done that back in August – otherwise you get stuck with all these painful splinters.'

'I have an idea,' says Cecily, looking over at her bookshelves. 'If you ever do leave your mother's, pick whichever of these take your fancy.'

'No, Mrs Finn, I couldn't possibly do that.'

'Kate, I cannot take them with me.'

'True. But with all due respect, Mrs Madrigal's just turned a hundred and four, I can't sit it out another decade.'

'Which is why I say take them now.'

'I can't break up your collection.'

'You can, and then I can move the Existentialists out of the bathroom before one of the idiots soaks them while violating my privacy. Kate – it would make me feel useful for once.'

'Mrs Finn – why are you being so kind to me?'

Cecily shrugs. 'Because I can be.'

'I promise this is the last thing I'll say about him, and I know it sounds trivial compared to your losses, but losing Nick feels like I'm losing such a large part of my life.'

Cecily frowns at Kate through narrowed eyes. 'That's foolish even by your standards. I think it's quite evident who's lost more.'

'Sorry, Mrs Finn, I absolutely was not comparing my losses to yours. I can only imagine what you went through.'

'No,' says Cecily, shaking her head impatiently. 'That's not what I meant at all, I wasn't suggesting I'd lost the most but then neither have you. The person who's lost something precious, obviously, is Nick. But you, Kate? You haven't lost a thing. You've gained back your future.'

Kate sits on the bus home staring out of the window at the rainy grey day. After all that's happened, does she regret giving Nick that second chance?

If she hadn't carried so much hope in their relationship, she'd have said her last goodbye at Stansted; she wouldn't have given him time to figure out what he wanted.

If she'd done that, she'd have started to accept the loss – she'd have been miserable, of course – but she'd have had clarity. She wouldn't have become consumed by trying to decipher Nick as though he was the world's most cryptic crossword. The realisation that there might not even *be* a solution to Nick had driven her half mad.

If she hadn't teetered on the verge of a meltdown she'd never have opted to volunteer, which means she'd never have found her way to Lauderdale. So does she regret these last few months of pain and disappointment?

How can she, when without them she'd never have found Mrs Finn?

PART FIVE

Let food be thy medicine.

Hippocrates

Chapter Fifty-six

CECILY HAS BEEN ASLEEP in her chair for the last two hours. Even though she emits a low nasal whistle with each breath it doesn't disturb Kate, who sits opposite, her gaze drifting to the pink-and-white cherry blossom on the branches outside.

April: at last. Some years you doubt spring will ever arrive. This winter has been particularly harsh, claiming Olive Paisner, who died from complications after a fall, and poor Bessie, from a stroke. It's taken its toll on Cecily too. She's eating such tiny portions, looking ever more frail, and her naps have been starting earlier and lasting longer. Kate hopes that with the coming of spring Cecily will perk up. In the meantime, Kate's content to sit here reading while Cecily sleeps, in the warmth and almost-quiet.

Kate has been reading rather a lot since the break-up – which *is* The Break-up, not The Wobble Two. It has been distressing for Kate to realise that even though this break-up wasn't their first (and in retrospect could have been predicted and thus avoided), it hasn't hurt significantly less than the previous one. A key reason she'd been *so* patient with Nick was that she'd been desperate to avoid the harsh realities of a broken heart. On certain days over Christmas and New Year she'd felt like she'd woken under cement sheets, her body immobilised by sheer misery.

She's coming to accept that this is the price of loving wholeheartedly, of taking a risk and losing. Her dreams are still occasionally disturbed by a vicious happy memory, but that's happening less often now. If a sad song comes on the radio, she no longer has to rush to change the station – unless it's The Magnetic Fields singing 'The Book of Love'. Painful though it is, time is changing Nick from the man she loved dearly into an increasingly disconnected memory.

On Rita's insistence, Kate allowed her mother to buy her six therapist sessions as a Christmas present, though she'd have preferred a one-way ticket to Hawaii. In fairness, her therapist has proved helpful. He's stopped Kate blaming herself for Nick's inadequacies. Whenever she berates herself for being a fool for sticking around for more punishment, she's meant to tell herself she is a generous person who gives people the benefit of the doubt – she just needs to choose better people.

Her therapist has made her realise that while she'd spent so long pitying Cecily because Cecily's life is so shrunken, Kate's own lack of ambition has kept her life small too. Kate had wrapped herself in the comfort of her relationship duvet, treating the parts of her life that weren't 'her and Nick' as if they were secondary – no wonder she feels bereft without him. And living with Rita has made Kate feel like a teenager in all the worst ways. As of last month, Kate's been staying in Bailey's spare room for low rent in exchange for free babysitting and help around the house.

Kate hadn't wanted to get sucked into years of paying for a therapist to listen to her moan – she has friends who'll do that for free, and they can drink wine while they're at it – so she'd asked the therapist, what would be the single most helpful action she could take for her future. The answer was succinct: radical self-care. Anything bad for her is now out: smoking, staying in bed ruminating about the past, being self-critical and Cara. If anyone was allowed an *I told you so* it was Cecily, because, well, she did. But if Cecily managed to bite her tongue, Cara should have, too.

Conversely, Kate's only allowing good things in. This includes all the usual suspects – vegetables, water, exercise – but any time she feels bored or lonely, she must nourish herself with the things she loves most: books and food. Over the last four months Kate has listened to the rest of Cecily's life story – the decade spent in Italy, the travels she took herself off on in her sixties and seventies, the reluctant slowing down in her eighties, the first fall, then the second and, finally, the painful process of accepting her diminishment and having to let go. Now when they meet, Kate spends time reading to Cecily, and when Cecily is asleep, reading to herself.

Cecily's cookbook collection has been inspiring – Kate's tried so many new recipes. In December, when she was hibernating and at her most fragile, it was all about soups – simple, comforting and perfect to come home to after a day on her feet. She'd started feeling more ambitious as the new year arrived, making ribollitas and laksas, and now she's making complex, delicious meals as a matter of course, getting up earlier even than Bailey's girls to make marinades and gremolatas and picadas.

One particularly bleak January weekend when it was sleeting and grey outside, she was inches from calling Nick, either to tell him she missed him or hated him, she wasn't sure which. Instead, she turned on her computer and started writing down some of the menus she'd been cooking that had comforted her, in the style of Cecily's book. She'd realised that all her different painful feelings were distinct – sadness, loneliness, anger, regret – and each required a slightly different menu to battle them. Her recipes for the sick of heart was just a dumb thing she did while trying to distract herself – but she showed Cecily anyway, and Cecily pointed out that writing about the different flavours of unhappiness was all well and good, but the plan was to get Kate back to happy, and to focus more on that.

She'd loved doing it, though, and by the time she'd written down 'Lunch for When You're Thoroughly Bored of Yourself' – slow-roast chicken with lemon and harissa, with a butter-drenched baked potato, followed by warm chocolate cookie pudding with cream – any urge to contact Nick had passed, and she was back to thinking he was a pillock – and that *she* was not only the icing but the whole entire cake.

She'd carried the satisfaction from writing into work with her on Monday along with the leftovers. When William had mentioned that his husband Chris was holding his book club in the café the following week, Kate had offered to recreate the chicken dish for them, followed by some salted caramel brownies. Chris had given her £50 for her troubles. It was the most fun £50 she'd ever earned. Cecily was right, of course: life is full of opportunities once you're open to them.

And then as Valentine's Day was looming, she'd decided the best way to take away its sting would be to hold an Anti-Valentine's supper club for a couple of dozen Aposta regulars. William was up for it, and waived any hire fee in exchange for tickets for him and Chris. It turns out some couples think 14 February is just another day. And other couples don't like being ripped off at some poncy place in town. And still other couples don't want to sit opposite each other at Pizza Express *yet again*, and would much rather flirt with the nearest stranger.

The night had been such a success that William asked her to do something regularly, and she's working on the follow-up. She might even make a few hundred quid too, and best of all it doesn't feel like work. This has been one pleasant surprise since the break-up – just how much comfort she's found at Aposta. When she was at Fletchers signing off shelf-edge stripping, it was all too easy for her mind to wander down slippery slopes and get stuck at the bottom. There's no chance of that here – there's no time or headspace, and what a blessing that is. Kate is too busy chatting to customers, washing up, mastering her latte art – her hearts are now flawless.

Kate checks her watch. It's finally getting dark outside. The other day Rita said that she thinks Kate is hiding at Lauderdale – but that is classic Rita, unwilling to accept that her daughter might think and feel differently to the way Rita does.

The truth is that these last few months Kate has needed a safe place to recover. Cecily is gentler with her nowadays. It might simply be because Cecily has less energy; she is fading. Or perhaps it's because Kate's relationship with Cecily has evolved into true friendship, of a type it pains her to realise she never had with Nick. Both women have been brave enough to be their vulnerable, imperfect selves. What a gift: to know another person, and to be known. Cecily has seen Kate at her most broken and did not walk away. To be fair, Cecily isn't much of a walker, but Kate thinks she'd have found a way, if she'd been inclined.

Kate looks up as Cecily emits a sudden snore. It's loud but not quite loud enough for her to wake herself, and it resolves into three frilly little echo snores. Kate will leave Cecily to it. She quietly puts the book she's been reading back on Cecily's shelf, tucks a blanket over Cecily's lap and heads for the door.

Chapter Fifty-seven

THROUGHOUT THE WEEK Kate has been pondering the menu for her next supper club. Today, while Cecily's been napping, Kate has been browsing Cecily's copy of Marcella Hazan's *Classic Italian Cookbook* and when Cecily wakes, Kate talks her through the plans.

'I thought I'd take a page out of your book and theme it, something like "Dinner for Pasta Lovers who Aren't Embarrassed to have Pasta as a Starter Followed by Pasta as a Main . . ."'

'Only two pasta courses?' says Cecily, with mock outrage.

'You don't think it's too gluttonous, do you? If I do a lighter pudding?'

'I used to eat double pasta all the time when I lived in Italy. Once in a trattoria in Rome I ordered three carbonaras in succession. It wasn't the done thing, but when was that ever my concern? The chef came out from the kitchen to inspect this mysterious greedy eater – he must have assumed I was a fat American man. We started talking and he ended up teaching me how to cook the perfect carbonara – relies, of course, on the cheek.'

'Ooh, I could do a carbonara for main, perhaps with new season's asparagus. Then I could start with tagliarini, maybe with crab and a hint of chilli?'

'Where do I sign up?' says Cecily with delight.

'Oh my goodness, would you come?' says Kate. 'I can arrange for you to be driven there and back.'

'Dear Lord, no – I was joking, it would be far too much excitement.'

'Mrs Finn, will you promise me when it gets warmer you'll at least sit in the garden with me?'

Cecily shakes her head.

Kate sighs in defeat. 'Oh – I need to call the event something, if I'm doing it regularly. What do you think of the name Nights and Weekends?'

'Night and weekends?'

'You once said that before you met Samuel your nights and weekends were spent desperately seeking fun. Those are often the times people feel loneliest. And I just like the sound of it.'

Cecily pulls a face Kate hasn't seen since Cecily was last commenting on Maud's excessive use of cream blusher.

'Or I could call it Thought for Food?' says Kate, looking up to see Cecily nodding, but rubbing her chest agitatedly.

'Far more apposite,' says Cecily, emitting a small belch. 'Be a dear – fetch me a Gaviscon, that alleged kedgeree is repeating on me.'

Kate heads to the carers' station but no one's there, and after waiting a few minutes she walks down the corridor in the direction of noise from the dining room. She pokes her head in and sees Mrs Gaffney and Bernadette seated at the front of the room, along with the sandy-haired man who has the young girlfriend. They've set up a projector with a slide reading 'Quarterly Food Survey – Feedback'. Seated in the audience are two dozen of the residents and the room is lively with the sound of grumbling. Mrs Gaffney catches Kate's eye and beckons for her to listen in.

'So it's agreed?' says Mrs Gaffney. 'Keep teriyaki chicken on the menu but lose Thai curry?' The ladies call out their assent. 'Good,' she says, ticking off her paperwork. 'Next on the agenda, omelettes: *The omelettes used to be much better. They're too dry . . . need to be fluffier.* Is that a generally held view or just one resident's?'

'You should make them runny, like they used to at the Savoy,' calls out Maud.

Bernadette puffs up in her chair irritably. 'We have to make thirty omelettes every morning, I'm afraid we can't offer you personal butler service.'

'And your eggs are *not* fresh,' continues Maud. 'I'm used to an orange yolk from when we had the farm in Africa.'

The man with the blue eyes shifts in his chair, looking mildly uncomfortable.

'There's *nothing* wrong with our eggs,' says Bernadette. 'They could hardly be fresher if we kept our own hens and I am not running around after a bunch of chickens *and* you.'

Mrs Gaffney squeezes Bernadette's arm sternly. 'Next item,' says Mrs Gaffney briskly. 'Fruit salad: *The fruit is cut wrong, there are too many grapes, the melon is hard as glass* . . . again, is this a widely held view or just Mrs Rappapot's?'

Why hasn't Cecily come to *this* meeting? She'd be in her element.

By the time Kate's located a carer and some medicine, Cecily is fast asleep. Kate resettles in her chair and picks up the cookbook again. Yes – screw etiquette, she's definitely cooking double pasta. She'll post the menu online in advance so the faint-hearted can avoid it – but it'll sort the wheat from the chaff, or rather the double wheat from the gluten avoiders . . .

She starts scribbling provisional costings, then decides she needs a bigger piece of paper than the scrap from her bag. She heads back down the corridor to find one, and as she approaches the admin office, she sees the sandy-haired man emerging with a biro in hand.

'Hello!' he says cheerily. 'Pen ran out.' He has beautiful deep blue eyes, and when he smiles, laughter lines form at their edges.

'Are they still ripping apart that poor fruit salad?' says Kate.

'We've moved on! To liver – underdone or too well done. Those ladies have strong opinions on food.'

'And so they should! It's one of life's few reliable pleasures. It's important, no matter how old you are.'

'Huh. You're right I guess – it would be a shame if they didn't still care. Were you in the room when they were talking about Mexican night?' he says, trying to stifle a giggle.

'Oh no, what?' says Kate, giggling even though she doesn't know what he's about to say.

'Edith Constable said the guacamole was grounds enough to send Bernadette to Qantas. I believe she meant Dignitas, but either way, Bernadette was not amused.'

'Oh my goodness, Mrs Constable ruder than Maud Rappapot? Though I have to agree, bad guacamole is a total missed opportunity, don't you think?'

'Er, I haven't given it much thought,' he says, looking mildly taken aback. 'I just buy mine from Tesco's.'

'What?' says Kate, stepping back in horror. 'You can't *buy* guacamole. It has to be freshly made. Anything you buy from a supermarket has loads of acid in it.'

'What, like LSD?' he says, laughing. 'I'd better stop feeding it to my kids, then . . .'

'Yeah,' says Kate, nodding and trying to hide her surprise, though why she's surprised that a man her age has kids is beyond her – it is the norm. 'Acetic acid or lemon juice, I meant – for shelf life. Kills the flavour. There's a great recipe online from a restaurant in New York, Rosa Mexicana – you'll never look back.'

'I'm Ben,' he says, extending his hand.

'Kate.' It's her favourite type of handshake – firm, dry and strong – and it's accompanied by some rather intense eye contact. 'Are you involved in Lauderdale's catering?'

'Jackie asked if I could sit in on the drinks feedback.'

'You're a nutritionist?'

'Me?' He laughs. 'Kind of the opposite. I supply the wine. We haven't got to it yet but I'm sure the ladies will have feedback.'

'No doubt Maud will have something to say about the substandard Beaujolais,' she says, laughing, then stopping as the uncomfortable look returns to his face. Ah. Oh. Ew. That's why he looks so familiar (and uncomfortable): it's that long, slim nose, same as his grandmother's.

'Well – good to meet you, Kate. I'd better get back in there,' he says cheerily.

Kate's trying to think of something apologetic to say about the fact she's mildly dissed his grandmother twice in two minutes, but her mind's gone blank. 'Er, enjoy your liver . . . I mean, enjoy talking about liver, to eat – not enjoy your liver before you develop psoriasis, cirrhosis, you know what I mean – er, I'm going to go now,' she says, turning and heading back down the corridor, feeling colour flood her cheeks.

Talk about missed opportunities . . . and she's forgotten to grab that piece of paper, but she's not turning back now.

Anyway, what is she even thinking? He has some age-inappropriate girlfriend. And it wasn't an opportunity. And besides, she's not in the market for a date. She's not looking for a relationship with anyone other than herself.

Chapter Fifty-eight

'WHERE HAVE *YOU* BEEN, stranger?'

Kate is busy at work clearing tables, but when she hears his voice she freezes. She turns, tray in hand, and, sure enough, there's Martin looking tanned, surprised and delighted to see her. She thought he'd have been in before now – after all, he'd claimed he was an Aposta regular – but then again, he'd claimed he'd meet her for a picnic six months ago and she hasn't heard a word from him since.

He smiles so broadly it disarms her. She grips her tray, half turns back to the table she's clearing, then back to him with a wry smile. He spreads his arms wide to give her a hug which forces her to put the tray down. He wraps his arms tightly around her and she feels the strength of his upper body as she breathes in the scent of clean laundry, then hurriedly disentangles herself.

'You're *working* here?' he says, pointing at her apron with confusion.

'So it would seem. Where did *you* disappear to, more to the point?'

'Me? I just flew in from LA, been filming a pilot there since January. Gosh, you look well. What happened to your pork pies?'

'*My* pork pies? I could ask the same of *you*,' she says, laughing. 'Birthday in December, indeed!'

He smiles as though he hasn't heard the comment. 'Hey, this must be fate. Are you doing anything tomorrow night?'

'Why do you ask?'

'My friend Archie's in a show at the National, it's totally sold out. I've got seats in the stalls, we could head to the Ivy after for supper?'

Kate turns back hesitantly to her tray and adds the two remaining coffee cups from the table before turning back to him. 'Martin?' she says gently.

'Yes, sweetheart?'

'Are you going to give me any sort of excuse as to why you stood me up, or are you pretending that never happened?'

He looks confused and frowns. 'Did we have plans? Oh God, we had a plan?' he says, his hand covering one eye in embarrassment. 'It was a definite plan, was it?'

'Very.'

'Oh Kate,' he says, grabbing her hands and squeezing them. 'I'm sorry, darling. I was having a bit of a terrible time, if I'm being honest. Did I mention I was in the middle of my divorce?'

'You did.'

'My ex is an incredibly difficult woman, and, er, she must have been doing something batshit crazy – that must be what happened.'

'Right . . .'

'Oh Kate, you should have called and given me a hard time.'

'Er, I tried to – but you didn't answer your phone, and also I had a rather heavy picnic hamper in my hands.'

He brings both palms to his cheeks in horror. 'Oh, Christ. Did we arrange a picnic?'

'You approved the menu.'

'Bollocks. Kate, I can't believe what an arse you must think I am. I'm so sorry if I let you down.'

Kate smiles at his use of 'if' rather than 'that'.

'Well, you must let me make it up to you,' he says, dropping his head in embarrassment, then looking up at her with a sheepish grin.

She looks past him to the shelf of coffee beans on the back wall. They're running low on Colombian, she'll need to grab some from the stock room later.

'Martin,' she says, smiling as her gaze returns to his. 'Thank you for the invite, it sounds lovely, but – well, the thing is, I'm just not interested in unreliable men anymore. I can't do it.'

He takes a step back and pulls a wounded face. 'Kate, darling, I've totally ballsed this up but it wasn't my fault. Everybody deserves a second chance, don't they?'

Kate thinks about this briefly as she scratches her eyebrow. 'You know what? I'm not sure that's true.'

'You don't believe me, do you? About my ex? I swear – I'll show you some of her texts, you'll see she's insane,' he says, reaching for his phone.

Kate puts her hand out to stop him. 'It's fine, Martin, really. I don't care either way.'

'You've got to let me make it up to you, honestly, I can't have the sexy waitress at my favourite coffee shop hate the very sight of me.'

Kate laughs. 'Honestly, there's no need.'

'No, please, let me do something, I feel dreadful,' he says, clasping his hands in prayer.

'Gosh, you're very dramatic, aren't you?' she says laughing. 'But . . . if you do want to make amends, there is one thing . . .'

'Anything.'

'Buy a ticket for my supper club. You won't be able to eat half the menu, but come anyway. Twenty quid's a small price to pay for three courses and redemption, don't you think?'

Chapter Fifty-nine

Don't let that be the doorbell, please do not let that be the doorbell.

Kate is back at Rita's, summoned to await a Tesco delivery while Rita's out for the night, and has taken the opportunity of a quiet night in to engage in some radical self-care, specifically a home-made avocado hair mask. Kate's scalp is half smeared with green mush, with a scoopful more in hand. The shopping's not due for another hour. But that is definitely the doorbell, again.

It must be a neighbour, no doubt John Pring moaning about rodents, or Lizzette, moaning about John Pring. When Kate calls out to ask who's there, she's surprised to hear it's Gerry's son, Jeremy.

'Mum's out – with your mum, and Patrick? At the Odeon? The new Tom Hanks film? Back around eleven p.m.?' says Kate, hoping to hear the sound of footsteps retreating.

'Yes, I know. I've got something for you.'

It'll be books, for Rita. 'Oh right, leave it on the doorstep would you?'

'I fear it won't keep well.'

Kate's fingers form green mushy claws as she struggles to open the door with her elbow. There's Jeremy all

387

right, in a tweed jacket and mustard cords, his grey hair combed neatly to one side. To Kate's surprise he's carrying a bottle of wine and a bag full of food.

'Hello, there,' says Jeremy. 'Rita mentioned you were home alone and might like a bite to eat.'

'Did she really?' Kate steps back to let him in as her stomach emits a low gurgle. 'I'm afraid I'm not really dressed for supper, though I do have a salad in my hair . . .'

He squints at her hairline but is too polite to comment. 'Right-oh,' he says, following her through to the kitchen. 'Shall I crack on with the cooking?'

Kate holds her hands up in resignation. She looks at the food he's unpacking, initially with hunger but then with rapid cold dread: Chicken schnitzel and mash followed by blueberry lattice pie. No! But of course *yes*. Come and wait for Tesco? More like come and let me pimp you out to a neighbour. Page thirty-five, *Dinner with Intent to Make A Match – It is better to marry than to burn, St Paul* . . .

'What exactly did Mum say to you?' says Kate, warily.

'Oh, nothing much.'

'Nothing much . . . like what, exactly?'

'She mentioned you were back for the evening, that you might like company.'

'Er, why?'

'Well, since you lost your boyfriend and your job.'

'Huh. I wouldn't say I lost Nick exactly – and I certainly didn't lose my *job*, I finally had the guts to leave, but a-ny-way. It's fine, I love my new job. I cannot *believe* she said that.' And she cannot believe Rita's set her up like a complete patsy.

'So what are you up to now, then?'

'I'm waitressing at Aposta, on the high street. And I'm starting this supper club thing – it's inspired by that book your mum borrowed.' Which Kate should have insisted was returned months ago.

'Ooh, I've never been to a supper club.'

'Come to the next one. There're a few tickets left, it's two weeks on Saturday, Dinner for Serious Pasta Lovers. Not serious as in solemn, obviously,' she says, her gaze shifting to the floor.

'Sounds great,' he says enthusiastically. He's only fifty or so, not much older than Nick, but he looks so middle-aged – his cheeks are ruddy, and in that outfit he'd be right at home at his local Rotary club.

'Listen, I was going to wait till after dessert to ask you . . .' he says, smiling nervously. 'But seeing as you've already brought up the book – that is the main reason I'm here.'

'Oh . . . OK . . . Gosh! Super-awkward,' says Kate, biting her lip. 'Look, Jeremy—'

'Call me Jerry.'

'Your mum's Gerry.'

'It's spelled differently.'

'Oh, right. Sounds identical, but OK – well, Jerry, I'm terribly flattered, but I'm not in the market . . .'

'For what?'

'You know . . .'

'I'm not sure I do.'

'Please don't think it's your age. Or the fact you live with your mum,' she says, laughing awkwardly. 'I did too, until recently.'

'I'm sorry, Kate, I've totally lost you.'

'You said the reason you're here is because of the book,' says Kate, wincing at how excruciating it is to have to spell this out.

'That's correct.' He nods, but his face still registers incomprehension. For a man with a big job in publishing, he's pretty damn slow.

'You obviously came round because Mum told you I was here.'

'Yes, though I would have phoned you otherwise.'

'And you brought me schnitzel? Schnit-zel?'

'I'm not sure I understand how you get from breaded chicken to romantic intrigue?' he says, looking perplexed.

'It's *the matchmaking dinner*,' says Kate, feeling her blush deepen.

'Oh *gosh*, no!' he says, a little too forcefully for Kate's ego. 'I chose that menu because I like schnitzel, not because I want to *go out* with you,' he says, laughing. 'You took it literally? Ahhh, that's very flattering.' He lets out another laugh that's closer to a guffaw. 'I'm sorry, Kate, but I'm actually spoken for at present.'

Kate shakes her head in mortification.

'Look, let's put the schnitzel on hold for ten minutes,' he says. 'I'll open this wine. And I'll explain what I actually do want.'

Twenty minutes later, Kate feels like she would very much like to give this man a hug – a platonic hug, but a large one nonetheless.

'I've always thought a modern version with new recipes would be brilliant,' says Kate excitedly.

'And you have such a great PR story, you'd potentially follow it up by rereleasing Mrs Finn's original.'

'And you really think a contemporary version could work?'

'Kate, we've published a dozen titles on clean eating in the last year: off the record, they're all identikit quinoa-filled pap. One of the things I love about Mrs Finn's book is that it has such a clear voice – so I'd brief any writer we commission to capture the spirit of the original.'

'Mrs Finn will be overjoyed her book's having a new lease of life,' says Kate as Jerry refills her glass. 'She's got this bee in her bonnet about how she's had no sense of purpose for so long. She never had kids, so she hasn't got a "legacy" – this book was sort of her baby, if that makes sense? Did Mum mention I own the copyright?'

'Yes – you should see around a thousand pounds from the modern version, and if we republish the original, you'll receive a hundred per cent of the royalties – perhaps five grand? Not enough to retire on, I'm afraid, but not to be sniffed at.'

'I'm not sure what Mrs Finn will do with the money, but she'll be delighted.'

'So in principle you're happy for us to commission a food writer next week?'

'Oh, absolutely.'

'You don't want to ponder it over the weekend?'

'Nothing to ponder! Now bring on that schnitzel.'

Two hours later, and the Tesco man *has* actually been and Jerry has gone, leaving Kate in high spirits. She's leaning over the side of the bath washing her hair and thinking through logistics for the double pasta supper club, when the thought hits her, flooding her with warmth like a shot of Jägermeister but without the regrettable acid after-burn. Hurriedly, she rinses the last of the avocado from her hair, and without even bothering to put on shoes, grabs her key and races downstairs, running along the corridor to Jerry's front door.

'Did I leave something behind?' says Jerry, greeting her warmly.

'I'm sorry,' says Kate, barely pausing for breath. 'But I shouldn't have said yes so quickly, I've had second thoughts.'

'That really was quick,' he says, his face falling in disappointment.

'No, not about publishing the book, I absolutely want that to happen. But I don't want you to brief someone next week,' she says, shuddering at the thought.

'OK,' he says, looking perplexed. 'Is the timing the problem?'

'It's not the timing,' says Kate, hurrying her words out before she loses her nerve. 'It's the writer part. The thing is, Jerry, I *know* this book, it's like a part of me. I've carried it with me – literally – ever since she first lent it to me. And I'm passionate about food – and I was a copywriter, for a long time . . . And it's just – if anyone's going to write a modern version of this book, it should be me.' Now she's started asking for what she wants, she can't stop. 'I'm sure another writer could do a good job, but I'd give it so much more – more thought, more love, more attention. I'd give it everything.'

He laughs a small, embarrassed laugh. 'But you've never written a book before.'

'Nor has anyone who's a first-time writer. I can do this book, I know I can. I can write menus and test them, I know how to make food delicious. And I think a lot, far too much, in fact, about what goes on inside other people's heads.'

He folds his arms and looks uncomfortable. Kate hasn't even thought what she'll do if he says no. This book saved Cecily's life, and more than anything Kate wants to use it as a raft to a different life for herself. Could she live with the idea of someone else writing it? Probably. Will she fight for the chance to do it? Absolutely.

'I did a mini-version of the book in January,' she continues. 'My supper club's basically an event version of the book. And I can think of nothing that would make Mrs Finn happier than if I wrote this book myself.'

He sighs. 'Well, I'm afraid that last point's not a hugely commercial reason, but why not have a stab at something, show me some sample chapters? I'll brief another writer in the meantime, and I'll need to be fairly convinced in order to persuade my team. Do you think you can get me a proposal and a synopsis, around thirty pages, in, say, four weeks?'

'You'll have them in two.'

When Rita and Patrick get home from the cinema that night, Kate wraps Rita in an enormous hug. This time it's Rita who struggles to free herself.

'See?' says Rita, draping her coat over the sofa and kicking off her heels. 'Your mother's not entirely useless after all. See, Patty Cakes? My daughter's finally giving me some credit for being a great mother.'

'Thank you, Mum, for being the sort of mother who opens my post and steals my book and gives it to a neighbour,' says Kate, as Rita laughs in spite of herself. 'I'm sorry I gave you such a hard time along the way.'

'As long as you dedicate the book to me, we'll call it quits.'

It's rather obvious who Kate would dedicate the book to, but that's OK, she can stick Rita in the acknowledgements.

Chapter Sixty

KATE HAD WANTED TO wait until she'd convinced Jerry about the book before telling Cecily, but the following Sunday she's unable to contain herself. 'And they're planning to publish next summer. And they're asking Nigella to write the foreword, they think she'll love the idea.'

Cecily has for once remained speechless, eyebrows raised in delight as Kate has breathlessly been sharing the news.

'But Jerry's briefing another writer, and now I'm worried he'll choose the other person.'

At this Cecily shuffles forward in her chair with a frown. 'How could anyone do a better job than you?'

'I've been scribbling down ideas all week,' says Kate, proceeding to talk Cecily through her proposed structure and menu ideas. As she's talking Cecily stares into the distance, lost in concentration. Occasionally, she gives a small dip of her chin. Occasionally, a smile creeps over her lips or her brow creases in confusion.

'What do you think?' says Kate with a hint of desperation she's embarrassed to hear in her own voice.

Cecily lets out a loud sigh. 'Did I ever tell you about the time Papa humiliated me at school?'

'You told me he threatened to embarrass you if you didn't become a teacher.'

'No, years before that, while I was still at prep school. English was my favourite subject. Every week we had to write a piece to read in class. I had rather an aptitude for making things up.'

'You don't say . . .'

'And I'd realised the more often I used the word God the higher my grade, so I'd sprinkle him in liberally. This particular week the homework was to write a letter of condolence to the mother of a friend who'd lost her husband. What a challenge!' she says, her eyes widening. 'In a weak moment I asked Papa's advice. He peered at me impatiently over his glasses and said, "Write *Thank God she's been left well provided for*".'

Kate shakes her head in embarrassment.

'I didn't realise what that meant – I was only six – so I wrote it down word for word, smugly confident I'd get top marks. When I came home from school with a detention I asked Papa why he'd set me up like that, and he said, "To teach you to think for yourself".'

Kate blushes. Cecily still hasn't lost her bite. 'Would you at least let me know what you think of the titles? "Second Helpings"? "The Heart of the Kitchen"? "Recipes to Cure Loneliness and Longing" . . .?'

Cecily feigns a yawn that turns into a real one. 'I need to lie down, dear – it's time for you to go.'

'Oh that's OK, I'll sit here for a while and read.'

'No, dear,' says Cecily, patting Kate's knee softly but decisively. 'It's not a time for reading, it's a time for writing.'

Cecily's right, of course, but seeing her sitting hunched in her chair looking so frail makes Kate loath to go. She has a strong sense that their time is running out.

Kate starts gathering her things but then pauses and turns back to Cecily, who looks at her enquiringly. Kate holds Cecily's gaze until it is Cecily who finally blushes.

'Mrs Finn – thank you.'

'For what?'

'For saving me.'

'From what?'

'From myself. For making me borrow the book. For giving me the copyright.'

Cecily waves the comment away, as if dismissing an inept waiter.

'No, listen, Mrs Finn, please. Your book made me laugh when I was down, it made me hungry when I'd lost my appetite. It's changed my life for the better because whatever happens next, it's given me back something I thought I'd lost completely: it's given me back hope.'

Cecily's smile lights up her entire face, and for a moment Kate sees a much younger woman, a woman who still has a whole life ahead of her.

'You're welcome,' she says, reaching out to touch Kate's arm. 'It's nice to know I made a difference. Oh, and by the way, Kate, I think it's probably time you called me Cecily.'

It turns out to be a lot more fun writing menus than writing lists of reasons whether to stay in or leave a confusing relationship. Every morning Kate sets her alarm for 5 a.m., starts writing, and in a heartbeat it's 7.30 a.m. and it's time to help Bailey get the girls ready for school, and then for Kate to head to work. Kate's writing till midnight, having to force herself to go to bed or she'd never get any sleep. It's a little like being in love; she's consumed by the book. Except often when she's been in love she's lost herself – trying to make another person happy without enough care for her own happiness. Writing the book, she feels like she's finally found herself.

Dinner at your Mother's House after a Surprise Break-up on Holiday

Aim: to minimise face time with your mother so as not to transfer blame onto her for your ex-boyfriend's uselessness

Large Breakfast Before a Wedding Where You'll Be the Only Single Guest

Aim: to line your stomach sufficiently to prevent disgracing yourself – and to prevent alcohol skewing your thinking and causing you to reach out to your ex, which will only result in months of further and unnecessary pain. Menu: Eggs, toast, more toast, coffee, toast.

Supper to Nourish Yourself During Heartbreak

Aim: to combine the perfect balance of Ben & Jerry's and Netflix, alongside dark leafy greens and berries. To encourage self-soothing, not self-pity

Early Supper for Two Overexcitable Easter Bunnies Under the Age of Ten

Later Supper for Your Best Friend and Her Marvellous Boyfriend to Celebrate their Five-Month Dating Anniversary While You Make Yourself Scarce . . .

Kate will have enough menus to write two books by the time she's done. Maybe she could persuade Jerry to let her write a travel-inspired sequel. She could spend a year in Italy, write an entire book on pasta alone . . .

That has been the only downside to this creative flurry: the timing. She could still do the supper club the night after she submits the proposal, but she wants dinner to be perfect; it deserves more attention than she can currently dedicate to it. It's not ideal, but she has all the ticket holders' details. Only four guests can't make the following Saturday, and Kate offers them a refund and a free ticket to her next event. The other guests will get free Prosecco for the inconvenience. She won't make a profit, but if they enjoy themselves, they'll come back again.

The night before she's due to send Jerry her work, she sits with Bailey in her kitchen sharing a pizza and a bottle of wine, watching as her friend studies the pages. Cecily told Kate not to seek other people's advice, but Kate has so much hope invested in the project she's worried she might have done something dire. She watches, her hands covering her mouth as Bailey reads through to the last word and finally puts the document down on the table.

'Well . . .?' says Kate, her fingers crossed tightly on her lap.

'I know I'm your friend and you think I'd say this anyway – but honestly, it's perfect.'

Now all Kate has to do is wait. She still hates waiting, but nowadays she's rather good at it.

Chapter Sixty-one

KATE HAS BEEN SO focused on the book and then the food for the supper club, that it's not until she's leaving Lauderdale the following Sunday and spots Ben talking to Mrs Gaffney, that she remembers she's completely forgotten to order the Prosecco.

She doesn't know Ben well enough to ask a favour, but he must already think she's rude for insulting his grandma, and besides, Cecily has taught her many things, including: if you don't ask, you don't get.

Still, Kate does have some dignity, there's no way she's asking for a job lot of cheap booze within Mrs Gaffney's earshot. Instead, she heads out into the warm spring evening and loiters awkwardly in the car park, pretending to look at something on her phone while surreptitiously trying to figure out which car might be Ben's. He always dresses stylishly – today in classic Levi's and a navy T-shirt, but he doesn't seem flash, so not the BMW, not the Mercedes . . .

When Ben emerges, sure enough he heads towards a VW Golf, but when he sees Kate, his face lights up and he heads over.

'Speak of the devil, I was going to ask Mrs Gaffney for your number but I thought it might be weird if you got a random text about avocados . . .'

'Avocados?' says Kate, totally wrong-footed.

'I forgot the name of that restaurant. My daughter's doing a vegan thing and guacamole's one of her favourites.'

'Oh right, yes – it's Rosa Mexicana.'

'Veganism seems to be all the rage nowadays. I'd miss bacon far too much.'

'And butter,' says Kate. 'How can people live without butter?'

'Ah, a woman after my own heart,' he says, laughing.

'How old are your kids?' she says, trawling her memory for anything Maud mentioned. All Kate can remember is that Ben used to bring back mochi cakes from Japan, and that his ex-wife is difficult.

'Martha's seventeen going on thirty, and Josh is eleven.'

'Seventeen? Does she visit her grandmother often?'

'You mean her great-grandmother? I drag her here once a month, but she'd much rather be doing anything else. On which note, I'd better get home and check she hasn't cracked open my vintage Château Margaux.'

'Oh, actually . . . there was something I wanted to ask *you*. I'm hosting a supper club for thirty next Saturday—'

'Are you a chef?' he says, looking impressed.

'Just a keen eater. I need to get hold of twenty bottles of decent Prosecco without breaking the bank. I thought you might know which supermarket has the best own brand, because I do know it isn't Fletchers.'

'What's on the menu?'

'Well, we're starting with tagliarini with crab, followed by pappardelle with cream, pancetta and new season's asparagus . . .'

'Pasta followed by pasta? Sounds like my dream dinner.'

Kate blushes with happiness. 'On the side I'm doing a simple tomato and basil salad, and I've got warm ciabatta rolls from Brick House, this amazing bakery we use. Then for pudding an intense dark chocolate mousse with cherries.'

'Where is this supper club and are there any tickets left?'

'You want to come?' she says with surprise.

'Absolutely.'

'Do you want to bring a friend?'

'Just me, I'm afraid. Right, so, you'll want a fairly dry, good value Prosecco. Give me your number and leave it with me. And put me down for a ticket.'

Kate's quite relieved she bumped into Ben as she was leaving Lauderdale rather than arriving, or she'd be forced to explain the dumb grin on her face to Cecily. Cecily will surely not approve, though hopefully it'll stop short of a blood feud.

Later that night Kate receives a text from Ben Wine Guru:

I'll never buy guacamole from a shop again – genius recipe. And I can get you a decent Prosecco at £3.74 per bottle, retails at £11.99 – will that work? If so, shall I come early on Saturday and help you set up?

Chapter Sixty-two

THERE ARE MOMENTS IN life when everything actually does go right; when you've taken a chance and things turn out even better than you'd dared hope.

There is a point halfway through her supper club where Kate stands in the doorway between the kitchen and the dining area, quietly looking out at what's in front of her. The room is buzzing, everyone in high spirits brought on by Prosecco and amazing carbs. Thirty guests are seated at the two long wooden tables, eating delicious Italian food, drinking great wine and enjoying themselves. The tables look beautiful – adorned with pretty little vases of yellow and white freesias, and antique cut-glass tea lights that make the candlelight dance and sparkle around the room. The food looks even better. The diners are midway through their main pasta and if the first course was anything to go by, there won't be a scrap of food left. Warm bread has been piled up and devoured, luscious platters of glossy tomato salad and fragrant basil have been passed around, tangles of tagliarini have been heaped onto plates, fingers have tracked every last drop of pasta sauce across them.

Of course there are some familiar faces – Bailey, looking happy and relaxed, sitting between Adam and Ben. The three are laughing uproariously at something

Martin has just said. There's Jerry and his date, chatting animatedly to a couple next to them. And then there are twenty-four other people who have chosen to spend their Saturday night here, sharing this experience, enjoying a home-cooked meal and, above all, the conviviality.

Earlier this afternoon when Kate was unpacking the food delivery, she'd suffered a mild meltdown when she realised she'd ordered raspberries not cherries, there wasn't enough asparagus and she hadn't allowed enough time to factor in more shopping. But then Cecily's advice, from 'Dinner in a Bed-Sitting Room', had popped into her mind: *What can't be disguised must be utilised. Don't apologise – improvise.* Kate had turned the raspberries into a sharp, fruity purée for Bellinis, kept the chocolate mousse simple and ended up asking Martin to find more greens – if not asparagus, then frozen peas or broad beans. The pasta had turned out even better, the peas adding sweet little bursts of freshness to cut through the rich, creamy, smoky sauce.

Kate takes one last look at the diners before she heads back into the kitchen to prepare dessert. She smiles to herself, and at that moment Jerry looks up and catches her eye. She wonders if he's read her pages yet – she can't read anything from his expression other than the fact that he's having a good time.

And maybe that is enough, for today at least – to know that she's done the best job hosting that she could have. Cecily would be proud of her, and more to the point, Kate is proud of herself.

Even though she's not expecting to hear from Jerry about the book for another week, every night as she leaves work, the first thing she does is check her inbox. There must be something in the air, though, because while there's nothing from Jerry, there are two emails she wasn't expecting.

The first is from Cara:

> Hey, hon, long time no speak. Saw your supper club on Instagram – looked #AMAZING. Can I get two freebies to the next one, and I'll get you some free PR? Xxx

When Kate thinks back, she realises that as harsh as Cara was about Nick, she wasn't exactly wrong. Kate had always confused Nick's cleverness with thoughtfulness – but they're entirely unconnected qualities. When Nick said *No one's ever loved me the way you do*, it wasn't a romantic compliment, it was narcissism. And Kate had always given him credit for being so uncritical of people such as Rob – she thought it meant Nick was nicer than she was, but actually all it meant was that he had bad taste in friends. On which note, does she want Cara back in her life? Perhaps or perhaps not. She replies:

> Come to the coffee shop and let's discuss.

The second email stops her in her tracks:

> Hey, Kate. I hope all is well. Saw your double pasta photos online – wish I could have been there. Anyway, I'm doing a big tidy-up in the flat and wondered what to do with your cookbooks. Shall I bring them round/do you want to meet for coffee? I think of you often. N xx

She hasn't had any contact with him since her fortieth last year, which feels like a lifetime ago. Still, the sight of his name in her inbox makes her stomach lurch. She is suddenly hijacked by a flashback of standing opposite him at Stansted airport on that sweltering August day, feeling shell-shocked and traumatised and utterly lost.

Six months ago she would have hoped for something more from an email from Nick – an apology, an acknowledgement that his behaviour had been crap – anything that might make her feel better. But she's learned that 'closure' is something you only get in an episode of *Friends*. In real life you live with mess and loose ends and unsent draft emails in your inbox. You go through pain, and then one day it doesn't hurt quite as much as it did the day before, and then one day, rather a long time later, it doesn't hurt that much at all.

One of Rita's dreaded buzz phrases is, 'If you spot it, you've got it'. It always reminds Kate of 'He who smelled it dealt it'. Still, it has made Kate examine her own role in the relationship. In her mind she'd often berated Nick for his cowardice and his lack of honesty with her. But Kate's hardly the bravest person who's ever lived – she'd stayed in a job she didn't like for aeons because she was terrified to leave. And she'd hardly been honest with herself about Nick – she'd told herself the crumbs he could offer were enough, when so often she was left hungry.

A few days later she replies:

Hope all is well with you too. Keep the books, enjoy them.

At some point, perhaps already, some other woman will love Nick, will wake up next to his sweet smile, will sit down beside him for a hundred delicious meals. But she too will have to find real nourishment elsewhere. Nick can only offer basic sustenance. Kate doesn't need that anymore – she's learned to feed herself.

Kate takes one last look at his name in her inbox. It no longer has the power to make her feel unwell. She presses delete.

That chapter is done. She's writing herself into a better story.

Chapter Sixty-three

*R*ING ME. PLEASE RING ME. *Just ring me now, please.*
    Kate hasn't felt this insecurely attached to her phone since those first horrible days after France. Jerry said he'd call at the start of the week, but it's not till the Thursday morning, as she's sitting on the bus on the way to work, that his name finally appears on her screen, and she scrambles to answer.

'Kate! I hope it's not too early to call?'

'Not at all,' she says, keeping her voice low as the woman next to her turns to her with a sour look.

'Great. First, thanks so much again for dinner the other week, we loved it. You're a talented cook.'

'My pleasure,' says Kate, her stomach gripped with anxiety as she wills him to cut to the chase.

'Also, we had our commissioning meeting yesterday. We discussed your proposal. I felt you deserved a phone call rather than just an email after all your hard work.'

'Uh-huh,' says Kate, feeling her throat go dry.

'I'm not sure if I mentioned this before, but we also briefed the project to Celina Summer – her agent's looking for a new project to make Celina more relatable.'

'Oh. I didn't realise I was up against her,' says Kate with dismay. Cara's hosted several food events with

Celina Summer and reported back that she's an epic bitch who loves cocaine far more than she loves food.

'Well – Celina has a lot of fans on social media, and she's now on her sixth book . . .'

'Uh-huh . . .' says Kate, because Celina's books are as thin and lazy as Celina and the thought of Celina doing a half-botched job on *this* book is rather upsetting.

'Her brand is very strong among key demographics,' says Jerry. 'Mums with young kids, millennials . . .'

'I see,' says Kate with a sinking feeling.

'And the thing is, our sales team would have a far easier job selling Celina in to the trade rather than an unknown. It's just the way the industry works.'

Kate's nodding because she's worried if she opens her mouth all that will come out is a strangled sound of disappointment.

'But I don't care about making my sales team's job easier,' says Jerry. 'I care about publishing great books – books that have heart and integrity.'

'I understand,' says Kate. How is she going to break the bad news to Cecily?

'So would you like to come in and meet the team tomorrow, and in the meantime we can draw up a contract? I'd suggest getting an agent. We can give you some names.'

'Sorry, an agent for what?'

'I loved what you wrote, Kate. Your voice is distinctive, it's likeable. Your menus are delicious, not a grain of quinoa in sight. Plus you're clearly highly committed.'

'You mean you've chosen *me*?' she says, her voice getting louder as she breaks into a massive grin. Who cares if the woman next to her thinks she's too loud!

'I'm pretty sure that's what *come in and have a look at your contract means*, yes!' he says, laughing. 'We've chosen you.'

The following morning Kate leaves Jerry's offices clutching a provisional contract, buzzing with excitement. It's a beautiful sunny day and William isn't expecting her till 1 p.m., so she heads over to the fancy haberdashery in Soho, buys a length of their finest red satin ribbon, and asks the assistant to wrap the seven pages in a perfect bow. Then she hops in a taxi straight to Lauderdale and rushes through reception and down the corridor to Cecily's room.

She knocks but there's no response. It's 11 a.m. With the amount that Cecily's sleeping nowadays she's probably already having a nap. Kate knocks again, then gently opens the door.

The bed is empty, as is Cecily's chair. Kate checks the bathroom: empty. Cecily had seemed particularly frail last Sunday, and Kate has the sudden absolute conviction that after everything that's happened, the evil and ironic universe would choose today to claim Cecily. She rushes back to reception and knocks on Mrs Gaffney's door.

Mrs Gaffney comes out from behind her desk and gently takes Kate's arm. 'Come with me,' she says conspiratorially, leading her back down the corridor and through to the garden doors. Mrs Gaffney points to a bench near the rose garden, where a lone figure dressed in a navy skirt suit is sitting on a bench.

Kate looks at Mrs Gaffney in amazement; Mrs Gaffney merely shrugs. 'She said she fancied some fresh air for a change.'

410

Kate races across the lawn and as she approaches she sees Cecily's eyes are closed. Kate can't tell if she's asleep or not but as she nears, Cecily slowly opens her eyes and gives a faint smile. Kate sits down next to her and without a word hands her the ribbon-tied contract. Cecily raises her eyebrows in hopeful enquiry and Kate nods, unable to stop the smile spreading across her face.

Cecily takes the paperwork and rests it on her lap, patting it with a deep sigh of contentment. She grabs hold of Kate's hand and squeezes it. Cecily's fingers are cold and bony but her grip is fierce and she holds onto Kate and does not let go.

The two women sit in joyful silence for some time, their faces turned to the warmth of the sun.

Chapter Sixty-four

Spring turns to summer, and Kate's life is in full bloom. She's so busy enjoying herself, sometimes she has to stop and remind herself that what's making her happiest is her work. Her time is filled with menu testing, writing, waitressing and supper clubs. She's three quarters of the way through the book, ahead of schedule for her September deadline. Jerry's sent the cover design, and a framed copy now hangs on the back of Cecily's bathroom door.

Kate's seen Ben a few times for dinner and a couple of walks on the Heath, but she's been so focused on everything else, he's been put on the back burner. One afternoon in June, Kate had been sitting in the garden with Cecily when Ben had come over to chat. Cecily had been in a deep sleep but the moment Kate began a whispered conversation with Ben, Cecily's eyes had snapped wide open and she'd insisted he join them for tea. Cecily has been getting increasingly confused, tripping over in her memories. When Cecily had asked Ben how he came to know her granddaughter, Kate had been on the point of correcting her, but then had caught the sparkle in Cecily's eye and had realised Cecily's mistake had not been a mistake at all.

Since then, though, Cecily has deteriorated, becoming increasingly disorientated and frail. She now sleeps most of the day and has developed constant, intense pain in her joints. She'd been in such discomfort a few weeks ago, the nurse had resorted to giving her morphine. When Kate had visited the following afternoon, Cecily was barely lucid, and her hair, usually so bright and buoyant, lay flat and limp on her fevered head. Kate had watched as she slept, Cecily inhaling and exhaling so slowly Kate held her own breath, praying the old lady would keep on taking just one more breath, just one more.

Ever since that day they've kept Cecily on heavy painkillers and in the last fortnight she's been struggling to eat or drink at all. Last Sunday when Kate visited, Cecily had barely managed more than a few words. Kate had sat beside her on the bed, scared her weight on the mattress would disturb Cecily, but Cecily had reached out one finger and silently, tenderly, stroked Kate's hand. The gesture had made Kate's heart ache.

Kate is on her lunch break the following Thursday when she gets the call. Even though it's a sweltering day, when she sees the name Lauderdale on her phone she turns cold.

It's Mrs Gaffney, calling to tell her that Cecily Finn died in the night, in her bed, in comfort and in peace.

The morning after the funeral Kate sits on Cecily's bed, her eyes fixed on the empty chair opposite. The room still smells so intensely of Cecily, Kate's half expecting her to emerge from the bathroom with a frown and a spiked comment.

When Kate arrived earlier, Mrs Gaffney handed her an envelope with a note Cecily had left. Kate stares at her name on the front, then gently opens the seal and slips out the piece of paper, a lump forming in her throat at the sight of Cecily's familiar looped writing.

Dear Kate,

I'm not one for grand goodbyes but I wanted to write a few words while I still retain a modicum of my faculties.

I shall be leaving you my entire library – not merely to educate you on the finer points of twentieth-century history, nor illuminate the fact that a novelist named George may actually have been born a Mary Anne. The gift is to nourish you in the widest possible sense.

When I was younger these books kept me from the worst of loneliness by providing me with companionship, and in these final months you have done that job admirably in their place. I don't believe I ever got around to saying thank you – so let me say it now: thank you, Kate – thank you.

Oftentimes when making a dessert you'll find a pinch of salt brings out the sweetness in the dish far more than extra sugar. It sounds counterintuitive but it is a fact, and one I've thought about often. What's true in the kitchen is often true more generally in life.

With my dearest Samuel I was lucky enough to experience love that was an enrichment beyond anything money can buy. When he was taken from me so unexpectedly I felt it was a profoundly bitter misfortune, but in some ways it was a gift. It forced me down paths I would never have chosen, yet on that journey

I discovered that a good life is about so much more than romantic love. A good life is about the books we read, the things we care about, the friends we love and the care with which we love them. And a good life is also about how we choose to treat ourselves. That is why I have always been firm with you, Kate. If you are not on your own side, who ever will be? I wish you could see yourself the way I see you. I know you can do anything, I know you will do everything. You are kind and hard-working; your heart is good – your cheese toasties less so.

Yesterday, I was a young girl, yet now, when I look in the mirror, I see a wizened crone. Beneath the outward signs of deterioration the same spirit dwells and looks on with dismay at the devastation the years have wrought. Inside there is still an urge to dance under the stars, to walk swiftly across the fields, to lie on the shore under a blazing sun. All I have left now are memories: a perfect strawberry ice cream with Mama after school in the shade of the garden, Samuel's smile on our wedding day, his hand in my hand, always. Today's choices become tomorrow's memories in a heartbeat – do make them count.

I've always had a voracious appetite – for words, for food, for more. Now I have read and eaten everything I ever wanted to and I am ready for death, but recently I've come to believe that I will probably miss this life. It's been a wonder and a glory.

I can't believe it's over so quickly.
Cecily

What a debt of gratitude Kate owes this woman. Cecily gave Kate the courage to let go of the things that didn't serve her, and the inspiration to pick up a pen and paper so she could start serving herself. All Kate can do to repay her is ensure that this book is the best she is capable of writing.

Kate slips the note back into the envelope and rests it on her lap, then turns her gaze back to the bookshelves – so many books, so many stories. Ben's offered to help pack and store them in his garage until Kate moves to her own place. She'll do that once her own book is finally handed in, and one of the first things she'll do after she's settled in a new flat is head back to the pet care centre round the corner and find a kitten in need of a home.

Male or female, that cat will be named Cecily because all cats are like Cecily – contrary, exquisitely stand-offish, fussy about food – and sometimes they pretend they don't need you or love you even though they do.

EPILOGUE

*It will never rain roses; when we want to have
more roses, we must plant more roses.*

George Eliot

Dinner For An Absent Friend

Aim: to celebrate a wonderful friendship in absentia

Scandinavian fish pâté served on lightly toasted challah, served with a cold white Montrachet

Slow-roast shoulder of lamb with cumin, and rosemary for remembrance – served with a Rioja Reserva

Toffee tart with milk chocolate ganache – served with Passito di Pantelleria dessert wine

THE TABLE IS LAID WITH Kate's new old china. The stylist on the book cover shoot had found some fantastic 1950s dinnerware, and while he claimed the plates had cost a small fortune he'd eventually sold them to Kate for a price that was affordable. They're not perfect – there are a couple of small chips, and five plates are cobalt blue, the other three teal – but Kate feels a small thrill every time she sees their beauty. There are seven places laid, though there'll only be six sitting down to eat – Kate, Bailey and Adam, Rita and Patrick, and Ben.

Cecily had once told Kate about the ritual of the traditional Jewish Passover supper, where a place is laid and a glass filled for the prophet Elijah in case he comes to call. Kate had asked if it was the equivalent of leaving mince pies for Santa's reindeer, and had received a withering look in response.

Kate's not sure whether Cecily would approve but she's laid a place for her anyway, and filled her glass, half-full, with vintage champagne. (That's one of the many bonuses of having Ben in her life – excellent wine, all the time.) This is a dinner to celebrate the book being published – how could Kate not pour a glass for Cecily?

It has been nine months since Cecily's death, and not a day goes by that Kate doesn't remember her. Kate cannot imagine what her life would be like if she'd never met Cecily – or rather, she doesn't want to imagine. She'd still be at Fletchers; chances are she'd be giving Nick his fifth chance by now, still making excuses for him, still allowing him to disappoint her.

Kate sits and takes a sip of champagne then gently taps her glass against Cecily's. Her stomach emits a low rumble. The lamb has been slow-cooking in the oven for hours and has filled the flat with the aroma of comfort, of spices and of home.

She jumps as she feels feline Cecily curl himself around her ankles. She reaches down and scoops him onto her lap. Cecily the kitten is now five months old. When Kate rescued him he was a tiny, blue-eyed ball of black fluff; now he's a slightly bigger, adorable, food-obsessed companion who hasn't objected to having a girl's name and who is far friendlier than his namesake. She tickles the kitten's ear, then carries him through to his play area in the bedroom.

She checks her watch – it's nearly eight o'clock, her guests are due any minute. She heads to the kitchen and takes the fresh bread from its bag and cuts six generous slices. She takes a lemon from the fruit bowl. The guy at her new local farmers' market claimed these Amalfi lemons are the greatest in the world. He probably bought them from Asda, but he was so charming Kate bought half a dozen anyway. She grates a final sprinkling of zest – a burst of freshness to sprinkle over the lamb. In the fridge the chocolate ganache is still setting over the toffee cream. Kate has to stop herself dipping her fingertip in, it looks so perfectly delicious.

Kate sits back down at the table and takes another sip of champagne. Her life has definitely not turned out according to plan, but then again, whose ever does? She is forty-one, she rents a tiny flat below another flat that has wooden floors and a flat-footed wannabe opera singer as a tenant. Kate's plates don't match, and she doesn't care. She has unshakeable friendships and her life has meaning. She has everything she needs for today.

She checks the place settings one last time and straightens Cecily's glass. There are sounds of life from outside the front door and a moment later the bell rings. Kate heads to the hallway to welcome in her guests.

There's a time to be sad and a time to be thankful – but right now it's time to eat.

A Note from the Author

The character of Cecily Finn was inspired by a real woman named Cecily Finn, who in the 1950s wrote the cookery book *Thought for Food*, with her good friend Joan O'Connor. Certain extracts from *Thought for Food* appear in their original format, others have been edited, some I have made up entirely.

Much like Cecily I have taken huge artistic licence in the telling of my tale – freely mixing truth and fiction. However, the following are facts:

Cecily Finn was born in 1904, in the East End of London, to Joseph and Eva Finn, who ran an ice cream and sweet shop in Forest Gate. The youngest of three, she was bright – winning a scholarship to West Ham High, then one to Saffron Walden teacher training college. Her father gave her a hard time about being an 'old maid' in her twenties, and it was Joseph who introduced her to a recently arrived young Polish émigré, Solomon, who became her husband (an engagement secured after a mere six weeks.)

Solomon, known to friends as Zimmy, was the seventh child of Leon and Shindel who were from Galicia, Poland. After Cecily and Zimmy married, they spent most of the 1930s travelling in Europe. They were parted during the Second World War for three years, during which time Cecily lived with her parents in Bournemouth, and Zimmy, based in Stockholm, worked for Allied Intelligence. She eventually joined him in Sweden, flying out on a bomber plane in order to do so. The majority of Zimmy's family refused to leave Poland in the late 1930s, despite his best attempts to convince them they weren't safe. During the war his parents, three of his siblings and all their children were transported by the Nazis to Auschwitz, where they were killed.

Cecily's father died during the war, and shortly after Cecily and Zimmy returned to England, so did her mother. Along with *Thought for Food*, Cecily authored a children's book, *Tell Me Again* (also published in Sweden) and various radio plays and two films, *The Man Who Liked Funerals* and *The Crowning Touch*. She was also a travel, fashion and food journalist, and in later life was heavily involved in charity work, and did indeed have tea with Ingrid Bergman.

But this is where fact and fiction diverge, because Cecily and Zimmy did have a child, a son, Jeremy, who is my father. Cecily and Zimmy remained happily married for 53 years. My grandpa died in 1987; Grandma survived him by nearly two decades. She died peacefully in her sleep, at home, at the age of 100, shortly after welcoming her first great-granddaughter into the world (and receiving a birthday card from the Queen).

Unlike the eponymous Cecily, in real life Cecily was good-natured, though she did complain of boredom, a lot. She adored art, food and books, and always encouraged me to write. This is not the first time she has featured in a work of fiction. Prior to *The Woman Who Wanted More*, I published four novels under the pseudonym Stella

Newman. In my first, the bestseller *Pear Shaped*, the heroine's grandmother is based on Cecily. I suspect she'd have been pleased about that, and even more pleased to be taking centre stage now.

I was privileged to have her as a grandmother.

Acknowledgements

This book would not exist without the support of so many.

Thank you first to Felicia Richardson, Joan O'Connor's daughter, for letting me use Joan and Cecily's words so liberally. It was such fun working with their text; I wish they were here to read the end result.

When I was writing the Stella Newman novels, my sister would accuse me of pretending to 'research' when all I was doing was eating. (Those four books are full of food.) Actually I do research – a bit – so thank you Elizabeth Watkins, Anita Morgan, and all the incredible staff and residents at the Mary Feilding Guild – spending time with you was a privilege. Thank you to Phil McCreery and Keoni Kailimai for advice on all things Hawaiian.

Thank you to my amazing agent Victoria Hobbs, for your immeasurable patience and hard work, and to Jo Thompson for your insightful feedback.

The fabulous team at Bonnier have been fundamental in making this book happen. To Eli Dryden, Sarah Bauer, Margaret Stead, Katie Lumsden, Ruth Logan, Alexandra Allden, Clare Kelly, Ellen Turner, Sahina Bibi, Stephen Dumughn, Felice McKeown, Nico Poilblanc, James Horobin, Vincent Kelleher, Victoria Hart, Angie Willocks, Carrie-Ann Pitt, Jamie Turner, Isabella Hannah and Kate Parkin – I am exceptionally grateful for all your hard work, talents and enthusiasm.

I'm indebted to Write Club, a superb group of published and soon-to-be-published writers, for constructive feedback and constructive wine: Irena Brignull, Kathryn Arbour, Courtney Clelland, Tash Bell, Jess Kimmel and Camilla Hill.

To Mum and Dad, H, Giles, Cookie – thank you, sorry, I love you. To Tabby and Frannie – you are magnificent young women. You fill my heart with delight.

Above all this book is about the power of friendship. I'm incredibly fortunate to have had so many exceptional people to hold my hand during the last few suboptimal years. Thanks in particular to the following – your love is a gift:

Alexia Da Silva – your grace and courage are exemplary.

Ali Bailey – the woman I want to be when I grow up.

Andrew Hart – thirty years of loyal friendship, surely you're due a sabbatical?

Ann Farragher – my sunshine.

Anna Potts – for cat therapy.

Dalia Bloom – for forgivenesss.

Debbi Adler – for curry and understanding, and understanding curry.

Ed McDonnell – dear, beautiful man.

Felicity Spector – for so many fabulous nights out.

Graeme Dunn – for maxillofacial A&E rescue and that extraordinary walk in the park.

Hannah Gladstone-Bacon – for the Sainsbury's late-night top comedy moment of all time, for being a magical, glittery friend and a daily, sometimes hourly, inspiration.

Heather Ingram – noodle twin, for unparalleled generosity and thoughtfulness.

Isabelle Broom – for so much, not least finding awesome nicknames for un-awesome individuals.

Jenny Knight – super talented writer, you are the best.

Jill Halfpenny – your fortitude and gentleness astound me.

Kathryn Finlay – the best mother-in-law I never had.

Madeleine Muir – life-saver, for so much support.

Michelle Gross – gelato partner extraordinaire, I'm so proud of you.

Philip Thompson – for dancing like no one was watching, even though everyone was.

Rachael Lloyd – for making me laugh all the time, particularly when it's wildly inappropriate.

Samantha Matern – Guru – for helping me choose better stories.

Sarah Birkett – my hilarious spirit animal, for reminding me, repeatedly, not to sell myself short – sorry it took a while to sink in.

Steve Beale – quality mate.

Toby Finlay – for keeping me company in Cali, and your endearing attempts to turn me into a better writer.

This book starts with a dedication to Matt Janes, and it will end with one too. Matt was my dear friend for more than twenty years. He was creative, wise, generous, courageous, and the most fun you could have at any party. He encouraged me to be braver and kinder, to live life better. He introduced me to so many joys in this world. The debt I owe him is immense.

Matt died very suddenly, at the age of forty-three, in his local gym. If they'd had a defibrillator he might have survived. If you belong to a gym with no defibrillator, please ask if they'll consider getting one.

I miss Matt every day. He has left a giant hole in many people's lives. How lucky I was to have shared such a long, rich and meaningful friendship with him.

His memory is a blessing.

Turn over for photographs from the author of the amazing woman who inspired this novel

Cecily Finn as a young girl in East London, c. 1908

Cecily and Zimmy on their wedding day

Cecily in the prime of her life

Cecily with her husband, son, daughter-in law and grandchildren, as well as the author's other much-loved grandmother, Esther Shavin, 1978. Author – the short one to the right of Cecily

Cecily on her 100th birthday, holding her first great-granddaughter,
Tabby, who is two weeks old. Cecily died a few weeks later,
peacefully, in her bed